WHAM!
BANG!
ERICA DOES IT AGAIN!

In *How to Save Your Own Life*, Erica Jong picks up the
story of hot-blooded, cool-witted Isadora Wing three years
after the events of *Fear of Flying*. With two marriages and
a bestselling book behind her, Isadora's search for the
ultimate sexual and emotional encounter is far from over.
This time Isadora's adventures take her to Hollywood
where she meets a variety of sharks, knaves, fools, gurus,
friends – and one real lover. As one by one she explores
and explodes the myths of literary fame, the short-term
solutions of lesbianism and group sex, Isadora eventually
comes to realize that it is possible to save your *own* life.

John Updike has said of Erica Jong that 'the Wife of Bath,
were she young and gorgeous, neurotic and Jewish, urban
and contemporary, might have written like this.' And
Henry Miller adds that Erica Jong 'will make literary
history ... and give us great sagas of sex, life, joy and
adventure.'
For all the millions of people around the world who
laughed with Isadora, loved her and saw themselves in her,
How to Save Your Own Life will ensure that now you will
never forget her.

SO FASTEN YOUR SEAT BELTS AND FIND OUT WHAT HAPPENED
WHEN ISADORA LEARNED TO FLY!

By the same author

Erica Jong

How to Save Your Own Life

A PANTHER BOOK

GRANADA
London Toronto Sydney New York

Published by Granada Publishing Limited in 1978
Reprinted 1981 (twice), 1982

ISBN 0 586 04737 9

First published in Great Britain by
Martin Secker & Warburg Ltd 1977
Copyright © Erica Mann Jong 1977
Portions of this book first appeared in *Playboy*,
New Dawn, and *Family Circle* magazines.
Grateful acknowledgement is made for use of portions of
the following:
'Because' © 1969 and 'A Day in the Life' © 1967, words
and music by John Lennon and Paul McCartney. Used by
permission of Northern Songs Ltd. All rights reserved.

Granada Publishing Limited
Frogmore, St Albans, Herts AL2 2NF
and
36 Golden Square, London W1R 4AH
866 United Nations Plaza, New York, NY 10017, USA
117 York Street, Sydney, NSW 2000, Australia
100 Skyway Avenue, Rexdale, Ontario, M9W 3A6, Canada
61 Beach Road, Auckland, New Zealand

Made and printed in Great Britain by
Richard Clay (The Chaucer Press) Ltd
Bungay, Suffolk
Set in Linotype Pilgrim

Granada ®
Granada Publishing ®

For Jon

Acknowledgments

Love and thanks to Elaine Geiger and Sterling Lord for support and encouragement beyond the call of duty, Grace and David Griffin, Alice Bach, Jonathan Fast who read and reread through all the drafts, Marjorie Larkin who typed and commented, Jennifer Josephy who edited and commented, Louis Untermeyer who liked the happy poems better than the sad ones, and all the people who wrote even when I could not answer.   E.J.

What is the end of fame? 'tis but to fill
    A certain portion of uncertain paper:
Some liken it to climbing up a hill,
    Whose summit, like all hills, is lost in vapour;
For this men write, speak, preach, and heroes kill,
    And bards burn what they call their 'midnight taper,'
To have, when the original is dust,
A name, a wretched picture, and worst bust.

—LORD BYRON,
    Don Juan

Experience, though noon auctoritee
Were in this world, is right ynough to me
To speke of wo that is in mariage ...

—CHAUCER,
    The Wife of Bath's Prologue

To cheat oneself out of love
is the most terrible deception;
it is an eternal loss for which
there is no reparation, either
in time or in eternity.

—SÖREN KIERKEGAARD

Using another as a means of satisfaction
and security is not love. Love is never
security; love is a state in which there
is no desire to be secure; it is a state
of vulnerability ...

—J. KRISHNAMURTI

I left my husband on Thanksgiving Day ...

I left my husband on Thanksgiving Day. It was nine years since I met him and almost that long since I'd married him – time enough to know something isn't working, and yet it wasn't easy.

Thanksgiving was an odd day to choose – or was it? On and off since I was two I had lived on the same block in Manhattan: that row of apartment buildings opposite the Museum of Natural History and the only street in New York privileged to be the launching pad for the giant balloons of Macy's Thanksgiving Day parade. As a little girl, I was allowed to stay up all night on Thanksgiving Eve to watch the trucks carrying the helium cylinders arrive and the great wrinkled latex balloons begin to take shape under their sandbagged cages of netting.

Starting at nine or so the night before the parade, the trucks would begin pulling in, and gradually the enormous outlines of Mickey Mouse, Donald Duck, Superman, the panda, and the dinosaur would be spread out on the black asphalt of the street. Later, Bullwinkle and the Smile balloon were added to the menagerie, but I was already older and the whole event was not as magical as it once had been. I had a special fondness for Bullwinkle though. He and I had something in common: a sort of quintessential silliness and an incurable naïveté.

I was not the only one on Seventy-seventh Street who was allowed to stay up all night that one special night a year. The other kids on the block were similarly blessed. We felt we *owned* the parade, and we would go downstairs and chummily feed sugar cubes to the policemen's horses (I was always terrified of losing a finger), thinking ourselves the luckiest kids in New York City – special, singled out, rare.

If we managed to keep ourselves awake that long, we could see the balloons swelling up toward our apartment windows by five or six in the morning. The process took all night, and sometimes, hard as I fought against it, I was asleep by two. I'd set an alarm for six, sleep in my clothes, and run downstairs to admire *my* balloons before the rest of the world possessed them. At the age of ten or so, I used to dream of mutinies in which I was the ringleader who convinced a gang of kids to steal a balloon. We kidnapped it to the center of Central Park, and held it captive while all the adults threw their hands up in despair.

But there I was leaving my husband on Thanksgiving morning. Leaving the seven-room co-op passed on to me by my grandfather, leaving my books, my typewriter, most of my clothes. Hurrying out at 7:30 A.M. past a giant Bullwinkle who seemed much more wrinkled than I remembered. I had three suitcases: beige linen imprinted with violets. One contained all the notes for the book I was writing: another was a dress bag with clothes varied enough for chilly New York, cold Chicago, warm Los Angeles, and the unpredictable weather in between; and the third was a cosmetics bag containing two hair driers, twelve bottles of vitamins, two bottles of perfume, various makeups, creams, and shampoos, assorted books, notebooks, and most of my good jewelry. I was on the lam, an exile from a bad marriage, a wandering Jewess, a lifelong New Yorker heading west. Released from a dying union by the news of an old adultery, reborn through a friend's suicide, I was off to meet a lover and my destiny – with my excuse for going to a movie I supposedly had to work on in Los Angeles.

But I was leaving for good. Even if my husband didn't know it, I did. And I was scared. Exuberant one minute, terrified the next. Two things sustained me: a new love, and a vision of my friend Jeannie dying in her mother's old fur coat in the back of a car idling in her locked garage on Cape Cod. Live or die. There are only two ways to go. Jeannie took one fork in the road and left the other to me. The legacy of her suicide was *live*. And suddenly, at thirty-two, I was released from my irrational fears, and at last took flight.

I had wanted to leave my marriage for years ...

Why is it harder to leave a loveless marriage than a loving one? Because a loveless marriage is born of desperation, while a loving one is born of choice ...

I had wanted to leave my marriage for years, had saved it up like a sweet before bedtime, like a piece of bubble gum put on the childhood bedpost, like the evening out you promise yourself after a day of writing. It was never any good – not from the beginning. But I deformed my mind to believing it was. I told myself nothing better was possible. I convinced myself that sadness and compromise were the ways of the world ...

A booksellers' convention in Chicago in early June. There were thousands of people surging through the lobby of the Sheraton and every third one seemed to know my face. I was grabbed by the hand, jostled, yoo-hooed, asked for advice, and solicited to read the budding literary efforts of nephews in Schenectady. I was smiling so hard I felt my face would crack as I plowed through the masses of booksellers, agents, editors, publicists. The air conditioning seemed to have given up the ghost. There was a line at the registration desk, a long line at the coffee shop entrance, and a still longer one at the taxi stand outside. All I could think about was somehow plowing back to my room. I tucked my chin under as if I were about to dive, seized firm hold of my shoulder bag, and marched, wove, waltzed, and sidestepped through the crowds that attempted to block my way on every side. I was not wearing a name tag, but my face had become public property.

Back in my room – with its two double beds (awaiting some mysterious *ménage à quatre*, no doubt), its gigantic color TV, its funereal flower arrangements sent by my publisher – I kicked off my sandals, stripped off my clothes, ran the bath, double-locked the door (so I wouldn't be killed like the lady in *Psycho*), and stepped into the steaming water. Whenever my life seems most unmanageable, I take a bath. I leaned back in the tub and let the water fill my ears. My hair flowed out around me.

What the hell did I want, anyway? I had everything I'd worked so hard for – and it somehow all seemed like ashes

15

in my mouth. I had lusted after fame, notoriety, adulation all my life. From the moment my father saw me in the hospital and asked my mother 'Do we have to take it home?...' my life had been a constant struggle to get attention, not to be ignored, to be the favored child, the brightest, the best, the most precocious, the most outrageous, the most adored. And now I had it – not from my parents or my husband, maybe, but from the rest of the world. And now it all seemed like some sort of nightmare.

Perversity. Three years before I would have been ready to kill for what I had now. I had envied published writers, envied and adored them. I had imagined them to be demigods, invulnerable to pain, blessed with a constant supply of love and self-assurance. Now I was learning about the other side of the fun-house mirror of fame. It was as if I had entered a room which very few are allowed to enter and which everyone on the outside believes to be incredibly beautiful, opulent, and magical. Once inside, you discover it is a hall of mirrors and all you see are myriad distortions of self, self, self.

There are the distortions of the press, the distortions of strangers who project their fantasies and frustrations on you, the distortions of all those people who envy you and imagine they would like to replace you. If you tell them that you are trapped in a hall of mirrors, they don't want to hear it. They need to believe in the magic of that locked room. They need it in order to justify their own envy, their own climbing.

I thought of my marriage to Bennett and of the past year. I wished I were home with him. Our marriage could be dead at times and dreary, but on some level it seemed we were working ourselves closer and closer together. And after all our ambivalence about it, we were finally talking about having a baby.

Why not? The time had come. I was thirty-two and panicked about getting older. I had written three books, knew that my vocation as a writer was firmly established, and we had enough money for housekeepers and babysitters, even a nanny – if I wanted one.

Then why did it all seem so wrong? Something kept

stopping me. I'd yearn for a child all day when Bennett was off at the hospital, and then when he came home at night and I saw his glum and sorrowful face, I'd rebel. Having a baby with him meant marrying that face forever. There had to be something better, something lighter and more joyful than that. Bennett was hooked on the myth of his unhappy childhood. He had been in analysis for seven years and he regarded life as a long disease, alleviated by little fifty-minute bloodlettings of words from the couch. He was a horizontal man, and I was beginning to suspect I was a vertical woman. But I felt so guilty about my misgivings. He was a perfectly nice man. A bit sad and self-absorbed, but perfectly nice. Loyal to me, supportive of my career. All year people had been telling me how *lucky* I was to have him: a husband who'd put up with my success.

Put up with – those were the words they used. And, though the words bothered me, I never really questioned them. I felt grateful to Bennett, grateful and obligated. He was my Leonard Woolf, I thought. My soothing live-in muse. After all, he hadn't left me when my novel *Candida Confesses* (which everyone but me seemed to think was so outrageous) became a best seller. And he hadn't left me when all his patients asked whether he was a character in the book. And he hadn't left me when I did the unpardon-able thing of becoming a public figure whose mail he had to help answer and whose escort he had to be at literary parties.

All my friends and acquaintances seemed to think of him as long-suffering, patient, and terribly secure – *for a man*. Didn't they realize what that *implied*? Didn't they realize how condescending that was to *both* of us? And to all men – if you wanted to stretch the implications? Was my success some sort of allergy that had to be tolerated? In my position, a man would be crowing; I was forever apologizing. Thanking my husband for 'putting up with' my fame. Apologizing to less successful friends by telling them how awful it really was to have what I had. And I *felt* apologetic. And obligated. The *least* I could do for Bennett was make it up to him by producing a child.

But there was his glum face, his nervous cough, and his perpetual analyzing. Though psychiatry was his vocation, his real passion seemed to be for his unhappy childhood. He nurtured its myth the way he might have nurtured the child we never had. And he was forever trying to convince other people to nurture their unhappy childhoods too.

Though I'd had more than my share of therapy myself, I'd begun to regard his attitude toward his childhood as a species of vanity. All people believe their suffering is greater than others'. Just as they secretly believe they are smarter, and more deserving of fame.

Everyone except me, it seems.

Bennett's childhood *was* worse than most, actually. A widowed mother who had to go on welfare, and numerous brothers and sisters, two of whom died of rare childhood diseases. It was harsh – but not as harsh as the fates of some of the other kids growing up during the Second World War. Besides, there is suffering even in castles. Hamlet is troubled by his bad dreams. And some people survive even concentration camps without forgetting how to laugh.

Humor is a survival tool. Perhaps that was why Bennett's childhood oppressed him so. He had no sense of humor. This showed up even in his practice of psychiatry – which was earnest, bookish, but essentially blocked by his lack of access to his feelings. He'd tried to establish full-time private practice but finally gave up all but a few patients and went into institutional psychiatry. His passion for security had led him to shelter in a hospital job.

In a way, I disrespected him for this and my disrespect had begun to eat away at whatever love I'd once had for him. But all this was semiconscious. I told myself, Marriage is ever thus, and men and women never really speak the same language. My friends pronounced me *lucky* to have such a supportive spouse, and I believed it myself. Who was happy? Where was it written that I ought to have *fun* with my husband as well as be tolerated, fucked, and supported in my creative ambitions? Most creative women had had it *much* worse. Bullying husbands, lovers who drove them to suicide, tyrannical fathers who forced

18

them into lives of sexual renunciation and daughterly dutifulness. At least I was blessed with a household saint – boring as that might be. And the fact was: Bennett barely intruded on my consciousness at all in either a positive or negative way. I used up no psychic energy on him at all. He was increasingly a sort of fixture in the house – like an oven or a dishwasher or a hi-fi set.

How had we drifted so far apart? Or were we apart from the very beginning? Does eight years of marriage erode all points of contact between two people – or weren't they *ever* there? I no longer knew. I only knew that I never looked forward to going on vacation with him – or being alone with him at night – and that I filled my life with frenetic activity, hundreds of friends, casual affairs (which, of course, I felt guilty about) because being alone in his company was so curiously sterile. Even when we were home together, I was forever retreating to my study to work. Surely some of this was my fierce ambition (or, as my astrology-nut friends would say, typical Aries woman married to a typical Cancer man); but surely some of it was a desire not to be with Bennett. His presence depressed me. There was something life-denying about his very manner, carriage, and monotonous way of speaking. How could one create life with someone who represented death?

I got up out of the bath and started drying myself, applying perfume and powder, blowing out my hair. Then I made up my face carefully – as much to hide from the world as anything else. Hide! This was a hell of a time to start hiding! Yet, it wasn't *I* who was famous, it was Candida – Candida, whom I'd modeled after myself as painters do self-portraits or depict their children as cherubim, their wives as seraphim, their neighbors as devils.

I came from a family of portraitists and still-life painters. It was family wisdom that you painted what you had at home. The reason was obvious. What you had at home was what you knew best, what you could study at leisure, learn from, dissect, analyze. You could learn chiaroscuro, color, composition as well from an apple or an onion or your

19

own familiar face as from the fountains of Rome or the storm clouds of Venice.

I had modeled Candida after myself, yet she was both more and less than the real Isadora. Superficially, the likeness was easy enough to spot: a nice Jewish girl from the Upper West Side, a writer of poems and stories, a compulsive daydreamer. Yet Candida was frozen in a book, while I was, I hoped, growing. I had outgrown many of the desires that motivated her, many of the fears that trapped her. Yet my public insisted on an exact equivalency between her and me — because my heroine, astoundingly enough, had turned out to be amanuensis to the Zeitgeist.

This amazing development surprised no one more than me. When I invented Candida Wong (with her wise-ass manner, her outspokenness about sex, and her determined bookishness), I was convinced that she was either unfit for print or else so precious that no one but a few other wise-ass Jewish girls from the Upper West Side could relate to her. But I was wrong. As Candida felt, so felt the nation. And no one could have been more surprised than her creator.

Millions of copies later, I began to wonder whether I had created Candida or whether she had, in fact, created me.

My mask completed, I ventured out into the teeming lobby again.

That night I was to attend a cocktail party for an aging stripper who had written an autobiography, another cocktail party for a chimpanzee TV star for whom a human had ghost-written an autobiography, and a dinner for a convicted felon who had just been paid a million dollars to write a memoir about his adventures as a high government official in the Nixon administration. Of the three authors, I found the chimpanzee the most honest and engaging — yet all evening I seemed to be conversing with animals and humans alike across a black hole in space.

Oh, I was on when I had to be: chatting everyone up, being delightful to book salesmen, embracing the public-relations game with what might have appeared to be my

20

whole heart. I'm a born performer and I play the smiling celebrity while anxiety pumps away in my gut. But inside I felt that I might as well have sent a wind-up doll to the party as to have gone myself. Instead of bringing me closer to people, those millions of books had separated me from everyone – even, it seemed, from myself.

Inevitably, I drank too much, talked too much, smiled too hard, swallowed back too much bile.

A vicious woman columnist waltzed up to me, told me that she wrote poetry too, but unlike me did not write 'commercial poetry,' and then confided that she had only read the first three pages of *Candida* before throwing it against the wall – because she couldn't stand 'pornography.'

Though Candida would have had an immediate snappy comeback, I was tongue-tied. I stood there dumbly for a minute or two reeling from all I'd had to drink, and then said 'Excuse me' and headed in the direction of the ladies' room, where I collapsed on the can and dozed a little with my cheek against the cool ceramic-tile wall.

Eventually, I forced myself to get up and go back to my double-double-bedded room with six gin and tonics in my blood and at least a half-bottle of wine pulsing through my temples.

I was even lonelier and sadder than I'd been when I'd left the room before dinner. Men I didn't want to sleep with had propositioned me, and I got into bed alone, mourning the waste of both those mattresses, masturbating over and over again in the hopes of putting myself to sleep.

Alcohol has a strange effect on me: wide-eyed insomnia. The feeling that my heart will fly out of my chest on its own wings. My mouth felt like the inside of a sand trap, my headache was monumental, and I realized that, short of three Valiums (which I didn't have), I was doomed to consciousness for the duration of the night.

What was I going to do? I knew I had a standing invitation to press my psychic wounds against the fleshly bandages of an aging editor who had repeatedly made his affectionate lust for me plain, but that was hardly what I wanted. Perhaps Candida would have done it, but I wasn't

21

about to. If anything, I knew it would only depress me more.

I revolved in the bed like a chicken on a spit, hoping to discover one more side to my torso than the mere four I'd already tried to span the abyss with. My back seemed camel-humped. My right side teetered over the edge of the hideous chartreuse-carpeted chasm between the two hotel beds. My left side was suddenly riddled with cramps, pins and needles, ancient aches. My beloved belly, usually so comfortable for sleeping on sleepless nights, also betrayed me. It sank down into the too-soft mattress as into quicksand, and it seemed that my mouth and nose would soon follow and asphyxiation would set in. I rolled over on my back once more, studied the ceiling, reached down to fondle my breasts, felt for lumps, thought – or did I imagine it? – that I found one, was perversely glad to have a *real* worry to occupy me, then reached lower down to fondle my cunt. I began to masturbate again desultorily, but quickly lost interest. Nothing so mundane would tranquilize me on this particular night. Black, winged presences were already gathering in the clammy air-conditioned hum of the hotel-room torture chamber: my Greek chorus had come to visit me.

They assembled one by one and hovered near the ceiling; I called the roll and each of them answered (in the most acerbic words he knew).

The first to arrive was an aging midget-*cum*-literary critic who combed his hair over his bald spot, wore elevator shoes to reach the willowy college girls he seduced at writers' conferences, had owed five different first novels to five different publishers for the past twenty years, and once, many years ago, had paid a visit to my college writing class, where he told the tender, pre-Fem-Lib sophomore maidens that women were biologically incapable of writing poetry or prose. He now reviewed books for a magazine of awesome influence and he had broken pub date to call Candida 'a mammoth pudenda.' He also hated Franz Kafka, Saul Bellow, Simone de Beauvoir. Anaïs Nin, Gore Vidal, Mary McCarthy, and Isaac Bashevis Singer – so it was almost an *honor* to be attacked by him, but still, on a

22

night like this, his words rang in my ears like the thundering voice of Truth: 'a mammoth pudenda,' 'spoiled by success,' and, finally, 'Ms Wing would do well to realize that popularity, too, may be a form of purgatory.' I didn't know, really, what the last thundering judgment *meant*, but it terrified me. The hostile tone was riveting – and so very *final* somehow. Why were my bad reviews so irresistibly mnemonic, my good ones so instantly forgettable? A mystery. The bad reviews all had the authoritative sound of my mother's voice.

Herbert Honig checked in with his jaunty black eye-patch, his auburn goatee, his psoriasis (and the heartbreak that accompanies it), his penchant for 'borrowing' his graduate students' original research, and his half-dozen remaindered novels. He pronounced me 'a polemical pornographer' and left immediately for Yaddo (with an adoring female PhD candidate for whom he had craftily obtained a fellowship there concurrent with his own). Next, I heard from Darryl W. Vaskin (the gray-bearded professor of seventeenth-century literature at Harvard) that my poetry was not as good as George Herbert's (with whom I had not realized, till that moment, I was competing). After that, Reah Taylor Carnovsky appeared (behind her shelflike bosom and her mustachioed upper lip) to pronounce me 'a piddling poetaster.' (Reah made her living putting other women writers down, so it could not be said she was biased toward her own sex. She had studied with Herbert Honig at Yale and shared his fondness for pontifical judgments.) She too immediately left for Yaddo to complete her new book on adumbrations of the Industrial Revolution in the imagery of Keats.

When the critics had all checked in, reassuring me that I was totally talentless, an egregious exhibitionist, and a panting publicity hound, my fans followed. Not my rational, well-beloved fans, my faithful readers who wrote me notes of gratitude – but the crazies: the proctologist from Mississippi who wanted me to send him my soiled underthings in a plastic bag and who enclosed a check for fifty-three dollars (a mysteriously arrived-at figure) so that I might replace them; the 'pastor' from New Jersey who said I sounded like 'a very broadminded individual' and who wanted me to correspond with him now that his wife had 'passed on' (the pastor's epistolary style resembled a page torn from an 'adult' novel, shrink-wrapped against prying fingers on Forty-second Street); the industrialist from Buffalo who called at midnight to ask if he might visit me 'for a cup of truth'; the self-styled 'scrap-metal millionaire' from San Diego who just wanted to know how I 'felt about coprophagia,' and didn't I agree that 'love juice' was 'packed with vitamins'?

What had I done to deserve the attentions of such people? Surely they correctly perceived something twisted in my own personality, some warp in my soul that corresponded with theirs, some high-pitched whistle of perversion that could be picked up only by their own finely tuned perverts' ears.

I was dying. Under the beating of the critics' black wings, under the perverts' urine-stained sheets, in the hum of the stone-cold 'conditioned' air, I was sinking into the grave as surely as my cancer-ridden grandmother had, as surely as any derelict in the Bowery, as surely as the Jews gassed at Auschwitz had. My body was flesh, which was only one step removed from shit, from clay, from dust. I seemed to see through to my own bones (which glowed greenish, as under a fluoroscope), and to actually *feel* the flesh falling from them, softening and rotting. I thought of hanged men letting go of their bowels, shitting in their pants even as they hug limply in air, rotting corpses on carts during the London Plague, rotting corpses stacked against the walls of Siena during the Black Death. There would be nothing left of my face but black eyeholes and glaring teeth. Isadora, Candida – it was all one. The woman, the portrait of the woman – both crumbling and dying; the flesh rotting, the paper turning to dust, the canvas peeling, and the critics' voices of death thundering above all my struggles to be heard, to live, to celebrate life.

I was a fish gasping on the bed and they were the fishermen reeling me in from the ceiling. They had me on the hook of my own mortality; fame was the bait I had swallowed and now it was stuck in my throat, stopping my screams. All my attempts at poetry, my love of Keats, of Whitman, of Blake – had come to this. They were going to silence me, silence me, and go on talking about the adumbrations of the Industrial Revolution among the dead.

Dead. You have to be dead to make the grade. But the flesh is already falling off the bone and there is no pyramid to mark the tomb where I lie, no plaque to mark the house where I write, no place even in the anthologies because they have declared me dead.

The dead have declared me dead! I know, with the absolute certainty of a nightmare, that I am dying. My uterus is a stone in my rotting carcass; I have no child; my three books have been declared dead by the thundering voices of the critics; my readers have forsaken me; only the perverts care. The necrophiliacs come forward to fuck my corpse – and as they pound away at my cunt, the flesh falls away like rotting meat, leaving only the gleaming greenish-white shark-jaw of the pelvic arch.

I am covered with sweat. My heart is pounding as if it is about to take flight, leave my chest cavity, shoot to the moon. I bound out of bed, turn on the light, pace, look at myself in the mirror to see if I'm still there, race back to the night table, pick up the phone and stand there stupidly, wanting to call someone, wanting to talk to someone, anyone who'll comfort me.

Bennett. It's three in the morning – but what if I call Bennett? A cold wind passes over my body with that thought. Bennett would be angry at being awakened. Bennett might not be home (and if he isn't – I don't want to know). Bennett would never understand.

My soul sinks still deeper with this realization: my husband – I cannot even call my own husband at a time like this.

I stand there holding the phone. I think of calling Jeffrey, my closest male friend, my occasional lover. He would call me if he were panicked in a hotel room. He *has* called me. But what about his wife? I'd wake his wife – and she'd suspect something about our relationship which, despite the occasional once-or-twice-a-year mercy fuck, really isn't true. And she's too paranoid not to be upset by my call.

25

Well, maybe I *should* call Bennett. Maybe I'm being neurotic to think he won't want to talk to me. It's absurd. I *will* call him.

I dial the hotel operator, wait fourteen rings to get her, and give the New York area code and number. I'm shaking as I do this. Whenever I call Bennett from out of town, I'm somehow always sure he's with another woman or not home. *Why* I think this, I can't say. To my knowledge Bennett has never ...

'Hello?'

'Hello,' comes Bennett's tentative sleepy voice.

'Bennett darling, I know it's crazy calling like this but I have to talk to you. I had such a panic just now. I can't sleep and I'm sure I'm dying. I know it sounds crazy, but ...' Somehow, I feel the need to apologize, to explain.

'What time is it?' he asks.

'I don't know. Maybe three o'clock. I can't sleep.'

'I have a patient at seven-thirty,' he says grumpily. 'I can't sleep late like you can.'

'Please talk to me – just for a little while, okay? I called because I had the weirdest fantasy. My flesh was rotting, and falling off my bones. It was horrible.' I shudder just thinking of it again.

'Well, why don't you get up and write a poem?' Bennett says sleepily and with what seems to be – or do I imagine it? – an edge of snideness. Then he goes on : 'If you can't tolerate separation like this, maybe you shouldn't leave me for three days.'

I am momentarily speechless, but already anger is replacing panic. 'Well, it's certainly clear I can't tell you when I feel lousy,' I say.

'What do you mean?'

'I mean you're certainly not very sympathetic, are you?'

'Why don't you write it down to tell your analyst?' Bennett says flatly. 'Or write a poem. *I* have to get back to sleep or I'll never get up in the morning for my patient.'

'I know, Bennett,' I say bitterly. 'You sell it. I know you can't be expected to give it away free.'

'Don't be angry,' he says, missing the point.

'Who's angry?'

'See you tomorrow?' he asks.

'If you're lucky.'

'Good-bye, Isadora. I refuse to fight.'

He hangs up.

I stand there, holding the phone, listening to the hundreds of miles of static between Chicago and New York, between Bennett and me.

Bennett tells all in Woodstock ...

Jealousy is all the fun you think they had ...

In the morning the demons were gone, burned off by the sun, banished by daylight. At 10:00 A.M., I participated in still another panel on women and creativity (probably my tenth on the subject that year), and flew home, totally exhausted, longing for my own bed, my own man, my own child.

A cab from Kennedy, a long discussion with the driver about how *he* could write a best seller if he only had the time – and finally I was home.

Let me invite you into my house – the rambling co-op I shared with Bennett on Seventy-seventh Street. It was the block I'd played hopscotch on, learned to ride a bike on. We were living there because my grandfather had given us the apartment – the same apartment Bennett's lawyer later claimed belonged solely to him.

His part of the apartment was middle-aged and middle-class. I was never allowed to hang posters or buy bright-colored furniture for the living room or foyer or dining room because a patient might be shocked. Bennett subscribed to the totally inexplicable theory that psychiatrists – who, after all, deal with all that is kinky and imaginative about the human soul: dreams, fantasies, sexual obsessions – ought somehow to comport themselves like accountants. And furnish their offices like dentists' waiting rooms in the suburbs. Why he believed this, I cannot tell you. But he was as fierce about it as if he were a Roman Catholic fighting the Protestants on the issue of transubstantiation. As a result, the *front* of our apartment looked like a dentist's waiting room in the suburbs and the *back* of it was a riotous gallery of my rebellion. Posters of me covered the walls; strange art objects made by my friends were strewn about; books were stacked on the floor, clothes draped over chairs, baskets of cut flowers from various admirers of mine distributed here and there on littered surfaces. Everything seemed clashingly colorful, messy, homey, and warm.

31

A European journalist once came to the apartment to interview me and used up all her resultant column-inches on a description of the place and what it reflected about my marriage. A cheap shot, perhaps, but nevertheless accurate. The apartment *was* the key to our marriage in many ways. In fact there were times when I doubted whether Bennett would have married me at all if I had not come with a co-op.

It's always nice to come home — even if home has a 'white-sound' machine in the foyer and resembles the interior of a dentist's office. The first thing I always do is kick off my shoes, strip naked, and open the mail. I read my fan mail in the nude — one form of nakedness greeting another.

During the previous spring, I ought to say, the mail had become as unmanageable and guilt-provoking as the Sunday *Times*. For six months after my novel was published, I had done nothing but answer all my correspondents at length, and now, though I'd largely stopped that, I still felt torn about it.

Though I'd certainly had my share of the crazies who came to haunt me in lonely hotel rooms, I had to admit in daylight that most of my mail was touching, heartfelt, and serious. The trouble was: there was no way to answer it. Even if I'd had the time to write to them all, there was absolutely no way to answer the questions my correspondents posed. I didn't know the answer *myself*. If I did, would I be in such lousy shape?

Dear Candida/Isadora,

I have never written a fan letter before, and I am very nervous writing this to you. But what-the-hell.

Youre book hit me right between-the-eyes like nothing I have ever read. Your right about men and women and sex and the man-woman relationship and EVERYTHING!!! I used to think all Womans Libbers were a load-of-shit, till I read you. (Youre book, I mean). Then I knew how right you are.

The problem is I have three children (they are loveley kids 3, 6, and 8) and my husband is very jealouse and there is no way for me to go away like you did and get Adventure or Sex or even have time to think about my Development as a Human Being and Woman. I am frequently horney, never have climaxed (Come) with my husband who says women don't need it. Is he right? Should I argue with him? He is a nise man though he gambles a little and their are the kids. I would like to be a Woman Libber like yourself but my husband blows up if I even go to a girlfriend's house and stay until midnight. Or even Eleven.(P.M.) He says I can't go out unless I can earn the money for the babysitter and how can I earn the money for the babysitter when the kids bug me all day and I never finished High School because my first boy was born right before graduation? I tell him their youre kids too but he says the Mother is the responsable one and I feel guilty. Maybe he is right?! He works hard earning money for us all to eat and life is no picnick for him either I am aware. What would you do in my position? I am writing to you because youre books shows how intelligent plus warm you are. I spoke to our minister who is supposed to be very forward-minded but he didn't say anything really that was Practical. I know your Jewish and maybe that doesn't apply but the Old Testament people were Jewish and they certainly knew alot us Christians could be helped by. Hope you won't think I'm a bigott. Actually my girl-friend is Jewish and youre Main Character (which is also you I believe) is exactly like me in all respects though Jewish. Please write right away or even you could call me Collect in San Antonio because I am so desparate plus beside-myself and I hope this is not an Imposition. I married my husband for security but I think he also fools behind my back (I have Proof too) and why shouldn't I have a night off to see my girlfriend not to mention other men though I am not that kind-of-girl.

Thanking you in advance for all youre help.

Sincerely yours,
Mrs Henry Laffont
(Celia)

P.S. I love the Book!!! My Girlfriend also does too.

P. P.S., My husband told me I better not read it or he would beat the shit out of me but I read it anyway!!! He thought it might give me ideas!!!

Dear Celia Laffont: (Please don't call yourself Mrs Henry...)

I love you, and your letter made me laugh and cry, but I don't know where to *begin* to tell you what to do. Come to New York and I will baby-sit for your children and put you all up in my apartment while you finish school...

But of course I never sent such a reply. Nor did I phone. I sent a card, with no return address, which read: 'Dear Celia Laffont, Thank you so much for your beautiful letter about my book. I wish I could answer all your questions, but I am hard at work on a new book which I hope will be more help than the first. Warmest wishes, Isadora W.'

Salvation. Everyone in the world wanted salvation. *Candida* had stated the problem but hadn't begun to *solve* it. And who *could* solve it? I had everything, supposedly, and couldn't solve my own dilemma; what on earth could I possibly do for Celia Laffont? If I ever get the time to write another book, I thought, I am going to call it *How to Save Your Own Life* – a sort of how-to book in the form of a novel. Hah. That was ridiculous. Imagine me saving lives when I couldn't save my own. Actually, *How to Save Your Own Life* was the title of a notebook given to me by Jeannie Morton who'd encouraged me to use it as a journal. But I had stopped keeping a journal. Keeping a journal implies hope and in the last year, I had given up hope. Was it because I had gotten everything I *thought* I wanted?

Bennett's key clicked in the lock at 6:15. I was still sitting at the round dining-room table pondering my stack of letters. Mooning over it. Not knowing how to go on after my perfunctory answer to Celia Laffont. There were forty-five calls to return (from the three days I'd been away) and a dozen bills to pay and ten book-length manuscripts by my writing students, and a stack of galleys to read. Three were friends' novels; I would have to read each one with care and think of tactful things to say. But the others were by strangers and could be put aside for the moment. Reading was becoming more and more of a chore. I yearned for the days when I could sit down with a copy of *Bleak House* or *Tom Jones* without thinking guiltily of the galleys on the floor by my desk. Besides, the books I was sent always seemed to reflect badly on my writing – or my character. I felt misunderstood by the galley-senders. Typecast somehow.

One was the sexual journal of a man who'd left his wife to jeep through California with two nubile teen-agers. One was a treatise on male superiority, tricked out as a 'breakthrough book' and 'the first cogent male response to the Women's Movement.' And one was a young woman poet's attempt to write a porn novel with literary pretensions. There were any number of novels about couples who had discovered swapping or about runaway wives or 'Jewish Princesses' – whatever *they* are. (I had used the term ironically in *Candida* and everyone had taken it literally, and thrown it back in my face.)

All the galleys came with sycophantic letters from editors tucked in. Some were the same editors who wouldn't return my calls before I'd had a best seller. I remembered their names. It was human enough, I guessed, but nonetheless depressing. People had to set priorities somewhere. I could certainly use a few more of those myself.

The only thing was: I knew Celia Laffont was more important than all the blurb requests put together. But how could I begin to help her with her problems? She needed nothing short of total salvation – and that was what I needed myself.

The door opens and Bennett appears. I continue to stare at my mail. Though we haven't seen each other in three days, I somehow have no desire to get up and face him. I force myself.

'Hi darling,' I say, embracing him in the foyer. He pecks

35

me on the mouth and moves away, unable to give himself to the greeting. He has missed me, but he hasn't yet seen his mail. It must be gotten out of the way like a bowel movement before screwing.

His rigidity angers me. Embracing him is like embracing a tailor's dummy.

'Aren't you really going to kiss me?' I ask.

He returns dutifully and kisses me very wetly (as he has ever since I ran off with a man whose kisses were wetter than his). He presses his pelvis against mine with consummate technique. I feel he is using craft. *The Craft of Fucking* or *The Well-tempered Penis* by Bennett Wing. Our greetings and kisses seem rehearsed, unfresh somehow. Like actors who have been in the same Broadway play for eight years. The longest run in history. With the original cast still playing.

'How was your day?' I ask. (We speak to each other like parodies of married people.)

'Oh, okay, I suppose. Auerback is fighting me on hiring Sy Kelson for the adult department ...' He wanders off to go through his mail and play back his Record-O-Fone. God forbid he should miss a single phone message or pay his shrink later than the tenth of any month.

Vaguely pissed, I drift away into my study and sit down to look at the galleys. I open the top set – a novel by my friend Jennifer about her Hollywood childhood. I read with apprehension, lest it be dreadful. But it's not. It's beautifully written. Delighted, I get up and run into the living room where Bennett is ...

'Jennifer's book is marvelous,' I say, 'really well-written.'

He is writing a check to his analyst, Dr Herschel W. Steingesser of 1148 Fifth Avenue, a building at Ninety-sixth and Fifth where you apparently cannot buy an apartment unless you have graduated from medical school, residency, and some accredited psychoanalytic institute or other.

'What's it about?' Bennett asks, absently.

'Oh, Hollywood, her father, her marriage ...'

'The whole oedipal drama, huh?'

At this, I become enraged. Bennett can never react to

36

any book, any movie, or any play without using the words *oedipal*, *anal*, or *primal scene*.

'Could we have a moratorium on the word *oedipal* for about forty-eight hours?'

Bennett wheels around in his chair: 'What are you so goddamned hostile about? I haven't seen you in three days.'

'Yes. And you don't even bother to kiss me.' I say this automatically and then realize it isn't true. He *has* kissed me. Why then do I feel so unkissed?

'What did you call that thing out in the foyer?'

'A kiss, I suppose.' I bury my anger, and go back to reading Jennifer's book.

The next day we are supposed to leave for a writers' conference at, let's call it, Pastoral U. I'm to teach the Craft of Writing for three days, read student manuscripts, and inhabit a beautiful bungalow by the lake. For this I'm actually to get money. Bennett has, for the first time in our history, consented to go with me. He has consented because everyone at the conference has told us that this will be more of a vacation than a teaching stint. The bungalows are said to be luxurious and the countryside beautiful.

We leave for the airport in the morning, but we never get to Pastoral U. In the car, it becomes clear that Bennett resents going. He is still mad at me for having been to Chicago and he picks a fight on the way to the airport.

BENNETT: You said you were going to cut down on all these activities, but I don't see you doing it.

ME: Bennett, please, I'm so tired and beat anyway, don't make it harder by nagging me. This is the very *last* appearance, I swear. In August we'll go away together.

BENNETT (*snidely*): Sure.

His mouth is tense under the Fu Manchu mustache he has grown in honor of my newfound fame, and he stares at the road in an almost-mean way. I look at him and am overcome with guilt. This poor man, shlepping his wife on literary junkets. What a sacrifice. I decide to sacrifice too.

ME: We don't have to go at all. I'll cancel right now.

BENNETT: That's ridiculous.

ME: No it's not. We'll have a weekend in the country, together, be alone ... You're always complaining we're never alone.

BENNETT: You can't cancel ...

ME: Of course I can – you're more important than any conference ... (*Lies, lies.*)

BENNETT: We planned to go and we're going. I gave up a tennis tournament to do this with you.

ME: What a sacrifice! This is the first fucking time you've come with me at all – and it ought to be *fun*. A free weekend in the country. Which we get paid for. (*I always refer to the money I make as 'ours' – though secretly I regard it as mine.*)

Bennett looks ahead in silence. I stare at his profile. Something is seething behind his set mouth but I can't tell what. My having gone away to Chicago for three days? Something older than that? Something borrowed?

Suddenly it explodes.

BENNETT: For a whole year you've done nothing but run around being nice to everyone but *me*. Any idiot who calls you in the middle of the night gets your time. You spend hours answering letters and hours with all your friends and students and hangers-on, but I never get to see you ...

That's because I feel depressed when I'm alone with you, I want to say, but don't. I SAY THE OPPOSITE: I'd *rather* be with you – it's just that I find it hard to say no to people.

BENNETT: You don't find it hard to say no to *me*.

ME: I do – really I do ... Look, let's not go to Pastoral U. Let's cancel.

By this time, we have entered the road to the airport. JFK.

BENNETT (*angrily*): Where's the sign to the Pan Am terminal? I missed it.

ME (*crying by now*): We won't go.

BENNETT: Yes we will. We have to.

ME: No – we'll call and cancel.

BENNETT: And then you'll hate me for sacrificing.

ME: No I won't.

BENNETT (*brightening*): You really would cancel?

ME: If you want it.

BENNETT: And what do *you* want?

ME (*hysterical and no longer knowing what I want*): Anything *you* want.

BENNETT: Bullshit. We're going. We said we'd go and we're going.

We park the car near the Pan Am terminal (the flight to Albany which connects with a smaller plane to upstate New York takes off from there) and begin taking out our bags. I look at Bennett's angry face – all the accumulated hurts of forty years – and I sob uncontrollably.

BENNETT: What the hell is the matter with you? Cut it out.

I am sobbing and shaking and speechless, suddenly terrified of the tiny plane, the students who will thrust manuscripts at me, the obligation to be *on, on, on* for another three days. I simply haven't the energy. And I can't stop crying.

BENNETT: Will you cut it out? It's not as if I hit you or something.

We lock the car and drag our bags into the terminal. The flight is in fifteen minutes. While Bennett gets the tickets confirmed, I run down to the ladies' room, splash cold water on my face, and try to stop crying. I can't. The year has dissolved me: Celia Laffont, perverts propositioning me through the mail, hotel rooms, Bennett ...

'There's nothing to cry about,' I tell myself in the mirror, but everything seems worth crying about. My whole life seems unmanageable; a disaster.

I race upstairs to the phone and call the director of the conference at Pastoral U., trying to sound sane. I've never cancelled anything before in my life. And for a thousand dollars. Sacrificial.

The director sounds nice. He calms me and starts persuading me to come. Bennett gesticulates madly that the plane is about to leave. Let it leave, I think, but I listen to the director's siren song about beautiful views, twelve to fifteen carefully chosen students, and luxurious bungalows. I have just been convinced when I see through the large glass windows that the only plane for Albany that day has just taken off.

On the way back from the airport, Bennett and I discuss what to do with the weekend, which suddenly belongs to us alone. Instead of being exhilarated about it, we are depressed. Now that the conflict between us has been removed, there is nothing at all connecting us. Dead air. And my remorse at having cancelled something I had been looking forward to. How had *that* happened? His anger? My exhaustion?

'Woodstock,' Bennett suggests. 'Let's go to Woodstock for the weekend.'

Now, Woodstock was a curious place to choose. Ominous almost. I can't hear the name *Woodstock* without thinking of that terrible August weekend in the third year of our marriage when Bennett was studying for his psychiatry boards and I was obsessing over the manuscript of my first book of poems (due to go into production the following week), and I went up to Woodstock in search of some reassurances from my friends Ronald and Justine (both writers) – while Bennett (who had refused to go with me, because he was supposedly studying) disappeared elsewhere for the entire weekend and would never tell me where.

We went through one of our familiar emotional hassles before I left. I begged Bennett to come. He refused. I told him Ronald would give him his guest-house study to work in. He still refused. He wanted me to stay in New York with him so he could rage at me periodically about his boards. But I was anxious too and desperately wanted Ronald and Justine to look at the manuscript before I turned it in. It was my first book and I reconsidered every punctuation mark hundreds of times before I let it go to press. I read every word into a tape recorder and played the tapes back over and over again, crossing out words, putting them back, crossing them out again.

Bennett refused to understand why I had to go. I refused to understand why he had to stay. Finally, I offered to sacrifice my interests to his and I called up Ronald and Justine and said I wasn't coming. Then Bennett mocked me for my indecisiveness, so I called them up and said I *was*.

'Go already,' he said. 'I can see you have to go.'

Weeping, I left for Woodstock. On the bus, I thought of Bennett with sudden empathy. He was nervous and upset; I should *never* have left him. As soon as I got to Woodstock I called. He was out. I called and called all night. He was never there. I called all weekend and he was never there. I became terrified. Bennett never did anything unpredictable. He must have been mugged in the elevator or axe-murdered in the living room. There was no other explanation.

And yet, somehow, as the weekend wore on, I was sure he was with another woman.

I never found out. When I returned on Sunday night, Bennett was there, looking mournful and mysterious.

'Where were *you* all weekend?' I demanded. 'I was frantic with worry.'

'Your fantasies are better than anything I can tell you,' he said aloofly. It was my problem, in other words. *I* was the neurotic, the daydreamer, the inventor of imaginary adulteries.

'Who *is* she?' I asked over and over again, but Bennett was mute. He smugly repeated the line about 'my fantasies.' But in my bones I knew I was right.

Woodstock.

We ride up in virtual silence. Something is brewing between us. Some marital thunderstorm. I try to make conversation and pretend I'm having a good time. I feed Bennett fruit I've brought. I try to draw the words out of him as I feed the fruit in. But he is hard to talk to. Every conversation ends on the second exchange. We are like two ill-matched tennis players, unable to maintain a rally. Finally, I pull out a book and begin to read. Side by side but apart, we drive to Woodstock.

Once there, we simulate companionship. We stop at an

41

antiques fair, a hamburger joint, an old quarry. We walk in the woods.

'Did you ever fuck in the woods?' I ask him.

Bennett smiles secretively.

'Well, *did* you?'

'Not with you,' he says, putting his arm around me.

'I *know* that. We never did anything romantic like that.'

'I think *this* is romantic,' he says.

And I think, Yes, everything is romantic but the way I feel.

At six, we decide we're hungry. We have walked and browsed and shopped, but time hangs heavy on our hands. We drive back to the main drag and ask a local hippie about restaurants. He recommends one nearby, an outdoor pub, with tables on the grass.

Just as we are about to sit down, a young girl comes up to me and asks tentatively, 'Are you Isadora?'

'Yes.'

'I *loved* your book! I think you're so brave!'

I blush, half pleased, half embarrassed. Part of me wants to hug her and the other part to shrink away.

'Thank you. I know that's hard to say. Thank you so much.'

We sit down at a table. After salad and wine, our attention wanders to another table where four adults are sitting with two children. The children are about five and seven and they are both very restless. They finally nag the adults into letting them go play on the grass. But Bennett and I can't seem to figure out which are the parents and which the parents' friends. We make a game of it. Not having children ourselves (and both longing for them), we always make much of other people's children, theorize about them, discuss them, philosophize about child-rearing. It is a shoddy substitute for parenthood, like nursing the myth of one's unhappy childhood.

'I think the woman in the Mexican shawl must be the mother, because she seems so blasé about the kids. The other woman keeps humoring them – obviously an aunt or friend ...' I say this, thinking of my own nieces and nephews, whom I adore. How stupid it is of me to deprive myself of children. I'd probably love them. I vow to myself to get pregnant as soon as possible.

'You know, when Penny broke up with Robby, she let her kids decide which parent they wanted to stay with. That's important. That way the kids don't feel powerless and pushed around ...'

I look at Bennett. *Penny.* Penny was an army officer's wife we knew in Heidelberg seven years ago. Why bring up Penny at a time like this? And Bennett is always so tender and concerned when he mentions her. He never sounds like that when he speaks of *me*.

A flash. Suddenly it all comes together. Penny, Woodstock, Heidelberg, now.

'Bennett, did you have an affair with Penny?' My heart is pounding. I seem to know the answer already.

'Do you really want to know, or ...'

'Yes, I really want to know.'

'Well – I did ...' A knife twists in my heart with the utterance of that simple monosyllable. And the pain is not undone by his continuing, 'But I haven't seen her for three years at least.'

'You seem to know a lot about her kids ...' My heart is galloping now: a wounded runaway horse.

'I spoke to her while you were in Chicago.'

'Oh.' I am overcome; I stare hard at him, obviously getting pleasure from his own revelation. *Seven years ago! Three years ago!* This is ridiculous. Ancient history. Why should it come between us now?

'Did you love her? Whenever you mention her name, I feel you still love her ...'

Bennett hedges: 'What's love?'

'When you speak of someone's kids in that tone of voice.' I am choking on my words. My salad sits on my plate dying in its vinegar. 'You never speak of me in that tone of voice.'

Bennett shrugs.

'You loved her, didn't you?' I hate the sound of my voice, saying this. So plaintive, so betrayed.

43

'Why does that matter?'

'That means the answer is yes.'

He shrugs again.

'Oh come on, Bennett, *tell* me. It's worse if you hedge like this. At least you loved *some*one if you didn't love me ... At least you *loved* ...'

'Don't raise your voice like that. People know who you are ...'

'And why not?' I scream. 'I don't *care* who knows. I really don't.'

'Shut up,' Bennett says, his voice a steel trap.

Later, in the car going back to New York (what point is there staying in Woodstock when the purpose for our trip has already been fulfilled?), I interrogate him about Penny, that cold copper bitch. I hear myself sounding like a betrayed wife in a novel – and I hate it. But I'm unable to stop. Some demon speaks through my mouth while my body looks on, amazed, ashamed.

'How often did you see her?'

'I don't remember.'

'How can you not remember?'

'I just can't.'

I think of my two part-time lovers (both of them named Jeffrey) who seem totally irrelevant to my life, but still I can remember everything. Every meeting, every meal, every mouthful.

'Was she good in bed?'

'I refuse to go into detail.'

'*Was* she?'

Bennett hesitates. He has unleashed something he cannot now control. He wants to take it all back. Salvage begins.

'I don't think she ever came. She moaned and writhed a lot, but I think she was inorgastic.'

Inorgastic. I recognize the voice of Dr Herschel W. Steingesser prompting from behind the couch.

'How did you know?'

'I never knew for sure.'

'Didn't you *care*?'

'Look, Isadora, not all women are like you. Some of

44

them get a lot out of sex *without* coming. They like being held, stroked, fondled.'

Snidely: 'Tell me about all those other women.'

'There *weren't* any others.'

'Sure.'

'It's true. There was just Penny. I felt I was dying and she saved my life. It was mostly that I needed someone to talk to. I couldn't talk to you in those days.'

'Saved your life? That's pretty strong stuff. We'd only been married a year. Why didn't you leave me if you felt so trapped? I was miserable too. It might have been a blessing.'

'Because I was conflicted. I knew you were warm and cuddly. That you came and she didn't, that my need for her was probably all my unresolved oedipal problem ...'

'That word again.'

Bennett bristles: 'Look – do you want to hear or don't you?'

'I do. I do.'

'She had six children – like my mother – and a husband she hated. I saw her as a damsel in distress – the mother I could save ...'

'I thought she saved *you*.'

'It was mutual.'

'It sounds great. It sounds like you should have gotten married.'

'No.'

'Why not? You apparently had a rapport with her you never had with me.'

Bennett concedes part of this. He is torn between boasting and contrition.

'She said she'd leave her kids for me. It was flattering, but after a while it began to bug me. It seemed unmotherly somehow ...'

'And you didn't want a cold bitch *shiksa* with six kids ...'

'If you want to shut me up – keep using that tone of voice, okay? I won't say another word.'

'I don't give a shit. *Don't* say a word. You haven't for eight years anyway.'

We ride for a while in silence. My tears are blurring the approaching headlights into nebulae. But Bennett has opened a Pandora's box sealed for too long. He cannot *not* talk now.

'She did other things that bugged me too. Like calling men "creatures." She always referred to her ex-lovers as "those creatures." '

Out of my hurt, I invent something to hurt him with: 'You don't suppose you were the only one in Heidelberg she was screwing, do you?'

'I thought so. Why?'

'She bragged to me and Laura about screwing Eichen the cellist and also two colleagues of Robby's on the army base.'

Bennett doesn't rise to the bait. He continues steadily: 'Well, I can only say that I *thought* I was the only one.'

Me, goading: 'You weren't.'

'Well, I thought I was and I suppose that's all that counts. I thought I made a deep impression on her. She was interested in my work with children – and she went into analysis.'

'How convenient! What did you do? Screw in the child-guidance clinic? Or on the couch in your office?'

I know I sound inane. The worst thing about jealousy is how low it makes you reach. How you stoop to conquer! I hate my words even as they tumble out.

'We used to meet on the nights you taught. In your study.'

'I thought you didn't remember.'

'I thought it would hurt you.'

'You thought right.'

And it's true. Somehow the fact that he was screwing a housewife while I was working makes it all worse. My drivenness. My need to teach, have a career, make money, not be dependent. And whom does he seek out? An army officer's wife who never finished college, has no career, and spends her day between the PX and her various lovers. No. Not various. I'd better not begin believing my own lies. I don't know for sure that she had various lovers. But it seems to fit. *And in my study.*

'Look,' Bennett goes on, 'when I got to Germany, I panicked. It was a terrible idea, really – doing three years there – but I was terrified of going to Vietnam, and I thought I could stand it, conquer my paranoia about the army. Well I was wrong. I freaked out, cut myself off from you entirely – and you were deep into your own thing: your writing, your teaching, your own paranoia about Germany ... Penny was so goyish, so American. The wife of an army officer ... she seemed so Aryan ... dumb as that sounds – and she was a mother, American as apple pie...'

'What an original phrase!'

'Isadora, I'm trying to explain ... I was terrified. I wanted someone un-Jewish, cool. But after a while I realized I didn't want that either. It was just a reaction to my feeling so trapped in the army. It reevoked my childhood – suddenly being trapped in Hong Kong and not speaking Chinese. You never took that part of me seriously. Penny did. She'd never had an Oriental lover before – and I was exotic to her. She made me feel special. Really. She did.'

I am moved. I know that what Bennett is saying is true, that he is trying to be honest. I should be sympathetic, but I am just so hurt. I was terribly lonely during those three years in Heidelberg and there were many occasions when I turned down affairs which might have solaced me. Now I feel like a damned fool. So much needless suffering. So much guilt for my fantasies. And he was actually *doing* it. On the nights when I taught. And in my *study*! This saintly Leonard Woolf who never resented my work actually screws in my *study*!

'Did you read my manuscripts too?'

'What?'

'When you screwed in my study – did you also read my manuscripts?'

'What a bizarre idea.'

'Not at all – I think that was partly the point, wasn't it? Getting even with my writing.'

Bennett says nothing. Then he says: 'That's absurd. Penny admired you enormously. She was actually quite jealous of you. Spoke of you constantly, envied you your

47

talent, your degrees, loved your poems, your short stories ...'

'I never published any of the stories – remember? How could she have read them if you didn't show them to her? What a pretty picture! Two of you, *post coitus*, reading my short stories aloud to each other and sipping *Spätlese*!'

'It wasn't like that. We both loved those stories. I told you you should have published them ...'

'You *both*! You *both*! Oh how terrific to know that Penny was honing her powers as a postcoital literary critic on my first attempts at fiction! I didn't *want* to publish those stories. I thought they were timid. And derivative! Just right for you and Penny.'

No need to detail the rest of this. Finally I shrieked at Bennett until the car echoed with my voice. I shrieked that at least he had loved someone and that was better than no love at all. I had thought him incapable of love and surely this revelation – painful as it was – was better than that verdict. I shrieked until my throat hurt and my eyes teared and I forgot what I was shrieking about.

You can demand deceit, I suppose, but not fidelity – and yet this revelation seemed spectacularly badly timed. He could have told me so many *other* times and it would have been a bond between us. He could have told me when I came back to him from my European adventure or when he read the finished manuscript of *Candida Confesses* or when I begged him to tell me about the Woodstock weekend. But no. He'd saved it up. Saved it until I was ready to have a child with him, saved it until I needed his affirmation most, saved it for the year of my sudden visibility, saved it to remind me of how dependent I'd been on him then, how helpless, how lonely, how unloved.

'So you were with Penny the weekend I was in Woodstock?'

'I really only went to say good-bye.'

'But why did you torture me so about "my fantasies!"

when I was right all along? What a cruel thing to have said!'

Bennett isn't aware of this. 'I didn't think it had anything to do with you. It was *my* problem.'

'To discuss with your analyst, right?'

Bennett says nothing.

'Right?'

'Yes, Isadora, it was *my* problem.'

'Bullshit. I happen to disagree. For seven years we've lived with a major falsehood between us and I happen to think it concerns *both* of us. I don't give a shit what Doctor Steingesser thinks. The vibes were there, the withholding was there, and a whole pattern of falsehood was set. You went to your analyst. I went to mine and we both continued to lead separate lives, drifting farther and farther apart. I think it stinks—'

'I didn't see any point in hurting you . . .'

'So you hurt me now – the worst possible time.'

'Now you're stronger. You can take it.'

At home, we fucked with more passion than we had in years.

From then on, we had a third person
living with us ...

In any triangle, who is the
betrayer, who the unseen rival,
and who the humiliated lover?
Oneself, oneself, and no one
but oneself!

From then on, we had a third person living with us in our house. I went to sleep with Penny at night, and woke up with her in the morning. I dreamed about Penny night after night. I remembered things I hadn't thought of in seven years: Penny's stretch bikini underpants hanging on the towel rack in the bleak bathroom of her bleak army apartment in Heidelberg. Penny sitting in the living room of that same apartment, pushing the thin strands of copper hair away from her freckled forehead and saying 'After you've had six children, it takes a lot of cock to fill you up ...' and then smiling lasciviously – first at her own husband, then at mine. Penny calling me up when I was in the hospital with a broken leg and asking me what she could do for Bennett. And me saying how *considerate* she was and thanking her, thanking her, thanking her.

I was plunged into the past. Time reeled backward. I was in the army again – that sad rainy army base, that sad, rainy second year of marriage.

Penny's face obsessed me: her ski-jump nose, her washed out *shiksa* eyes, her Norman Rockwell freckles. I was unable to concentrate on anything. At my desk in the morning, all I could do was reconstruct our apartment in Heidelberg, and my little gray-walled study – in which Bennett's cock is entering Penny's stretched-out *shiksa* cunt, while a stack of my early writing looks on ...

I was obsessed with details. How *long* did their assignations last and how often did they meet? How many *times* in a row did they fuck and in what *positions*? Did they moan or scream or whisper terms of endearment? Did they speak of their spouses afterward? Did they compare notes on our sexual techniques? Did they fall into each other's arms laughing about how clever they were at deceiving us? Did they give each other gifts, exchange tokens of love?

But mostly it was the sexual organs I focused on. Again and again and again, I saw Bennett's cock enter Penny's cunt. I would wake up screaming at three in the morning

53

after I had dreamed of this. And Bennett would comfort me, in the kindest words he knew.

Now that my life had stopped dead in its tracks and was nothing but a museum to my jealousy, Bennett became enormously sympathetic. He had reestablished himself at the center. Nothing could rival him now – not my career, nor my friends, nor my lovers.

Bennett didn't know about my lovers – at least not until the weekend he told me about Penny. Then in desperation I told him. It was all I had left.

Sunday number one, post-Woodstock: I have begun dating my life pre- and post-Woodstock. Bennett and I are at home. We have fucked all night – like thieves who don't know each other's names. And I have dreamed of Penny and awakened screaming. In the morning Bennett brings me breakfast in bed: a perfect cheese omelet and *café au lait*. He is smiling with the inner peace of a man who has demolished his wife and can now afford to be generous. I have only been up a few minutes and I am already weeping into my omelet. Eight years of tears! I never knew I had so many.

'I'm sorry I hurt you,' Bennett says.

I choke on the eggs and tears.

'I am. I really am.'

I pick at my omelet.

The coppery color of the cheddar cheese is Penny's hair. The blue of the china is her eyes. The white of the napkin is her bikini underpants.

'Have you had any other affairs?' I ask, not wanting to know the answer.

'Only one,' Bennett says smugly, sitting on the edge of the bed.

'Last night you told me none!'

'It was when you were so immersed in writing your book,' he says. 'I guess I felt shut out. I had no one to turn to.'

'So who did you turn to?' I ask, bitter.

'Robin McGraw,' he says, naming a blonde social worker from his hospital clinic.

54

And suddenly I spin off into the past. Robin and Penny. Intuitively, I knew about *both* of them. I remember the time Robin came skiing with us in Vermont. One afternoon we were having drinks in the hotel room and I looked at Robin, registered the resemblance between her and me, and had a sudden flash: my husband is fucking her. That's why she looks at him with such mournful blue eyes. The blue of her eyes, the blue of Penny's, the blue of mine. Three women refracting off each other.

'You certainly run to type,' I snap.

'Robin is really terrified of men,' Bennett says matter-of-factly. 'She practically has dyspareunia.'

'What's that?' I ask.

'Spasms in the vagina that make intercourse painful.'

I marvel at his colossal *chutzpa*. First he fucks them; then he annihilates them with analysis. *Inorgastic, dyspareunia.* The depth of his hatred for women is just becoming apparent to me. I am starting to hate him. I married a monster, I think. And all those years, it was *I* who felt guilty.

'What are you thinking?' he asks.

'What a monster you are.'

'*Me?*'

Bennett is incredulous. He has so convinced himself that his unhappy childhood makes him a perpetual victim that he cannot fathom himself as a monster.

'Why did you bother with them if you felt such contempt?'

'What contempt?'

'*Inorgastic, dyspareunia,*' I say mockingly.

'That's not contempt. It's just factual.'

'Sounds pretty contemptuous to me.'

'Robin came into my office crying one day,' he goes on. 'She was terribly upset about some patient who had yelled at her, and I had to comfort her. That was when you were so engrossed in your own things – I began seeing her every other week or so. I guess I always knew she had the hots for me. I remember telling Doctor Steingesser about that *months* before. "Why does it surprise you so that a handsome woman should be attracted to you?" he asked . . .'

A handsome woman, I think. I turn the antiquated phrase

over in my mind like an old coin. Why do analysts cultivate these Jamesian locutions? Can't they join the rest of us in the twentieth century?

'Anyway, I was flattered,' Bennett continues. 'She was pretty, and obviously crazy about me – and you were working so hard . . .'

'What a marvelous muse you are!' I say with considerable fury. My anger is bubbling to the surface again like boiling mud in a region of volcanos. Once again this long-suffering patient husband is acting out his rage against my success. Fucking Penny in Heidelberg, fucking Robin in New York.

'I'm human too,' Bennett says, unconvincingly.

'Then why did you always make yourself out to be such a saint?'

'Did I?'

'You certainly fucking well did! You let me writhe in guilt and fantasies, thinking myself a bad little girl, while you pretended to be above it all, above sexual peccadillos, above lust. It's *that* I can't forgive you for. Letting me sweat it out and pretending to be so pure yourself! If only you had *shared* it with me . . . If only you had said, "Okay, don't feel so guilty – I've done it myself." But you pretended you never even had such *fantasies. I* was the only one. You could have leveled with me instead of letting me feel like some sort of freak.'

'What was the point? It was my problem . . .'

'I've heard that before and it's pretty goddamn self-serving. You simply didn't want me to feel free to have affairs too – that's what I think. But you know what? – I had them *anyway* . . .' I feel sick about the revelations I am about to make, but I can't help myself. The words carry their own momentum. A confession in motion tends to remain in motion. Newton's first law of jealousy.

'Who with?'

'Oh Jeffrey Rudner, for one, and Jeffrey Roberts.'

'Jeffrey *Rudner*?' Bennett is stung by this. Jeffrey – his fellow shrink, his tennis partner. I am delighted to have this additional dart up my sleeve: 'He used to cancel a whole afternoon of patients for me – something you'd never do.'

Bennett looks crestfallen. 'I thought that English asshole was the last ... I thought when I took you back you *promised* ...'

'I promised nothing.'

'I thought your analysis ...'

'Ah analysis – the universal panacea ... The cure for lust, for restlessness, for every sexual itch ... As a matter of fact Jeffrey and I used to bump into each other *after* our analytic sessions. That was how it started. I'd be walking out of 940 Park and he'd be walking out of 945 Park. We'd collide in the middle of the avenue, and go for coffee. After a while, we'd spend the odd Friday afternoon in his office, making love ...'

I say this coolly – as if it had been easy, as if there had been no angst, no misgivings, no anxiety. Not true at all. The whole silly little affair had been fraught with guilt and misgivings. The only good thing about it was being able to pull it out now, like a rabbit out of a hat. Talking about it was far more fun than living it had ever been. But I don't intend to tell Bennett this. For his sake, I embellish:

'Jeffrey happens to be a great fuck. I even think he's *orgastic* – to use your jargon. And he would try things you'd never *consider* – like eating apple butter out of my cunt ...'

'In the office? On the analytic couch?' Bennett goes from incredulity to contempt: 'Boy, you two were certainly acting out against your analysts weren't you? – doing it on the *couch* ...'

I suddenly remember that we never actually *did* it on the couch (Jeffrey was too superstitious) – but I won't give Bennett the satisfaction of knowing that.

'It's great fun on the couch,' I say gleefully; 'you ought to try it.'

'I have,' he retaliates. 'With Robin.'

'And I suppose you don't call *that* acting out?'

'I certainly do. And I certainly spent *hours* on it with Doctor Steingesser.'

'I guess that makes it kosher, huh? Fuck first, analyze later.'

'Have it your way,' Bennett says. 'At least I didn't do it with a *friend* of yours ...'

'I think it's kind of nice that Jeffrey was willing to cancel patients for me, don't you? An extremely gallant gesture – especially for a shrink.'

I look at Bennett, his face set in anger, his eyes hard and narrow. I wish I had even more peccadillos to display. I wish I had fucked his entire medical school class, all his colleagues, every doctor in New York. I scrape the bottom of the barrel: 'Jeffrey Roberts was in love with me for years, and then there was Bob Lorrillard when I went to Chicago to do his TV show, and Amos Kostan, the Israeli poet.' (The last isn't even true; Amos and I once embraced in the kitchen, but never had an affair. Still, I know it will get Bennett mad.) I am feeling as helpless as a child who suddenly realizes that dirty things are going on behind locked doors and that she is left out in the cold. I would do anything to inflict the same feeling on Bennett. But he isn't biting.

'I suspected all of those,' he says defensively – 'and I'm prepared to forgive you.'

'Forgive me! Forgive me! And what if I don't *want* forgiveness? What if I want the right to my own anger?'

'I understand that artists tend to be a bit unstable and I understand that you —'

This enrages me still further. 'Don't give me that patronizing shit, goddamn you. I had one or two dumb fucks – and you had a serious passionate affair – for which you nearly left me. Don't give me that artist crap. It's insulting and condescending. Once again you're playing the big daddy who deigns to take me back. No thanks! Can't you see how controlling you are? Don't you *realize*?'

And with that I begin to cry. The dams break, and eight years of tears pour forth. Where had I been storing all these tears?

When I am utterly dissolved in my own tears, Bennett opens his arms to me and wants me to crawl in. All the way back to the womb. And I crawl. But I am raging within. I let him embrace me like a crab embracing its dinner – but inside I am furious. The marriage has begun to end.

A day in the life ...

*Advice is what we ask for
when we already know the answer
but wish we didn't ...*

There is a rumor abroad in the land that women today leave their husbands at the drop of a hat – or some other appropriate garment. I am living proof that it isn't so. With no children to 'tie me down' (or anchor me to reality), with a profession and livelihood of my own, leaving was still the hardest thing I ever did in my life. I tried everything I could think of to postpone the decision – or reverse it – and the very process of leaving took years, not months. Even the flings and affairs I had, even the rebellious things I wrote were, in reality, ways of postponing the actual terrifying decision to leave.

It was a far cry from what one overhears from a neighboring luncheon table or, fleetingly, on the crossed wires of the telephone: '*And then she just up and left him.*' That classic line is inevitably pronounced with a mixture of contempt and envy – but vicarious elation underlies them both. Another prisoner has escaped! Another bird has flown her gilded cage! The line stirs us, no matter how many times we have heard it repeated. Freedom, freedom is the theme.

I was not insensible to the call of freedom. Every time I heard of *any* woman who had left her husband – whether it was a friend, a friend of a friend, a distant acquaintance, or some media personality compounded of two parts rumor, two parts projection, and the rest wishful thinking – I yearned, palpably *yearned*. I became a ready customer for paperback originals with titles like *How to Do Your Own Divorce, The Joys of Divorce, The Natural Incompatibility of Love and Marriage,* or *The Challenge of Single Living.* I was obsessed with leaving, yet I could not leave. In the manner of psychotics who project their own delusions on the environment, I began to convince myself that the entire world was obsessed with leaving its husband, that leaving one's husband was the *only*, the cosmic, theme.

My friends were crucial to me then. In a bad marriage, friends are the invisible glue. If we have enough friends,

61

we may go on for years, intending to leave, talking about leaving – instead of actually getting up and leaving.

I have always been blessed with friends. At no time in my life, no matter how miserable, have I lacked friends to share my misery with. Friends *love* misery, in fact. Sometimes, especially if we are too lucky or too successful or too pretty, our misery is the only thing that endears us to our friends.

Right after Bennett's revelations, I found myself calling on each of my friends in turn, as if they were healers, gurus, shamans. Each of them was a mirror that reflected only its own distortions – yet even this was comforting in its way.

That hot Monday morning post-Woodstock, I called them all: Gretchen Kendall, the feminist lawyer; Michael Cosman, my best friend and almost-lover in Heidelberg; Jeffrey Rudner, the shrink who cancelled sessions for me; Jeffrey Roberts, the WASP advertising man and poet who had wanted to marry me for years; Hope Lowell, my muse and fairy godmother; Holly, the perpetual loner whose paintings make it absolutely clear that she would rather be a plant than a person. The friends that I neglected to call somehow called me. Before eleven that morning, my entire week was booked solid. Not a sliver of time was left to see Bennett. It might even be said that I never saw Bennett again until long after I left him. Only then could I look at him without rage, and understand. But by then it was too late, what I understood made it absolutely clear to me that I could never go back.

Gretchen is five foot eight, blonde, has enormous boobs, a raunchy tongue, and professes Marxism, feminism, and a passion for baroque music. Two years ago, during the gay-chic phase of the Women's Movement, she and I talked a lot about having an affair – but, of course, we never did. We never really wanted to. It was only the *idea* that seemed appealing. Instead, we went to London together, when my novel was published there, and we had what can only be called a ten-day-long primal therapy session in our hotel room at the Dorchester. It was a pretty hellish experience, which convinced us both that we should never again attempt to live or travel together, but it left us fast friends. Secretly, I am a little intimidated by Gretchen. Her domineering nature (Leo, Leo ascendant), her professed radicalism, her fast mouth, her extraordinary beauty. She has so much life-force that she makes everyone else in the room feel drained. She overwhelms me.

Once, when I was being interviewed by a London women's magazine, Gretchen sat in the back of the room saying 'bullshit' after nearly every one of my responses. 'It's *my* goddamned interview!' I finally said in a rage – and of course the snotty journalist made *that* the headline of the piece. Our friendship nearly faltered over that, but it survived because, in some strange way, Gretchen and I are sisters, and need each other – even to yell at. I love her (and I think she loves me). The fact is – you can't really write about somebody you don't love. Even if the portrait is vitriolic, even if the pen is sharpened with old grudges, there has to have been love somewhere along the line, or the sheer, brute energy of pushing that pen across the page will not be there. And writing takes energy – more energy than you ever think you have. And energy comes from love. It takes a spasm of love to write a poem, and several spasms to write a short story, and hundreds of them to write a novel. A poem (surely someone has said this before) is a one-night stand, a short story a love affair, and a novel a marriage. From time to time, you get tired of your subject and your passion wanes – but you hang in there for a long haul. Occasionally, you succumb to temptations: a poem or two, an occasional short story: but the novel binds you with its long apron strings. You may stray – but never for good.

Gretchen runs her one-woman practice out of a tiny windowless office on Madison Avenue in the Sixties. It's in the back room of another, more successful lawyer's suite. The walls are covered with political posters, the desk is heaped with briefs and feminist books, pictures of her kids are pasted up on the wall, and there's a large male nude hanging over her cluttered desk. It's a hard-edged painting of a naked black man holding a giant watermelon in front

63

of (what we presume is) his penis, and grinning devilishly. To ward off any suspicion of racism, Gretchen tells you at once that the artist is a black woman client of hers. Her clients seldom can afford to pay, so they give Gretchen paintings, Christmas fruitcakes, original manuscripts, or, more often, nothing at all. She barely has enough to cover her rent and answering service – and money is always a sore point with her.

When I walk into her office, she's got her feet up on the desk, one welfare mother on hold, and an abortion reformer on the line.

'You look terrible. Sit down,' she says, and goes on talking. Sometimes I suspect that the phone conversations I overhear in Gretchen's office are partly performed for my benefit. Gretchen has a great sense of the theatrical. The female Clarence Darrow of feminism.

'Of course he's a pig. Who did you expect – John Stuart Mill?' A peal of infectious laughter follows. Gretchen has a delightful laugh – which is fortunate, since she often has a very sharp tongue. Without the laugh, she might be totally terrifying.

'Look – that bastard came into the hospital dressed up as a doctor and molested five women. But nobody gave a fuck until he molested a *white* woman. Then the shit hit the fan.'

I smile at Gretchen, her knee-jerk radicalism. She grins back.

'Well, what are we going to do? Let the fuckers get away with it? Believe me, he'll be out in six months and doing it again. Maybe to you or me. I'd give him a karate chop so fast he wouldn't know what hit him – the son of a bitch. Okay. Check it out and call me back. Good. I know. Bye.' She presses the other button on her phone. 'Hello? Mrs Brown? You're going to have to come down to my office and tell me the whole story in detail so we can nail the son of a bitch, okay? Do you know how to get here? You take the Lexington Avenue subway to Sixty-eighth Street and then you walk three blocks downtown and two blocks west. You have the address? Good. Tomorrow? Well, if I'm out to lunch, make yourself comfortable here.

64

I should be back soon. Okay. Bye.' And then to me: 'God –
you look like the roof just caved in. What the fuck happened?'

'I'm leaving Bennett.'

'I've heard *that* before.'

'This time it's true.'

Gretchen laughs. 'I'll believe it when you change the
locks.'

'Do you know what the son of a bitch did?'

'Joined the Tong? Quit analysis? Took a male lover?
Actually *talked* to you?'

'Very funny. Actually, he *did* talk for the first time in
eight years and you know what he told me?'

'That he's actually a robot? I suspected it all along.'

'No, you idiot. He had a *lover* for years. In Heidelberg.
And after. The sanctimonious son of a bitch. Remember all
his outrage about *your* open marriage? Remember how
guilty he tried to make us *both* feel about going to London? Well, it turns out he even got laid during the time
we were away – even though *we* never did.

Gretchen laughs. 'I always wondered why you were so
sure he didn't. They're all pigs underneath, you know.
Even my illustrious Alan – with his cute vasectomy scar
and his men's c.r. group. You can take it as a rule of thumb.
Pigs is pigs.'

'But Bennett was so straight.'

'Not straight. Just rigid, uptight, and boring. They all
cheat sooner or later. You might as well have one who isn't
a bore the *rest* of the time.'

'I guess.' I look down, about to cry.

'Look – don't flagellate yourself about it – at least you
know now. At least you don't have to delude yourself anymore. You always did this *shtik* about how virtuous *he* was
and how bad *you* were. At least you can cut *that* crap
now.'

'What a colossal waste of energy. All that guilt. *Christ.*'

'I know. But it's better this way, isn't it? Maybe you can
leave the shmuck now. And that useless analyst you go
to.'

'She's not so bad. She's pretty good in fact.'

'Then why are you so stuck? You've been going round and round with the same old Freudian garbage for years now. You'll never get *any*where with that. And you'll never move from A to B married to that *deadpan*.'

'You know what kills me?'

'What?'

'The way I needed to see him as my daddy and protector, the way I needed the *illusion* of being protected. Why do we do that? We all do it, you know. Even you.'

'Well, I'm reconciled to the fact that I'll always be with men. I'll never make it as a lesbian – but at least I don't Uncle Tom it up the way you do.'

This hurts. 'I don't think I Uncle Tom it up.'

'Bullshit. Of course you do. Whenever Bennett enters the room, you start *accommodating* him. It's sickening. What did *he* ever do for you? Treated you rotten until you got successful and now treats you like the goose that laid the golden egg. And he patronizes you like crazy. All that "woman artist" horseshit. As if being a writer were a *disease*. The sooner you get rid of that stiff, the better. I'd start your separation agreement right now, if you wanted. Only I can tell you're not really ready.' Gretchen gets up, stretches, retucks her shirt in her jeans, and begins making faces in the magnifying mirror on her desk. She unscrews a jar of vitamin E cream, massages a little of it into her neck, and starts dabbing herself with perfume out of a Youth Dew bottle. The best-smelling Marxist in New York. If you smell good, you can conquer the world.

'I'm so mad at the bastard, I'd like to castrate him, not divorce him. Divorce is too good for him.'

'You're mad at yourself, babe.' The room is beginning to reek of Youth Dew.

'Yeah. I guess. The thing is, why did I need that myth of having this glorious daddy and protector? That's what gets me so pissed. We're alone anyway – so why don't we just admit it from the outset? Bennett's function in my life was mostly imaginary, wasn't it? I've been making half the bread for the last few years. I don't have fun with him. He doesn't like most of my friends. And we practically never

66

see each other. We don't have kids – so what am I *doing* there, really?'

'I thought he was a good fuck – though that's no reason to stay *either*.'

'Well, he is. But Jeffrey Rudner does better back rubs and goes down on me with a lot more gusto. And I'm sure there are plenty of fucks as good as Bennett. For god's sake, he screws in his *socks and pajama-top*.'

'You never told me that.'

'If I had, you'd have made fun of me even more.'

'You're damn right.'

'Do you know what he *did*?'

'Are there any variations on cheating I don't know about?'

'That stinking hypocrite was having an affair the whole time he was being so pious about everyone else's sex life. On the army base. When he was going on about how *infantile* they all were. And how they were *acting out*. And he was so superior to you and Alan. He said your tolerating each other's affairs, baby-sitting for each other on nights out was unconscious oedipal something or other. God – I'd like to kill him.'

'Don't. I couldn't get you out of *that* one.'

'When I think that I was ready to have a baby with that son of a bitch. When I think of it! I'd be stuck with that hypocrite forever.'

'You could still leave, but it would be harder. Anyway, I'll believe you're leaving when I see it. I still don't think you're ready. All this *rage*. When you're ready, you'll walk out calmly.'

'You know what the oddest thing is?'

Gretchen fixes me with her large blue eyes and then starts to laugh. 'I know what you're going to say.'

Me, defiantly: 'What?'

'You're going to tell me that since he laid his sexual history on you, you've been fucking more and better than since you first met.'

'How'd you know?'

'Kendall's first law of jealousy: jealousy makes the prick grow harder. And the cunt wetter. It's so common you

67

wouldn't believe it. Also, just when you've finally made up your mind to split, the sex gets great, to stop you. But, you know what? It doesn't last. *Thank* God.'

I put my feet up on Gretchen's desk too. 'You know the weirdest thing? I don't believe I'll ever find anyone else.'

'You should only be so lucky,' Gretchen laughs.

When Gretchen leaves for her lunch date, I drift on up Madison Avenue. It's one of those hot June days when the air feels slightly wet, and you feel like you're swimming, not walking. I linger, gaze in shop windows, stop in a fancy Italian boutique to try on a pair of expensive sandals I know I won't buy, stop in a drug store to buy contraceptive jelly and a bottle of perfumed body oil (I am going to see Jeffrey Rudner later), stop at a florist's to buy a long-stemmed rose for Hope, my fairy godmother.

Hope is exactly twenty years older than me, born on March 26, 1922, and ours is one of those curious old family connections. Her mother, now a terrifically bouncy old lady named Selma (who also appears to have cornered the market on *kvetching*), had an affair with my grandfather, circa 1908. Both of them deny it – but Hope found the letters to prove it. When pinned down, Papa will only say, 'Well, Selma was an anarchist, a follower of Emma Goldman,' and Selma will say : 'Ach – Stoloff – all he ever does is talk, talk, talk. Believe me, if you want to know from affairs, I could tell you better ones than *that*.' And she could. But the fact is, Hope and I are convinced that, cosmically speaking, we are sisters. There are too many coincidences. The same birthday, a mother and grand-father who were lovers, identical taste in poetry, jokes, food. All the really important things. And, of course, sex. Unlike my mother, who seemed to regard sex as a barter-able commodity, Hope always understood that there's nothing wrong with being an easy lay. Except that she's also a romantic, and when she falls in love (as she is now with a second husband she met at the age of fifty) she is com-pletely, delightedly monogamous. We have that in common too : being romantics. And yet through all the crazy, guilty little affairs I had during the denouement of my marriage to Bennett, she was immensely comforting. I would come to her with my guilt, my misgivings, my constant chafing to leave, and she would say : 'Let it be. Float. When you're ready to leave, you'll leave. Don't punish yourself.' She knows me like she knows herself. All that Jewish guilt. That constant appeasing of the evil eye. If something good happens, something bad is right around the corner. If you have pleasure, watch out for pain. If sex is good, you're going to get clap or pregnant or caught.

Hope had been a background figure in my life throughout my childhood. I heard about her from my grandparents and parents, but never really got to know her. She was referred to as 'Poor Hope,' apparently because she married a musician who 'never made a leeving,' as my grandmother said. But instead of dumping him – as any sensible Jewish girl would have done – she stayed with him and supported him. This was thought to be a sign of great foolhardiness. Hope was extremely attractive to men, was highly thought of as an editor, and made a good living. My grandparents clucked their tongues over her guilelessness. How could she stay married to that bongo drummer from Rego Park? Love is love, but marriage is an investment. And for an attractive woman to squander her 'best years' on a bongo drummer from Rego Park could only be a sign of weakness. 'Poor Hope. She's too good.'

But poor Hope knew more than any of them. She understood that the cornucopia returns upon itself. She was always immensely generous with her money, her love, her time. The result was thousands of friends, a life crammed with lovers, and, at mid-century, an idyllic romance with a man who turned out to be her mental and emotional double. My mother and grandmother, who hoarded and calculated their love, my sisters, who chose their husbands at eighteen and never budged, wound up with less than Hope, who gave everything away. She was a human potlatch. Gifts dropped from her like fruit from a tree. You dared not admire anything in her home or office or on her person for fear she would give it to you. Anything at all :

69

a painting, a first edition, a piece of jewelry. She gave and gave and gave. Things fell out of her pockets. And everything eventually came back. Doubled, usually. Or tripled.

Hope and I became really close friends during the summer of 1968, when I came back to New York from Heidelberg for a week to watch my grandmother die of cancer. I walked into her office and felt I had come home. It was a sunny room with thick gold carpeting and a large desk covered with trinkets, photographs, flowers. People were always sending Hope flowers.

'Let me look at you,' Hope said. I looked at her while she looked at me, and it was love at first sight. Hope was plump, gray-haired, and gave off warmth like an open fireplace. Her presence had a way of smoothing out all one's lumps and bumps, of making one feel *mellow*. My mother always made me feel nervous; Hope made me feel calm.

She sat there reading my unpublished poems while I looked around the room, mostly for something to do. I was terrified whenever anyone read my poems, convinced they were dreadful, convinced I was going to be revealed as a fraud. At the time, I had an unpublished book of poems about living in Europe, Germany, Nazis, and the silences in my marriage. Hope read. I pretended not to be terrified. After a page or two, she looked up and said : 'Poetry manuscripts always knock me out. Such simple white pages – and someone's entire soul behind them.' Then she went back to reading.

Well, I could always go back to graduate school. *That* path was open to me. Or I could find a job in a publishing house. It was not such an awful thing to have *tried* to be a poet and failed. It was worse never to have tried at all. Wasn't it? But then I thought of all those pompous bores who thought themselves poets and weren't. The hopeful boobs who mailed off their sentimental effusions to *Writer's Digest*, who signed up for correspondence courses at the Famous Writers' School, who went hopefully to vanity presses with eight-hundred-page poetry manuscripts in hand and the firm conviction that somehow their vanity-press books would 'catch on,' would become word-of-mouth best sellers. What if I were one of *those*? It was one thing to be a mediocre prose-writer. Mediocre prose might be read as an escape, might be spoken on television by actors, or mouthed in movies. But mediocre poetry did not exist at all. If poetry wasn't good, it wasn't poetry. It was as simple as that.

I thought of my grandmother, from whose house I had just come. She was jaundiced, cadaverous, eaten away by cancer of the pancreas and beaten down by the side effects of the chemotherapy she was being given. For as long as I could remember, she had had a cancer phobia, but now that she actually had cancer she never breathed the word. She sat in a chair by the window, sewing, taking in her clothes. 'They're all too big,' she said, 'and I want to have something to wear when they let me go out again.' Of course, they never did let her go out again. She was dead two months later. But before she died she sent me to Hope. It was she who was responsible for my going over there, poems in hand. I never would have done it without her prodding and without wanting to please a dying old lady. In those days I was afraid to show my poems to anyone. Especially an *editor*. Editors were deities to me. They *knew*.

'You're going to be the most famous woman writer of your generation,' Hope said to me, looking up.

The woman is mad, I thought : gushy, overenthusiastic, wholly lacking in any critical judgment. She is just being nice to an old family friend.

'You don't really mean it,' I said.

'I never say anything I don't mean,' Hope said. 'I may seem gushy to you —'

I lie : 'Never.'

'But I care too much about poetry to lie. People bring me manuscripts all the time. And most of them stink. I say so, in the nicest words I know – but this book is something special. I want to send it around to publishers. May I have this copy?'

'Oh god – that's not a good copy. It isn't ready. I have to revise it – and have it retyped. My typist is in Heidelberg – I'll have to send you a good copy. I will. I swear I will.'

Hope looked at me and read my mind. 'I think I want to have this xeroxed right now – so I can keep it. What with Mama dying, and you going back to Germany in two weeks, I don't want them out of my sight that long.' She smiled mischievously.

While the poems were being xeroxed, she asked me about my marriage. She had never met Bennett, wanted me to describe him. I thought for a while. There was nothing I could say. His dour face, our fights, his urging me to come to New York and stay with my grandmother while she died, his insistence that I go alone, 'face her dying' alone, his insistence that I remain in analysis, his sullenness, his lack of humor.

'He's very supportive of my work,' I said.

'But do you love him?' she asked.

'What's love?'

'If you have to ask,' she said, 'you don't.'

Now, six years later, I am back in Hope's office to tell her what she's known all along.

'Remember the summer we met? Remember when I brought you my poems?' I am sitting in the chair opposite Hope's desk, just as I did that summer. 'Remember when Bennett insisted that I come to New York to "face Mama's dying"? Do you know why he did that?'

Hope is clairvoyant, as usual. 'Another lady?'

'How did you know?'

Hope makes one of her characteristic hand gestures that indicate parabolas, infinity, circles within circles. 'I just know.'

I start to cry. 'Oh Hope, I'm so mad at him I want to kill him. I can't see an Oriental on the street without wanting to murder him. Sometimes I lie in bed with Bennett, thinking I'll get a kitchen knife and cut him up. I feel like such an idiot. All those years of obsessing about sex, sex, sex – and all the while he was *doing* it. And making me feel guilty. I'll never trust him again. I know it. And you know the worst part? He doesn't even know why I'm mad. He doesn't understand that it's the *hypocrisy* that makes me crazy. He doesn't begin to grasp it.'

'Look, darling, you know what I always tell you. Take it if you can take it, and if you can't take it, get out.'

'I can't take it.'

'So get out. But don't sit on the razor's edge and cut your beautiful pussy.'

And so on up Madison Avenue to the analyst's office. Oh god. This is your life, Isadora Wing. Still living on the West Side street where you grew up. Dividing your life between the writing desk and the telephone table and the analyst's couch. Is *this* the woman everybody envies? Is this the woman who's supposed to have the answer? Ask Kathryn Kuhlman. Or Clare Boothe Luce. Or Helen Gurley Brown. Start your own religion. Become a faith healer. Marry money. Start a magazine. *Those* people have answers. But not writers. We are paid for our pain. And our nightmares. We are paid to drift foggily from the typewriter to the kitchen stove (where we make still another pot of coffee and remark to ourselves irresolutely that *one* of these days we really ought to mop the kitchen floor). Then we drift back. We get paranoid from too much solitude and believe our publishers are ripping us off or our readers pestering us. We get a dozen raving mash notes and one unsigned, illiterate hate letter and remember only the hate letter. We spend so much time alone, brooding, that we become obsessed with sex, with fame, with chimerical business deals. We hunger for love, ache for sex – and yet, when we get it, dispose of it quickly so as not to let it interfere with our writing. Unhappiness is our element. We come to believe we can't function without it.

The analyst's office. There is the constant hum of the 'white-sound' machine, thick wall-to-wall carpets, bokhara rugs over them, crystal chandeliers, velvet chairs, prints that are neither obscenely banal nor lewdly avant-garde. The proper Piranesis and Picassos : the two P's. I go from my husband's home to my analyst's office and the sounds are

73

the same. A whole life spent on the couch. A whole life blurred into the 'white-sound' machine.

The first time I entered the office of Abigail Schwartz, MD, I thought: How can *she* help me? This slender brunette with her Kimberly knits and her Evins shoes, with her Oriental rugs, and her inoffensive art, with her crystal chandeliers and her Irish maid who shops in Gristede's, and her children in private school. She probably never leaves the East Side – except to take a Caribbean cruise. I had been to plenty of analysts, and with the exception of my German mentor, Dr Happe, they were all paralyzed by their banality. Not that they didn't help me. Every one of them made some contribution, made me a little less afraid (or else life did it; I will never know for sure). But at some point, every one of them became trapped in the method itself. It became a solipsism: *I analyze, therefore you are a perpetual patient.* At times, I could hear Dr Schwartz's technique actually *creak.* I would say something about Bennett – something critical usually. And she would say, inevitably, 'Didn't your mother do something like that?' or 'Didn't your father do?' or 'Didn't your sister do do do do do?' I told her I could make a tape and play it to myself – for all the good she was doing me. I told her she bored me. And yet I liked her, her mildness, her gentle sense of humor. I kept coming back. In all the boredom, there was something good happening. We went on and on and on about my marriage to Bennett. Why was I so restless? Why was I so ambivalent? Why did I always want to leave? For a long time I'd believed that that was *my* failing. For a long time I'd believed I couldn't love any way but ambivalently. I had come back into analysis to overcome a writer's block. That accomplished, I stayed because I wanted to leave my husband and didn't know how.

But that Monday something strange happened in my analysis. After years and years on various couches I refused to lie down. I sat in a chair facing Dr Schwartz, unwilling to be horizontal anymore. Of course she interpreted this – but gently, as was her fashion.

'Do you think it could be because unconsciously you're afraid of things happening behind your back?'

'Damn right I do,' I said.

Analysis: the apotheosis of the obvious! If some of the banalities spoken to one by one's analyst were uttered at a dinner party, everyone would think: *how moronic.* Yet we pay for them. Often at a dollar a minute. I was just about to tell Dr Schwartz how banal she was, again, when suddenly, I spun off into the past ...

I see myself lying asleep on a spare mattress on the floor of my study in Heidelberg. It is about 8:30 A.M. and Bennett has already left for the hospital. His bed – I gave him the one extra bed and slept on a mattress on the floor – is tossed. We are sleeping in the study because friends from the States, a couple and their two children, are occupying our bedroom. As I struggle to wake up, I hear them talking in the kitchen.

I told Bennett if he wanted this marriage to work, he had to commit himself and give up the other ...

What did he say?

That he didn't know if ...

More breakfast noises. A siren going *derdee derdee derdee derdee* down Panoramastrasse and all the little American army brats in Holbeinring imitating it *derdee derdee derdeeeeeeee.* Sirens like the Nazis used. All those old movies. People being awakened in the middle of the night ...

Does he realize what he's? ...

I don't know. I only told him that he had to make a choice ...

My heart is racing, my ears burning. I feel sick. I try to hear and not to hear at the same time. I could leap up out of bed and confront them, but wouldn't they be embarrassed? Wouldn't I? The last thing I'd ever want is to embarrass them. Rhoda and Lionel. Bennett's old friends from New York. Both on their second marriages. Both having been through hell and come back. They *know* they want to be married to each other. Bennett and I are only hanging on with our fingernails.

I roll over and bury my head in the pillow, cover my ears as I used to when I was a child. I try to pretend that what I heard is not in the kitchen but in an adjoining chamber of a dream. And then I fall asleep again.

Dreams of Bennett, Penny, and my friend Michael Cosman. We are all on skis, skiing endlessly down to some beautiful little Austrian town, smaller than Kitzbühel, bigger than Lech. I am skiing as I never ski in life: effortlessly shifting my weight, paralleling around bumps and boulders, *wedeln*, and actually circumnavigating fir trees. Penny and Bennett are skiing arm in arm, smiling at each other, and oddly using only two poles between them. They are going to get married, but I don't care because Michael Cosman is following close behind me, grinning from under his bushy blond mustache, and he is going to marry me. I turn around to smile at him and fail to notice a fir tree right in front of me. Suddenly I am so close upon it that there's no time to avoid it. I am zooming head-on into the fir tree. I am surely going to be killed. I try to scream, to wake up, to fall backward, or to change the dream, but I am as stuck in the dream as I am in my marriage to Bennett. When you are stuck like that, you either bend or break. And then – as if by magic – the tree becomes substanceless and I ski straight through it. And Michael follows me. And Bennett and Penny are nowhere to be seen. 'Where are Benny and Pennett?' I ask Michael. 'That's terrific,' he says. 'What's terrific?' 'Pennett and Benny,' he laughs. And the dream fades.

When I wake up an hour or so later, Lionel and Rhoda are still puttering around the kitchen. I have consciously forgotten everything I heard earlier, but it lingers – like an aftertaste of onion, or a bad dream. All day I am fogged, off-key, unable to concentrate on the smallest task. When it's time for me to go to my analyst in Frankfurt, I drive to the railroad station and somehow manage to miss my train even though it's standing right there on the platform. I look straight at it – the same train I always take – and am convinced it's the wrong train. Another train pulls in, and I'm convinced that too is the wrong train. I miss two trains in a row to Frankfurt, and go home weeping, having missed my only session with Dr Happe in all my years of analysis with him.

'Do you understand now why you missed those trains that day?' Dr Schwartz asks.

'Of course – it's all so infuriatingly obvious – if I'd gone, I'd have had to discuss what I knew about Bennett and Penny.'

Dr Schwartz nods. 'Why do you think you didn't want to know?'

I look down at my green sandals, then up at her bland, pleasant face leaning on her bland, pleasant palms over the bland, pleasant French provincial desk on which she has rested her bland, pleasant elbows.

'Oh, I suppose it's something disgustingly oedipal. Mommy, Daddy, locked doors – all that.'

'What does it remind you of?'

I think terribly hard, as if my brain would break with the strain and a crimson stream of blood shoot out of my forehead. This is it, the dead center of analysis, the point where, after years and years of paying in your money, you are finally supposed to have a blinding vision of Mummy and Daddy fucking in the clouds and be cured of your neurosis forever. That great parental bed up in the sky. Those cosmic bedsprings creaking.

My mind is utterly blank.

Oh, when I was fifteen, I *did* accidentally open the door on my mother and father in a thigh-lock in bed – but fifteen doesn't count. Too old. Not formative years. And then there was my older sister Randy necking in the studio of the crazy gothic triplex we moved into on Central Park West – our 'step up' from West Seventy-seventh Street. Did she go 'all the way'? I thought so. But do older sisters *count* as primal-scene material?

'What are you thinking?'

'Oh, just a lot of junk I've told you before ... Seeing my parents in bed that time I was fifteen and Randy necking in the studio when I was a kid.'

'What about Randy? ...'

'What about Randy? What about Randy! She was always up there in the studio playing records and necking with her various boyfriends, while I was studying away to get A's in school like a little jerk. She was the rebel, had temper tantrums, never studied, had millions of boyfriends.

And there *I* was – flat-chested, skinny legs, potbelly, long stringy blonde hair, little smocked dresses and knee socks, leather leggings – no, that must have been earlier ... But the point is: I was forever a child and she was *born* a woman. She was tall, had breasts, pubic hair, her periods ... And she knew about things like diaphragms and condoms and saltpeter and Spanish fly ... I was the little jerk trying to please, please, *please* everybody by being a damned overachiever and she was getting more attention for necking in the studio. She drove me crazy. I wanted to *be* her. But I was five inches shorter and looked like a little kid. All I could do, for god's sake, was get A's in school. And that's all I still can do! While the whole world is fucking away behind closed doors, all I do is write, write, write!'

'Didn't you do that in Heidelberg too?'

'Exactly. While Penny and all the other army wives amused themselves by playing *Peyton Place*, I was writing. For all the good it did me!'

'It did you plenty of good.'

'Oh sure. Fame. Books on the shelf. Crazy people sending me love letters. What I wanted was a man to love me. I *didn't* get that.'

'Well, why does that make you so bitter? You got everything else you wanted.'

'Everything else is nothing without that. Empty. Meaningless.'

'I don't think so. Your work is very important ...'

Suddenly I laugh. 'Hey, Doctor Schwartz – you know what? Our roles are reversed. You're supposed to be the Freudian saying "*The love of a man is all*" and I'm supposed to be the feminist saying "*Work is all*." *Arbeit macht Frei*. What they had over the gates at Auschwitz. Did you know that?'

She shakes her head.

'Well, they did. Funny, isn't it. The Nazis coming up with that. Was it ironic, do you think? A cruel joke on the prisoners?'

'Let's get back to Penny. When was she born?'

'Why?'

'I'm just curious to know her age. She was older than you, wasn't she?'

'Yes. I think she was ... Let's see, I married Bennett in 1966. I was twenty-four – boy, was that dumb! – and the next year I had my twenty-fifth birthday. Penny was thirty that year. Five years older ... God – she must have been born the same year as my sister Randy, 1937 Jesus.'

'Do you see why it makes you so mad?'

'My older sister fucking in the studio all over again. While I play the little good girl and *write* about my fantasies instead of acting them out. Sublimation and its discontents. Christ, Doctor Schwartz, I hate to admit it, but sometimes you really know what you're doing.'

She laughs. 'Your fury isn't so mysterious, is it?'

'No. But do you really mean to imply that because it's all a reenactment of me and Randy, that explains away my anger at that creep I married – what's his name – Bennett?'

'It doesn't explain it away, but at least you understand some of the ingredients of the anger.'

'Are they always from the past? Can't I just be furious about being duped?'

'Both. But if the component from the past weren't there, you wouldn't forget things, blank them out like you did when you overheard your friends talking in the kitchen. You would have taken it all in and done something about it then instead of getting angry now, do you see?'

'You mean I would have left Bennett then?'

'I can't really say. I know I don't know for sure. But at least if you had discussed it with Doctor Happe, you would have had a choice in the matter – instead of feeling so trapped.'

I mull this over. It's really true. I deliberately deprived myself of the choice of leaving Bennett. Every jailor requires a prisoner to continue being a jailor. I was my own jailor, my own prisoner.

'The thing that interests me, you see, is your blanking out. If you can get to the bottom of *that*, you'll be a lot freer. You don't have to be Hear-No-Evil.'

'True.'

And then the time is up. I wander out onto Park Avenue thinking, *analysis isn't so bad*. The point is well-taken: if I can unscramble the tricks my unconscious plays on me – the blanking out, the not hearing – I can be a lot freer. In my life. In my writing. Not bad, huh? But analytic insights are like Chinese food. Two hours later, I'll feel hungry again.

Jeffrey Rudner, MD, is striding toward me along Park Avenue. When I see him loping along from his analytic session (just as I have completed mine) I always think of how he looked to me the summer I first met him at the Cape: a little foolish, an overgrown hippie with a manic giggle. He affects a beard and stringy Mexican ties and walks as if he had springs under his soles – a sort of pogo-stick bounce along the pavements of New York. He is always contemplating psychoanalytic studies of Euripides or Sophocles – which, of course, he never writes.

'Hello, pumpkin,' he says, grinning at me. If eyes could salivate, his would.

'Hi,' I say brightly. I always feel like something of a fraud with Jeffrey because secretly I think him not very bright. Likable enough, but slightly puerile. Would I ever have fucked him in the first place if he hadn't told me he had lupus?

There we were on the nude beach at Truro, drinking white wine under the sun and smoking dope and pretending not to be examining each other's bodies nor interviewing each other preliminary to an affair – when suddenly he injected a note of solemnity into the proceedings by talking about his rare, incurable disease. Our spouses were not along (they both disapproved of nudity). But we were not going to let *that* bother us. We were free spirits, after all, tra la. We did not have to be governed by our stuffy spouses. I was getting the first sunburned nipples of my life. He seemed to be getting quite a lot of infrared rays on his circumcised but otherwise unsurprising *shlong*. We were joking and bantering and generally pretending not to be undressed

– when Jeffrey declared that he might die any month, year, or decade. 'So might I,' I joked, looking down and admiring my snatch-hair (which I hoped was beginning to bleach in the sun). But no, he was serious; he had learned to live with his incurable disease and it had liberated him. Formerly an uptight psychiatrist, he was now a hedonist. Once, in fact, on this very beach, he had come swimming at 6:00 P.M. (when the dunes were empty of kids and the naked matrons and beachboys had all gone home) and coming out of the water he had spotted a 'mermaid,' a teeny-bopper of fifteen or so, who apparently wanted a back rub, which became a front rub, which became a fuck, and they parted without exchanging names.

'Very *Last Tango*esque.'

'Unzipped, as you say.'

I scowled. I hate being misquoted. 'Zipless, you mean.'

'Unzipped,' he persisted.

'Well anyway, it sounds nice. Was it a good fuck – apart from the excitement of the *idea*?'

'I don't remember, actually.'

And then he went on to detail the other elements of his liberation: an affair with a young male painter (so that he would not die without having experienced homosexuality), an affair with a radical feminist (so that he would not die without having experienced radical feminism), an affair with his Swedish *au pair* girl —

'So that you wouldn't die without having experienced a Swede?'

'Well, it may sound silly to you, my dear, but you don't *have* an incurable disease. It changes everything.'

And it did. When Jeffrey made a definite pass at me, I thought and thought about it and finally said to myself, *Well, after all, he does have an incurable* ... I was making love to death, enlivening death, denying death. What a ploy! How did *I* know the guy had lupus anyway? But even more important, would I *catch* it? I never fucked Jeffrey without wondering. And I never washed so much when I came home.

Our first encounter was a farce anyway. Gretchen had a loft where she used to meet her various men (after we had

81

both read their 'F' Questionnaires* and given them clearance) and from time to time she would lend it to me. Jeffrey claimed to have some cocaine and he wanted to try it with me. That was the excuse, anyway. If *I* had known anything about coke then (I know slightly more now) I would have realized that *he* knew nothing. He had scarcely enough coke to get a roach high (and there were plenty of them in that loft, too) and he had no idea of how to snort it either. But what did *I* know at that point? I hadn't yet been to Big Sur to meet the experts. I was just a psychiatrist's wife from the Upper West Side and hot for adventure. Coke it is. Clear all the patients out of a Friday afternoon in September. Lock up the co-op, tell your husband you're in Bloomingdale's for the afternoon, and head for the loft.

Much cloak and dagger. Jeffrey and I are both feeling so illicit that we take separate cabs to Gretchen's office, meet in the lobby, exchange conspiratorial glances, and, while I go upstairs to get the keys to the loft, he goes off to get some beer and sandwiches. Then we take separate cabs to West Nineteenth Street.

We meet on the rickety wooden stairs, both of us looking around nervously (nice Jewish kids that we are) for fire escapes. The place is a trap. SHRINK AND WRITER TRAPPED IN LOFT FIRE. But we persevere in pursuit of adventure. You

---

* The 'F' Questionnaire, invented by Gretchen Kendall (patent pending), is described as 'a simple quiz for feminists to determine which men are safe to fuck.' It contains such questions as : 'When referring to members of the opposite sex, do you use the term (a) chick, (b) girl, (c) woman, (d) bird, (e) Ms, (f) your highness, (g) cunt, (h) the distaff side, (i) the little woman . . .' and : 'In any relationship, who should be responsible for contraception? (a) the man 50 percent of the time, (b) the woman 100 percent of the time, (c) the man 100 percent of the time, (d) all of the above . . .' There are numerous trick questions and an elaborate scoring system to 'smoke out' (as Ms Kendall describes it) 'the numerous phony male feminists in our midst.' Almost no one passes, and I have often thought that Gretchen would be better off instituting a sort of 'Open Admissions' policy – much like the City University of New York.

know the loft. Creaky floors, a dozen skinny avocado plants in pots. A mattress on the sooty floor. Dirty sheets. Dirty old couch with cheap Indian throw. Windows begrimed with all the pollution of New York. And then Gretchen's special touches: a fruit bowl full of Reese's Peanut Butter Cups by the bed, a silver tray with a vast selection of condoms, vaginal jellies, diaphragms, a bottle of Youth Dew. God bless Gretchen.

Jeffrey and I pace around nervously, giggling a lot, then finally settle on the couch and begin unwrapping our sandwiches.

'Would you like to try the coke now or later?' my smooth co-conspirator asks.

'Why not now? ...'

He pulls two little foil packets out of his pocket – they look like the wrappings for salt brought on a picnic – and extracts two battered sawed-off straws from his jacket pocket. Oh god. I am terrified. Will this weird drug make me into a sex-crazed lunatic? Will I lose control totally?

'Snort,' he says expertly, not knowing what the hell he's doing; and of course I breathe out and disperse the tiny quantity of white powder over the dirty couch and dirty Indian throw.

'Here,' he says patiently, 'try again,' and he also offers me the contents of the next packet.

'No, I can't. I'll ruin that one too.'

He insists. '*Please.*'

'No. You try it.'

'No, really, I insist.'

'No, you try it.'

'No, *please* ...'

'No, really. After you.'

'No, I *insist* ...'

'No. You try it.'

Jeffrey tries. He snorts deeply. Then his face lights up – as if there really were enough powder to make him feel anything.

'Do you feel anything?'

'I don't know.'

'Then you don't, silly.'

Jeffrey leans back on the pillows. 'I *think* I do. Here . . . You try too.'

'There's no powder left.'

'Yes there is. Here.'

He sticks it under my nose and I breathe in. It tickles. It could be the dust in the loft. Then we both sit there for a while staring at each other, waiting to become raving nymph and satyr, totally devoid of inhibitions. Nothing happens.

'What do you feel?' I ask.

'Hmm . . . interesting,' Jeffrey says.

'Interesting what?'

'I wonder if this is it.'

'If *what* is it?'

'This.'

'What?'

'This . . . this . . . *je ne sais quoi* . . .'

And with that inanity, I begin to giggle. Jeffrey assumes it's the effect of the coke so he giggles too. Which makes me giggle more. Which makes him giggle more. Which makes me giggle more. Which makes him giggle more. Which makes me giggle more. Which makes him say, smoothly, 'Shall we go to bed?'

Aha. The question has been popped. The long-unphrased, entirely inevitable, nude-beach-ripened, adjacent-analysts-inspired question has been popped. Popped. Here goes.

'I think not.'

'Why?'

'Well, for one thing, your wife's my friend, and for another, you play tennis with my husband, and for another, I'd feel too guilty.'

'What if we only give each other back rubs?'

'Which lead to front rubs, which lead to fucks . . . like with your mermaid.'

'Not necessarily. Would you feel less guilty if we only went down on each other?'

I grin at him. This is what my old high school buddy, Pia, used to do while touring Europe. To keep herself pure. It does, somehow, feel less like a commitment than fucking.

'Or else we could use one of Gretchen's vast selection of condoms.'

'Why a condom? Don't you have a diaphragm?'

'I do – but how can I use the same one with my husband and with a lover?'

'You use the same cunt, don't you?'

And we both get the giggles again. Somewhere mid-giggle, Jeffrey points to the bed and says 'Shall we?' and I think, What the hell, the guy has lupus, the patients have already been cancelled, and we've gone to all this trouble to get the keys to the loft. The cocaine seems to have been forgotten – if it ever existed.

To my surprise, Jeffrey is not silly in bed. He stops giggling and becomes wholly concentrated on rubbing my back, eating me till I come three times in a row, and then finally fucking me. He is slow and meditative about it, and a terrific lover. All that's missing is my *feeling* anything for him. Except that he *is* a dying man. But then, again, aren't they all?

Jeffrey and I greet with innocent cheek-kisses under the canopy of 943 Park. Midway between his shrink's office and mine – a discreet compromise.

'Shall we take separate cabs to my office?' he asks, rolling his eyes around, obviously enjoying the intrigue.

'Not necessary,' I say. 'In fact, I rather hope Bennett sees us.'

'But what about Roxanne?' he asks nervously. His wife, Like all adulterous husbands he assumes she's pure. And unsuspecting.

'Oh you're right.'

'Anyway, why are you so cool about Bennett?' Jeffrey asks. 'You didn't *tell* him, did you?'

My heart leaps. God – I did. And after promising Jeffrey I would never.

'Of course I didn't tell Bennett, silly, but after what Bennett told me, I don't suppose it matters much if he finds out.'

'What is it, pumpkin?' Jeffrey asks sympathetically.

'I'll tell you when we get to your office.'

Once there (having risked the one cab) I spill out the whole sad story of the Woodstock weekend to Jeffrey, who is immensely understanding.

'I always thought Bennett was a sadist at tennis,' he says. 'What are you going to do?'

'Leave him,' I say, decisively. 'I can't go on living with a hypocrite. I mean fucking around occasionally is one thing, but Bennett was immensely cruel. That time I came back from Woodstock, you know what he told me?'

'What?'

'I repeatedly asked him if he had been with another woman and you know what he said?'

Jeffrey shakes his head. 'No. What?'

'He said, "Your fantasies are better than anything I could tell you." Can you *imagine*? I mean if he had said, "Look, I fucked someone else, I'm fallible too." Or even told a *lie* about where he was, it would have been *human* at least. But to lay it off on me and *my* fantasies ... I call that sa*dis*tic. I had enough problems with my fantasies without his tormenting me about them further. He made me feel that I was crazy. Like in *Gaslight*. That seems to me the cruelest thing anyone can do – making the other person feel crazy. It's almost kinder to beat someone up.'

'Poor pumpkin,' Jeffrey says, coming over to my chair and putting his arms around me. 'The guy really is a bastard, isn't he?' And he begins gently easing off my shoes, kissing the soles of my feet as he does, and unzipping my green-and-white voile dress (under which I am wearing nothing but flesh-colored bikini panties). And then his hands are cascading over my body, cooling my anger, soothing my hurt. We move down to the floor (we have always been super-stitious about fucking on the analytic couch) and he gives me one of his expert back rubs, massaging each vertebra separately, concentrating for a long time on my coccyx and then on my shoulder blades. When Jeffrey makes love to me, I relax entirely – maybe because I have never felt the slightest stirrings of romantic love for him and therefore feel wholly safe. It is just sensation. Sensation and friendship. In friendship now, he buries his head between my legs and begins eating me – something he does as if he really enjoyed it, unlike the majority of men. Perhaps it is just a virtuoso performance – a species of male narcissism – but what do I care, lying back, being teased and licked and probed and licked again, being made to come and come again until I am weak in the knees and shaking all over. I try to reciprocate, take his cock in my mouth and begin teasing it with my tongue, but he won't let me. 'This is your day,' he says, and begins massaging my back again.

By the time he looks at his watch and declares it time for the seven o'clock analytic patient – the one he can't cancel – I have come five times, and still he won't let me reciprocate.

'Women's Lib,' he says, with a twinkle in his eye.

I leave Jeffrey's office and wander out onto Central Park West. It's still light out, with those warm breezes wafting up under my voile dress where my cunt is wet and throbbing from all that attention. Sure enough, every man I pass looks me over, and one even starts to follow me. It never fails. After making love for three hours, I must walk with a special lilt or exude some odor like a cat in heat.

It used to astonish me that men followed me in the streets after sex, that they grinned and winked as if they *knew*. I'd be coming from Jeffrey's office (or Gretchen's loft downtown) and before long I had a retinue, a string of chorus boys, a following of tomcats.

Usually I felt wonderful after an assignation. Before, I would be tense, obsessive, terrified. I'd call Bennett at the hospital and be exceedingly sweet to him and also set up my alibi for the afternoon. Somehow it was always shopping. 'I'm going to Bloomingdale's, darling,' I'd say, quite unconsciously affirming the deep connection between sex and shopping, between bloom and Bloomingdale's.

Ah Bloomingdale's! Would it be as crowded as it is if every woman in New York had two lovers named Jeffrey? One afternoon, I had the brainstorm of strolling through Bloomingdale's main floor after walking all the way back uptown from the loft on Nineteenth Street. I looked around me like a dreamer and suddenly *understood*. All those women promiscuously spending money, stuffing shopping bags with *things*, charging, charging, charging to their husbands' accounts, were starved for sex! So many holes to fill! So much misplaced passion!

The only difference between the shoppers and me was that they failed to recognize their hunger for what it really was while at least I admitted it. They scarcely *knew* why they cared about a new gloss stick for the lips, a free sample-kit of wrinkle creams for the face. They wanted their wrinkles plumped out, their valleys filled, their pores plugged. They would pay *any*thing for that. They were excited when some vapid model on the main floor handed out cards saying FREE CUSTOMIZED PERSONALIZED MAKEUP BY MR X or LEARN TO LOVE THE FARM-FRESH FACE or FIND A NEW YOU. Suddenly I had a vision of a whole world of women starved for sex and making do with all sorts of buyable substitutes. Making up.

A woman who spent her afternoons with a lover would never again find herself in Bloomingdale's fingering Mary Cunt or lusting after Elizabeth Ardent. She'd go barefaced as a baby and throw her charge plate in the nearest sewer. Isn't that the problem? That women have been swindled for centuries into substituting adornment for love, fashion (as it were) for passion? The main floor of Bloomingdale's by Hieronymus Bosch!

All the cosmetics names seemed obscenely obvious to me in their promises of sexual bliss. They were all firming or uplifting or invigorating. They made you *tingle*. Or *glow*. Or feel *young*. They were prepared with hormones or placentas or royal jelly. All the juice and joy missing in the lives of these women were to be supplied by the contents of jars and bottles. No wonder they would spend twenty dollars for an ounce of face makeup or thirty for a half-ounce of hormone cream. What price bliss? What price sexual ecstasy?

Normally I would be high after those hours with Jeffrey Rudner, but on this occasion despair very quickly sets in.

I suddenly realize that I could fuck a different man every weekday afternoon and still not feel contented. Adultery is no solution, only a diversion.

To clear my head, I walk all the way to my dinner date with Jeffrey Roberts (almost forty blocks downtown), and all the way across town to Madison Avenue again. Jeffrey is working late and waiting for me in his office. He knows nothing of the existence of the other Jeffrey, has no idea that he is the other half of what is, in fact a double Jeffrey.

Not that they are at all alike. Jeffrey Rudner is brown, long, and lean, Jewish and tawny, bearded. Jeffrey Roberts is fattish, porcine, and pink. WASPish, Southern, clean-jawed. Whereas Jeffrey Rudner is fucking me to stave off death, Jeffrey Roberts practically never fucks me at all, but loves me with a tenacity which would put Pyramus and Thisbe to shame. For years I thought we'd wind up together. Right after we met, he went to live in South America with his family and we wrote each other long, literate letters. Almost love letters. Or love-for-literature letters. Jeffrey is a frustrated poet who works in an advertising agency writing cosmetics ads. Those beautiful goos they sell at Bloomingdale's are his poems. Not that he creates them. Only God (or Elizabeth Arden) does that. But he names them. He is the Adam of hormone creams and lipsticks, the primal poet of eyeliner and false lashes. Barefoot boy with cheek gloss.

I fell in love with his letters. He wrote so well I thought him handsome (in a way I used to think certain radio announcers handsome because they had such handsome *voices*). Of course I had seen him – his pinkish mottled skin, his stubby white lashes, his beady blue eyes – before he left for Brazil. But his letters were so beautiful I forgot his face. We conducted a whole love affair on paper for two years. An epistolary novel almost. An eighteenth-century Richardsonian romance. And then he returned. Face-to-face with that piglike face, I could not love him. Oh I was sorry. Very sorry. It was not at all democratic of me – but when was love ever democratic? There is, in this imperfect world, the sheer irreducibility of looks. We love for funny reasons: a slightly crooked smile, front teeth that are a trifle too long, the way the chest hair feels to the cheek that lies on it. Sorry. I did not invent the system. Next time, I will try to improve on it.

But nevertheless I *tried*. Old I.W.W. never gives up on any man without a struggle. I hang in there year after year trying to make the unlovable lovable. I believe the imperfections of the system are all my fault. I *want* the world to be democratic when it obviously isn't. So I tried with Jeffrey. Every morning at eleven we checked in on the phone. Long literate conversations. We were both immensely lonely and married to people we couldn't talk to. I think we may have saved each other's lives. Those conversations were lifelines to us both. I was writing poems and novels at home. He was writing haiku on hand cream and sonnets on suntan lotion at the office. We lunched together once a week at least, getting drunk and merry, eating too much, giving each other books and manuscripts, cards, gifts, furtive propositions. Eventually bed reared its ugly headboard. Another six months went by. (I suspect Jeffrey was really scared of me.) Then it reared again. We met at my house, ate lunch and then each other on the old velvet couch in my study that used to belong to my grandparents. Jeffrey belched after eating me as if I were a mug of beer. I couldn't bring myself to touch him for another six months.

That was pretty much the course of our 'affair.' Six months of letters, phone calls, and lunches for every fuck – or even every naked lunch. After every physical encounter, I vowed, *No more*. The physical attraction simply was not there. But then the months would go by and I would forget. I would forget what a terrible lover he was. And then six months later I'd try again. And suddenly I'd remember. 'We never really gave it a chance,' Jeffrey would say. He was thinking technique, the joy of sex, foreplay, foreskin – all that jazz. I was thinking, *Never*. But I loved him. He was my *friend*. I thought him terrifically funny and clever, found him affectionate, witty, charming, intelligent, a great critic of my work. So I always tried just this one more time – and every one more time was just as terrible as the time before. That was the interesting thing about my double

Jeffrey: one half I loved but couldn't fuck. The other half I couldn't love but loved to fuck. Fragmentation, I thought. The dichotomy between lover and friends. I blamed myself, as usual, for the inability to bring them both together.

Now I am striding into Jeffrey's office at 8:00 P.M., to see him sitting, and *davening* over the story boards for a suntan lotion commercial.

'Tan-tan makes you feel like a *shvartzeh*,' I say, entering laughing. 'Don't be merely tan – be *Black*. Get the benefit of Equal Opportunity Employment without being traumatized by your peers. *Or* by your early years.'

'You really want to get me fired, don't you?' Jeffrey says. And then: 'Hi beauty. You look smashing.'

Jeffrey may be ugly, but he knows how to make women feel beautiful. That and a little phony feminism can get any man laid in two minutes flat.

'How are things?' I ask.

'What can I tell you that you don't already know about suntan lotion?'

'Does chicken fat really work?'

'Only if you're Jewish,' he says.

I sit down in an armchair, relieved to be in Jeffrey's office. My friends' offices – up and down the isle of Manhattan – are havens for me, homes away from home, places I can go to escape from Bennett or writing or myself.

'How's Rebecca?' I ask. Rebecca is Jeffrey's wife, born a Southern Baptist, now a Seventh-Day Adventist and confirmed schizophrenic.

'Crazier than ever. She made me take down the picture of Flannery O'Connor I had over my writing desk because – get this – O'Connor is an Irish name, and the Irish are the enemies of the English – and her family was English. That kind of logic is abundant around our house. I'm really ready to move out.'

'Funny. So am I.'

Jeffrey brightens. 'If you ever need a roommate ...'

I feel a terrible pang of guilt for not loving him that way.

'Oh Jeffrey, I *wish* it could be —'

'Nonsense. We've just never given it half a chance. I honestly think it would save both our skins. You keep saying you're leaving Bennett, but you really don't want to live alone. We could take care of each other, not get married or anything, just see if it would work out. I'm a terrific cook, honey.'

'I know it.' For a moment I let myself drift into a fantasy of living with Jeffrey. Shelves laden with Flannery O'Connor criticism, the comforting sound of two type-writers going against a background of Scriabin, bouilla-baisse simmering in a huge enamel kettle (Jeffrey is a great maker of bouillabaisse), cats with silly literary names like Percy Bysshe, Childe Harold, Frankenstein. But then I would have to fuck Jeffrey. At least once in a while, out of politeness. If only I cared less about that aspect of life, I could do it. I really could. Who in the world would I rather read books aloud with, cook with, browse in the Gotham Book Mart with, travel with, observe the passing scene with, laugh with, drink with? No one but Jeffrey. *Damn* sex. If only one could lobotomize it out of one's system. Without sex it would be so easy to choose appro-priate people to live with. Sex was the joker in an other-wise rational deck.

'You know I love you, don't you?' Jeffrey says.

I nod. 'I love you too.'

'But not the same way I love you.'

'Nonsense.'

'Nonsense to *you*. You know goddamn well what I mean. We've been friends too long. And I know you too well. Miss Transparency. I read your mind. If I looked like Robert Redford, we'd have been cooking together and waking up together for the last four years.'

I look down at the floor. What in god's name have I just been doing with Jeffrey *Rudner*? I don't love him *at all*. Perhaps I should try again with Jeffrey Roberts. I *do* love him. I *do*.

'Love,' says Jeffrey, 'is a joint experience between two persons – but the fact that it is a joint experience does not mean that it is a similar experience to the two people involved. There are the lover and the beloved, but these two come from different countries. Often the beloved is only a stimulus ...'

'Carson McCullers?'

'You read the book! You actually read one of the books I gave you! I was beginning to give up hope.'

'Look,' I say, 'I *wish* we inhabited the same country.'

'Me too.'

'I had a hell of a weekend with Bennett, and I really feel I'm ready to leave.'

'I've heard that before.'

'This time I mean it.'

'I've heard that before too. What kind of a hold does he have on you? You can't really believe you'll wind up alone. It's so *obvious* you won't.'

I thought about it. From Jeffrey's point of view it must seem bizarre, but each of us only feels the torn lining of his own coat and sees the wholeness of the other person's. I *was* sure I'd wind up alone. I was certain I'd fall apart without Bennett. What held me? Panic was the glue. Besides, I didn't see myself as Jeffrey saw me. To him I was confident, sane, strong, beautiful, with a million choices before me. To myself I was a bundle of indecisions, crazies, irresoluteness, overweight. I was also over the hill, too old, too set in my ways, too used to having a keeper and feeling kept. To be told that I was a young woman with myriad possibilities before me made me laugh. At least *then*. I would have to get considerably older to realize how young I was.

Jeffrey walked over to me, lifted me out of my chair, and gave me a bear hug. Out of friendship, I hugged back. Soon he was panting, pressing his cock against me and asking, asking for my reassurance that he wasn't ugly, wasn't unhappy, wasn't trapped in a job he hated, a marriage he hated, a whole way of life he hadn't bargained for. And soon I was down on my knees sucking his cock to prove to him that somewhere in all that unfulfillment and unhappiness he had a friend.

My mouth was in it, but not my heart. I couldn't wait for him to come and for the thrusting and gagging to be over. It was a Good Samaritan gesture – like taking a blind person across the street or giving blood – but it was

somehow also loathsome to me because sex is too powerful a force to misuse it that way. I was being dishonest
with him – as I'd been dishonest with Jeffrey Rudner.
Doing it out of pity was not much better than doing it
out of selfish lust. They were both sides of the same
counterfeit coin. That Jeffrey Roberts sighed and moaned
and thanked me profusely later only made it worse. What
was he thanking me for? Pity was no gift.

'Let *me* buy you dinner tonight,' I said. And we left his
office and headed up Park Avenue to the Trattoria, where
we gorged ourselves on pizza and *zuppa inglese*. We were
always more comfortable together at table than at sex.

After I'd insisted on paying for dinner and walked him
to his 10:10 train to Greenwich, I called Holly from a
phone booth.

'Christ,' she said sleepily, 'what time is it? I've already
had three Valiums.'

'Can I come over?'

'Of course, love. Of course you can always come over. I
ought to be insulted by the question – but I'm too tired.
Where the hell are you?'

'Grand Central Station.'

'Crossroads of a million private lives?'

'You said it.'

'What time is it?'

'It's only ten-twenty.'

Holly groaned. 'Come on. I'll get out the mint tea and
we can take our midnight Valiums together.'

Holly's apartment is the sanctuary the analyst's office
should be but isn't. Another loft (this one on lower Fifth
Avenue), reached by a dark staircase. But when you enter
the apartment, there is a sudden revelation of lights, plants,
air, space. There is a skylight with a jungle of ferns growing up toward it. There are numerous stands of African
violets, flourishing under fluorescent lights that go on and
off on timers. An artificial pebble walkway between the
sleeping area and the cooking area is flanked with potted
avocados, lemon trees, gardenias, kumquat trees. How she
makes all this tropical stuff grow in dreary, sooty New

94

York, is nothing short of a miracle. But I guess Holly makes it grow because making things grow keeps her alive. That and her painting, numerous examples of which cover the walls.

How to describe her style? Georgia O'Keeffe crossed with Francis Bacon? No. Holly is herself alone. But she does have this tendency to zero in on the everyday objects we don't usually bother to look at, enlarge them to heroic size, and force us to see them as if through the eyes of Blake – if not God. Holly is the painter I would be if I had three times as much talent to paint as I was ever born with and hadn't given up at the age of twenty for fear of competing with my mother. Every canvas of Holly's is a vision out of one of my nightmares. I have never had this sort of relationship with an artist friend before. Friends of *mine* have told me that my poems spoke their thoughts and feelings, but I have never before felt, as I do with Holly, that every new canvas of hers is a revelation of my own inner life.

Holly is tall, thin, buxom, with a mop of curly brown hair, and a small mouth that usually has a rather wry expression. She is one of those odd people who has never had a weight problem, who, when she gets depressed, stops eating and gets thinner and thinner until her analyst threatens to hospitalize her. She and her plants nourish each other. She lives on oxygen, herb tea, and Valium. She has often explained to me, with considerable passion, that the fern, that ancient botanical specimen, has the ideal life situation. It is self-nourishing, self-fertilizing, contains sexual life-styles within its own lifetime, and it is actually immortal. Or at least some part of it is always alive. I have never before met anyone who clearly wanted to be a plant, but Holly makes it seem extremely attractive.

The door opens and I am hugged. Holly has only recently learned, after a lifetime of WASP boarding school *coolth* – as she calls it – to hug people, so she hugs a lot. Especially me. I like it.

The fluorescent lights over the violets are on, but otherwise the loft is dark. A soft tangle of ferns grows up towards a gray skylight.

'Come on in, love,' says Holly, who is wearing a caftan she made herself and no shoes. She smells of sleep, warmth, somewhat stale Jungle Gardenia perfume. I sit down in the bentwood rocker, dispossessing the cat, Seymour, and several patchwork pillows.

'Where the hell are you coming from?' she asks.

'I just had dinner with Jeffrey Roberts, actually.'

'Oh? The Pillsbury Dough Boy.'

'He's really very nice – and very lost.'

'I would be too, if I were living in a haunted house in Greenwich with Aimee Semple McPherson. Boy – she sure ain't playin' with a full deck ...'

'He wants out too.'

'And you're planning to save him? Let me take my Valium right now and go back to sleep.'

'No, Holly, I'm not planning to. I don't love him that way – though sometimes I wish to god I did. But I don't think I can stomach Bennett anymore.'

'Well, that doesn't mean you have to instantly move in with someone else. There *are* those of us who live alone and like it. It's *not* a fate worse than death.'

I look around at Holly's nest, which even with the lights out is cheery and warm. Better to have spent the day here, working, as she did, than to pound the pavements of New York, seeking salvation. What on earth did I do with a whole day? Gretchen, Hope, Dr Schwartz, Jeffrey Rudner, Jeffrey Roberts, here. And all to avoid having to go home to Bennett. When a marriage reaches *that* point, surely it is not worth keeping.

'The thing is, Holly, I don't even know why I'm so angry at him. I mean – I've had affairs myself. At times I've even *wished* he would have affairs – to prove he was human.'

Holly is fogged. 'What the hell are you talking about?'

'You know, the stuff I told you on the phone this morning.'

'You mean the dame he had in Europe?'

'And also here, when we got back.'

'I *would* say that it was pretty sadistic of him to tell you about it *now*.'

'But *why* does it make me so furious and ready to leave? It doesn't add up somehow. I've done it myself. I'm not exactly Miss Fidelity. So *what*? So he had a couple of affairs ... He's forgiven me *my* affairs ...'

'Forgiveness isn't the issue.'

'What is?'

'Love.'

'Oh god. I'd be happy never to hear *that* word again.'

'If you loved Bennett, if he gave you something besides lectures, guilt, and grief, I don't think the affairs would really matter at all. So he put his penis in someone's hole. Big deal. *Who cares?*'

'Boy – *your* analysis must really be progressing. I've never heard you say *hole* before. When do you think you'll come up to *cunt?*'

'Fuck *you*.'

'Bravo. Very good.'

Holly often says that she spent the first three years of her analysis learning to say *fuck*, and the next three years learning not to feel guilty about saying it, and the next three years getting up the courage to *do* it occasionally. She still doesn't do it much. But then, neither do ferns.

'Do you want me to level with you, love, really level with you?'

'I guess that's why I'm here.'

'Okay. Truth time. Here it comes. I have *never* heard you say anything positive about Bennett except that he was a good fuck.'

'*Really?*'

'Cross my heart and hope to die. In the three years we've really spent time together – *never*.'

'You know what? He isn't even such a good fuck ...'

Holly lowers her eyes. 'You can spare me the erotica. Save it for your new book. I just wonder why you don't ask yourself why you're so bloody afraid of being alone. It ain't half bad compared to living with the walking dead.'

'I thought you *liked* Bennett.'

'What's to like or dislike? He's completely inaccessible to me. Of course he was very riveting one time about the re-analysis of the ten-year-old, but other than that, I don't remember ever having a conversation with him that had any emotional content whatsoever. I haven't the faintest idea *what* he's about. Is he happy? Is he sad? Only his analyst knows for sure.'

This gives me a pang. 'I feel sorry for him. I think I represent life to him – how can I up and leave?'

'And what does he represent to you? Death? Look, lovely, you don't stay with a person out of pity. Not at thirty-two, you don't. Life just ain't long enough for that. Sorry.'

'But he'll fall apart without me ...'

'*Bullshit*, he will. That's the biggest piece of narcissism I've ever heard. He'll do just *fine*.'

'How do *you* know?'

'I just *know*. Besides, will *you* do just fine if you stay? For years now, you've been anguishing over leaving. It's bad for your work, bad for your head, and fattening. It's obvious you two are never going to get it together to have a child together. You really don't *like* each other well enough for that – so what the hell? Why don't you take off and find someone you really love?'

'Maybe I'm incapable of that. Bennett really has me convinced I can never love anyone because I'm so neurotic. He says the only way I'll ever straighten out is to stay in analysis.'

Holly looks exasperated. 'Boy – is *that* ever a self-serving theory. *If you don't love me you must be sick.* How can you *believe* such crap?'

'Well, maybe I'm just too committed to writing to ever love anyone. Maybe I couldn't *live* with anyone but the walking dead. He *has* been good for my work. You've *got* to admit that.'

'I'm not so sure.'

'What do you mean?'

'All your poems are about unfulfillment, emptiness, bitterness. Who knows what you could write if you really loved someone? How can you box yourself in that way? How can you lock yourself in that kind of self-fulfilling prophecy?'

98

'You're a fine one to talk – you and your plants.'

'Look – cutie pie – you and I are not alike. I don't *want* to live with anyone. I don't *want* children. I'm not even very into sex. But you *are*. You're not a fern; you're a god-damned mammal ...'

'God. For a moment, I thought you were going to say something devastating.'

'Didn't I?'

'I've been called worse things than a mammal,' I said.

Holly lit a cigarette and did not laugh. She was intent on getting her message across. 'What's the point of hanging on like this? *Any*thing would be better than this god-awful cliff-hanging.'

'I suppose.'

'Look, what do you think *my* life is like? Not really so different from yours. I work, see my friends, go to parties. You do that anyway. Bennett is merely an appendage to your life, an inconvenience as often as not. Tonight, you don't even want to go home. It's obvious you don't. Where is he, by the way?'

'Who cares?'

'Does he know where you are?'

'Probably not.'

'Then the whole marriage is a farce, a sham, a security blanket. *I* think so anyway.' She emphatically exhaled a mouthful of smoke.

I thought about it. Holly was right. Our lives really *were* much the same. Bennett and I practically never saw each other. And by design. Or at least by my design. Then what did I need him for? So I could say 'my husband' and have a figurehead monarch – like England has its Queen? So I could disguise my rebellion with token convention-ality? So I could have the illusion of being protected by a man?

Suddenly, I panicked and decided I had to go home. Suddenly, I had to be with Bennett.

'I'm going,' I said.

'Thanks a whole lot. You wake me up, get me going, and then walk out. I thought you were going to stay the night, sleep on the couch.'

'I can't,' I said, shaking. 'I really have to go.'

'You keep yourself on a very short leash, don't you?'

'Please understand if I go. Will you?'

Holly looked pissed off, but she understood. 'I was going to make something terrific for breakfast,' she said. 'Now I have no excuse.' Holly was, in addition to her many other talents, a *cordon bleu* chef who never had anyone to cook for.

'Some other time,' I said.

Back on Seventy-seventh Street the light was on in the foyer, Bennett's briefcase was stowed neatly on a chair, and the man himself was stowed neatly in bed, sleeping without rumpling the blankets. Just being back calmed me considerably. I looked in briefly at Bennett, then went to my study, sank down in my leather chair and tried to make sense of my feelings. Why was I suddenly so calmed by seeing him sleeping there? And was that a reason to stay married? It was really odd how, especially if I had fucked someone else during the course of the day, I was utterly panicked until I'd come home and touched base with my husband.

My husband. What security was in that phrase! It was almost like 'In God We Trust' or 'Guaranteed by Good Housekeeping.'

What magic did the phrase *my husband* have? It was a seal, an imprimatur, an endorsement that I was a *bona fide* woman. It was like saying, 'Look, I have a man, therefore I am a woman.'

Why did I need this? Why did we all need this? All my life I had known women who supported their families, did their own work, did most of the housework – yet needed to be married, often to men they clearly did not enjoy. I knew rich women who had husbands as baubles, career women who treated their husbands as sort of extra children in the family, frenetic housewives who raised kids and cooked and also kept their husbands' stores, businesses, or medical practices from sinking into total confusion. There was no doubt about the strength of these women. Except perhaps in their own eyes. Did every one of them need that phrase *my husband* as badly as I did? Did every one of them need that sleeping man whose presence scarcely ruffled the bedclothes?

I had tried to leave Bennett so many times, and each time I had come back. Each time I'd come back, things changed for the better. The marriage had become freer, more open, less restraining. It was so free by now that if I didn't come home at night, he simply went to sleep. Yet that wasn't what I wanted either. It was as if we were two strangers living in the same house. We really weren't free – just indifferent. Loving someone *is* a loss of freedom – but one doesn't think of it as loss because one gains so much else.

But I could scarcely even remember why I had married Bennett in the first place – as if that had been in another life, and I had been a different person. We all go through various transformations in the course of growing older, and become several different people even in our own brief lives. The soul is a process, not a thing; therefore you cannot put it in a box (or a book) and close the lid. It will crawl out and keep changing. The woman who married Bennett in 1966 was as different from the woman sitting in that leather chair, as the woman who endured that crazy summer of fame and jealousy is different from the woman writing this book. I keep trying to recapture myself at different periods of my life and it is impossible because even as I write, I change. Both the passage of time and the process of writing change me. And though I try to skewer bits of pieces of reality with the point of my pen, inevitably memory fails me, words fail me, and the picture is fragmentary and false. Worse still, this false-hood will be seen by the reader as literal truth and only I will realize how many discrepancies and holes there are, how many sins of omission I have committed, how many tattered fragments masquerade as the tapestry entire.

There is a rhythm to the ending ...

Many people today believe
that cynicism requires courage.
Actually, cynicism is the
height of cowardice. It is
innocence and open-heartedness
that requires the true courage
– however often we are hurt
as a result of it.

There is a rhythm to the ending of a marriage just like the rhythm of a courtship – only backward. You try to start again but get into blaming over and over. Finally you are both worn out, exhausted, hopeless. Then lawyers are called in to pick clean the corpses. The death has occurred much earlier.

Everything I did that summer was part of the unraveling of the marriage, though I didn't know it until later. The first symptom of distress – just as it is the first symptom of falling in love – was that I was unable to work. I went frenetically from one friend to another, one activity to another, avoiding my home, avoiding my writing desk, unable to eat or sleep.

It wasn't odd, really, that I was drawn back to Michael Cosman that summer. Michael was the friend of my broken leg, the friend who had cheered me through the grim three years in Heidelberg, the friend who had given and given of himself without ever trying to take me to bed. He was also the only person in the world who could tell me about Bennett and Penny – and I was hungry for such information, ravenous for every detail. With Bennett's Woodstock revelations, I had slipped back into the past and I was once again remembering Heidelberg, turning the pages of my life as if it were a book, flipping back and forth between past and present. The one event that symbolized the fracture in my marriage to Bennett more than any other was my broken leg, and what Bennett had helped to break, Michael had come to heal.

Michael Cosman was a general practitioner from Great Neck for whom the army had found no medical use whatsoever. He was assigned to spraying mess halls for roaches and interviewing the contacts of VD victims (who, in truly democratic spirit, often offered to infect him). The army was driving him about as crazy as it was driving me. But his response to it all was to grow a handlebar mustache and plant marijuana outside the hospital (where, along with marigolds and pansies, it helped to spell out *USA-REUR*) – while my response was to break my leg. (Is there a psychological difference between men and women? A rhetorical question.)

Sometimes I think I could tell the story of my life through the scars that mark my body. I could write a whole novel in which the heroine, standing naked before the mirror of her memory, enumerated the scars up and down the length of her body, and for each scar told the story of how it came to mark her flesh, the pain she suffered, whom she shared that pain with, what healing was attempted and by whom. Each chapter heading would name the scar, and each chapter would begin with a re-counting of the accident that 'caused' the scar. Except that the reader would instantly become aware that the 'cause' was much deeper than mere accident.

I would tell of the opalescent, crescent-moon-shaped scar on my right knee, made by an equally opalescent shell fragment on the beach at Fire Island the summer I was eight. I would tell how I sank to my eager knees in the sand, not feeling the shell pierce through to the moony white bone until I stood and bright-red arterial blood spurted out onto the white sand. I would tell of the six pale stitches on my left palm, made by a huge bread knife the summer I was fifteen, miserably unhappy with my job as kitchen maid and waitress at Camp Merryhill, and wanting a reason to stop slicing sandwiches so I could languish in the infirmary, read Dickens and feel like an orphan along with Pip and Oliver Twist. I would tell of the twelve-slice-high stack of uncut peanut butter and jelly sandwiches and how I suddenly brought my palm down on the blade I had unwittingly pointed towards the ceiling, slicing open my own white flesh instead of the spongy white flesh of the bread. I would tell of the strange fibrous lump in my back-side, made by the quarts of blood released into the tissue of my back and thighs when I was deliberately given a too-spirited horse at the Ft Sam Houston Riding Club and was later thrown spine first onto an outcropping of rock. I would tell how I was lucky enough to lose only blood rather than the use of my legs, how I landed on my ass rather than my spine, how my guardian angel spared me paralysis, how I was taken to the army hospital, and suddenly, in the middle of 1966, realized that a whole secret war was being fought in Vietnam as I passed my three weeks in the hospital among baby-faced quadruple amputees and napalmed children from Vietnam.

Then I would go back in time more than thirty years and tell of the tiny hole in my neck, created in my mother's womb, the disturbing remains of some mysterious prenatal event whose traces remain to this day. I would tell of the three stitches above my left eye, made when I catapulted over the cord of my electric typewriter in one of those fits of despair about writing which are as much a part of the writer's trade as the typewriter itself. I would save for last that almost imperceptible swelling in my left shin, the remains of my fractured tibia, snapped on the icy slopes in Zürs in 1967, when Bennett was so deeply involved with Penny that he hated having to go on vacation with me and consequently bullied me into skiing on slopes which he knew were icy and anyway too difficult for me to handle.

Oh I could tell the story of my marriage to Bennett through the accidents we had together. Interestingly enough, *I* was always the one who got hurt. And he – who felt like a perpetual victim of the world's injustices and therefore justified in committing any cruelty – was always angry at me for getting hurt. But one accident will have to do, will have to serve for all the rest.

I rewind the film backward seven years and my life flashes past in reverse: The sunny room in which I am writing this changes to humid overcast New York during that summer of jealous madness, then changes to rainy Heidelberg the winter of 1967–68. We are driving south on the autobahn and the wiper blades are smearing the windshield with arcs of mud. It is two and a half weeks before Christmas and Bennett has gallantly insisted that I drive to the Austrian Alps with friends and get in two weeks

107

of skiing before his leave schedule permits him to join us. His 'leave schedule' – unbeknownst to me – is actually Penny. And once again Bennett has made me feel guilty about going away – when in fact he has chosen to stay in Heidelberg so that he can have a full two weeks to fuck Penny in my study without fear of any witnesses but my manuscripts.

Our parting has been grim. Bennett has duly reminded me about what a 'spoiled brat' I am – because (at his suggestion) I am getting extra vacation time and he is not. All the guilt he feels about getting rid of a wife to fuck a mistress has been reversed and projected onto me. And I, who am so very good at feeling guilty, feel terrible. Poor Bennett, I think, as we speed south on the autobahn, and me the lucky one, going skiing.

Not that I ever wanted to go skiing in the first place. Just as a glittery blue ocean puts me immediately in mind of sharks, sugary alps piercing a bright blue sky make me think immediately of broken limbs, falling chair lifts, and hapless skiers impaled on their own poles. The first time Bennett took me skiing (in the Black Forest, that spring), I'd never even had the damn things on before, and he left me to struggle with the laces and bindings while he took off over the hills and wasn't seen again for six hours. That was pretty much the course of our outdoor-sports relationship. He was the athlete; I was not – and whenever he prevailed upon me to do anything athletic with him, it was usually a prelude to his leaving me stranded on a mountain or a beach or a baseball field or a muddy track.

But there I am going skiing and trying for the life of me to feel lucky about it. The skis are on the roof of the Volkswagen Squareback, the boots are in the trunk, the mud is on the windshield, I am in the back seat with the dog, and my friends Chuck and Ricey Higgins are telling me not to feel bad about Bennett, for whom my heart is breaking.

'Oh, he'll be okay,' Ricey is saying – probably knowing full well that he's stayed home to screw Penny.

'He'll get in plenty of skiing *after* Christmas,' says

Chuck. 'Don't *you* feel guilty.' In retrospect, they probably *both* knew about Penny.

Two weeks of skiing in the idyllic Austrian town of Kössen, in the foothills of the Alps. Though it is early in the season, there is plenty of snow, and with my two supportive friends beside me, my skiing is progressing beautifully. All day in ski school I perfect my stem turns, hoping Bennett will be proud of me when he arrives. At night, we three wander through the snowy, blue streets of the village, past the cemetery with candles marking the headstones ('So they can read?' Ricey asks), past the war memorial where all the names of the dead who were buried under other snowdrifts are incised in cold black granite. The blue snow blows up in little gusts like the smoke of risen souls. It covers the names, uncovers them, covers them again – making the dead seem like sons and fathers to each other.

Alone in my room later, I am sad and frightened. I never would have seriously entertained the idea of sleeping with anyone else during the first years of my marriage, but I wonder about Bennett. Is he really alone? Why hasn't he called me in ten days? Is he mad at me for going away without him?

After eleven days, I call him, wanting reassurance. Bennett sounds pained. The strangeness of his voice panics me.

'Oh, Bennett *always* sounds strange,' Ricey says later.

'He isn't the warmest guy,' says Chuck, philosophically. I try to reassure myself. He's always strange, I tell myself – which is true. But then the other question inevitably comes up: what am I doing married to a guy who is always strange?

Bennett arrives three days before Christmas, bringing the rain.

The rain begins pissing down over the slopes, washing away the snow, revealing boulders, tree stumps, haystacks, the black obelisk of the war memorial, now unsoftened by snow. The four of us languish indoors, praying for the rain to stop.

'If it stops today, the snow will still be good.' we say

hopefully, every day. And every day it goes on raining.

Somehow, the rain is my fault. The rain is the result of my having been comfortably off in childhood while Bennett was poor, the rain is the result of my having skied so well during the two weeks Bennett and I were apart, the rain is the result of my suppressed anger and suspicion.

And I am duly apologetic. I apologize to Bennett for the rain. And he rages at me. And I apologize again – which only makes him madder. One thing I have only lately learned is that apologizing to people sometimes produces the reverse effect that one intends. If you apologize for something that isn't your fault in the first place, you, in effect, confirm their belief that it is your fault. Thus the weather is my fault. I believe it. Bennett believes it. Ricey and Chuck don't believe it – but who are Ricey and Chuck, after all? Just friends. Bennett and I are the weather gods.

With the fanatical zeal of the frustrated athlete, Bennett insists that we all pack up and head still higher into the Alps. Surely, higher up there will be snow. So we take off for Kitzbühel.

Now, Kitzbühel is usually one of the more bustling ski resorts. Cafés, people strolling down the main streets, discotheques, tanned ski instructors in their red sweaters and red caps, their hip pockets filled with flasks of brandy – but today even Kitzbühel is deserted. The main street is blustery, slick with sleet, desolate. Ricey and Chuck have stayed in their room playing cards. Bennett marches resolutely up the Hauptstrasse, determined to ski no matter what the weather. I trudge resolutely behind him.

The cable car swings up the mountain in a strong wind. A few red-faced stalwarts – veterans of an Arctic expedition, perhaps – join us in the cable car, laughing and slapping each other on their well-padded backs, taking light snorts of some Teutonic firewater as the car creaks on its icy cable. I am, of course, sure it's going to break – and actually, that alternative seems not much more unattractive to me than what awaits us at the top of the mountain. One of our compatriots in the cable car is a hearty one-legged skier – one of those indomitable veterans of Germany's imperialist past. He may have lost a leg in battle –

but he skis twice as well with the other. This is the sort of counterphobic madman who tackles the slopes on such a day. Normal people don't. Except my beloved husband – whose mouth is now set in absolute determination. Our car swings into the upper dock of the cable landing. Bennett shoves me with his pole to get a move on, as one might prod a cow.

Outside the cable landing, there is such a blizzard that one literally cannot see the path ahead. We stop and put on our skis here, even though the wind already threatens to knock us over. I press my boots into my ski bindings with a satisfying snap. Once I *have* the skis on, it's another story what to *do* with them. My knees are buckling. I have maneuvered on skis perfectly adequately with Bennett away, but now that he's *here*, I am suddenly incompetent. It feels like coming to the top of a staircase, looking down, and forgetting how to walk.

We form a single-file procession (Bennett behind the hearty one-legged skier, me behind Bennett, some idiot behind me, treading on the backs of my skis). We trudge blindly along in the blizzard, stabbing the ice with our poles, sliding one quaking leg in front of another. To the left of me is a whitish blur which I assume is a mountain. To the right of me is a bluish blur which, my ski pole tells me, is sheer drop. How did I get myself into this predicament – me, a simple Diaspora type from the Upper West Side? The skating rink in Central Park was my winter Olympics. The Great Snow of '47 nearly buried the Museum of Natural History and the cars on both sides of the street looked like giant loaves of snowy bread – but what in god's name am I doing on an icy ledge in the Austrian Alps with a crazed Chinaman and a one-legged Kraut? And who is that idiot who keeps stomping on the backs of my skis? I say a little prayer to God, my mother, and my beloved analyst, Dr Happe : *Please let me live long enough to publish one book; I swear I won't ask for anything at all after that.*

Eventually, the narrow icy ledge gave onto what seemed like a mountainside : another white blur, descending. As we left the ledge and came out into the open, a gust of wind hit us with such ferocity that I was nearly knocked over backward and managed to keep my hold only by digging my poles into the frozen ground.

'For god's sake, Bennett, let's go back,' I shouted in the direction of his red parka.

'I didn't come all this way to turn back. I've already missed nearly a week of skiing!' he snarled.

Missed a week. Already. That was the essence of Bennett's personality: feeling cheated. I couldn't see his face and yet I knew how it must look – scowling, self-righteous, twisted with determination not to let the weather cheat him. And so the reddish blur took off down the mountain while I stood at the top, paralyzed with fear, digging my poles into the ground to keep from being blown over. Bennett was blown over a few minutes later, in fact, but I couldn't see how it happened, nor could I have helped him even if I'd wanted to. And at that point, I didn't much want to.

After several struggles with the wind (which the wind invariably won) Bennett relented and deigned to descend by cable car. On the way down he made sure to call me chicken and accuse me of having ruined his day of skiing. Oh, there is no sense in blaming *him* for that. The world is full of petty tyrants, stingy souls, woman-haters. There is no end to the supply of them. They are themselves, as the snake bites and the scorpion stings. But those of us who get involved with them and stick with them are the fools. *We* deserve the blame for not picking ourselves up and walking away. We think we are buying security with our slavery – and then, a decade later, we leave and let them keep the furniture, realizing that it is a blessing to be rid of their tyranny at any material cost and that there is no such thing as security anyway.

The next day we continued driving higher and higher into the Alps. If there was no good snow in Kitzbühel, perhaps we should try Innsbruck or St Anton or Lech or Zürs. Chuck and Ricey went along. They were happy enough wherever they were, playing cards in front of the fire and drinking *Glühwein* and eating Austrian pastries.

The rain was still pissing down when, on the third day of our wanderings, we drove into Zürs am Arlberg – a bleak, treeless ski resort whose barren peaks were shrouded in rain clouds.

The resorts highest in the Alps, above the timberline, all have a similar naked aspect to them : a group of elegant chalet-style hotels on the lower slopes of severe jagged peaks and, on sunny days, an intense blue sky – blindingly blue, because of the thinness of the atmosphere. When the mountains are covered with snow and the sun is out and the lifts are all running, these 'serious' ski resorts are not entirely without cheer, but when the butterscotch-candy sun slides down between the peaks and the shardlike purple shadows cut into the snow, the whole landscape becomes dismally lunar and cold.

On rainy days, it is even worse. You are there to ski, but you cannot ski because there is no snow. Neither is there anything else to do – but play cards and eat. Or else read – preferably some long, inscrutable tome. We spent four days at the Sport-Hotel Edelweiss, watching the rain come down, playing hearts, overeating dumplings and schnitzel and roast pork with apples. Feasting on pastries *mit Schlag*. And *Kaffee mit Schlag*. And drinking ourselves insensible on *Glühwein* every afternoon by the fire.

I was perfectly happy with this routine. I was reading *Ulysses* at the rate of about five pages a day, gaining weight at the rate of about five pounds a day, and feeling content never to put on skis again as long as I lived.

The slopes were dangerously icy. I had heard terrible stories about what happened to even expert skiers on icy slopes. There was nothing preventing me from staying in the hotel with Ricey and Chuck the morning Bennett decided to tackle the slopes – nothing except Bennett's challenging glare. Or was there more? Bennett's affair with Penny had begun (I now realize) the previous fall and he had become more and more rejecting toward me. Even though I didn't 'know' about Penny, I *knew*. My antennae were too good for me not to know. In fact – this flashes back to me with a shock – I'd been thinking

113

seriously of leaving Bennett. A broken leg was the perfect punishment for thoughts of running away.

Christmas Eve, Zürs am Arlberg

It has rained all night, the rain has frozen and the slopes are glassy as the slopes of some fairy-tale mountain. Toward morning, light flurries of snow begin and settle on the slopes just enough to resemble two days' cover of fresh powder. Sheer ice camouflaged in fluffy snow. After a breakfast of croissants and coffee, I trudge along after Bennett toward the nursery slope T-bar.

'We'll start on the easy slopes, okay?' he says, appeasing me. And I nod, thinking, *There are no easy slopes*. But already, Bennett is on the T-bar, heading upward, and I follow. I remember the words of my first ski teacher, an American college dropout: 'All you have to worry about is gravity.' *All*. At the top of the T-bar, gravity strikes and I fall, ass first, on the icy ground. A brisk German girl snaps at me as if my falling were a rude gaffe, an antisocial gesture like a fart or a belch. I scramble to my feet, look for Bennett, and realize that there's a terrible cramp in my leg. The days of sitting around the Sport-Hotel Edelweiss have left me out of shape. Meanwhile Bennett is already whizzing down the slope.

I follow. My leg is cramped, I can't bend my knees, I am doing the sort of straight-legged panicked snow-plow they show in ski manuals as an example of what never to do.

Bennett does two graceful parallel turns and I mimic him, looking like something out of Chaplin's *Gold Rush*. The poles are lethal weapons in my hands, my knees are absolutely rigid, my eyes closed in panic. Just then, I must have hit a patch of ice because I got going so fast that I suddenly understood the expression *greased lightning*. I fell – deliberately, I think, in order to stop myself – and lay in the snow, twisted into a pretzel of arms and legs, wondering what in the hell I had done to deserve so much pain.

'Are you all right?' Bennett yelled. I answered in groans. I was looking melodramatically up at the blazing blue sky and thinking of *The Snows of Kilamanjaro* – the part where the hero says something about how you are supposed to black out from the pain, but, alas, you never do.

'Don't move,' Bennett admonished, but I was stuck in such a painful position that I had to *try* to move. One ski stuck in the snow, my foot wedged in the boot, the special quick-release bindings not releasing and all the pressure on my own nonreleasing leg.

Bennett came over and pronounced it 'just a sprain.' Then he tried to extricate my foot from the boot. The pain was excruciating, but the humiliation was even worse.

Help came in the form of two young men on skis who arrived at the top of the T-bar with a cunning aluminum gondola contraption between them. One was wearing bright yellow sun goggles, and the other had a gap between his teeth. My whole being was focused on that gap. They got me out of my ski boot somehow (the leg was already swelling up) and slipped a long plastic balloon over my leg, zipped it up, and inflated it. I was lifted onto the gondola, covered in blankets (like a corpse), and my skis were strapped alongside me. My rescuers clicked into their skis and we were off down the mountain, the neon-blue sky above and the blinding snow below, and my presence evoking looks of curiosity, relief, and fear from the skiers we passed. We zigzagged down the mountain with incredible speed and lightness, then we trudged along the slushy Hauptstrasse (where I was jostled considerably). More vulture-like looks from my fellow humans, to whom I smile and wave, trying to be brave. Cars passing. People staring down at me. Pain. That intense physical pain which cannot be remembered except as a kind of blinding whiteness. White sound.

I am taken to the office of an unforgettable shark named Dr med. Holger Kapp (an avaricious Austrian who'd learned all the latest medical shenanigans in Boston), and there I am X-rayed. Bennett appears, assuring me once again that it's 'just a sprain.' The X-rays appear, assuring us that it's an impressive break, a spiral fracture above the ankle and the tibia shattered into bits the shape of sharks' teeth. In German the diagnosis sounds even more menacing: *Schien-*

beindrehbruch am distalen Ende (Aufsplitterung in mehrere Bruchstücke)! This is what happens to a woman who even *thinks* of leaving her husband!

Then I remember Dr med. Kapp, waltzing in, trying to sell us bone-hardware, special crutches, and a week (at least) of chicken soup at steak prices. Anything might happen on the way home, he warned. Severe skids on icy roads, fogged-in autobahns, drunk drivers. But Bennett insisted on getting me back to the good old army hospital, where the doctors did not have funny accents and believed in 'conservative treatment' of fractures. And so we hit the road that very night.

Deserted, rainy autobahns all the way back to Heidelberg. The grimmest Christmas Eve I've ever spent in my life – and, believe me, I've spent some grim ones. Ricey and Chuck drove our VW bug and Bennett and I took the Squareback so that I could stretch out on an inflatable mattress in the back. I was by then delirious with pain, and alternated between weepy remorse for having ruined Bennett's vacation and deep embarrassment for having to pee into wadded-up Kleenexes and then toss them out the window.

The next thing I knew I was in the army hospital flying high on Demerol. Nothing much seemed to bother me then. I skied in and out of sleep, weaving, looping, sailing over icy slopes, rocks, and boulders. Each time I awakened from my Demerol dreams, there was some new diversion. Chaplain Glascock, for example, came bearing mimeographed copies of the latest Character Guidance Briefing, blessed me, and then hastily departed – as if afraid of opening some theological dispute he couldn't resolve. Pete Hatch, the well-named head of ob-gyn hung around telling gynecologist jokes which all dealt with vaginal odor. Phyllis Stein, the president of the Jewish Officers' Wives Club (or JOWC) wished me the obligatory *mazel* and assured me that she had the clout to get me kosher meals if I desired them. Even the hospital CO appeared to tell the stories of his two broken legs (Davos and Kitzbühel) and to admonish me to get right back on skis the following year. Only my husband made himself scarce. Guilt and anger kept him away, but as long as I was on Demerol, it didn't much matter.

A week later, though, trapped at home, a prisoner of my cast and Bennett's wrath, the full horror of my disability struck. I couldn't drive with the cast on or walk up stairs or bathe. Bennett refused to let me sleep with him at night because he said the cast 'disturbed' him. He refused to come home for lunch because he claimed I was so hysterical and weepy that I depressed him. I was in constant pain, and without the drugs I'd had in the hospital I was a wreck. Dreams of mutilation replaced the dreams of flying. I hopped glumly from one room to the next, trying to clean up the house, trying to work, trying to block out my nagging, constant feeling of betrayal. I'd drink coffee. I'd read the junk mail. The entire army seemed afflicted with the doggerel-writing bug, and in the morning mail there was always something diverting. The Medical Wives' Club Newsletter (MWCN) reminded me: 'As you go through life/ Never forget:/Strangers are friends/You've just never met!'

But where *were* these friends? And where was my husband? Missing in action. Off with another officer's wife. And I was home with bound feet, like a good Chinese wife.

Somehow, just when the day seemed most unbearable, Michael Cosman would arrive. He arrived with hand-rolled joints or little bottles of champagne, with handfuls of flowers, with books, with strawberries, with brandy. My neighbors probably thought we were having a torrid affair when they saw his car parked outside my house for hours and hours. But we were talking. And laughing. Telling each other stories. Remembering New York together. Telling Polish jokes. Drinking. Getting stoned. Making fun of Germans and the army. And giving each other marital therapy.

On the days when Michael couldn't come, he'd call. I'd hop madly to the phone on my good leg, plop down on the couch, rest my cast on the ugly army coffee table, and we'd settle down to two hours of mutual therapy at government expense.

He'd call ostensibly to ask me how I was doing and to

let me cry on his shoulder about my problems with Bennett. But it wasn't long before he'd start talking about *his* problems, telling me his reaction to DeeDee's much-vaunted affair with a local hippie, what he blamed it on, how he rationalized it, and so on. Then he'd reminisce about his youth, treat me to long Jean Shepherdesque monologues about his violin teacher Mrs Traumstein; his third-grade teacher Mrs Gletscher; his sexual explorations in the bathrooms of PS 103; his fraternity days at Cornell; how he once put barbecue sauce on his penis and asked this girl to lick it off; how Harriet Finklestein had the biggest clitoris he'd ever felt; how Mr Weinburger (of Weinburger Window and Shade) once caught him in bed with Sally Weinburger; what different girls said (moaned, yelled) when they came; how he had this recurrent dream that he was involved in an orgy with the characters in Archie comics; how one day he would forgive DeeDee for her affair and then the next day start imagining it in vivid detail and haul off and slug her. Et cetera.

I was more grateful to Michael than I've ever been to anyone. He called out of his need; I listened out of my own, and, while perhaps this wasn't the best possible basis for a friendship, a real friendship grew. Even after my leg had mended, Michael remained my best friend and confidant. In seven months the bone had healed, leaving a slight thickening in an otherwise slender shin – and Michael and I were still just talking.

Six years later. Summer. Michael and DeeDee have been divorced for almost four years, Bennett and I have 'lasted' through much gritting of molars (mine) and the fact that we've arranged our lives so that we practically never see each other. Ever the rebel without a cause, Michael has still refused to do a residency and has a thriving clap- and birth-control-pills practice for young singles in a brownstone in the West Seventies.

'What can I do for you?' Michael asked, offering me a seat in his sooty back garden, where not even marijuana would grow. The place was littered with bottle glass and cinders, but one cheery, yellow umbrellaed table stood in
118

the center of the soot garden. We drank vodka and ate Greek olives. Michael looked me over.

'What's up? You enjoying being a famous lady? I haven't seen you in ages.'

'You really want to know?'

Michael looked at me over his bushy yellow mustache and beard and amber aviator glasses. He seemed to know exactly why I'd come.

'If Bennett was having an affair in Heidelberg, who would it have been with?'

Michael stared hard at me, hesitated, realized I knew, and then said firmly: 'Penny. I thought you knew *years* ago.'

'Bennett just told me last weekend.'

'What made last weekend different from all other weekends?'

'I don't know. Maybe he resents all the attention I'm getting and doesn't know how else to express it. Maybe he wants to destroy me. Certainly it's working. I've never felt more hysterical in my life. I walk through the streets absolutely seething with rage. I want to kill every Oriental I see.'

'Christ – I'm astonished. I thought you knew *ages* ago.'

'Why?'

'When you came back from Vienna, got back together, you told me you'd discussed everything ...'

'*I* thought we had. Apparently, *I* discussed everything. Bennett didn't. That's one of the things that makes me so mad. I was always cast as the bad girl. He had to have *that*.'

'God,' Michael said.

'Why didn't *you* tell me?'

Michael sucked on his pipe: 'The same reason you didn't tell me about DeeDee, I guess. I knew about Penny and Bennett almost from the very beginning – just like you knew about DeeDee and her hippie. Why didn't *you* tell *me*?'

'I thought it would hurt you. And I didn't want the responsibility for breaking up your marriage. Probably it was

119

a way of shucking responsibility as much as anything else. I plead guilty.'

'Me too.'

We sat and contemplated each other, thinking how different things could have been if we both had known. Would we have had an affair, gotten together, left our spouses sooner? We were both momentarily silenced by the unreeling of the years.

'When did you find out about Bennett and Penny anyway?' I asked.

'Almost at the very start of their affair. You remember where Penny and Robby's apartment was?'

'Right upstairs from you?'

'No. It was one stairwell over. But anyway, one afternoon, I came home for an alert, and because our stairwell was full of kids, I ran up the *next* stairwell and thought I'd take a shortcut through the maids' rooms. Who do I see at the top of the stairs – looking like a commercial for strychnine – but Bennett. He looks at me. I look at him. He averts his eyes. I think immediately: Penny and Bennett? Holy shit! He says "Hello Michael" with that psychiatric snideness of his. I want to say *"You motherfucker!"* – I always thought he treated you like dirt anyway – but I don't, of course, being a professional coward, and he trots down the stairs. After that I knew. Then DeeDee confirmed it. Penny told her everything in lurid detail, it seems. Everybody knew.'

This reopens my wounds. They bleed invisibly.

'Everybody?'

'Yeah. It used to kill me when I saw you and Bennett and Penny jogging around the track in your sweatshirts. Everybody knew about it but you. And Robby, I think. But then, he was having an affair with his secretary ... Frankly, I thought Bennett was immensely cruel to you.'

'Why didn't you *say*?'

'Nobody in their right mind messes with anyone else's marriage. *You* know that.'

I hung my head. 'I thought DeeDee treated you cruelly too.'

'And you didn't tell me either. In fact, you *drove* her into town to meet her lover on one occasion.'

'I *had* to, she ...'

'Don't explain. I'm not blaming you, Really, it's just ironic. You had such a need to rationalize your relationship with Bennett, to tell yourself it was all okay. I don't think that even I – with all my conflicts about breaking up – hung in there as long as you did. You really tried.' He took my hand. I was beginning to weep very steadily, very quietly.

'Why do you think I hung on so?'

'Oh I don't know. We all have this peculiar need to rationalize our choices. Partly it's an inability to admit mistakes. Partly it's to present a united front to the rest of the world. If we admit our marriages are for shit, we're in part saying our lives are for shit. That's very hard. All those years committed to a mistake? Very hard to admit. So we defend the marriage, we rationalize. Until something jolts us really hard. In my case it was my father dying. You can't live with a person you despise – even if you're terrified of living alone. Life is too precious to spend it being contemptful.'

'I know. It's terrible to have contempt for the person you're married to – isn't it? That's the way I've felt for years. It's corrosive.'

'Remember the fall after we got back from Germany?' I nodded. 'That was the closest we ever came to having an affair. You even seemed to want it – and I was ready for it in a way I just wasn't in Heidelberg. I was *incapable* of having an affair then – even though I knew about DeeDee's. Anyway, do you know why I didn't press it?'

'No. Why?'

'Because I knew that if we got that close, I'd have to tell you about Bennett and Penny – and I didn't have the heart to.'

'Oh Michael,' I said, springing out of my chair and hugging him. I was grateful to be reminded, after eight long years of marriage to a robot, that there *are* men in the world for whom sex and intimacy are related.

121

Michael rocked me in his arms and we both cried a little over the past, the miserable years in Germany, our broken marriages, the love affair we never had. Then he moved out of my arms decisively, but tenderly.

'I'm going to make you chicken livers for lunch, okay?'

'Okay,' I said, somewhat disappointed. 'I was rather hoping you'd fuck me – after all these years.'

Michael stood in the doorway smiling. 'Listen. If a month from now you still want it, I promise I will. But I don't want to do it when you're in this state. I don't want to exploit your hysteria.'

'Who's hysterical?' I said, licking the tears from the corners of my mouth.

In the kitchen, he told me Polish jokes and recounted the anecdotes generated by a West Side clap practice. The livers were sizzling in the pan, my heart was aching, and all was wrong with the world. Except that, at such times particularly, it's nice to have friends. Especially friends who cook you chicken livers.

'Do you remember my broken leg?'

'How could I forget it? You were so fucking sexy in that cast. One time, I remember, you wore a black net stocking over it – and a red velvet rose at your knee. You were always hot for me, weren't you?'

'You *know* you're irresistible,' I said, not altogether mockingly. I was thinking of all the men I knew with whom I had tender, bantering, good-humored friendships. Why was I married to the one man in the world I couldn't talk to?

'You know the worst thing about Bennett's affair with Penny?'

'I don't know if I want to hear.'

There was a pause, during which we both listened to the livers sizzling.

'Well, do you?'

'No ... Yes, I *do*. I want to hear *every*thing.' I wanted to open my wounds again, rub salt in them, and shriek my pain until I got it all out of my system.

122

'Her car was parked outside your apartment practically the whole time you were in the hospital.'

His words had the desired effect. I was crying again, long, choking sobs that seemed born out of my gut, my womb, my cunt. Michael put his arms around me and rocked me for a long time.

'Leave the bastard,' he said, 'and then come back to me. Okay?'

That night, at home, I asked Bennett how he could have raged at me for breaking my leg when he was fucking Penny the whole time I was in hospital. He looked impassive. At first he didn't seem to know what I meant. He was brushing his teeth methodically. I was sitting on the toilet seat cover staring at him hatefully. Finally, he took the toothbrush out of his mouth.

'You were always getting into accidents to deprive me ...' he said, as if he hadn't the slightest idea what he was implying psychologically.

'To deprive you! You! We were skiing on *ice*, if you remember. And it was *your* idea!'

'So I had an affair – big deal. Doctor Steingesser doesn't think that's any reason to break up our marriage.'

'What marriage?' I shrieked. 'What marriage are you talking about? Your marriage to Doctor Steingesser or my purgatory with you?'

'Very funny.'

'Oh, I'm not being funny at all.' I got up from the toilet, marched into bed, and pulled the covers over my head. I lay there, savoring my rage. After a while, I could hear Bennett methodically turning off all the lights, locking the doors, padding down the hall in his scuffs. Finally he climbed into bed beside me. There was a moment of silence during which we lay side by side like two sarcophagus sculptures. The king and the queen. Both dead. Cathedral-cold marble.

Finally my lips moved. They were saying:

'I think you ought to get out of bed this instant because if you stay here a minute longer, I swear I'm going to go into the kitchen, get a knife, and cut your balls off. I don't want

123

a divorce, I want to castrate you – simple as that. And you don't even have to interpret anything because I'm saying it straight out. GET OUT OF THIS BED!'

Bennett grabbed his pillow and scurried into the guest bedroom.

Minutes went by. The clock ticked. My lips trembled and tears slid down my cheeks and into my ears. I remembered a song we used to sing in high school. *'I have tears in my ears from lying on my back in my bed while crying over yoooooo . . .'* but it didn't seem funny anymore. Someone walked by, down Seventy-seventh Street, carrying a transistor radio loud enough to pierce the hum of the air conditioner.

This was the bottom, the lowest point in marriage. Sleeping alone in the same house, unable to comfort each other. More alone than if we'd never met. Better to live in a cave like a hermit or to haunt singles' bars, cruising for one-night stands. There is no loneliness like the loneliness of a dead marriage. The bed might as well be a raft in a shark-infested sea. You might as well have landed on a dead planet with no atmosphere. There is nowhere to go. Nowhere. The soul sinks like a stone.

And out of that stony coldness, the flesh stirs – as if to affirm its own tentative life-force. The woman, degraded past all degradation, gets up out of bed, tiptoes down the carpeted hall, and slides into the narrow guest bed occupied by that stranger, her lawful wedded husband. The blue moonlight creeps in past the blackout shades. The old air conditioner whirs like a gardenful of crickets, and she presses herself to his still-warm body.

They might as well be strangers who met in a bar for all the intimacy between them – and yet it is also oddly exciting.

'Hey – what are you doing?' he asks.

'Feeling you up,' she answers.

'I thought you wanted to castrate me.'

'I do.'

The seriousness of her voice makes him hard immediately. It is their old familiar dance. Her broken bones, her

124

accident-proneness, his sadism, his familiar cruelty. It excites her. He might as well be a rapist, a night prowler, a deliveryman invited in for a quickie. They are ice-cold and expert. She opens his pajama-bottoms. He feels for her cunt. He savagely stabs a finger in. It hurts, but somehow hurt feels right on this particular night. He stabs another finger in. She pivots on the bed, swiveling on his fingers, and takes his hard cock in her mouth, wanting to bite it off and seeing nothing but a bleeding root, a fountain of blood spurting all over the moon-blue sheets. But she teases it with her tongue instead. She nibbles around the root with her teeth, almost letting herself hurt him, but not quite. He moans. He is frightened but aroused. It would be so easy to hurt him – but still, she can't bring herself to. She would sooner hurt herself. Now he is rubbing her clitoris rather roughly and she wants him. She hates him, she despises him, but she wants his strange root-shaped cock inside her. It waits there for her, dark as an old tree stump, gnarled, almost inanimate – or dead. The sight of it excites her still more. He lies motionless, silent, the man who died with an erection and then grew harder as rigor mortis set in. She climbs on his upraised penis, swiveling on it, rhythmically rocking, using it as a dildo, coldly. Her orgasm comes in great concentric rings like the water in a still lake when a heavy rock is dropped from a great height. And then he is suddenly thrusting, thrusting, in search of his own. It is as if his orgasm were somewhere deep inside her and he had to find it, fish for it, hook it, reel it in like a wriggling fish. There. It catches. No, not quite. There. A nibble. He gropes blindly, then establishes a rhythm again. *Now.*

She observes all this as if from a great distance, as if she were reading a book – and yet it also excites her. Reading often excites her. And often she does not know if she is writing or living.

There. He's got it. *There, there, there, there, there ...* The thrusting stops and he lies still again. No words. No grunts. Fisherman and fish both gasping at water's edge. What kind of a man is it who makes no noise at all when he comes? A dead man?

She feels tainted, ashamed, slightly necrophiliac. She climbs off his dead penis and lies at his side, thinking. How could two people couple for eight years and yet be so far apart? They might as well be freight trains, locking together for a time, and then going off to opposite ends of the earth. And yet *he could woo me with words,* she thinks, *words would warm me* ... But he doesn't know any words. Words are the only language he cannot speak.

My posthumous life ...

To name oneself is the first
act of both the poet and the
revolutionary. When we take
away the right to an individual
name, we symbolically take
away the right to be an individual.
Immigration officials did this
to refugees; husbands routinely
do it to wives ...

Bennett left early the next morning. He was already gone when I awoke, alone in the big bed. What had happened? I dimly remembered creeping back into the bedroom to sleep alone. I wanted to fuck him, but I didn't want to see him afterward. After eight years, our marriage had all the intimacy of a one-night stand.

What was I doing there? I lay in bed, thinking of my posthumous life. Keats had been twenty-five and dying of TB when he used that term. I was thirty-two and dying of deadlocked wedlock. An incurable disease? I thought of a man I knew who had come home and told his wife he was in love with another woman. 'I'm in love with her, but I haven't fucked her,' he said, thinking to spare her feelings. Incredibly enough, she seemed to believe him. 'Can't you fall in love with me again?' she asked.

So many marriages, so many deaths. People getting up in the morning and going to work, coming home at night, fucking, feeling dead. No wonder they left, ran off with their secretaries, smoked dope at forty-five, discovered sex as if they were Adam and Eve in the garden, and paid and paid and paid for it. Lawyers' bills, alimony, houses sold for half of what you paid for them, children going to therapists, looking up at you with wounded eyes, furniture carted away, family heirlooms kissed good-bye, wounded husbands, wounded wives – it was all worth it if it made you feel alive again. In a pinch, we all know the truth: survival is all. The life-force is the one thing you can't afford to lose. Bennett and I had lost the life-force.

Didn't *he* feel it? Was he satisfied with this half-life we were leading? Bennett was a man who could have steak and steamed rice for dinner every night of his life and never get tired of it, never want a taste of caviar, a taste of tropical fruit. He got up every morning at 6:30, came home every night at 9:00, worked all week like an automaton, played tennis all weekend on a similar schedule, even skied that way on ski vacations, and was content to

129

spend every August in the same shrink-infested sea. Were they in Vienna? Very well, then, we would go to Vienna. Were they at Cape Cod? We would go to Cape Cod. Follow the shrinks! Every August for the next forty years would be like that. We would have children and Bennett would stand over me, coaching me on penis envy (for the little girls) and castration anxiety (for the little boys). When the kids were old enough (five?) we would put them in child analysis. (How could child psychiatrists remain in business without the children of other shrinks? Who but a shrink's wife would shlep a kid to a shrink's office five times a week at a cost of forty-five dollars per session?) *That* was something to look forward to! Once my own protracted analysis was over, I could look forward to my kids'. We'd all be getting bettah and bettah all the time, and life would slip by in fifty-minute hours.

New York from September through July, the Cape in August. Every few years a Psychoanalytic Congress in Europe – just to break the monotony. We'd buy a bigger co-op – maybe on the East Side. There'd be an *au pair* for the kids, a summer house in some kosher shrink community like Wellfleet or Truro, the proper progressive private schools. Mommy would write little books. She'd be shocking, but not so shocking that Daddy would leave her. She would not, for example, write that her husband was a complete hypocrite in his private life. Oh, he had made that quite clear. It was one thing for her to write a book about a runaway wife and take the rap for having sexual fantasies *herself*. Oh, he approved of that. Women were rapacious, incorrigible, 'infantile.' They had to be tolerated, patronized, shrunk. Did they choose badly in the bedroom and fall in love with heartless bastards? That was natural enough; they were hung up on their Daddies. Oedipal problems. Back to the shrink with you, little girl. Five more years of analysis. At least it fills up the afternoons when you might be seeing a lover. But how about your husband, Dr Know-it-all, Dr Face-up-to-yourself? What's *he* doing in his spare time? He's just 'forgiven' you for your sexual fantasies, remember? He's just told you it's okay to act them out every now and then (as long as you feel too

130

guilty to enjoy them, repent at once, come home to Daddy and go immediately back into analysis; as long as you admit that sexual fantasies are 'immature'). He's 'mature.' He is fucking a housewife in your study on the nights you teach (even though he doesn't resent your writing one bit). Mysteriously enough, he begins this passionate affair just as you begin to write seriously, just as you begin to feel that finishing a paragraph is perhaps more important than cooking a soufflé. The timing is very interesting, isn't it, Doctor? And what about this past year in which everyone has been praising you for being such a patient husband? Your outrageous wife, the notorious Isadora White Wing, bestselling poet/novelist, wrote a book whose heroine, the notoriously candid Candida, confesses to actually experiencing lust! And doing something about it! How revolutionary! Men all over America are commiserating with you for having such a filthy-minded wife and yet bearing it all so manfully. The heroine of your wife's book actually runs off with another man – and everyone believes that's the whole story – but marriage is far more complicated than fiction gives it credit for being. Your wife may have taken a flier, but you knew how to turn it to your advantage. It only consolidated your hegemony, didn't it? Especially because you made her feel good and guilty for it, didn't you? Especially because you never thought of telling her *then* that long years before her little fling, her miniaffair with a man who couldn't get it up, you had been having a serious, passionate affair with someone you really loved. Now you have told her – but you have also told her that if she ever writes about *this*, if she ever dares to expose the fact that you have sexual fantasies too, you will surely leave her. Some things cannot be tolerated. It is one thing to demythicize women, to expose one's self – but it is quite another to demythicize men, to expose one's husband. A man's hypocrisy is his castle. Tread softly; you tread on my hypocrisy.

Good. We have set the ground rules. I lie here in my bed on a New York summer morning, not wanting to get up, not wanting to be married to the man I'm married to, not able to write (because the most momentous event in

131

my recent life has been declared off limits to me). Jealousy is what I want to write about. Jealousy is the subject of my new novel. But I have been told I cannot write it. Bennett has made it quite clear that if I write explicitly about jealousy, he will not tolerate it.

He wants to tell me what to write about! He wants to tell me and yet at the same time be seen as patient and long-suffering by all the husbands in America.

He points out to me frequently that he and I have the same name and that my writing might be an 'embarrassment' to him in his professional career. How did we get the same name anyway? An interesting story. We are linked by this name as some people are linked by children. We are linked by a name embossed on the bindings of books.

My name. Isadora White Wing. I am stuck with the 'Wing' forever – whether I leave Bennett or not. My *nom de plume*: Wing. Whoever else I marry, whoever else I love, my name is stamped in gold on those fine morocco presentation volumes publishers give authors for Christmas, emblazoned on all my luggage, stationery, bookplates. The name used to have a certain crude irony – when I was still afraid of flying. It pointed toward a future of flight. It was ambiguous: perhaps Oriental, perhaps not. It was a little odd; no other writer had that name.

My maiden name was counterfeit also. Isadora White. My father was born Weissmann, shortened it to Weiss, anglicized *that* to White. So neither White nor Wing is authentic. Neither father nor husband supplies me with an honest identity. I should have taken matters into my own hands and *invented* a *nom de plume*. I thought about it for quite some time. Isadora I would have to keep – farcical as it is. It tells so much about my mother and me. Isadora *must* be the heroine of a comedy. And yet there is something touching in actually having been named that. My mother wanted me to be her wings, to fly as she never had the courage to do. I love her for that. I love the fact that she wanted to give birth to her own wings.

So I took Bennett's name – perhaps unconsciously realizing the appropriateness of the pun. I had begun to publish poems under my maiden name, my little-girl name, the name that got A's in school, the name that was mocked in camp. You'd think that Bennett, with all his Freudian clap-trap about the formation of character in the first three years of life, would have respected my attachment to my childhood name – but he was adamant. He looked at one of my early poems, published in a literary quarterly, and said ominously: 'The poet has no husband.'

'But *lots* of women poets use their maiden names. It's almost a *tradition*,' I protested. He only glowered and coughed nervously. (Bennett's nervous cough was always more of a put-down than someone else's 'Fuck you.') It was clear that he considered my attachment to my maiden name to be a sign of my 'oedipal problem.' Greater loyalty to father than husband. Unmistakable proof of infantilism.

'Does anyone ask *men* to change their identities when they get married? Would *you* like to be Bennett *White?*' More nervous coughs and more silence. Bennett stalks out of the room, leaving me feeling guilty. Perhaps he's right, I think. Perhaps I should show my commitment to the marriage by taking his name. And yet, it seems so illogical. My maiden name *feels* right: an old shoe. It *is* my identity. To give it up seems like an amputation. I am *not* Chinese, after all. And though White may be a fake, it is my own *father's* fake – while Bennett's name is an accident of transliteration made up by some American embassy clerk in Hong Kong. Some members of his family are Wong, some Wang, some Weng, some Wing – depending on the capriciousness of immigration officials. Why should I take this fluke of history as my identity simply because I happen to go to bed with its bearer?

But Bennett was one of the great guilt-inflictors of all time. Whenever I showed him my work in print, he glowered at the name attached to it. So much so that I had no pleasure at all in showing him my published work. Quite the contrary, I would try to hide it. He wanted to assert possession of me, and of my poems. He would not rest until he had stripped me of my name.

I thought of using my grandfather's name – Stoloff. But

133

that was wrong too. Papa was not my father. To use his name would be to suggest incest between him and my mother. (That the incest *is*, in fact, there in spirit made me less than anxious to betray it in print.) And then there were the invented names I contemplated.

Isadora Orlando, after Virginia Woolf's androgynous protagonist; Isadora Icarus, after Stephen Dedalus; or just plain Isadora, after Colette. But none of those were right either. Too affected – all of them. Underneath the portrait of the artist as a young woman there is a blank area of canvas. *You* fill in her name.

I was still vacillating about names when my first book was accepted for publication. Isadora White or Isadora Wing? Isadora Orlando or Isadora Icarus? Isadora Isadora? I felt the decision to be momentous and irrevocable. I was in great pain about it. I could either please Bennett and displease myself or risk his wrath and keep the identity I had been honing since childhood. What a cruel choice! Like cutting off a foot to stay out of the war. And yet I was so in need of his approval that I did it. I became Isadora Wing – and Bennett opened his arms to me and my poems, and never had anything but praise for my work after that. Not until *now*, at any rate. Not until I hinted I had bartered my birthright for approval. Women always do. Or *girls* do anyway. I was not a woman then or I wouldn't have done it. But I am now. And now it's too late to do anything about the name.

I was trapped. Now that I had made the name *Wing* famous, Bennett wanted to tell me what to write. Apart from that I wouldn't ever care about the name anymore. Sometimes, it's true, I look at my name on a book and remark on the strangeness of it all. My grandparents from Russia and Poland, my parents from Glasgow, London, and Brownsville, and me with a Chinese name. At times I feel I have no identity at all. I float in and out of different souls. And, who knows, perhaps that is the best state for a poet.

Yet at times I still feel bitter toward Bennett. What right did he have to confiscate my childhood like that? (And why did I let him? Why was I so desperate, so unable to stand my ground?' I needed his love so badly that I gave him the deepest part of myself: my work. Bennett, who read and wrote so haltingly, had secured his place in American literature. From Hong Kong to *Who's Who* in one generation – and none of it by his own efforts.

Bennett should have married Penny. It would have been better for all of us. I would still be Isadora White. She would be Penny Wing – and I would be free to fly. I could write about jealousy – or anything. I would not have to keep myself within certain approved limits of rebellion. Lying there in bed, thinking about names, marriages, the past, I suddenly had the desire to call Penny, confront her, commiserate with her, scream at her.

As if possessed by a demon, I leapt out of bed, raced into the living room, and began looking for Bennett's address book. I found an old Week at-a-Glance and became entirely engrossed, reading the appointment schedules, trying to figure out which appointments were really perhaps trysts (now that I knew about Penny, I didn't trust Bennett at all), and remarking with considerable astonishment on the fact that Bennet had noted down none of our social engagements or weekend activities but only his work-appointments. The Week-at-a-Glance was a complete microcosm of his personality: all work, no play.

At the back of the book were telephone numbers. I looked up *P* for Penny Prather. She had remarried. Her new husband's name was Forbes. There it was, under *F*: Penny Forbes. A true patriarch, Bennett had crossed out the old name and lettered in the new. A woman keeps changing identities with each husband. She never has a last name she can count on. With my heart thudding, I dialed the number from Bennett's phone. It was an area code in Pennsylvania. Faintly, the phone rang – and with each ring I grew more and more terrified. Finally, there was a click and the phone spoke in a robotlike electronic voice: THE NUMBER YOU HAVE REACHED IS NOT IN SERVICE OR TEMPORARILY DISCONNECTED. PLEASE BE SURE YOU ARE CALLING OR DIALING THE RIGHT NUMBER. THE NUMBER YOU HAVE REACHED IS NOT IN ...

I hung up the phone with relief.

What was the point of calling Penny anyway? What was the point of dialing the past? Penny and I were not antagonists. We were fellow sufferers. My rage at her was what Bennett might have wanted. She was not so bad really. An intelligent girl who quit college to marry a West Point cadet and almost immediately had six kids. She found herself moving from one part of the world to another every two years, having her babies while Lieutenant, Captain, Major, and finally Lieutenant Colonel Robby Prather was in Korea, Vietnam, Cambodia, or on field maneuvers in rural Germany. He came home chiefly to knock her up. And for a while it wasn't so bad – or at least, she thought there was nothing better. She was like me. She rationalized her marriage. But she was braver than I was. With six children, at the age of thirty-two, she picked up and left Robby, saying there had to be more to life than shlepping from one army base to another as he collected more and more spaghetti on his hat. Her affair with Bennett had been the catalyst for her leaving. It had opened her eyes. Good for her. It had opened my eyes too. But *she* was the courageous one. At thirty-two, she went back to finish college and got a degree in psychology. Had Bennett helped her to do that? Very well then, he had helped *some*one. Maybe there are times when we can help other people's spouses and not our own. And maybe that's better than helping no one at all.

The phone rang in my study and I made a dash for it. I was thinking so hard about Penny that I was sure it was going to *be* Penny.

'Hello,' I said, breathless.

'Hello.' The voice was unfamiliar at first, but nothing like Penny's.

'Who's this?' I asked.

'Who's *this*?' came the petulant Brooklynese reply. I was suddenly frightened. The very intonation was intimidating. 'This is Britt Goldstein,' the voice went on. 'I just got in from the Coast.'

Hello to Hollywood ...

Where is Hollywood located?
Chiefly between the ears.
In that part of the American
brain lately vacated by God.

Britt Goldstein belonged to a subspecies of human I had not been privileged to meet before I became famous: the Compleat Parasite. She had no talents, no abilities, no charm, and boundless *chutzpa*. She lived by ripping-off the achievements of others: their work, their lives, their money. The money was the least of it. What was so infuriating about Britt was the way she identified herself with me, claimed to 'understand' my book and to be more candid than the real Candida.

Britt and I were as different as Adolf Hitler and John Keats, yet I think that for a while I was as fascinated by her as I was repelled. Writers always get into trouble because they become fascinated by charisma – if utter vulgarity is a form of charisma.

Britt referred to herself as 'B.G.,' the air conditioner as the 'a.c.,' her birth control pills as her 'b.c.' pills, her Rolls-Royce Silver Cloud as the 'S.C.' She was born in Flatbush, made a brief detour to Manhattan's Upper East Side, then went directly to Hollywood without passing Go. She lived in 'Bev Hills,' loved 'Mex' food, snorted 'c,' rolled the tightest 'j's' in the history of middle-class marijuana-smoking, had her 'l's' waxed at Elizabeth Arden in Beverly Hills, her 'h' frizzed at Kenneth in New York, and her two favorite expressions were 'No pain, no gain' and 'That's junior.' ('No pain, no gain' really meant "*Your* pain, *my* gain,' and 'junior' meant 'It's tacky if you do it, classy if *I* do it.') She might have been entirely comical if she didn't cause so many people so much pain, in the process of grabbing so much gain. The key to Britt's personality was her voice: it whined, wheedled, and insulted the intelligence of the ear it slithered into. It was such a bad imitation of guile and cunning that in the beginning nobody ever took it for what it was: guile and cunning. Britt threw everyone off at first because they could never believe she was what she appeared to be: a shark in shark's clothing.

I met Britt through my unscrupulous New York agents –

a firm with the improbable name of Creativity and Glory, Ltd. (better known as C&G). Britt had done time in publishing houses in New York (where she read slush piles), in an advertising agency (where she wrote ads for cunt sprays), at a ladies' magazine (where, monthly, she made up horoscopes), at a lecture agency (where she learned to falsify expense records). As a producer, she was able to bring all these nefarious skills together.

With the lack of imagination peculiar to her profession, Britt stayed at the Sherry-Netherland. She had a big suite with yellow-and-green silk curtains and telephones even in the bathrooms. This is the 'Sherry' and the 'Bev Hills' have in common: telephones everywhere. God forbid you should miss a call while taking a shit or drinking cocktails. Every one of the plusher suites in each hotel has telephones by the can, and the cocktail lounges feature plug-in phones, which can be brought to the tables. Both, I humbly submit, are strictly for show. What producer, however crass, would negotiate on the phone while grunting out a large turd? In a profession in which appearances are all, and substance is the one utterly dispensable element, no one would ever think of putting a telephone to that use. Nor would anyone dream of having any significant business conversation in a cocktail lounge filled with one's eavesdropping competitors. So the plenitude of phones is strictly to impress the greenhorns. Like me. Enter Isadora Greenhorn, hapless author about to say hello to Hollywood.

Britt always made you meet her on her turf. She had come to New York to woo *me*, but began insisting that I come to *her* hotel. Big gangsters do likewise, I'm told. So did the Wizard of Oz. Always bring the trembling supplicant onto one's own turf. And the Sherry-Netherland bears the same relation to Hollywood as the Russian embassy does to Russia: once within its portals, you are no longer a citizen of your own country.

If only I had trusted my first impression of Britt Goldstein! What grief could be avoided in this life if we trusted our first impressions! But I deceived myself. I was, like most members of my generation, in love with movies. I loved the unique ability they had to insinuate their way

140

into our dreams, making the dreamer forget which images were celluloid and which were spontaneous generations of the synapses. I was also fascinated with Hollywood – its legendary evil, its Medusa-like power to destroy those who gazed at it. Of course, I pooh-poohed the stories. I knew which of my high school cronies had wound up in Hollywood – and they were, with a few notable exceptions, the least promising, the least imaginative, the most likely to be pacified for the world's injustices with Rolls-Royces, mansions, swimming pools, and a ready supply of cocaine. Still, I was fascinated. I had tested out most of the other clichés and found them wanting. It was time to test out the cliché of the evil of Hollywood.

The test begins in the Sherry-Netherland the day after Britt's fateful phone call.

First impressions. Britt Goldstein lies in a yellow chaise drinking a gin and tonic while her old high school friend from Flatbush, Sue Slotnik, gets up to let me in. That in itself tells the story: she does not get up to greet me. She reclines, her waxed legs from Elizabeth Arden exposed in the slit of an Indian caftan from Bendel's. She is tiny (about four feet ten), thin (I never trust anybody that thin), passionately orange-haired, with icy eyes and a hard little mouth. Her nose is bobbed into that curious S curve (a cheese paring? a crescent moon?) possessed by fully half the Jewish women in Beverly Hills. (If all the missing pieces of nose in Beverly Hills could be put end to end, they would reach all the way back to Poland!) But her mouth tells all. The tight muscles that pull on either side of her thin lips reveal her spiritual stinginess, her total lack of generosity. Apparently 'No pain, no gain' is not a life credo that leads to the growth of the spirit.

'Hi.' The voice is nasal, almost a vaudeville parody of the voice of a Jewish girl from Brooklyn. '*Hoyyy*' would be the dialect-writer's transliteration. 'This is my friend, Sue Slotnik – we're just catching up on old times.'

'Hoyyy,' says Sue.

'Hi,' say I.

The grouping of figures signifies everything – as in

141

a Michelangelo *pietà*. Britt still reclining, Sue fumbling with her purse, me standing awkwardly above the couch to extend my hand.

Now, I should tell you – tell myself, really – that I have met Nobel Prize winners, living legends, mayors (if not presidents), and princes (if not kings) without the least nervousness, but there with Britt (whose diction alone would have caused me to snub her in my younger and more snobbish years) I was frightened. She had some weird kind of authority. The authority of the street urchin, perhaps. The authority of the playground bully – but authority nonetheless. You sensed at once that Britt would win out over others – not because she was either more intelligent or craftier -- but because she would stoop to things no one else would even think of. I learned later, for example, from a former friend of hers (all her friends, as far as I could tell, were former friends) that when shopping for material to make curtains or slipcovers (back in the days when she did such mundane things) she would tear the fabric when the salesman's back was turned and then demand a discount from him without so much as a tremble in her throat. If I were a gentile, she would have confirmed my worst suspicions about Jews. If I were a man, she would confirm my worst mistrust of women. If I were old, she would have made me lose faith in the younger generation. But I was none of those things – so I quashed my mistrust of Britt and listened avidly while she told me what my book was 'about.'

Sue Slotnik soon withdrew. I seem to recall her walking out of the hotel room backward – as courtiers were once said to have left the company of the king – but surely that is memory falsifying. Anyway, she left. With humility. And Britt continued to lie there regally on the chaise like the queen of mudpies, the queen of leg wax, the queen of plastic charge plates.

'When I first read your book,' she said, 'I knew it was the story of my life – and I knew immediately we'd be lifelong friends.' (I have come to understand, partly through my experience with Britt, to mistrust anyone who attempts to begin a business relationship with the expression *life-*

long friends. The less friendship is mentioned the better. The more friendship is mentioned the less likely one ever is to see a check.) 'I see your book as the story of a woman's discovery that she can save her own life ...' (You will have to imagine the accent and the extreme nasality, coupled with the high-flown content.) And I just sat there like an idiot while she regaled me with the erroneous *explication de texte* of a book which, till that day, I'd supposed I'd written.

She wanted to option the screen rights and mentioned, that very night, an insultingly low figure. I'd consult my agent, I said, and instantly she switched into the role of bully. Nobody else would do it, she said; nobody else would buy it. Instead of saying 'So what?' I got scared and saw all my celluloid dreams being burned away.

'If you really like the book as much as you say, why are you telling me nobody else will buy it?' Asking the question was already a show of weakness. With bullies, one does not question, one demands. Or walks away. But, unfortunately, it took me two more years to learn that.

'Because I take chances, I take risks, and I'm willing to take a chance on you.'

Willing to take a chance on me! This was the essence of Britt's strategy. She had come to me – whose book had already sold millions of copies – telling me she was 'willing to take a chance.' She was doing me a favor, you see, like the saleslady at Saks who deigns to sell you a Trigère.

And it worked! Suddenly I was sweating, nervous, almost panicked. I visualized a wonderful Truffaut–Fellini–Bergman masterpiece based on *my* book – and all at once it went down the drain.

'You don't know what all those male-chauvinist producers would do to your work. They'll absolutely destroy it. This way, at least you know you'll have control.'

The old siren song: *Control. Artistic control. You have to give up money to get ... artistic control.* The Hollywood rag. So elegant. So intelligent. Because of course you *never* get control. So if you give up money, what do you get? Nothing. And all your old pals in the literary world accusing you of having 'sold out.' Ah, the literary world. They hate failure and despise success. They have contempt for authors whose books go unread and sheer hatred for authors whose books are too much read. Try to please the literary world and you will spend your life in a state of rage and bitterness. But Hollywood is simple, almost pure – if total venality is a form of purity. There, nothing at all matters but making money. And the more you make the better you are. And the end justifies any means at all.

That was why I was right to question Britt's insultingly low figure. It meant contempt for me and contempt for my work. If I accepted that, there would be no end to the insults they would ask me to accept. But if I walked away, they would suddenly get nicer. However, I had been trained by my mother to be insulted and come back for more, to be insulted and feel guilty toward my insulter. And Britt, with her street-urchin instincts, sized me up in a flash.

'Look,' she said, studying herself in a hand mirror – Britt was always studying herself in mirrors – 'nothing prevents me from getting my own writer to rip off your book. It isn't all that original.'

I stared at her in disbelief. In the space of about two minutes she had utterly contradicted herself. She had just said it was the story of her life. She had just said it was absolutely unique. And she had just said it could be ripped off with no trouble at all. What stopped me from telling her to fuck off right then and there? What prevented me from saying 'Go to hell' and slamming the door? Fear? Politeness? The inability to believe that anybody was really as rude, as crass, and as bullying as she appeared?

'I have to talk to my agent,' I said.

'Talk,' she said.

And in the days that followed, I did. But what I didn't understand was that my agent was also Britt's agent. Nor did I know that Britt had already announced to all of Hollywood that she 'had' my book – so *hands off.* Britt belonged to that ancient Jewish merchant class whose philosophy seems to be that you don't actually have to *buy* a thing if you can make everybody believe you already own it. Purchase by publicity. And of course she was so intimidating to everyone – not just to me – that no other producers dared make offers on the book. In essence, I was trapped. I tried to negotiate, but the negotiation went nowhere. I was like a Christian trying to negotiate with a hungry lion.

Lunch with my agent, Eliza Rushmore. Eliza is a saccharine-voiced, streaky-haired graduate of Skidmore who called me Isadora until the first million copies were sold, 'my love' after the second million, 'sweet one' after the third million, and 'darlingest' after the fourth. You'd pay ten percent of your yearly income not to have to talk to her at all.

'Darlingest,' she said (over a lunch of red snapper flambé at Laurent), 'we *tried* to sell your book *every*where, but there were just *no* takers at *tall*.' (She talked in italics like the Cosmopolitan Girl.) 'It really *is* a very hard book to film. All those flashbacks . . .'

'But movies *always* have flashbacks . . .'

'Yes, my love, but everyone was quite agreed that the literary *flair*, the *humor*, if you will, makes it all *harder* to deal with. The books that make the *best* movies are always, in*var*iably, the *worst* written. It's greatly to your *credit* as a writer that your book is so un*sale*able as a film.' She bit off a buck-toothed, goyish smile.

'I don't give a shit, Eliza, I absolutely refuse to accept a tiny option for a book that's sold all those copies. It's insulting. I mean when you sell out to Hollywood – you sell *out*. Or else you don't do it at all. They're likely to make a mess of it – so if all I'm ever going to see is that much money, I'd sooner not sell it at all.'

'But the movie will sell more books. And besides Britt is a *can-do* person . . .'

'A *what?*'

'A can-do person rather than a big talker – like so many of your Hollywood types.'

'If she's the best of them, I'd like to see the others. *God.*'

'Besides, sweet one, you'll make money off the percentage.'

'I've heard you *never* make a penny off a percentage of net profits. They have bookkeepers working in cellars to make it appear there *are* no profits.'

'Oh, don't believe that silly sour-grapes stuff. Of *course* you'll see a percentage. It could make you rich.'

'I'm not sure I want to be rich.'

'Darlingest,' she said, forking up some more red snapper, 'it never hurts.'

Britt summoned me to the Sherry-Netherland the next morning. She sensed my reluctance and realized that stronger measures were needed.

'Let's have breakfast together, okay? I really don't care about the movie at all – but I *do* want to get to know you better.'

I trotted off to the Sherry-Netherland at 10:00 A.M.

When I got there, Britt was not waiting in the café. I sat for about a half-hour feeling increasingly like an idiot and then got the brainstorm of calling upstairs. The line was busy, busy, busy for another half-hour – and when I finally reached Britt she seemed to have forgotten all about our date.

'Oh God, I've been on the phone with Bob Redford *all* morning, and then my lawyer called from the Coast – can you hold it just another minute and have some coffee?'

I held it another forty minutes at least, and still Britt did not arrive. I had an appointment at noon – so I called Britt's room again. Again she appeared to have forgotten my existence.

'Oh God, I am disorganized this morning. Why don't you come to the room?'

In the room it was apparent that Britt had never even tried to make it downstairs to meet me. She was just blow-drying her hair. She was dressed in nothing but black bikini underpants, and her shapely waxed legs ended in perfectly pedicured feet. She was manically fluffing her orange fizz with a blower, bending forward, bending sideways, almost as if blown by her own hot air. Her body was tiny. Somehow I was always surprised to find Britt so short. At four foot ten and virtually bare-assed, she should not

146

have been so intimidating – but she was. Her breasts were tiny points with wrinkled raisins for nipples.

I felt like a courtier at the king's levee. Tyrants always establish their dominance by making one watch them dress, eat, or shit. As I waited I felt increasingly drained of any ability to rebel, to plead my case, to establish my position.

'I have an appointment at noon,' I said feebly.

'With whom?'

'What business is it of yours?' I should have said, but I felt obligated to *tell*. Sometimes I spill the story of my life out of nervousness, and sometimes out of a wish to ingratiate and disarm.

'Actually, it's with this psychiatrist I've been having an intermittent affair with. You see, my husband recently told me that all during the early years of our marriage – when he was really brutal to me – he was madly in love with this woman – this army officer's wife named Penny, and . . .'

The phone rang. I was caught with my life history down around my ankles.

'Hello?' That nasal voice. The voice of a telephone solicitor selling ballroom-dancing lessons, or a street-corner vendor selling hot watches.

'No, I will not give him even his goddamned agent's commission – that son of a bitch . . . Why? . . . I hear you, Murray, but he's a creep who couldn't get arrested . . . No, we don't need him . . . What? . . . Tell him I'll put it on the auction block. Tell him I have another studio to indemnify me . . . Why the fuck should I? . . . I don't need him, I'm telling you . . . Don't you *dare* call me back till you've gotten rid of him. I mean it. Or I'll find another goddamned fucking lawyer, do you hear me? I mean it.' And she slammed down the phone.

To me, sweetly: 'Why don't you cancel that appointment and have lunch with me instead. Girl-talk, okay? No deal stuff.'

And I did, and she spent the next hour screaming on the phone or blowing her hair – while I waited, feeling dumber and dumber. And with that, I lost it all: my dignity, my resistance, my integrity. I had known her only one day and already I was waiting three hours at a time in hotels. The pattern was set.

At lunch, she tried to convince me we were sisters under the skin. It was true that a lot of people had responded to *Candida Confesses* – but what I didn't yet realize was that the book was a litmus paper for everybody's special craziness. It had the common touch – whatever that is. Scholars responded to it and so did totally uneducated people. It later became clear to me that just because people came up to me and said 'I am you,' that didn't necessarily make it true. Most critics are so misguided about the nature of literature that they lead even writers, who should know better, astray. Even autobiography is not interesting if it is only about its subject. Unless that subject becomes everywoman, unless that story becomes myth, it is of no interest to anyone but the subject – and perhaps her mother. And once it becomes myth – it is no longer merely autobiography. Or merely fiction.

So of course Britt identified. How could she not? She was a Jewish girl from Flatbush. She felt she had been victimized by the male sex, by the whole world. This was especially interesting, because if any victimizing was being done, you could be sure Britt was, as the N.Y. police say, the perpetrator. As for being victimized by the male sex, it was hard to imagine any man fucking Britt and coming away with his genitals intact. Just as her laugh was metallic, one could presume her inner organs to be made of the same unyielding stuff.

'The whole point,' she said at lunch, 'is how women are fucked over by men.' She said this looking very self-satisfied, as if she had just translated the Dead Sea Scrolls.

What was I to say? That I didn't think that the point of my work at all? That I thought she was smug and not very intelligent? That I thought she was making a mockery of the very real sufferings of some women in order to grab more profit for herself? We were in the Sherry-Netherland café and Britt, of course, had taken the banquette while she left me the outside chair. Trout meunière was about to be brought. The white wine had been poured and was cupping the light in long-stemmed glasses. We sipped. 'To the year of the woman,' Britt toasted. Just then, a roach crawled over the banquette behind Britt's bony shoulder. He made his way slowly toward her Hermès handbag, up one side, across the top, and then descended into its caramel-colored leathery depths in search of tobacco crumbs, half-smoked joints, one bent cocaine spoon, an assortment of French cosmetics, a handful of tarnished pennies, half a month's supply of birth control pills, an old Valium vial filled with the purest, whitest coke, a rolled-up hundred-dollar bill to snort it with (she'd forgotten she had the spoon), and a wallet full of charge plates, traveler's checks, and cards of people she'd never remember to call.

I saw the roach descend into Britt's handbag but said nothing. Britt and I would meet again.

The Rolls-Royce love affair ...

If I do it once, I'm a philosopher.
If I do it twice, I'm a pervert.
(WITH APOLOGIES TO VOLTAIRE)

My life was pushing me westward and away from Seventy-seventh Street – although I didn't know it at the time. Couriers appeared to bring the news that it was time to leave the old block, time to pull up roots, time to move on. Britt was one such courier – a female Mephistopheles in bikini underwear. Rosanna Howard was another. The day her Rolls-Royce Corniche pulled up on Seventy-seventh Street, it was clear to somebody – if not yet to me – that everything was bound to change.

Rosanna was a student of mine who had been pursuing a friendship with me for months. You couldn't fail to take special notice of her because she appeared at the writing seminar (which met in my apartment) in that chauffeured Rolls-Royce Corniche, satin jeans, and rhinestone-studded T-shirts suitable for a rock star. She also wore black lip-stick, platform sandals with six-inch spikes, and a heavy musk body-oil that suggested the very rich *were* different from you and me. Just *how* they were different, I was not to know until much later. She wrote poems about decaying family mansions and kinky sex. I found her moderately interesting but I was too busy for a new friend (I barely had time to see my old ones that year), and besides I had known lots of rich girls before and was not fascinated by them. The very rich like to collect writers and I do not like to be collected. It makes me nervous. But one morning, after a particularly bad scene with Bennett, Rosanna happened to telephone.

'This is Rosanna Howard.' The voice was crisp, mid-western, boarding-schoolish. I must have been disappointed to hear from her because she immediately went on to ask : 'Isn't this a good time to call?'

'No,' I lied, 'it's fine.' But I can never conceal my feelings. My voice gives them away on the phone. My face gives them away in person.

'You sound upset,' she said matter of factly. 'Is there anything I can do?'

'No. It's kind of you to ask, but really, I don't ...' Only with Rosanna would I have used the word *kind*.

'Are you free for lunch? I'd love to take you to lunch.'

What the hell, I thought, I won't get any work done today anyway.

Her car pulled up twenty minutes later. My ass-kissing doorman, an unctuous Eastern European named Valerian, genuflected before the chromium hood ornament. 'Nize car,' he said, 'nize peeples.' Valerian had no bleeding-heart liberal hang-ups. Money was good, poverty bad. Rich folks were 'nizer' than poor folks. Teach a kid communism from a young age, and when he grows up, he becomes a raging capitalist. Simple.

Rosanna and I had lunch at the Carlyle, and I made a point of paying, knowing that nothing endears one to the rich more than that.

Rosanna had grown up in Chicago, inherited a 'tiny railroad' (which just happened to surround the stockyards), gone to Bryn Mawr (and then graduated from Sarah Lawrence), married an uptight, boring lawyer who loved her money, had one son with him, and then left him for a swinging lawyer (who also loved her money, it turned out, but in a way that was less obvious to her). His name was Robert Czerny (and I later came to call him the 'bouncing Czech'). To a society girl from Chicago he represented rebellion, freedom, Stanley Kowalski, sex, self-destruction, excitement. He wore a gold cock-ring and twenty-five-dollar ties – and he went down on her when she had her period (which no WASP would do). The way to a woman's heart.

They maintained an apartment on Lake Shore Drive in Chicago (where the son and the nanny were ensconced), but Rosanna and Robert traveled. When Rosanna decided 'to Write,' she took a studio apartment in the East Fifties, hired a chauffeur for the Corniche, and set herself up in New York (like any struggling poet) to make her literary fortune. Robert commuted between Chicago, New York, and Washington (where he lobbied for mysterious causes and fucked around a lot). The Czernys had an ultraliberated marriage; they never saw each other. But Rosanna was fiercely defensive of 'Rob.' He was her rebellion, but he was also her respectability – because, you see, she really liked women. And every reluctant lesbian needs an absent husband to cover her. I never heard *any*one use the phrase *my husband* as often as Rosanna.

I uncork a bottle of musk oil to conjure Rosanna. I spread it on my wrist, rub it in, inhale deeply, invoke the genie within, and suddenly it all comes back: the oil-smooth ride of the Corniche, the people staring in at us with a mixture of resentment and awe, the polished parquet floors of Rosanna's writing 'studio,' the bentwood furniture, the hanging baskets of ferns, the practically bare rooms, the closet full of rock-star clothes, the bed with its white whicker headboard, canopy, and monogrammed sheets, and what we did there.

I went to bed with Rosanna out of curiosity the first time, horniness mingled with what I can only call 'bisexual chic' the second, and obligation the subsequent occasions. It was stylish to have a lesbian affair that year, I thought I might want to write about it, and Bennett was making me miserable. If men were the question, perhaps women were the answer. I had fantasies of setting up salon (if not house) with Rosanna – all very Vita Sackville-Westish or Colette-loves-Missy or Stein-loves-Toklas. We'd take care of each other faithfully, and occasionally bring in men we could share.

The first time we made love, I was chiefly exhilarated by the sense of doing something forbidden and not feeling the earth heave open to swallow me. There was something particularly liberating about breaking that taboo. It was not like losing one's virginity – which had been fraught with guilt and tender tears. And it was not like the first adultery – which had been a roller-coaster alternation of panic and pleasure. How can I describe it? The word *smug* comes to mind. The word *smug*, and the scent of musk. I felt so goddamned superior to all those people who wouldn't dare it; I felt I had gone down on my mother.

Ah sex. A very mysterious force. Was it Lawrence who said 'the more we think about it, the less we know'? I think so. Try to imagine oral-genital relations (as the sex manuals coyly call it) from the standpoint of a Martian or a low-flying UFO pilot from another solar system. How silly it would appear! It would seem like a form of cannibalism, perhaps. And perhaps it is.

What Rosanna was trying to eat through my cunt was my poetry, my vulnerability, my Jewish warmth. What I was trying to eat through hers was her WASP *coolth*, her millions, or perhaps the freedom which I imagined went with them. I had never felt more trapped or desperate in my life than I did that summer. I had tried everything: fame, fortune, adultery, never looking up from the page, living to write, running away, coming back, sitting on the razor's edge. Perhaps Rosanna had the answer. There had to be an answer *some*where.

I had never before made love to a student. It was against my principles. If I felt guilty for anything, it was for that — not for touching another woman's creamy, slightly rancid-smelling cunt. Yet I was also fascinated by the act itself, seeing my body's mirror-image in another body, not the cosmic crash of cock and cunt, but the lilting, soft, safe, rocking of woman against woman. *Safe*. That was the word I was seeking. Men were lethal; this was *safe*.

Rosanna must have sensed my need for safety the morning she appeared. She must have sensed my vulnerability. All year she had been hot for me, had looked at me across the writing-seminar table (also my dining table), wanting me, falling in love with me. To me, she was chiefly a curiosity: mannish haircut, tall stringbean body, Mick Jagger clothes, Cartier jewelry, and that musky smell. I needed no one new that year. I was so locked within that dying marriage; so hopeless about change; so cynical about love, freedom, breaking loose. Rosanna had to hammer her way through my cynicism to make me hear her.

The Corniche glides up, a chariot from another planet; Valerian genuflects; and off we go in a cloud of musk and carbon monoxide. At lunch we talk about men, jealousy, marriage, mothers, poetry, Bloomsbury, the vintages of wines. We consume two bottles of Mouton-Cadet — Rosanna's favorite. Or rather, she consumes them and I help a little. Not being Jewish, she has a hollow leg. As
156

I spill out my story of Bennett's betrayal – again! – she takes my hand. I feel mothered, cared for, vulnerable, understood. And I go on drinking wine.

And then the chauffeur is waiting and we go back to her 'studio.' How easy everything is with a waiting chauffeur! How little one has to think, to consider, to obsess.

More wine, more talk, hot rock-music at first, then Cole Porter. Rosanna has the situation well in hand. Her face betrays no emotion but calm and understanding. I am the child again, coming to mother with my scraped knee. Suddenly Bennett is nothing more than a scraped knee! A little injury on the smooth skin of my life.

Rosanna excuses herself, goes to the bedroom, comes back wearing a caftan slit to the waist and lots more musk. The top of the caftan opens when she sits down next to me on the couch. I see her small pointed breasts and want to touch them. She sees me looking and reads my mind. She takes my hand and guides it to her breast. The nipple is bumpy and wrinkled, but the underside is smooth, cool, sleek. Rosanna strokes my hair, then my cheek, then she tilts my chin upward so she can kiss me. I feel I am kissing my mirror-image, smooth womanlips, a trifle thin, cool, safe.

Here is a woman who addresses her letters 'Dear Heart' and signs them 'Fondly'; she makes love the same way— as if it were a course taught at boarding school. Does my heart pound and my cunt drip because of the exhilaration of breaking a taboo? Because I am hot for Rosanna? Who can possibly tell? My husband is a Freudian analyst who takes a harsh line on bisexual shenanigans. That's certainly part of the thrill. *He'd kill me if he knew*. Bennett has never much liked going down on me; Rosanna loves it. I lie there trying to think and trying not to think, trying to suspend judgment and judging like crazy, trying to justify and feeling no need to justify ... All these feelings rush at me at once. Meanwhile, she is gently nibbling my clitoris with her perfect, capped teeth, sliding one manicured finger in and out of my cunt, and stroking my nipples with her other hand, on whose fourth finger she wears a seal

157

ring with her family crest. 'Rush–Poland' meets the DAR! Brownsville meets Lakeshore Drive! Central Park West meets Beekman Place!

I shut my eyes and try to feel nothing but sensation, wine-blurriness, and the concentric rings of pleasure in my cunt – but inevitably, there is something more. She is probing the center of my Jewishness; I am being raped by old money. That slim finger sliding in and out of my wet, warm cunt belongs to a Mayflower descendant! That cool mouth eating my Jewish pussy is the mouth of the WASP Midwest, the mouth that made America great, the mouth that ate up the goodies of America and itself remained thin, the mouth that roared! But the roar is coming from me. I am moaning, crooning, ooohing my pleasure. That mouth of the American Jewish Bard singing the passions of WASP America! What Sam Goldwyn did on celluloid, what Saul Bellow does in ten-point type – I am doing here in bed with Rosanna (or so I rationalized at the time).

It was fun. She adored me, was an expert cunt-eater, and had lots of class. It was also very high-toned. It seemed less sexual somehow than cultural. Vita Sackville-West was big that year – and Rosanna wanted to be a contemporary Vita. It almost seemed she should be brought a silver finger bowl (with rose petals floating in it) after touching my cunt. And Irish linen napkins to wipe her fingers with. And, after that, some scrumptious dessert.

But then I had to reciprocate. Or anyway I *felt* I had to. That was more of a problem.

Oh let me be some ancient epic poet (or some Eighteenth-Century Mock-Epick one) and involve the Muses of Bilitis (Vita, Virginia, Gertrude, Alice, Sidonie Gabrielle, Missy – even our contemporary Kate, Robin, and Jill) before embarking on this one! God help me, I am about to tell about my first impressions of cunt-eating and risk the wrath (wrisk the rath?) of mine sisters: Gentle Reader, it did not taste good.

Art and politics, politics and art. Strange bedfellows. Stranger still than Rosanna Howard and me. Can any feminist dare tell the truth about cunt-eating in this day and age? Do I dare – knowing I will be attacked from both sides – attacked by the gents for being too ballsy, attacked by ladies for being not ballsy enough?

I *tried*. I put my best tongue forward and took the plunge. *You'll get used to the smell*, I told myself. I said to myself, *Self, you smell the same*; but it was not much use. Rosanna took forever to come, and my nose felt like it had spent its entire life in there. I was nibbling her clit as she had done for me, sliding two fingers in and out, trying not to think of the smell, the hairs getting stuck between my teeth, and the fact that my wrist was getting tired from moving back and forth, forth and back. How long had it been? An hour? Two? I began to sympathize with Bennett's not wanting to go down on me; I began to understand what it meant to be a man, fumbling around – is *this* the right place or is *that*? – getting no guidance from one's subject (who is too polite and ladylike to tell) and wondering, wondering if she is going to come now, or now, or *now* – or *has* she already, or *will* she next summer, or *what*? Help! I need some guidance. This is uncharted territory. If I keep sliding these two fingers in and out and revolving my tongue on her clit and nibbling with my teeth, will she eventually come? Will she come by 1984? Will she *tell* me when she does. Do WASPS moan? I know that Chinamen *don't* – but do WASPS? Goddamn my cosmopolitan family (who would never dream of telling me to stick with my own kind). Why didn't they warn me? Why didn't my mother ever say: 'WASPS don't moan in bed'? Therefore, it is impossible to tell *when* they reach orgasm. Or *if* they do.

Ah. A shudder shakes her pelvis. She is moving toward my mouth rhythmically, faster and faster. It's going to be all right! She's going to come! Whooppee! I won't seem like a pig seeking only my own pleasure! I won't be a female-chauvinist pig!

False alarm. The pelvis has stopped, the shudder has stopped, my heart is about to stop.

'Rosanna?' I said weakly. 'Was that okay? Did you come?'

'It's okay,' she says. 'I don't mind.'

'Did you lose it, did you miss coming?'

'It's all right, dear heart, really.'

'You didn't,' I say, my heart sinking, my wrist aching, my mouth full of hairs. After all that, no orgasm. I feel like a boob, an inept lover, a befuddled man in bed with a frigid woman. For the first time in my life I can identify with the athletic, exhausted hero of 'The Time of Her Time.' Oh dear. I really am in a bad way if my very first lesbian experience makes me think of Norman Mailer!

'I don't mind,' she says, smiling down at me, 'I really appreciate your trying.'

And then I seem to understand it all, the war between the sexes, 'selfish' man and 'unselfish' woman, the role-playing, the pillow diplomacy, the mattress *mishegoss* that has reverberated down through the centuries to the detriment of us all. Man or woman, vibrator or shower spray, I come in three minutes flat. If I don't, I am angry, resentful, snarling, biting, mean. None of that 'I don't mind' stuff for me; my feelings are right there up front. My cunt growls, howls, bays at the moon.

But Rosanna 'didn't mind,' she said. And after that, making her come was my personal challenge. I was going to *find* a way to make her come. If I had to become the Rube Goldberg of dildos, the Thomas Alva Edison of vibrators, the Luther Burbank of elongated fruit – I was going to make that WASP cunt come!

The Corniche took me home. I was not yet sufficiently daring to spend the whole night there with Rosanna. Back home to my husband – whom I hated, but with whom the fucking became ever more exciting as I interposed between our rigid bodies my anger at him – and now my lover Rosanna.

I was back at her house first thing in the morning, with my book, bag, my manuscripts, my toothbrush. Not that I ever stayed away all night – but I pretty much lived there on and off for the next couple of months. Rosanna tried to persuade me to go away with her. She had a vacation house in Aspen which she wanted me to share with her that summer. But I was torn. I was still, in my half-assed way, trying to sort things out with Bennett –

and besides, I wasn't so sure I wanted to be alone with Rosanna for a whole month. Bennett would have 'let' me go – in his usual resentful, guilt-inflicting way, but did I really *want* to? It seemed to suit my purpose better to divide myself between Bennett and Rosanna. Days with her, nights with him. Writing in her apartment, drinking red wine, retiring to the white-whicker canopy bed (so she could go down on me tenderly – and I could go down on her desperately). Later we'd drive around the city in the Rolls with the top down, enjoying the impression we made, in our identical rock-star jeans-suits, mutual scent of musk oil, conversations about Roethke, Virginia Woolf, Neruda. I helped her revise her poems, and she comforted me about my fits of jealous rage. We were good for and to each other. There was real friendship there – or at least the stirrings of it.

But bed was the problem. I pounded away with dildos, Coke bottle, green plastic vibrators from Japan. A big one in the cunt and a little one in the ass. All the colors of the rainbow. I put cucumbers covered with ribbed condoms in her cunt and bananas covered with French ticklers. I bought a shower spray that vibrated and we took long baths together. It was never any good. She'd always come right to the teetering edge of orgasm, and then draw back, shivering, shuddering, weak in the knees. She never blamed me, though. She was much too polite for that. She was always extremely gracious about not coming. And yet, as time went on, I began to believe her cunt was an unconscious anti-Semite.

But I'd never dare say so. There was something about Rosanna that made one tactful, delicate – maybe scared? She seemed to be above anything as base as orgasm. She seemed to be made of pure spirit – like a stock-market rumor.

Then, one day in midsummer, I arrived at her house with a bottle of icy Dom Pérignon (to celebrate her thirty-third birthday). We drank the champagne, munched on Jarlsberg Swiss and *pâté de foie Strasbourg truffé*. By the time the tempting dark-green champagne bottle was empty, we were drunk enough to look at its furled lip and have the same thought instantaneously. We went to bed with the bottle, hugged and kissed, sucked each other's nipples, and stroked each other's thighs until finally, finally, after a month of bottles, vibrators, fruit, and pulsating water, I had the pleasure of seeing Rosanna Howard reach tumultuous orgasm with the bulging green base of a Dom Pérignon bottle protruding from her reluctant cunt.

She thanked me and thanked me. She wept tears of gratitude. The only other time she could come apparently was when her husband went down on her during her period. She attributed her miraculous orgasm to my skill. I attributed it to Moët et Chandon of Epernay. Would she have come with Paul Masson or Taylor's New York State?

I think the answer is clear.

The housewife poet ...

The aim of my writing is to utterly remove the distance between author and reader so that the book becomes a sort of semipermeable membrane through which feelings, ideas, nutrients pass ...

In August, Rosanna left for Aspen without me. I was determined to make one last try with Bennett. However much I mistrusted him, however much I disrespected him, nevertheless I had a certain unshakable regard for marriage. We had been together eight years. We had shared all sorts of pains and pleasures. Eight years were not to be taken lightly. There must have been *something* to bind us together all that time – or so I supposed.

Why does my life always fall apart in the summer? Can it be the heat? It *does* seem to be true that in summer the glue binding up the ill-fitting fragments of my life tends to dissolve. The major crises in my life always happen between June and September, and I always meet the men I am going to marry in the fall.

All that summer, the marriage was dying. Between my desperate affair with Rosanna and my frantic consultations with friends, I replayed the jealousy scenes obsessively like a child setting out toy houses. Gradually, all the little pieces fell into place: the streets, the trees, the parked cars. Whose car was parked in front of whose house? I began to understand the missed innuendos, the fragmentary conversations, the overheard pieces of dialogue like dissolving puffs of smoke over the characters' heads.

Why did it anger me so? Why did it become such a total obsession? Perhaps because Bennett had always played saint while he cast me in the role of sinner. Perhaps because I had been so unhappy myself during all the early years of our marriage and because I had felt so guilty about even *thinking* of leaving or having an affair. In a happy marriage, jealousy is painful but not necessarily lethal, but in an unhappy marriage, jealousy is often the final straw. There had almost never been anything between me and Bennett but pain. And pain is a good adhesive only when you are young enough or foolish enough to believe it is somehow more virtuous than pleasure. I was no longer that young or that foolish.

From then on it was only a question of time. It was only a question of getting my feet to follow my heart. The shock of discovering that I had been living with a total stranger for eight years took a while to sink in. And I was not one to give up on a marriage easily. I tried hard to forgive Bennett. I tried hard to convince myself he was only human. He had betrayed all the things I believed in most – candor, honesty, openness. But I tried. We took an expensive vacation in Italy and attempted to repair our marriage. We took one of those vacations that never works: a honeymoon hotel in Capri with views of the Mediterranean and splits of champagne in a little re-frigerator by the king-size bed. Everything plush and romantic and nothing to say to each other. All night I'd lie awake with my heart beating the same tattoo: *I want to leave, I want to leave, I want to leave, I want to leave.* To which my head answered: *Coward, coward, coward, coward.* I felt that my entire soul was engaged in civil war. I'd smile forgivingly at Bennett – and then feel murder in my heart. I *wanted* to love him – but all I felt was guilt over the fact that I didn't. Love and guilt do not go to-gether – although sometimes one simulates the other. How could I love someone that low and sneaky? How could I love someone that sadistic? 'You should love him because he's your husband,' some nineteenth-century aunt kept repeating in my head. But I knew she was wrong. Having made one mistake at twenty-four hardly dooms you to keep repeating the mistake for the rest of your life. But it is not easy to unglue an eight-year marriage. There has to be more than betrayal. There has to be death.

Early October in New York. I am driving across town in a cab (to my analyst – again!) when suddenly I hear on the radio that Jeannie Morton, 'the housewife poet' – as the announcer calls her – has died. A locked garage door. An idling car. A tipped glass of vodka in her hand. Her bloodstream full of lithium – or Valium – or some other contemporary chemical to combat fear, loathing, and the sickness unto death. The announcer says a few banalities about her 'untimely death' (she was forty-five) and then goes on to quote some evil and envious literary guru about her 'narrow, self-absorbed art' which 'vacillated' between 'the madhouse' and 'the gynecologist's office.' The guru in question spends *his* life vacillating between AA and college symposia where he can fuck unsuspecting nineteen-year-olds – but no matter. He is judging her – not vice versa. And anyway Jeannie never had much desire to judge anyone but herself. She was the soul of generosity with everyone but Jeannie.

But she had no talent for happiness. It could be said she had a talent for misery, but I'd prefer to think of misery as the absence of joy rather than a deliberately cultivated condition. That's a moot point, however. Some poets cultivate misery the way banjo players cultivate long fingernails. But Jeannie was not one of these. Her misery was honest, and honestly come by. Death was her roommate, occasional lover, mother, and friend.

I had only met her a few times but ours was one of those instant friendships. We loved each other on sight. She addressed her letters 'Dearest Isadora' from the first and she signed them 'Love.' No 'Fondly' or 'Dear Heart.' She was not Jewish, but she was Whitmanic. Manic depressive too, alas. It was always clear she'd do herself in someday. Her poems were palliatives. Had she escaped suicide it would only have been by a knight's move. Through the looking glass, perhaps. Still, I was shocked when I heard the news. Shocked and guilty. I had owed her a letter for three months when she died.

Not just an ordinary letter, either – but a letter responding to the poems she sent me during the last summer of her life. They were strange poems. Not that all her poems weren't strange – but these were the strangest of all. In a godforsaken world, Jeannie dared to believe in God. In the midst of cynicism and materialism, Jeannie dared to affirm the spirit. In a world in which writers and critics make a cult of misery, hate fecundity, mistrust joy – Jeannie dared affirm joy, dared find God (and say so), dared lash out against misery – including her own.

It was easy enough to put her down. She was a woman – and her images (even of God) were kitchen images, plain aluminum utensils to serve the Lord, Pyrex casseroles to simmer the Holy Spirit. She was easy to mock. Where a male poet would have been taken seriously – even if he saw God in a hunting knife or the wound of a war buddy – she was mocked because it is hard for many people to understand that the womb (with its red blood) is as apt a vessel for the muse or for God as the penis (with its white sperm). Perhaps these are our contemporary wars of the roses. We live in an age that has forgotten how to honor Mary, forgotten how to love God, forgotten how to recite poetry, keep faith, kindle love. Greedy and envious, we doubt the existence of everything but greed and envy. And Jeannie had no use whatsoever for these two.

'Would you turn the radio up?' I asked the cab driver, a certain Seymour Asofsky.

'Whadjasay?'

'Would you turn it up?' The yellow taxi (a member of the Lucky Cab Corp. fleet) was only a year old, but it looked like a veteran of some desert tank campaign. It rattled and clattered up Madison Avenue and I scarcely caught the radio announcer's words. A sudden blast of hard-rock music. Jeannie's obituary was already over.

'A friend of mine just died,' I confided to Seymour.

We were twenty blocks from the analyst's office, and perhaps I had the desire to start my session early.

'Whadjasay?'

'My friend just died,' I shouted, wanting to share my grief – with him, with anyone. 'That poet the radio just mentioned – Jeannie Morton – she *died*.'

'Oh. Dat's a shame. I never hoida her. You a poetress too?'

'Yes,' I said, ashamed of confessing it to a cab driver. As if I were somehow boasting. And yet we were both manual laborers.

'I don't read much poetry myself. I do remember one pome in school though – "In Xanadu did Kubla Khan" – Kipling I think. I *loved* dat pome. I should read more ... What's your book called?'

'Well, I wrote two books of poems, but my most well-known book is a novel.' Suddenly, I'm stumbling with shyness.

'Oh yeah?'

'It's called *Candida Confesses*,' I said.

Seymour wheels around in his seat and nearly collides with a Gristede's grocery cart being pushed by a now-terrorized Puerto Rican kid. He strains for a look at me through the scratched Plexiglass divider.

'You dat Happy Hooker chick?'

I laugh, deeply offended.

'Hey – I seen you on TV.'

I smile my book-autographing smile – but I am already miles, light-years away. I am in Cape Cod with Jeannie.

From the moment I heard of it, Jeannie's death had a strange effect on me. I was grieving, yes. I missed her palpably. But I was suddenly light. Light – in both senses of the word. The baggage of my summer-long depression dropped away. Sometimes people reach out from the grave to have a more powerful effect on us in death than they had in life. To tell the truth, Jeannie's effect on me was almost always a long-distance one. Poets relate to each other through inky pages, through words, through the mails, from the grave. We dream each other. We dream while waking.

Our meetings in life were few, but each one was a revelation. Other than that, we met on the page. I first read her poems when I was in Europe, reading during those grim years of marriage, surviving Bennett's silences through printed words.

Jeannie's poetry was brave in a way I had not encountered before. She dared to be a fool. She wrote about all the things we had been told in college were unfit subjects for poetry – blood, madness, excrement, the transmigration of souls. I don't know how my own college generation got such curiously tight-ass notions of what poetry should be. Perhaps it was the influence of all the little Eliotasters who taught us. We might have read Whitman or Blake or any of the other great Dionysiac spirits and realized that

169

poetry was never meant to be a fastidious thing, that a certain kind of inspired insanity was the way into the unconscious and also the way into the cosmos. But these lessons have to be learned over and over again. One generation learns them, the next buries them. The generation after that unearths them as if it had invented them – and so it goes. But in this case, more was happening than just the usual generational Zeitgeist tango. There was the great upheaval of the female half of the species, the buried lives of women were suddenly surfacing, the earth was falling away from their faces as from the faces of the dead, and the Dionysiac spirit was reasserting itself through the breasts, the cunt, the womb.

It was time for women to lead and men to follow – at least in the spiritual realm. Lawrence had predicted it; so had Whitman and Mallarmé. Men who were wise and sure of themselves and willing to learn knew it and were not frightened. They felt no particular shame in taking spiritual instruction from women – any more than they would feel shame in taking spiritual instruction from other men. They would take wisdom wherever they found it and let it enrich them. But many men *were* terrified and reacted violently. Also, the women themselves had often made deep commitments to terrified men before they discovered their own strength. They had houses, children, lives of habit and habitation. They were trapped in an especially painful way. Their spirits free and yearning to travel, their bodies committed to men, to children, to houses. The classic conflict between freedom and duty. Jeannie was one who suffered from this.

We met on a couple of occasions at poetry readings. We exchanged passionate letters and phone calls – but our first long, live encounter came after she had left her husband.

She was staying at the Algonquin, preparatory to recording her poems for Bardic Records. Bardic was a classy outfit and Jeannie had fought for years to get her own solo record – like Yeats, like Dylan Thomas, like Auden.

'I'll only be the second living poet they've recorded,' she told me gaily when we met at the Algonquin. But not for

170

long. By the time the record appeared, she was speaking from the grave.

She was thin, hysterical, wired that night at the Algonquin. She had lost twenty-five pounds since leaving Bumby, her husband of twenty-five years. Both her kids were away in college. She had just lost a beautiful married lover – one of those struggling, straggling poor-fessor–poets who falls in love with great lady poets, promises everything and then goes back to his wife, his dog, his tenure. Gutless.

'Men today are gutless.' she said. 'But who can blame them? I'm often terrified myself,' and she laughed like a shower of gravel hitting a window.

She was merry in a hysterical sort of way. She was drinking Stolichnaya vodka on the rocks with little twists of lime and dashing around the room looking for fallen worksheets under the bed, refilling her glass, filling mine, answering the phone. There seemed to be many more people in the room than just the two of us From time to time, her huge blue-green eyes would fix on mine and she would say, 'Forgive me, please, please forgive me for being so hysterical' – and then she would recommence her dashing around.

No forgiveness was necessary. I loved her. There was an openness there, and a vulnerability in those eyes that made you forgive everything. Anyway, I am no stranger to disorder, obsession, fear of hotel rooms. I kept wanting to hug her and tell her it was okay. This was just shortly before Bennett broke his Woodstock news to me – and I must have sensed a fore-trembling in Jeannie's own marital disaster. I wanted to hug her as much for my own sake, perhaps, as for hers.

'I'm blind!' she said, staring at a page of one of her early books. 'The words are blurs on the page! They look like Rorschachs! Can you imagine – all these years I've fought for this album, this record, this goddamned Bardic *mishegoss*, and now I'm *blind*! Like Homer! Talk about success phobias! All my shrinks told me I had a will to fail!' Her voice was gravelly, yet somehow resonant. It

171

was the voice of a Sibyl, a Delphic oracle. Where they chewed laurel leaves, she drank Stolichnaya. It was all one. Anything to oil the unconscious.

'You know what I need?' she asked.

'What?'

'A magnifying glass. Do you suppose we could find a magnifying glass around here?'

It was ten at night. Everything was closed. All the art-supply stores and stationery stores were closed. I offered to go out looking for an all-night drugstore, but she wouldn't let me. She rang for the bellman instead.

He arrived – a bright-eyed Irish boy of eighteen or so with a thick brogue and curly hair – and she began flirting with him outrageously, using the desired magnifying glass as the excuse. Would he go out to an all-night drugstore for us, would he try to find a good one, a big one, not one of those crummy little plastic ones? It seemed as if the magnifying glass were a metaphor for something else. And the bellboy picked it up immediately. He was Irish, after all, and a born wordsman. He also had a poet's twinkle in his eye. The Playboy of the Western World – from Central Casting.

'A big solid one, is that what you fancy?'

'Yes,' said Jeannie, laughing, meaning the glass and not meaning it, knowing the transparency of the metaphor and pretending not to know it, magnifying the game as well as the illegible print on the page, delighting in her hys-terical Homeric blindness, eyeing the boy (for whom she was *not* blind), and enjoying herself thoroughly.

'I'll be glad to get you one and bring it back to your room later, ma'am. But right now I can't because I can't get off me work.' The brogue thickened, seeking a tip.

'Do you faithfully promise you'll come back later?' Jeannie asked seductively.

'I faithfully promise,' said the boy, more Irish than ever.

I felt that I had entered a time warp and been transported back to the days when the Algonquin was new. There were no Irishmen in New York anymore. That was tele-vision or Hollywood – not reality. But Jeannie had a way
172

of making you feel that you had gone back in time, were living in a legendary age – an age of myths and poets and chthonic deities.

The Irishman bowed out, promising to return later with 'a fine big magnifying glass.'

Jeannie made him promise six times not to forget, telling him she was a poet, after all, and had to read her work, batting her eyelashes, flirting, quoting herself until the poor man was quite overcome.

As soon as he left, having promised and promised, she became obsessed again. He would surely forget. She would never be able to read a single word. She would miss this golden opportunity to record her work. She was finished. Her dream of reading for Bardic Records was over and done.

'Why don't I call the desk?' I said brightly. 'Surely there must be a magnifying glass somewhere in the hotel.'

'Oh, you *are* brilliant as well as beautiful – aren't you, Isadora? Aren't you, my love?' She was absurdly, passionately grateful for this obvious suggestion.

Feeling terribly pleased with myself, I sat down on the edge of the bed and called the desk. I was drunk on vodka by then and had a drunk's verbal nerve.

'The Algonquin,' I said rather pompously into the telephone, 'is known to be a friend to poets. We have a very famous poet right here in this room – a Pulitzer Prize winner, in fact – and . . .'

'Say *Nobel* Prize!' Jeannie prompted, in her gravelly voice. 'They won't know the difference!'

'A Nobel Prize-winning poet,' I went on, 'and a bludgeon – I mean a legend – in her own lifetime . . .'

Jeannie laughed her wonderful throaty laugh.

'And we were wondering if, by any chance, you might have a magnifying glass – because, you see, she can't seem to find her glasses, and she has to give a poetry reading and . . . yes? . . . you do? Would you send it up? Thank you so much . . . room Six-fourteen. Yes. Oh thank you. Thank you.'

Jeannie was delirious. She waltzed around the room with her Pulitzer Prize-winning third book of poems, *Holy Fool's*

173

Day (whose epigraph was: 'Yes, to be a fool, that perhaps requires the greatest courage of all').

The magnifying glass came, the *other* magnifying glass came (with the Irishman), we all drank together, and the next day Jeannie read her poems for Bardic without mishap. By the time the record was out in the stores, it was all that remained of her voice.

Two nights after the Algonquin blindness episode, Jeannie came to my house to a party at which I had been instructed to have as many 'yummy single men' as I could find.

It was a hastily thrown-together party – because I was leaving for that fatal booksellers' convention in Chicago the next day, but it was gay enough. Bennett and I were always at our best at parties – when other people were there to fill the vacuum between us. The food was takeout Szechuan, with lots of good cheeses and wine; the guests were mostly literary – with the exception of Holly, who met Jeannie that night and fell hopelessly in love with her; but the one 'yummy single man' I found for Jeannie left without offering to take her home. This was not because she wasn't beautiful, but because she had an edge of hysteria everyone could feel. The man in question was pretty flaky himself – and this was clearly a question of his not wanting to fuck someone with more problems than himself. It was the first and only time I've known him to be so prudent. Both his wives were psychotic *and* alcoholic.

Jeannie was in rare form that night. She was (to use a much overused word that happens to be literally true in this case) incandescent. She sat in a straight-back chair in the center of the room (while all the rest of us sat on upholstered ones) and seemed to catch, with amazing grace and dexterity, questions that showered upon her from her enchanted, happily captive audience.

The guests were all fans of Jeannie's and they all wanted to interview her about her methods of composition, her life, her art. She was spectacularly patient with them. Also with me. I had to leave early the next morning and I was panicked about the flight, the public appearances, the lonely hotel room. I have this truly paradoxical gift of looking completely calm and fearless on public platforms. on television, in interviews. But I do all my suffering later, in the hotel room, or on a plane. I'm forever trying to convince my friends and family that I bleed when stabbed – but no one believes me because I look so jaunty.

And then there was the matter of sex. I was troubled about the way the public treated me and I needed Jeannie's advice badly. We live in a world so nutty on the subject of sex that a book of poems which uses it as a persistent metaphor can be confused with an exploitation book written by a former hooker. This disturbed me greatly and Jeannie knew it. I wanted her to tell me how to handle it. I was plagued by the confusion between natural earthiness and licentiousness, the mistaking of openness and lack of pretense for a desire to titillate and shock.

'What do I do when they come up to me and ask me for a zipless fuck?' I asked Jeannie.

'Thank them,' she said firmly.

'*Thank* them,' I was incredulous. 'Why?'

'*Thank* them,' she said again, 'because no matter how crude their expression, no matter how vulgar their speech, what they are *really* trying to say – what your fans are *really* trying to express – even when they pinch your ass, even when they send you obscene letters – is that they have been *moved*. They know no other way to express it but crudely. Yet they are really saying: *I have been moved. You have touched me in a very deep place which I do not dare call my soul, so I call it my cock.* So thank them and then say, "Zip up your fuck until I ask for it!" '

Jeannie's audience broke up.

'God – what a wonderful line. Can I steal it?'

'Steal – there's no stealing,' Jeannie said passionately. 'Your words, my words – language can't be appropriated by one person, one poet. The words belong to all of us. They belong to God, really.' And she stared ahead as if at a vision of Him.

This *is* the reincarnation of the Delphic oracle, I thought.

'Don't you see, Isadora, that there *is no* "your poem, my poem"? There is no "your line, my line"? There is the

175

language, and we are its vessels. We speak for the mouths that can't speak, we speak *their* thoughts – not our own. That's when we're writing, when we're pure. When we're not writing we worry about ego, ego, ego, and the critics talk about ego, ego, ego. Whose by-line? Whose book? How long? Which prize? But the gift for language has no particular by-line – just as a river doesn't care if it stays in a given state. It will flow across boundary lines, down mountains, from one country into another, from one civilization into another. The small minds sit there labeling, arguing about naming things, arguing about by-lines, but the river just keeps flowing. It doesn't care if it's called Jeannie River or Isadora River. It doesn't care if it's masculine in one state, feminine in another. It doesn't care how many copies are bought, or what the reviews are, or if anyone gets paid. All it cares about is flowing. And *you* are its servant. Your *only job*, and I mean *only*, is not to hold up its flow with your silly ego, your worries about approval or disapproval, about by-lines, about stealing this line or that, about second-guessing the public. Your *only* job is to go with the flow. The rest is not your business. Or mine.'

Jeannie's audience was speechless and transfixed.

'You see,' she went on, 'the river has more rights than the ego that wants approval. The river has the only rights there are. *Your* big mistake, Isadora, is that you think it matters what the river is called, or who says what about the river. Is it a "profound" river? Is it "deft and lyrical"? Is it a "break-through" river? Who *cares* – as long as it flows. All the rest is foolishness, distraction, jockeying for position and reputation – politics, in short. Your ego has *no* rights *whatsoever* in this matter. Nor do the egos of the critics have any rights whatsoever. The *river* has the only rights there are. And the river corresponds to the rights of the readers. Nobody else has any authority at all over the river – not the author, not the reviewer. It is only river and reader. The reader is like a fisherman, standing in thigh-high boots, in the midst of the rushing stream and catching what he can, trying to see his face in the moving water, trying to reel in his dinner. He has the rights – not you. You must only see to it that nothing dams up or diverts the river. You must let the river flow so he can see his face and possibly even catch his dinner. That's all. That's all there is to say about it.'

Before Jeannie left, she took me aside and gave me a slim, oblong package wrapped in tissue paper.
'What is it?'
'Something to remember me by,' she said cryptically.
'Remember you? I'll never forget you as long as I live.'
'Longer,' she said, smiling.
I tore open the package. Inside was a notebook covered in red marble-patterned paper, with a red morocco spine and red morocco corners. On the first endpaper, Jeannie had written (in a hand that seemed to flatten the lowercase letters into submission – but leave the uppercase ones standing taller as a result):

> Life can only be understood backwards,
> but it must be lived forwards.
> – Kierkegaard, via Jeannie Morton

'A notebook,' Jeannie said, 'to understand your life – or save it. You could call it, *How to Save Your Own Life.*'
'How did you know that was exactly what I needed?' I asked.
'Because I'm a witch,' she laughed, hugging me. 'Just make sure you fill up the notebook. Do it for me.'
'I'll mail it to you as soon as I'm through.'
'You may never be through,' Jeannie said.

My friends Louise and Robert Miller drove Jeannie back to the Algonquin at midnight, had a nightcap with her – and then wanted to head home.
She would not let them go, but held them captive in the lobby, ordering drink after drink, swallowing her sleeping pills with vodka, waiting for the pills to take effect, to quiet the panic, keep down the demons.
Jeannie clutched Bob's wrist with hysterical tightness, growing tighter and tighter as her fear of going upstairs

to her room increased. She tried to convince them to stay with her – but when, at 3:00 A.M., they pleaded exhaustion, she downed another Valium – and leaned back in the lobby armchair to doze. They finally left her there, not knowing what else they could do short of getting into bed with her.

In October she was dead. Already she was laid out in the funeral parlor, her children were called home from college, her husband and lovers all remarried her in death, and, the whole world over, schoolgirl poets were using her as the subject of their poems. She was ossifying into myth. Another suicidal lady poet. She, who had been so funny, so outrageous, so pure in her intuition and so warm, was being frozen into cult.

The weekend after her death, I was having my picture taken in Central Park by a fellow named Rod Thomas, who is a photographer and a poet and also a devoted fan of Jeannie's. Rod took me wandering through the park, where we reminisced about her and took pictures of me under trees, on rocks, in row-boats. They were supposed to be pictures for a new book of poems – but in all of them I looked so haunted that something kept us from using them. I'll never know whether or not the decision was wise. In none of the pictures did I look quite like myself – nor did I look like Jeannie, really – but some transmigration had taken place. Whether of the soul or of some other part is not for me to say.

Photographs, anyway, are the most curious indicators of reality. They are said to convey the exact nature of the material world, but actually, what they convey is spiritual and only partly the result of the masses of light and shadow in the world of rocks and trees and flesh. Things happen in photographs that do not happen in life. Or else we perceive in photographs what we cannot perceive in life. Is perception equivalent to existence? That is the premise on which we base our lives, yet it may well be a false premise. In these photographs, something new had entered my face: a special sort of daring, the courage to be a fool.

All this is retrospect, hindsight. 'Life can only be understood backwards, but it must be lived forwards' it said in the notebook which, in the months after Jeannie gave it to me, I had found too beautiful (and had been too depressed) to use. Of course I was not completely without the fool's daring before Jeannie's death. I had done plenty of dumb things, and suffered for them, and learned from them. But with her death, some new element entered my chronic, anguishing indecision. 'Live or die,' she seemed to be saying to me from the grave, 'but for god's sake don't poison yourself with indecision.'

Throughout our lives, we are brought in contact with spiritual advisors; the trick is not in meeting them, but in recognizing them when we do. I recognized Jeannie from the start, but if she had not died, would I have acted upon that recognition? I wonder.

It was Sunday, the day we took pictures in the park. Back at the apartment, Bennett was loafing around in slippers, listening to the same Bach cantatas over and over again and reading the same psychoanalytic journals. He had already played his obligatory tennis early that morning.

When Rod and I returned with our rolls and rolls of haunted film, all three of us had tea together. In the midst of the tea, the phone rang.

A blizzard of static on the line told me it was sunny California calling.

'Hello? Isadora. This is Britt.' (She scarcely had to identify herself – since the nasal voice said it all.)

'Hi,' I said, my heart pounding with the terror Britt always inspired in me.

'Hi,' she said, racing on to the point of her call. 'Listen, I don't have time to talk because Paul Newman is waiting for me at the Polo Lounge – but I think I can get you a fabulous deal. The only thing is – you'll have to come out to the Coast.'

The fortune-telling power of waves ...

*There are people in this world
who are joyful and they always
seem to have more energy than
the rest of us. This is because
they don't use it all up on
repression and self-delusion.
Being miserable is not a hobby,
but a full-time job ...*

The 'Coast.' I dreaded going to the 'Coast.' That was where writers went to die, where poets went to have their words snuffed out, where producers and promoters and parasites sapped the life out of flourishing talent, killed off dying talent, and made mincemeat of the fledgling talent that happened to get caught in their jaws.

Producers. They ate writers for breakfast, directors for lunch, and actors for their seven-course dinners. And yet, despite all my misgivings, and despite the fact that I already knew I feared and mistrusted Britt, I was strangely elated by her call. There was deadlock between me and Bennett. This was an excuse to fly

The last sight of Bennett at the airport. In some way, this was the last sight of him forever. His hair looked black and glossy, his eyes sad and small behind the reflections of his thick glasses, his posture frozen.

No – wait. There is another tableau preceding that one. The last time Bennett and I made love.

It was the afternoon before I left for California on the 7:00 P.M. flight. We had gotten up early, both nervous about my departure. He made my breakfast. I began to pack. He went to play tennis. I made lunch for his return. He returned. I was already packed. We went to bed.

But now there is a strange blank in my memory – a whitish blur like sheets over the eyes of a fearful dreamer just awakening at sunrise. Then a glassy, silvery object glitters up from the bottom of the pond of memory. What is it? Shaped like a small baton. Bright, brittle, moon-silvery, it is the silver baton of an elfin twirler – only it has glittering facets and numbers on its edge.

It is an Ovulindex thermometer! One of those things you use to find out when you're fertile – and it is on my bed table because (in the midst of my terrible despair about my marriage to Bennett and my constant chafing to leave) I have begun taking my temperature to figure out my fertile days,

183

and from time to time I have been omitting my diaphragm in an attempt to 'accidentally' get myself knocked up.

These furtive attempts to create an 'accident' fill me with ambivalence and panic. On the one hand, I know that babies cannot patch up sundered marriages, but, on the other hand, I want a baby to keep my life company in the desolation and loneliness that will surely overtake me when I do finally leave Bennett. Or else maybe the baby will transform us, give us back the will to live, make us love each other. Jeannie's death also points to procreation. I will have a girl and name her Jeannie.

And yet, on this occasion, because I am going to California, and because some extraordinary new fate perhaps awaits me, I find my diaphragm (deep in my suitcase where I have packed it) and put it on before Bennett gets home from tennis.

In bed, we talk.

'Are you pissed off at my going?' I ask, seeing Bennett's glum face.

'I'll miss you,' he says.

And I am touched. He is trying, for the first time in the whole of our marriage, to express tenderness toward me. It is still stinting, stingy, far from being unstoppered – but it is tenderness. I cry.

'I don't want anyone else,' I say, weeping.

And yet, why is everything between us always so grim? Even the tender moments are grim. We have never once laughed in bed.

He makes love to me expertly, mechanically, coldly. Neither savagely – as during our summer of jealous rage – nor really warmly. He is pressing all my buttons, as if I were a pocket calculator.

On the plane, something is missing, Fear. I sit back in my seat waiting for that familiar panic, that old friend fear, that certain knowledge that I am about to die. Yet I clasp my seat belt and feel completely calm. The takeoff is natural, uneventful. The plane rises as if on the power of Jeannie's death. I have the sense that my life is being fueled by her death, and whatever happens next is meant to happen. I am no longer responsible for holding up the plane.

184

Either Jeannie will do it or it will fall – and one way or the other, I am given over into hands stronger and steadier than my own.

Flying is suddenly miraculous! We dip and turn over the flats of Queens, where the inflated backyard swimming pools of the working-class row houses gleam like round blue eyes. I wish Leonardo da Vinci could be here beside me! If only he could ride in a 747! If only Jeannie could be here beside me, going off across the Rockies, going toward the big western sky, starting over, starting life over again.

Was it really Jeannie's death that suddenly released me from the fear of flying I'd had for years – or was it something else? Was it some new understanding of how uncontrollable life is, how little our anxieties influence our futures? Or was it suddenly growing up, growing unafraid of leaving home, leaving Mother, leaving the earth, leaving the street I grew up on, leaving Bennett, the man who made me 'Wing' and then tried to keep me from flying?

It was true, oddly enough, that even during all my worst panics about flying I dreaded takeoff and almost always enjoyed the landing. This was absurd because landing was, in fact, the most dangerous time. But perhaps what I really dreaded was leaving home – and suddenly leaving home was no longer terrifying. Home was wherever I was. And right now I was flying.

I struck up a conversation with the man next to me – a record-company executive in classy California clothes. A medley of Gucci, Hermès, and Cardin – and his silk shirt unbuttoned to his breastbone, revealing beads, chains, and plenty of curly hair over tanned skin.

We talked for three hours – through drinks, hors d'oeuvres, dinner, brandy – and we never exchanged names. Then, shortly before the flight was over, he asked me, 'Was your last name White? and did you have a big apartment with a circular staircase?'

'Yes,' I said, surprised. And then it flashed: this is the first guy who felt you up, who put his hand under your skirt when you were twelve! Christ! Isadora goes to Hollywood! Is this what Hollywood is – a bunch of kids you grew up with on the Upper West Side, now metamorphosed into walking testimonials to Gucci, Hermès, Cardin, and the tanning power of the southern sun? Suddenly Hollywood didn't seem threatening at all.

'Your father had drums,' my old pal said. 'I remember playing them.'

'I remember you feeling me up,' I said brazenly.

'Funny, I don't remember *that* part at *all.*'

'How insulting!'

'But your father's drums were *terrific.*' He thought a moment. 'I wonder why we only went out twice. You were considered an unusual girl ...'

Then I remembered what I'd thought of *him* (apart from being aroused yet terrorized by the speed with which his hand darted under my skirt): another snotty Horace Mann boy, another Jewish prep-school prince! I'd felt *superior.* But of course I felt superior to *everyone* when I was twelve.

My plane was thirty minutes late, and to her chagrin, chronically late Britt had arrived at the airport only twenty minutes late. When I spotted her she was smoking like the Camel sign in Times Square, chewing gum at the same time, and pacing like a caged tiger. She was wearing patched jeans that had been tapered to her every curve (not many) and a blouse made of old silk handkerchiefs and a little ring that said LOVE in gold block letters. Her hard mouth did not say love, and her woolly orange hair had been freshly fluffed out into the Beverly Hills equivalent of an Afro. A halo of friz surrounded her small, determined head, and a saddle of caramel-colored freckles spattered her nose and cheeks.

'C'mon,' she said as soon as we found my luggage on the carrousel, 'I have to drop you at your hotel *fast* because I have a heavy date later tonight.'

'What about your *husband*?' I asked, surprised.

'I left him as a direct result of your book. I *told* you how much your book meant to me. And you should *see* the guy I'm seeing tonight. God – is *he* beautiful. You'd love him. And I'm not going to let you meet him ...'

She paused, looked me over critically, and said: 'Oh I don't know. Maybe I *could* let you meet him – as long as you promise not to lose any weight.'

That was Britt exactly – competition and put-down at the same time. She'd never do a nice thing (coming to the airport) without simultaneously asserting how one-up she was.

Skinny. She certainly was skinnier than I was. Sheer meanness kept her skinny. That – and an assortment of hypochondriacal disorders that would fill the Merck manual.

The Beverly Hills Hotel. Who can do justice to a New Yorker's first glimpse of the Beverly Hills Hotel? It loomed before us, pink as a little girl's birthday cake, with slender, swaying palms instead of candles, and mysterious floodlights picking out the foliage. The scripted name of this pink stucco emporium was outlined in eerie greenish lights.

Rolls-Royces with curious license plates glided up to the door to be met by princely young men with platinum hair. If these were the parking attendants, what must the guests be like? Oh unimaginable splendor! I thought of the Land of Oz, of Alice's looking-glass world – and there was Britt as my Red Queen, leading me furiously into the lobby with its huge, unnecessary fireplace, past the smiling desk clerks, down the long halls (where a maintenance man was actually repainting the white sky between the jungle-green palm fronds of the wall-paper). Painting the roses red! This is Beverly Hills, where real grass has been made to look like Astroturf, where real palms have been made to look like plastic ones, where tropical flowers have no odor, and where lawyers ride around in Rolls-Royces with Vuitton briefcases on their knees.

This is the land of the Big Deal, of pay or play, of millions one year and bankruptcy the next, of meetings, meetings, meetings (interrupted by an occasional movie), of much talk and very little action, of hustle and hassle, greed and guile.

The license plate I saw on a Rolls parked outside the

Beverly Hills Hotel the night of my arrival summed it up: GREED. Britt was not that honest.

'I want to make a really quality movie of your book,' she said in the hotel suite (where we were eating our sumptuous room-service meal of roast rack of lamb, carved by the *maître d'* himself assisted by a flunky).

'I think we should get Truffaut or Ingmar Bergman – or maybe even John Schlesinger to direct,' Britt said, chomping down on a mouthful of lamb. She was nervous about her date later – and, with many apologies, she wanted to eat and run. I could almost see her brain ticking. She had done her bit for me (picked me up at the airport). Now it was time to attend to herself. Pretty soon she was gobbling a chocolate mousse (Britt ate lots of chocolate but never got fat – a sure sign of demonic possession) and reapplying her blood-red lipstick and running off to her late-night date with a man whose live-in girlfriend just happened to be away for the weekend.

I was left alone in the suite, waiting for my hotel-room panic to claim me – but somehow, it did not. I inspected the rooms, showered, turned down the covers of my bed, piled up the numerous pillows, and then went to have a look at my terrace, which overlooked the deserted swimming pool and cabanas. The air was balmy and mild. I was calm. I was delighted to be alone, delighted to have experienced an entire transcontinental flight without a moment of terror, and unequivocally delighted to be in evil, awful Los Angeles.

While I was out on the terrace, the phone rang. Though I was momentarily annoyed at having my reverie interrupted, when I picked up the phone and heard Holly's shaken voice across three thousand miles of telephone cable, I knew something serious was up. It was four in the morning in New York. Crazy as Holly was at times, she was not given to late-night long-distance dialing.

'What's up?' I asked cheerily, as if that way I could eradicate whatever was bothering her.

'Am I crazy, Isadora?' Holly asked. 'I want you to tell me the truth.'

188

'Of course not,' I lied.

'Come on, this is *serious*. I want you to tell me if you think I'm mad.'

'What's "mad"?'

'That's no sort of answer and you know it. I don't want cheap semantics or cleverness, I just want to know whether you've ever detected in me any sign of real insanity – not imagination or the sort of things I paint or anything like that – but delusions, conjuring up things that aren't there, *that* sort of thing.'

'No,' I said firmly, trying for the life of me to remember whether it was true or not. 'No, absolutely not.'

'Well,' Holly said, sounding relieved, 'for the last couple of days – I don't know why I didn't tell you this before you left, but I guess it sounded too weird – I've been thinking almost constantly of Jeannie Morton. I know this sounds insane, but it's almost as if she's here with me in the loft, hovering over the plants, watching me paint, a definite *presence*. I keep going to her books, reading them, painting some more, feeding the cat, reading a poem of hers, painting, thinking about her – but all the time I'm agitated, as if she's trying to tell me something, as if she's here, and all the time I'm also thinking I'm crazy, and that I have to call you, but I don't know if you're in L.A. yet and I'm also afraid you'll think it's weird ... So finally (and you know I *never* paint people) I take out a clean canvas and one of the jacket photos of her – the one where she's sitting in her solarium with the white angora cat on her lap – and I start doing a *portrait* of her. I *know* I'm not playin' with a full deck, but as I paint it, oddly enough, the room gets calmer, the agitation lifts, it gets peaceful again ... So I go on painting till I'm very tired (I used Seymour as the model for the cat, but Jeannie I painted from the photograph, at least I *hope* I did) and then finally, I'm so exhausted I fall asleep without any Valium even – which is some kind of *first* for me. And then – *this* is the weird part – I *dreamed* about her and she looked just like herself and talked like herself and she said something very strange which I don't understand at all but maybe you will ...'

'What?'

189

'She said, "Tell your friend to use the notebook." And she was very firm about it, very definite, like a command. Then I got up and called you.'

'How do you know the friend was me?'

'You're the only friend I *have*, dummy. Listen, Isadora, does that *mean* anything to you?'

'I'm thinking,' I said. 'Wait – could you hold the wire a second? I think someone's at the door ...'

'It's Jeannie,' Holly said, terrified.

'Don't be ridiculous.'

I went to my suitcase, pulled out the red-marbled notebook and returned to the phone.

'No one there,' I said, 'just some drunken producers in the hall ...'

'Thank God,' Holly sighed at the end of the long umbilicus. I opened the notebook to the first endpaper, where I was relieved to find no words but the ones that had been there before.

'I think you've just been working too hard,' I told Holly reassuringly, reassuring myself too. I leafed through the notebook with my free hand and in the sewn centerfold I saw something I hadn't noticed before :

*'How do I save my own life?' the poet asked.
'By being a fool,' God said.*

It was unmistakably Jeannie's handwriting. But more than that, it was unmistakably Jeannie's *voice*.

'Listen, Holly, I will *not* sit here and listen to this supernatural nonsense. You just miss her, that's all. I miss her *too*. Haunting by another name is love.'

'Hey – I like that. That's a good line. Did anyone ever tell you you should write greeting cards?'

'Very funny.'

'I mean it. You might even attempt a best seller someday, go to Hollywood, earn big bucks. It sure beats painting ferns.'

'Do you think you can go to sleep now?'

'I think so, I feel fine, really I do, it was just a passing lunacy.'

'Will you call me immediately if you get upset again? Call collect, it's on Britt, she can afford it better than you can.'

'I think I'm okay now.'

'Good.'

'I love you a lot,' Holly said.

'Me you too. Call me anytime if you feel weird again. Promise?'

'I promise.'

'Lots of hugs and kisses.'

'To you too,' she said.

And we blew a bunch of transcontinental kisses and hung up.

Britt put me through hell. In the week that followed, I got to know her, and what I got to know, I did not like. She was incorrigible, kept me waiting four and five hours for meetings, stayed for an hour or two, and then raced off to some boyfriend's house, leaving the bedspread in my hotel room scumbled with crumbs of marijuana and traces of cocaine.

She had me marked as a sucker, and she was right. Who else would have come to Hollywood for the price of a plane ticket and hotel bill? Who else would have worked days and days on outlining a screenplay that turned out to be wrong in concept, wrong in construction, and unplayable – because it was a botch of my book and her directives and because the truth was that at that point, neither of us knew anything about what we were doing. 'Trust me,' Britt said. And I did. Oh I am very good at trusting all the wrong people.

I knew *I* was ignorant, but I assumed Britt knew what she was doing. So I did what no writer should *ever* do: I put my words in her hands. I took instruction from her. I let her tell me what to write. And my naïveté set me up for disaster. The screen-play that resulted represented neither my book nor Britt's idea of a movie. It was a pastiche of mistakes.

We worked at the Beverly Hills Hotel, in Britt's office on the back lot of Paradigm Pictures, at her mansion in Beverly

191

Hills. *Worked* is a rather strong word for what went on. It was impossible to get Britt's attention for more than ten minutes at a time. She paced, smoked, snorted, answered phones, made dates, took breaks, left me baby-sitting with her two neurotic Lhasa Apsos, sent me shopping for food – and, in general, treated me like a menial or a personal secretary. I was so astounded by this treatment that I could barely find the words to protest. *Nobody* had ever treated me that way before. Did Britt *know* what she was doing or was she totally unconscious? I suspect the latter. Whenever I got up the courage to hint to her that I wasn't her caretaker, her wet nurse, her nanny – she broke down and cried, telling me she was my friend, telling me she loved me, telling me she identified with me completely and would never, never, *never* want to do anything to hurt me. By fits and starts, we managed to take apart the whole of *Candida Confesses* and break it down into scenes on index cards. Then we started crawling around on our hands and knees, arranging the scenes on the floor of the hotel room. My whole life on index cards under our knees! As we took the book apart, I realized that I would have to take my life apart the same way. But whether I would ever be able to put it back together again was another story.

In the middle of my second week in California, Britt disappeared. Neither her secretary nor her housekeeper nor her estranged husband knew where she was. I waited around for her an entire day, and when it seemed that nobody else was really worried (she had done this before – and had always wound up returning – often with a new boyfriend), I decided to take a vacation too. I flew up to Berkeley to visit a college friend, and spent the flight marveling at the remarkable shapes of the mountains. I had never felt so absurdly at home in the air. Or in the world. I had never thought of Bennett so little. He was gone, my depression was gone, and my whole life seemed about to start over.

I checked in with Britt's secretary the morning I got back, and when I learned that she was still away, I declared a vacation for myself and did other things with my time.

I rented a car and drove to Disneyland, I drove out to Malibu by myself and stood on the beach in a Santa Ana wind, thinking about my life and testing the fortune-telling power of waves with my toes.

The ocean was an astonishing medley of purple, azure, and green, with a glittering surface of scales being played by the wind. The air was so clear that the horizon was a razor's edge halfway to Japan, and the ocean kept falling into itself, gathering itself up, and falling into itself again.

I stood with my bare feet planted in the sand at the tide's edge and waited for the irregular lips of the waves to tell me what to do with my life. If the waves touched my toes, I promised myself I would leave Bennett.

Then I waited in increasing desolation while the waves kept missing my prophetic flesh. I stood still for what seemed like hundreds of waves, trying not to show the sea how badly it had disappointed me. Until finally it happened: one glittering cylinder of blue water crashed into white foam, sending its froth bubbling along the beach to my waiting toes, ankles, calves, and knees. I felt the wet sand cave under my arches and I knew panic – and exultation. The sea had just divorced me from Bennett.

Later that afternoon I had an invitation to visit a famous old American writer (formerly an expatriate in Paris) whose reclining years had brought him, like so many other frantic bohemians, to bourgeois comfort on the edge of the Pacific. Kurt Hammer had honed his underground reputation on tattered copies of his reputed-to-be pornographic novels, smuggled in through customs in the days when sex was considered unfit for print. Now that sex was everywhere in print, his royalties were fading. Censorship, which had once made him seem a modern Marquis de Sade, had receded, leaving him exposed as something of a romantic, a man in love with love – and especially in love with words.

Now eighty-seven, he spent the whole day in bed, writing and sleeping and entertaining disciples. They came from all over the world, and when they didn't come, he wrote to them in longhand on yellow pads. From his bed he communicated with the entire world! He wrote in a free sloping hand not unlike my own – and it was not unusual for him to write as many as twenty letters in the course of one day. I mailed a stack of twenty-two for him the afternoon after I visited him. They were addressed to Sweden, Japan, France, Yugoslavia, the Middle East. Kurt had been accused of male chauvinism by the women's movement, and that piqued and intrigued him. He corresponded with feminists all over the world and he admitted as often as possible that women were the superior sex. 'No man lives as long as I have,' he said, 'without discovering that.'

Seeing this whimsical, elfin octogenarian (with a freckled bald dome and the antic grin of a child who's just gotten into some delicious trouble), it was hard to make sense of his image as a monster of depravity and machismo.

'I'm supposed to be a dirty old man dontcha know,' Kurt said mischievously, in a voice that still said Brooklyn. 'Aren't you afraid to sit on my bed?'

I giggled. He looked pretty harmless to me. 'Whatever I answer, you'll be insulted.'

'I'm *beyond* being insulted. The whole world is cake to me. Every morning when I wake up, I say to myself: What? Not dead *yet*? Sometimes I feel so lousy I think I *am* dead. But all I ask is that the next world be as interesting as this one. I'm not *interested* in Nirvana. Nirvana is a goddamned bore. I can't think of anything *worse*, in fact. What I want are the extremes – the good, the bad, the shit, the Chopin. By the way, do you like Chopin?'

I nodded.

'I *love* him. For me, nobody touches my heart like Chopin. I'd give up every book – every book dontcha know – if I could just have written one prelude like Chopin. That's the truth.'

I stayed with Kurt for hours, talking about his writing, my writing, feminism, poetry, my marriage, his marriages. He had the intense interest in the young that comes to writers when they are beyond competition, when their life's work is a completed thing, when they know for sure that all books constitute a communal enterprise. I told him

194

how painful it was to read vicious things about myself in the press, and he blew up at me.

'I never want to hear you use that word *painful* again,' he said. 'Do you know what they said about Whitman?'

'No,' I conceded.

' "A pig rooting among garbage." That was the review when *Leaves of Grass* came out. Do you read *Leaves of Grass*?'

'Yes. I love it.'

'And have you ever heard of that review?'

'No,' I confessed.

'So don't let me catch you saying "painful." Pain is not something you waste on newspaper hacks. In fact, I've never seen the point of pain at all. The trick is not how much pain you feel – but how much joy you feel. Any idiot can feel pain. Life is full of excuses to feel pain, excuses not to live, excuses, excuses, excuses. When you wind up in bed at the age of eighty-seven like me, the only pain you'll feel is for all the *useless* pain you felt, all the times you let your-self not do something because of fear and cowardice, all the times you let the bastards and the kibbitzers and the life-shrinkers hold you back. Watch out for the death-people, do you see what I mean? The people who want to die and want everyone else to die with them. They're the ones to avoid. If you can learn to avoid them, you'll be fine. And in your writing too, don't listen to them. They don't know what they're doing, only how to destroy, to silence every-one – including *themselves* after a while. They *need* you – or they have nothing to write about – but you don't need them. Do you see what I mean? Do you see why I hate this word *painful*?'

Outside the window of Kurt's bedroom, the Pacific was about to swallow the sun. In New York, it was already night – if New York still existed. I was beginning to doubt it.

What was this myth, I wondered, driving up the Pacific Coast Highway, that literacy ended when you crossed the George Washington Bridge? Certainly no one could have been more chauvinistic about New York than I, who had spent nearly my entire life in the same neighborhood, so it was all the more exhilarating to discover that there was intelligent life west of the Rockies. I was thinking of my afternoon with Kurt as I raced back to the Beverly Hills Hotel to change for a party being held in my honor by friends from the East. Kurt made feel that it was okay to be eighty-seven – as long as you got there with as few regrets as possible

There would always be arthritis and arteriosclerosis and all the other mortal diseases of the flesh – but your spirit didn't have to die an untimely death. For the first time, I had a vision of myself at eighty-seven – a faint vision, perhaps, but a vision nonetheless. I was going to be a terrific old lady someday! I was going to be surrounded by students, disciples – maybe even grandchildren. My life – which a month ago had seemed over – was just beginning. What was thirty-two compared to Kurt's eighty-seven? Where did I get off talking to *him* about pain? I may have been born into this world against my better judgment – but I was staying as a matter of choice, and nobody was going to kick me out until I was good and ready.

I left my rented car in the lot and sprinted, skipped, and ran back to my suite, itching to put some words on paper. I slammed the door, kicked off my shoes, sprawled out on the bed with the notebook Jeannie had given me, opened to the first page and wrote, giggling all the while:

How to Save Your Own Life
The Wit & Wisdom of Isadora Wing
(Amanuensis to the Zeitgeist)
'Have pen, will travel!'

1. Renounce useless guilt.
2. Don't make a cult of suffering.
3. Live in the Now (or at least the Soon).
4. Always do the things you fear the most; courage is an acquired taste, like caviar.
5. Trust all joy.
6. If the evil eye fixes you in its gaze, look elsewhere.
7. Get ready to be eighty-seven.

(*to be continued*)

By 6:30 that evening, I was standing outside the Beverly Hills Hotel, not wearing my glasses and consequently not seeing the bleach-haired beachboys who valet-park the Rolls-Royces (with their poetic license plates), the tanned male agents in jeans by Fred Segal and loafers by Gucci, the yentas hoping to be mistaken for starlets, the starlets hoping to mistaken for stars, the talk-show hosts, the ghostwriters, the screenwriters, the ghosts.

'Ms Wing?' a young man asked, apparently wanting to be politically correct (like my pal Gretchen in Gristede's, hefting lettuces of various political hues).

'Call me Isadora,' I said (amazingly not laughing at this ridiculous line because I was studying the furry, warm, odd, likable face that had just swum into my myopic line of vision).

'Josh Ace,' he said, putting out his hand to shake mine and leading me to a double-parked pea-green MG with the top down. (That much I could register even without my glasses.) Josh was the son of Robert and Ruth Ace, who were hosting the party for me that night. They were a well-known team of screenwriters from the thirties, black-listed in the fifties, surviving McCarthyism by writing spaghetti Westerns in Rome for a dozen years, and now happily back in California, being honored by all the chic radicals – radical sheep, I liked to call them – in the film industry. I had met the Aces through writer friends in New York (where they had been living for the last five years). I never even knew they *had* a son until this moment.

Josh was tall, slim, red-bearded, and had a very gentle manner. I generalized at once: 'Flower child.' He closed the door of the MG and climbed back in behind the wheel.

'Fasten your seat belt,' he said (which I interpreted as an immediate sign of concern for me, but actually it was a new car which wouldn't start unless I locked myself in). And we were off to his parents' house in the Hills, where I, like other literary exiles from New York, was to be given a visiting fireman's welcome.

'It's really nice of your parents to make this party,' I said.

'They love you,' Josh said, 'They really *want* to do it. My

197

father would have picked you up himself, but I insisted.'

'Why?'

'Because I was curious. I've read your poetry and I think it's neat. Actually, from your image in the press, I expected you to be eight feet tall, wearing steel breastplates, and carrying a spear. I'm glad you're not.'

'I *write* tall,' I said.

'Yes, but I sort of expected you to be *scary*.'

'How do you know I'm not?' I asked, not knowing whether to be pleased or insulted.

'I *don't*, really, but my first impressions of people are usually pretty accurate. This may be the first time my father's ever been right about anyone. He's usually a *terrible* judge of character.'

'People always confuse writers with their ideas,' I said, 'especially lady writers.'

'Hmmm,' Josh said. 'It must be hard being a lady writer.'

'It's nice of you to say so. I usually encounter a lot more resistance.'

'I don't know how anyone could resist you,' he said.

What a gas, I thought, looking at his warm face, his aquiline nose, his freckles, his furry beard, his rabbit-toothed smile, what a gas to seduce a *kid*.

'You probably think I'm a kid,' he said, startling me by reading my mind.

'Not at all,' I lied. 'Why? How old are you?'

'Twenty-six, but I have a very old soul.'

God, I thought, *twenty-six*. 'I haven't been twenty-six for about half a century,' I said. He looked at me as if to say I was mad.

We drove to a gas station, where I gathered up the courage to ask him what he 'did.' The question seemed absurd. Why did he have to *do* anything besides be so charming?

'The family racket,' Josh said. 'I just wrote a screenplay for De Laurentiis – a real turkey for which I did what may have been the twenty-ninth rewrite. If I'm lucky, it'll never be released. Don't think I'm a hotshot screenwriter or anything. I have no credits at all. That job was gotten through sheer nepotism.'

When he said 'nepotism' I wanted to hug him. It was the honesty that was so endearing, especially after all the time I'd spent with Britt. Britt – who knew nothing and claimed everything. Josh claimed nothing at all – and knew plenty. I could tell by the modesty.

'Actually,' Josh said, paying for the gas, 'I haven't worked since then. I spend a lot of time waiting in line at Unemployment.'

'Work is much overrated,' I said.

'Only to your generation. I spent four years in college majoring in LSD. I can't think of anything I'd rather do than work – if somebody would hire me.'

'They'd be mad not to,' I said. Oh Brave New World, to have such gentle *men*. Why, I wonder, feeling increasingly like an old bawd or the Wife of Bath, why hadn't I looked into the underthirties *before*?

The Party. I had been looking forward to the party, but now it just seemed like a mob of irritating people, separating me from Josh. Even though he was the only one there I wanted to talk to, I pretended to ignore him and circulate dutifully, as if to undo the fantasies I was already having about him.

'Some house for communists,' I said to Robert Ace, inspecting the forty-foot room, with four-inch shag carpeting, the seemingly Olympic-size swimming pool, the black servants gliding by with trays of hors d'oeuvres. And Robert explained to me (gesticulating with a large cigar) that he wasn't a communist anymore but a Zen Buddhist and that meditation was neither abetted nor undone by large rooms. He was a slight man with a Groucho Marx mustache and glasses that kept slipping down his nose.

'He's a Zen Judist,' Josh said, lurking close behind me, and smiling that rabbit-toothed smile. The smile said everything. Affection for his father mingled with an infallible bullshit detector – an absolute refusal to be conned.

Meanwhile, there was this agent hustling me – a man named Greg Granite (possibly changed from Greenberg?) – who wanted to take me home that night, and failing that wanted to take me home the next night, and failing that, wanted me to write television scripts he could sell to the networks. Ah Hollywood – where pleasure is business and business is pleasure, where communists live in $400,000 mansions with Olympic-size swimming pool, and where agents change their names to igneous rocks and pursue writers through the landscaped Hills on balmy October nights! It was all worth it – the misery with Britt, the misery with Bennett, the fame crazies – if it had brought me here, here to the Land of Oz, where this sweet-faced munch-kin was flickering his green-gold eyes at me across the room and saying, Let me take you away from all this and into the funny, ticklish, warm world of my beard.

I was lionized, lambified, tigerated until two in the morning. Meditating Buddhist movie stars, affable agents (who studied Tai Chi) and wary writers (who practiced TM and *est*) monopolized me by turns. There is a certain kind of grayish, stoop-shouldered, beaten screenwriter one meets in Hollywood, a man with an income of a half-million a year and no hope. And I conversed for an hour with one of these – a certain Herman Kessler who said he *knew* he could never write a novel. Perhaps he could have once, but by now it was too late. And besides, how could he work three years for a $20,000 advance on a novel when he made that much in two months, writing screenplays?

'You have a problem,' I conceded.

He was rich, but he was not happy. He had seen his lifework rewritten by illiterate producers, his best apho-risms mangled by arrogant actors, his philosophical nug-gets crushed by directors, mushed by assistant directors, and trampled to dust by the Italian-leather soles of execu-tive producers' shoes. He was a beaten man, an intellectual derelict, a Bowery bum of letters. They had taken away his words and given him money instead. And it was a lousy bargain. He spent an hour wishing he were me.

Josh rescued me at 2:00 A.M., mumbling something about taking me on a tour of Mulholland Drive – whatever that was.

We exited to the disguised sneers and polite smirks of the other characters who had offered to take me home.

What the fuck am I getting myself into? I thought,

climbing into Josh's MG. I knew something was up – but I was pretending to myself it wasn't. I thought of Jeannie's notebook, which I had started keeping after my afternoon-long talk with Kurt. What would *Kurt* have done at a time like this? How would *he* have gotten ready to be eighty-seven? The same way Jeannie would, if she were here: by being a fool.

And yet I was also strangely shy with Josh. I was determined not to act like the heroine for whose sake I had become so fatally famous.

Josh and I drove around for hours. First we parked on Mulholland Drive and watched the lights that outlined the map of Los Angeles winking through the smog like tiny UFOs. Then we drove to the Strip, where he pointed out the Institute of Oral Love (a massage parlor), the Fantasy Fulfillment Center (another massage parlor), the Kosher-ama (a perfectly ordinary delicatessen), the Nosh on Wry (ditto), and various gotesque, enormous signs advertising Brobdingnagian rock stars. The air was still unbelievably balmy and I was calm and nervous at the same time, as if on some psychic form of Dexamyl. I wanted the ride never to end, just for us to keep on circling the city this way, talking, talking, talking, being together, side by side, close.

I knew that eventually we'd have to make a decision – to bed or not to bed (with all its concomitant possibilities of disappointment, pain, unrequited love, unrequited lust), but right now I was enjoying the suspension, the feeling that sleep would never come, that the journey, not the arrival, mattered.

It was three in the morning, then it was four, then it was five. Still we were driving around, not knowing what to do, not wanting to part, but not wanting to join ourselves yet either, wanting above all to prolong this delicious tingling sense of brinkmanship.

And then I blew it – blew it characteristically with my goddamn need to put everything into words.

'I feel there's something unspoken here,' I blurted out (as we were riding down the deserted Strip for what must have been the tenth time).

'Unspoken?' Josh said, vaguely.

'Possibly you want to take me to bed?' (My heart started pounding with astonishment at my own *chutzpa*.)

'Bed?' he said, as if he'd never heard the word before, as if the object itself were unfamiliar to him, an archeological find, a household item from early Greece no longer in use today and unknown except to specialists. 'Bed?' he repeated, with the same stupefied air. 'Oh – in New York, I'd be hustling you, but in L.A. everything's so *laid back*.'

'*So what?*'

'*Laid back*. An L.A. term meaning "relaxed." Do you want to come to my apartment? It's very pretty – 1920s Spanish L.A. architecture. Very *Day of the Locust* and nostaglic.'

I panicked. If I went to his apartment, it would be clear I wanted to go to bed. (It was clear anyway, but I wanted to go on deluding myself.)

'How about the Polo Lounge?'

'Okay,' Josh said.

He double-parked his car in front of the Beverly Hills Hotel, as if tentative about the whole venture, or perhaps he was just being polite, trying to show me he wasn't cock-sure of being asked to stay.

We went into the Polo Lounge and found it closed.

'Where can we get drinks?' I naïvely asked the weary desk clerk. (Josh and I were two babes in the woods, Hansel and Gretel in search of bread and water.)

'Room service,' he leered. So the decision was made, made by an impartial stranger.

We went obediently to my suite, chastely ordered Tab and ginger ale, and sat far apart, clothes on, with our feet up and our shoes on the bed. I was thinking, What a fling to seduce 'a boy.' He was perhaps thinking how he wasn't going to make the mistake of confusing me with Candida (thus branding himself forever in my eyes as an illiterate boob, a person who could not tell the difference between literature and life, art and illusion, fiction and autobiography). Perhaps he was determined to be cool, in deference to my authorial sensitivity. Perhaps he figured that men had been hustling me all year, and he wasn't going to join the ranks of the hustlers. But none of those speculations consoled me. All I knew was: I couldn't bear to let him out of my sight. That left it up to me.

We nursed our meager, teetotaling drinks. The ice cubes clinked, meltingly.

'Don't worry, I'm a gentleman,' Josh said ambiguously, with an unambiguous nod toward the bed. Awkward conversation as we contemplated it – that mass of king-size upholstery separating us. His sneakers were dirty and, touchingly, had torn laces. The laces on the one (the right) were undone. The presence of the bed between us had stopped our bantering conversation. Ice cubes clinked. I coughed. We smoked. Finally, perhaps not knowing what else to do, Josh got up to go.

I can't let him out of my life, I thought. So I looked up, asking to be kissed. And when our tongues touched, it was somehow all decided.

'Please stay the night.' (I shocked myself by saying this. So brazen. So woman-the-aggressor.) 'Go park your car.'

He kissed me again. We clung like two people who had just found life rafts.

ME: Park your car.

HE (*boyish*): Promise you won't change your mind.

ME (*womanly, reassuring*): I won't. Silly.

He went off to park and I (putting on diaphragm and filmy caftan and perfume) thought: I'm crazy. I'm married. He's only twenty-six and I'm his *parents*' friend. God – robbing the cradle.

He came back, he knocked, we hugged for dear life.

Then there were jeans on the floor, and his sneakers with torn laces, and I discovered his chest covered with reddish fuzz soft as mohair, his thick cock, his gentle wit in bed. He fucked as if he wanted to get back inside the womb. My heart was beating so hard I couldn't come. Our rhythms were not in synch yet. He came, groaning for me across forever. And then I slept in his arms as if I'd come home for the first time.

Breakfast in the Land of Oz. Crisp bacon. Orange juice in a bucket of ice. Cube-shaped, metal heaters, bearing Sterno

203

and eggs. I was under the covers, being naked. Josh was striding around in jeans and no shirt, answering the door.

One wilted rose on the room-service table. Josh took off his jeans to keep me company. In mutual nakedness we ate breakfast.

I was astonished at how comfortable he was in his skin. Bennett, who had a beautiful body too, was always hiding it. Pajama-tops, socks, shorts. He was always retreating from nakedness into clothes. But Josh filled the room with his suntanned skin.

Over the eggs and orange juice, he read me the funnies.

A fling, I was thinking, and then I'll go home to Bennett. I told myself all kinds of lies about how important it was to have this 'experience' with 'a younger man.' I was very pompous and self-important about it. I was doing research for life, not living. Next incarnation, when I knew all there was to know, I'd live. This was just a warm-up.

'You know what's astounding?' I said.

'What?'

'The way I slept last night. I've never slept that well before – with a stranger.'

Hurt, Josh said, 'Do you do this all the time – take men to bed the first night?' He didn't understand what I meant – that he was a stranger but didn't *feel* like a stranger. I had never before been able to sleep in the arms of a man I didn't know well. I would toss and turn, wake up panicked at 6:00 A.M., thinking: What am I doing? What have I done? But Josh felt like kin to me, my long-lost brother. How could I say that without sounding corny? So I held my tongue.

'Do you do this all the time?' he demanded again.

He was insecure, thought me an easy lay. I had to find some words to reassure him. It was premature, it would have scared him away. He was six years younger, my friends' young son, tender shoot. There was a husband at home, a life, a career, that curious houseguest, Fame. I had the feeling my whole life was about to change, but he was broke, young, another generation.

How could I have known that a year later, we both would miraculously become the same age?

204

Winging it ...

Of all human activities, none
is so useless and potentially
destructive as trying to predict
the future. The future is
merely a shadow which blocks
out the joys of the present and
emphasizes the miseries of the
past.

Wing it, I thought, waking up with Josh the morning after that. He was asleep, his light-brown lashes curled against his cheeks. I felt such tenderness for him that my fingertips ached. (Where do you feel love? In the chest, as a straining of the heart against the rib cage? In the fingers, as if the blood were reaching out beyond the skin?) For me, love had always been a battle – a battle with myself – or with a male adversary. A battle not to care too much, or not to *show* I cared. A battle against my own cynicism – or my own naïveté. Something was different here. I felt at home. This was no adversary, no opponent, no tyrant, no bully, and no victim either. This was my brother, my other half.

Even his body felt right to me. We locked together like two pieces of a puzzle. I slept in his arms as if I had never known the meaning of sleep before. And I woke up happy – as if I were understanding happiness for the first time.

But I wasn't going to look ahead or plan anything. I wasn't going to think of the future. Wing it, I kept saying to myself. Don't think. Just fly.

The telephone bell pierced our nest like the serpent in the Garden of Eden. I startled and grabbed the phone. Josh awoke to hear my half of a conversation with Bennett.

'I don't know when I'll leave. I'm still waiting for Britt to get back ... No, I don't know when. She hasn't been heard from in days ... Of course I miss you ... Of course ...'

Couldn't he hear in my voice that I didn't miss him at all, that he had never even existed, that he was a ghost, a shadow? I suppose not. Though Bennett was a psychiatrist, he was spectacularly tuned out to the nuances of human feeling. He was the easiest husband in the world to deceive because he was so self-deceiving. But I didn't like that either. What was the point of spending your life with someone you were always looking for ways to deceive? I knew most people lived that way – marital hypocrisy, 'white' lying, 'discreet' afternoon affairs that didn't tear the fabric of one's life. But of course they *did* tear it. And if they *didn't*, then why have them at *all*? What other point was there in bringing a man and woman together *except* to stretch the soul and expand the imagination, except to tear things apart and put them back together in new ways? Beyond a certain point in life, the mere rubbing that sooner or later results in orgasm was not all one looked for. A vibrator could do that.

But it was still not easy to let myself get close to Josh. I kept looking for snags, looking for him to show signs of being exploitive or manipulative, looking for failure, looking for disillusionment.

'This will never work,' I muttered, as he began stroking me, kissing me, and starting to make love to me again.

'But will it play?' he asked, with a twinkle in his eye. 'Can this love affair be saved?'

I laughed. His cock was sliding inside me, filling me up, making me forget my cynicism. It was big and hot and made me think of all-day suckers, candy canes, impossible melting sweetness. I love this man, I thought, feeling totally entered, totally his; and then I got so carried away with his pleasure, his puppyish exuberance, his excitement, his moaning happiness – that I went right to the edge of orgasm and wasn't able to come. This had happened the night before. And the night before that. And the oddest part of it was: I didn't care. We would both come together in time – or else we wouldn't. All my judgments were suspended. So was my need to control the future. All I knew was that I loved this funny face, this furry red-bearded bear. Loving someone that way was in itself such a miracle and such a gift that I wasn't going to think beyond just being grateful we had met.

'Do you know how lucky we are?' Josh said, kissing my eyes, the furrow between my brows, my chin, my nose.

'Yes,' I said. But I was still afraid to say 'I love you' – though we both knew.

That night Kurt Hammer invited us to join him at a Japanese restaurant for dinner. He was holding court at a table in the corner, surrounded by two ex-wives, a current lady friend, his secretary, his male nurse, and the struggling young actress who served as his *au pair* girl and cook.

She was a ravishing redhead named Liane (with Cherokee cheekbones and a terrific giggle) – and she had brought a current boyfriend of hers – a silly fellow named Ralph Battaglia, who was a self-made millionaire with a weakness for trendy self-improvement and a tendency to sound like a California Kahlil Gibran. He was tall, slim, gray-haired, had a mustache, and wore a dashiki (which I somehow deeply resented – almost as if I were black and proud).

'I no longer call my ex-wife my "ex-wife," ' Ralph explained earnestly (over sashimi), 'because that would imply she was an ex-person.'

'Not to me it wouldn't,' Kurt said. 'I got two ex-wives right here.' Two very young-looking Japanese girls tittered. They couldn't possibly have been as young as they looked.

'Twisting the English language into pretzels doesn't mean you've found a new religion,' Kurt said. 'Ex-person – what the hell is an ex-person?'

'I mean she's entitled to her identity as an individual even though she's no longer my wife . . .' Ralph said, fatuously.

'Maybe *more*, eh?' Kurt said, laughing. 'It could be the best thing that ever happened to her. You know, sometimes women *blossom* when they get rid of men. I've seen that a million times. It's the men who go to pieces dontcha know? There's no doubt in *my* mind they're definitely the weaker sex. Hmm.' He took another slug of sake.

'I don't like to use the words *stronger* and *weaker*. They're judgmental. Let's just say : different,' Ralph said.

'What the hell is *wrong* with *stronger* and *weaker*?' Kurt thundered. 'Do you want to cut the balls off the English language?'

Ralph seemed suddenly stymied, at a loss for another cliché. He excused himself to go to the men's room (perhaps to check whether or not his balls were still there).

'He's the dumbest one you've ever brought home,' Kurt told Liane as soon as Ralph was out of earshot.

'Brains are not his strong suit,' she admitted. 'But he

209

loves picking up checks' – which Ralph returned and dutifully did.

'Thank you,' said Kurt, grinning. In his Paris bohemian days, Kurt had made sponging meals into a fine art. Now that he was old and not terribly mobile – except on rare occasions like this – he most often fed others at his house. In Ralph's case, however, he was willing to make an exception.

'Good night,' he said, waving his beret and being led to the car by his two Japanese ex-wives. 'Come again soon! *Bonne chance!*'

'What a grand old man,' Ralph said, seeing Kurt depart, and obviously having no idea how he'd been made a fool of. (I've always mistrusted people who use the word *grand* – unless they are referring to hotels.)

And then he turned to Josh and me. 'I want to give you a special experience,' he said. 'Judging from your poetry, I *know* you'll appreciate it ...'

Josh and I looked at each other gamely.

'What the fuck,' said Josh.

So we followed Ralph back to where he lived. Chez Ralph. What can I call it? Ralph's 'house'? No. That would imply a certain hominess it did not possess. Ralph's 'bachelor pad'? Ralph's 'emporium'? But it was a mansion. There are certain kinds of people who would willingly live in a model room at Bloomingdale's if it could be proven this was the smart thing to do. Ralph was one of these. His 'home' was a special sort of dwelling existing particularly in California and inhabited by trendy middle-aged divorced bachelors with hair transplants. Future archeologists will marvel over such places and will probably wonder what they were used for.

We emerged from Josh's MG into a garage whose door closed electronically behind us. Around us were Ralph's cars: a 1936 Cord Phaeton (supercharged, of course), a recent Rolls-Royce Corniche in Mediterranean blue with white leather seat-covers and a license plate that said ZEN, a silver Jaguar XKE with a license plate that said PEACE, and a gold dune buggy with a license plate that said, coyly, BUGGY.

A chrome-and-steel elevator (with glass walls) took us to the upper floors on which Ralph 'lived' (or perhaps one should say on which Ralph 'Ralphed'). We entered a very dark hallway with cocoa-brown velvet walls, cocoa-brown carpeting, and cocoa-brown suede benches along the walls. (Someone must have told Ralph that cocoa-brown was a 'masculine' color.) Spotlights imbedded in a cocoa-brown ceiling) picked out certain *objects* ('objectionables d'art,' Josh called them): the head of a Siamese Buddha (who must have been appalled at the company in which he found himself); a rubbing from a medieval tombstone; a parchment scroll on which some funky California calligrapher had hand-lettered Fritz Perls's Gestalt prayer: 'You do your thing, I do my thing ...' (I would like to be around to see what future archeologists make of *that*.)

Ralph invited us into his cavernous cocoa-brown living room, drew up a cocoa-brown suede footstool, and lit a fire (in that distressing California way of merely lighting gas jets under the logs). Then he turned on the quadraphonic sound (taped chants from some Oriental monastery, passed around some joints (which he must have spent the whole afternoon rolling – or perhaps he had them prerolled at a hip tobacconist's), and then went off into his cocoa-brown electronic kitchen to make some Irish coffee and confer with the Oriental houseman.

'Wait'll you guys see the Jacuzzi,' Liane said, dragging deeply on a joint and passing it to us.

'What's a Jacuzzi?' I asked.

Pretty soon we were all naked and simmering in a great redwood tub of bubbling water – like *kreplach* bobbing in a vat of chicken soup. Above us were the stars, seen through a trellis over which bougainvillea had been trained. Below us were water jets, which made the hot, scented water of the Jacuzzi bubble up between our legs provocatively. We were all getting more and more stoned, the quadraphonic Oriental monks were getting more and more stoned, and our host was passing around more joints and more Irish coffee. This must be heaven, I thought – or California.

Meanwhile, Ralph had begun to make speeches – the

211

sort of woozy, unfinished speeches people make when they're stoned; but then I was too stoned to know if it was him being woozy – or me.

'The important thing,' Ralph said in pulpit tones, 'is to conquer possessiveness, to give and to take, to feel pleasure and to feel pain as if we were all flowing together, parts of one organism – because we all *are* parts of one organism, and ...'

'I think he means this to turn into an orgy,' Josh whispered, 'and I don't know what the *etiquette* is in a situation like this. I mean, are we being *bad guests* if we refuse?'

Everything Josh said was like a voice speaking out of my guts.

'I don't know what we're supposed to do,' I whispered back, 'but he sounds like the type you could jolly along with a dose of his own Gestalt rhetoric.'

'Become one with the water, the bubbles, the steam rising to the stars,' Ralph intoned.

'I feel like a chicken bubbling in a cauldron of chicken soup,' Josh said wryly.

Ralph was delighted. '*Be* the chicken soup!' he exclaimed, full of Gestalt enthusiasm.

Josh made bubbling noises in the back of his throat, and punctuated them with a gurgly *oy vay*.

Ralph was delirious. This was not only Gestalt – it was *ethnic*.

'Now you be the carrots,' he instructed me.

'I don't know *how* to be a carrot.'

'*Try*,' said Ralph, condescendingly. 'Don't *resist*.'

'What does a carrot *do*?'

'A carrot,' said Ralph, 'merely *carrots*.'

'Aha,' I said, 'I see.'

'So do it,' said Ralph.

'Wait a minute, let me get into it.' I sat in silence for a minute or so, feeling the steamy water bubble up between my legs.

'Well?' said Ralph, growing impatient.

'I'm *doing* it,' I said.

'But you're just *sitting* there,' said our host.

212

'I'm carroting,' I said, 'in my own *personal* way. Who are you to *judge* my way of carroting? Who are you to be so judgmental? Everyone has a right to carrot in their own way, don't they?'

Josh was cracking up. So was Liane. I continued carroting solemnly.

'Food for thought,' Ralph said ponderously.

When we were all so waterlogged that our fingertips looked like bleached raisins and our knees were weak from the steamy water, Ralph rang for the Japanese houseman, who brought us towels and more refills of the Irish coffee.

'He's not only my houseman,' Ralph explained with embarrassment. 'He also teaches me Zen.'

'What a handy combination,' said Liane. 'Perhaps we should invite him in.'

'Hates water,' Ralph said hastily.

In the living room, the lights were turned down low and we were all so stoned that we lay in front of the fire and gazed into it without speaking. Josh and I were stroking each other's backs in that dreamy way pot makes possible.

'Do you think we'll be invited back?' I whispered. 'I mean, I think I got water stains on the *suede*.'

'Just what I was thinking myself, Pooh,' said Josh. 'God – here we are at a potential *orgy* and all we think about is the *upholstery*. Boy – are *we* ever uptight and Jewish.'

'True-ish,' I said.

Presently, Ralph and Liane got the idea we didn't want to mingle and they slipped away to the bedroom without us. We were left alone by the fire. Hours, years, decades went by. The fire flickered. I stroked Josh's back. He stroked mine. Eventually, Ralph emerged naked to say: 'By the way, there's another bedroom down the hall you can use. Let me show you.'

We were led to still another cocoa-brown room with a vast fur-covered waterbed built into a platform under a skylight. LOVE, DON'T LOVE, flashed a neon sign 'sculpture' on the table beside the bed. Right under the sign was a half-used tube of K-Y jelly and a lethal-looking French tickler

213

with spiky pink rubber bumps. Conspicuous consumption of sexuality.

The waterbed had the obligatory black satin sheets, somewhat rumpled from what must have been Ralph and Liane's predinner fuck. Josh and I climbed into it, got under the fur covers and hugged. The Love, Don't Love sign kept flashing.

'I wonder if we can disconnect that monstrosity,' Josh said.

'I doubt it,' I said. Actually, I didn't want to let go of him and get out of bed. We resigned ourselves to the garish presence of LOVE, DON'T LOVE.

'You know, all my life,' said Josh, 'people have been saying, "Possessions don't matter" – yet would we be spending the night here if it weren't for the Jacuzzi, the pot, the fancy furniture? Probably not.'

I laughed and hugged him. Josh's vision of things was so clear, so dear. He managed to be honest in a world where no one was, where honesty itself had gone out of style.

It was not that I failed to feel guilty about Bennett. There was nothing to feel guilty for. I was not 'committing adultery,' or 'having an affair.' My marriage to Bennett had become the faintest of memories.

We talked all night. Under the flashing Love, Don't Love sign, above the sloshing of the waterbed, Josh held onto me for dear life and told me about himself. He didn't want to fuck that night; he wanted to talk. 'I lose the other person when I fuck,' he said. 'I go into my own pleasure and become autistic.' I understood. I understood everything he said. For the first time in my life, I understood what it meant to be a man, to grow up with a throbbing cock between your legs, to be scared of women and want them at the same time, to be told that men were supposed to be strong and yet to feel weak and vulnerable, to want shelter and protection in a woman's arms and yet to fear being trapped. I had always somehow assumed that men were insensitive – perhaps because the men I knew had always found it so hard to articulate their feelings. I had also felt contemptuous toward men – contemptuous toward their arrogance, their strutting, their need to deny their emotions. Women, at least, were in touch with their feelings. For all their faults, they were tuned-in to their own needs. But here was a man who seemed to know himself a little, and would share that knowledge with me. Was this a new thing, a generational thing? Were men under thirty an improvement on the older models, or was it just Josh? Whatever it was, I liked it. Suddenly there was no pretense, no playacting. We were just two friends, staying up all night, telling each other the stories of our lives.

We talked about growing up, about camp, about school, about parents. We talked about the way Jewish parents make their kids feel so breakable, so fragile. And then, having filled them with neurotic anxiety about perfectly ordinary things, they can seem to rescue them from all evil and harm. If you get the toast out of a toaster with a knife, you'll surely be electrocuted. If you pop popcorn over a fire, fat will fly in your eye and surely blind you. If the fat doesn't blind you, you'll die of botulism from eating rancid butter. If you don't die of botulism from eating rancid butter, you'll die of botulism from eating contaminated tuna fish. If you don't die of botulism from tuna fish, you'll get mercury poisoning and die. And if you don't get mercury poisoning and die, you'll surely cut your finger on the edge of a tuna fish can – so you better have a tetanus shot immediately! We talked about how we had internalized all our parents' (twice removed) ghetto terrors and then spent our lives, paralyzed with fear, craving adventure.

It turned out we both had had precisely the same dialogues with our families about how babies are made.

'How does your body *know* you're married so it can make a baby?' Josh asked his mother and sister when he was six. And they had laughed at him – just as my mother and sister laughed at me when I asked exactly the same question.

'The middle-*class*ness of it!' I laughed. 'I guess neither of us *knew* anybody who had had a baby without being married.'

'I guess,' said Josh. 'I mean, I used to sit around for *hours*
215

saying to myself, *How do their bodies know?* I was really *puzzled.*'

'Me too,' I said, astounded at the similarity. 'Me too. Me too. Me too.'

It was as if I had found a misplaced twin in Josh. Everything we said to each other found a knowing response; sometimes we even seemed to flash on the same things without speaking – until it seemed we had never *not* known each other, had never been apart. Oh, maybe someday I would feel bored living with my double – but right now it was such a welcome change from the silences and hostility I had known for eight years that I was willing to risk it, to risk everything. It seemed that I had spent the whole rest of my life being lonely.

'You know, there's one thing I really should tell you,' Josh said at about five-thirty in the morning.

'What?'

'I'm a secret male chauvinist.'

'Who isn't? Most of them, in fact, aren't so secret.'

'No – I mean it,' he persisted. 'I'm not trying to give you a more-raised-consciousness-than-thou number, but the first time a girl said to me, "Look, I don't come unless you mess with my clitoris," I felt one wall of my masculinity crumbling. I had thought that the insertion of the penis was *enough.* I never *knew.* And it upset me *terribly* to be told.'

I lay there dumbstruck, thinking of our last couple of nights in bed and how I hadn't been able to come – and I panicked. Isadora, old girl, I thought, you've done it *again,* thrown yourself headlong into the arms of another helpless, hopeless male ...

Silence. The waterbed sloshes.

JOSH (*gloomily*): Reassure me. Tell me it doesn't matter.

But no words came out of my mouth.

JOSH (*hurt, sad*): I tell you my deepest, darkest secrets, things I've never told *anyone,* things I'm ashamed of – and you don't even reassure me ...

'I guess,' I said haltingly, 'I guess all men really feel that way, but none of them are honest enough to admit it.'

'*Maybe,*' Josh said.

'*God* – it's so hard to be straight with someone – even someone you ... care about.'

'You were going to say "love," weren't you, but you chickened out.'

'I guess ...' I said tentatively.

'I love you too,' he blurted out, 'but what the hell *good* is it going to do me? You're six years older, married, famous – and besides, I like skinny model-types.'

He trailed off, knowing he had hurt me.

I stormed out of bed (almost impossible to do from a waterbed), and for the first time burst into tears. I had never felt so fat, so rejected, so vulnerable.

'Why do you have to back away before we've even *begun*?' I screamed. 'Why are you so scared of feeling *anything*?'

Josh buried his head in the pillow. I stood there watching, feeling uglier and uglier, fatter and fatter, determined not to comfort him. Finally, he looked up. 'What the hell's the point?' he shouted. 'You get me to tell you everything, to fall in love with you, to need you, to depend on you, but for you it's just another affair. Because pretty soon, you'll go back to your boring husband and leave me all alone – and then I'll be lonelier and worse off than I was *before*.' He sat up in bed, looking like a madman. 'I know you didn't come last night. I know it, I'm not an *idiot* – but what's the sense of working it out? What's the sense of satisfying you? making you come? You'll only go home to your husband and leave me *anyway*. You've certainly done it *before*. Anyway, you don't take me seriously. I'm just a kid to you, a "fling," a sort of sexual slumming trip. All your fucking lady-writer friends in New York will want to know, "What's it like to fuck a hippie?" And *you'll* say, "*Terrific*." But it's not so terrific for me. I'm the hippie. I'm the goddamned sucker in the piece. Oh go ahead and try *everything*, Candida – try an Englishman, a Chinaman, a *shvartzer*, a *lesbian*, a hippie. Meanwhile I go back to my apartment in Hollywood and my weekly fuck with a librarian, and I sit around reading your poems and seeing you on Johnny Carson and looking forward to your next book so I can see how I rated on your *score*card. Terrific, huh? Terrific for *you*. But not so terrific for the kid. Well, no *thanks*. You're not going to put me through that routine. I love you – but what the hell good is it going to do me? I don't want to wind up in a book. Frankly, I don't give a shit about immortality. I just love you.' And he buried his head in the pillow again, this time sobbing loudly.

I was astonished. I had never known a man who could cry before and I loved him even more for it. I walked over to the bed and took him in my arms, 'How the hell did you know? How did you know I slept with a woman?' I asked.

'Did I say that?' he asked, baffled. 'I didn't know at all. It just *figured*.'

'You amaze me,' I said. 'You keep reading my mind. How could I ever leave a man who reads my *mind*? I've been waiting for you my whole life. I always told myself that if I met someone like you and didn't do something about it, I'd be crazy. I'd blame myself for the *rest* of my life.'

'What about Bennett?'

'What *about* him?'

We looked at each other very hard, our faces smeared with tears and sleeplessness, both trembling, exhausted, on the edge of hysteria. The dawn was coming up. We both looked terrible in the light.

'Oh Josh, let's just *wing* it, okay? Let's not try to predict the future.'

'Okay,' he said.

Take the Red-Eye ...

*Every country gets the circus
it deserves. Spain gets bull-
fights. Italy gets the
Catholic Church. America
gets Hollywood.*

The next morning Ralph's houseman made an elaborate breakfast for us during which Ralph insisted on reading aloud from his favorite book, *If I knew Who I Was, I Would Tell You* (printed on rice paper in Big Sur and handbound in brown batik by hippies). It was written by a friend of his, a certain Dwayne Hoggs, who was, according to Ralph, a philosopher, a sculptor, and 'a beautiful human being.' His prose style left something to be desired, but what he lacked in style, he made up for in schmaltz.

'"I asked the brook, Tell me who you are,"' Ralph read piously. '"And the brook replied: *My name is written in syllables of water. My name bubbles itself to you. You may dip your foot in my name*." ... Isn't that *beautiful?*'

'Hmm,' I said.

'Hmm,' said Josh.

'*I* know why he can't tell us who he is,' Josh said of Hoggs as we were leaving Ralph's emporium. 'Because he's the village idiot. If he knew who he was, he'd be exceedingly *embarrassed*.'

'Isn't it, "if I knew who I *were*"?'

'Not in Big Sur, it ain't,' said Josh. 'Grammar is bourgeois and repressive dontcha know.' (He imitated Kurt's husky Brooklynese.) 'Also, I love you immensely.'

'Me you too.'

'Promise me one thing,' Josh said passionately.

'What? Anything ...'

'Promise me we'll never see Ralph Battaglia again.'

'Done,' I said.

We returned to the Beverly Hills Hotel, where we were astonished to discover our suite occupied by none other than Britt Goldstein, the tiny terror herself, and two gentlemen callers. They were cosily breakfasting in bed and the gentlemen (who were wearing nothing but gold neck-chains and St Christopher medals) looked extremely unsavory.

They jerked the covers up to their hairy armpits as we entered.

'Hi, Isadora,' said Britt (as nasal as ever). 'I hope you don't mind ...' (she glanced at her boon companions, who were shoveling in the crisp bacon as if this were the Last Breakfast) '... but we got in late last night, and I was so excited about this *deal* ...' (she glanced from side to side at her buddies) '... that I wanted to tell you *immediately*. When we found out you weren't *here* ... well, we thought we'd let ourselves in and *wait* ... and then we got stoned ... and you *know*.' She gave me a sheepish, trying-to-be endearing look. Her two bodyguards just kept on shoveling.

'This is Sonny Spinoza' (she gestured to the thug on her right) 'and Danny Dante' (the thug on her left).

'Hi,' they said in gruff unison.

'And this is Josh Ace,' I said.

Britt looked him over, with naked calculation. The torn shoelaces particularly caught her eye.

'Not bad,' she said to me – as if Josh were chattel. 'I see you've done okay for yourself. Do you want some breakfast?'

'Thanks a lot, we've already eaten.'

Josh looked as if he wanted out of there as fast as possible. I'd told him about Britt, but he hadn't really believed me till then.

'Listen, cookie,' said Josh, 'why don't I go home and do some work and I'll come get you later, okay?'

'That sounds like a good idea,' said Britt. 'I mean, nothing personal, but I wanna talk business.'

'Right,' I said wondering if they were going to put on some *clothes* before business or not. I wanted to take a shower too but the room was clearly Britt's now, not mine. She paid the piper and therefore called the tune. Producers – *Jesus*. Next time, I'd pay my *own* hotel bill.

'Would you mind steppin' out a minute, honey, while we get some clothes on?' one of the thugs said to me, as deferentially as he could. 'You could kiss your boyfriend goodbye.'

'Okay,' I said, flustered. Britt had only been back in my life two minutes and already I felt like a lackey.

In the hall I said good-bye to Josh. 'Better come back and rescue me later,' I said. 'It looks like one of the outtakes from *The Godfather*.'

'I'll see you about five, okay sweetie? Just holler if you need help, but they look pretty honorable to me. Sleazy, but honorable. Just remember, you're safer doing business with the Mafia than with any big conglomerate you can name. Anyway, they all use the same lawyers.'

'Oh god,' I said, with mock horror. 'It's a sequel: *Candida Meets the Mob*.'

'You bet your boobies,' Josh said, kissing me and hot-footing it down the hall. He waved before he turned the corner. 'Write if you get work ...' he called out.

'Very funny,' I yelled back.

I knocked at the door of my suite.

'Just a minute, babe,' said one of the thugs.

After about five minutes, the door was opened and Danny Dante stood there in buckskin jeans, bare feet, and bare chest. He was all of five foot two. Just four inches taller than Britt. I was beginning to feel like the jolly blonde giant.

'Hiya,' he said, 'welcome to our humble abode.'

'Thanks,' I said.

Coffee was pressed on me by a now caftan-clad Britt, who was out of bed, smoking furiously and pacing as usual. Sonny Spinoza was sitting on the edge of the bed slithering into his snakeskin loafers.

'Here's the deal,' said Britt. 'Danny and Sonny have friends – a very influential tax-shelter group – who want to finance *Candida Confesses*. They can get six million for the picture right now. All they ask is that we change the title to *Candida!* and change a couple of minor things – like the heroine should be Italian, not Jewish, but that's still open to negotiation ...' (she winked broadly at me) '... and we should get some major, bankable star in the lead. I frankly think – and I've really looked into the situation with the studios – that we'd be crazy not to take it. Up-front money is terrific – if we finalize the deal now. Because in exactly seventy-two hours some new tax law – don't ask me what it is – gets passed which really will dry up all these funds. So we have to act *fast* – which is why I brought these guys here so you can see how straight they are. All we really need from you is a signed option on the rights. The terms can be negotiated later. This is just for them so they can get the project off the ground. We'll work out all the lawyer–agent stuff later. Whaddaya think?' Britt blew smoke at me emphatically. 'I frankly think we'd be crazy to pass it up.'

I was baffled by the spiel. Six million only reminded me of the number of Jews killed by the Nazis and I didn't really know what a tax-shelter group was. I wanted to sound cagy but knowledgeable. So I said, 'Who's the bankable star you have in mind anyway?'

Danny was waiting for that question. He sprang to his feet (which still made him look like he was sitting down).

'Listen, babe,' he said, 'I don't wanna drop names or nothin' but for the past coupla years, I've been into arranging scenes for Robyn Barrow. She and I are very good friends – even though, frankly, she digs women – and I can tell you that I can get her to commit to this project for a hundred grand in a brown paper bag, and from there on, it's clear sailing.' *Whatever* I had heard about Robyn Barrow – the Italian nightingale from Flatbush – this description sounded totally off the wall. Scenes? Digging women? The hundred thousand – that was another story. Of course no one likes the tax man. And the richer they are, the more they hate taxes – but why would a classy lady like Barrow be hanging out with a guy like Danny? (Hollywood, after all, is run by a bunch of Jewish and Italian kids from New York who are really far more interested in real estate than kinky sex.)

'Okay,' said Danny, 'so maybe she wants the hundred grand in a Swiss bank, not in a brown paper bag. *Big* diff, you get me? But she's a good kid, sensible – and basically a buddy. Look, I once told her, "Robyn, anybody mess wit' you and I break bot' dere legs – and if you don' call me when you're in trouble, den I break bot' *your* legs," dig?'

I dug. What an interesting theory of life. A hundred thousand in a brown paper bag or a pair of broken legs to take care of all the many vicissitudes destiny has to offer. There had to be a how-to book in this *some*where.

'Puppy, I *like* you,' Danny said to me. 'I like her too' (he

224

nuzzled Britt). 'She looks like a poodle – and you look like a cocker spaniel. Listen, I'll break the legs of anyone who messes wit' either of you. When Danny's your friend, puppy, you know the meanin' of the word *friendship* for the first time.'

Danny's buddy Spinoza, a big bouncer of a man at least a foot taller than Danny, nodded his head gravely.

'It's true,' he said. 'Danny never lies.'

'So,' said Britt, 'whaddaya think?'

'She has to be *Italian?*' I asked, 'or was that a joke?'

'Oh, I was *kidding*,' Britt offered. 'These guys are very sophisticated. They love jokes like that. And actually, Robyn Barrow is not a bad idea. But nobody's going to make her Italian. You remember what I promised you: complete artistic control.' Sonny and Danny nodded their heads solemnly.

'You're the artist,' Danny said. 'You got the talent. We're just promoters. I tell you, if I had your talent, I'd be suspicious too. So take your time. Get to know us. The more you know us and the more you know this crummy god-damn business, the better it is for *us*. This business is filled with sharks – and they ain't in *Jaws*, either. This business eats it.'

Britt nodded. 'I frankly *hate* the picture business,' she said, 'and one of these days, I'm just going to retire and *write* ... That's what I *really* want to do. But the problem is, we don't have a hell of a lot of time. Seventy-two hours – or the deal is *no go*. And in those seventy-two hours, we've got to wrap it up here, and then go to New York and wrap it up with the tax-shelter lawyers. Also, I want to make you a real Hollywood party before you go ... In fact, I've already invited fifty people to my lawyer's house for to-morrow night – and after that I've booked us all on the Red-Eye to New York – so the best possible thing is if you sign the option now – and then we can hassle out the other stuff in New York.'

From her caramel leather bag, she extracted a tattered piece of paper, which she handed to me. It was densely printed with fly-speck-size words, but I could read the heading: UNIVERSAL OPTION FORM. And then somewhere

225

toward the bottom of the page there occurred the chilling phrase: *World Rights in Perpetuity.*

'What am I supposed to do? Sign in blood?' I quipped. (Typical of me to have exactly the right gut reaction and then disregard it completely.)

'Oh, don't pay any attention to all that lawyer talk,' Britt said, 'we'll work out all the details later. The main thing is to get the project off the ground. Later on, we'll make a real deal-memo – get the lawyers, the agents – do it *right.* But for now all they need is a piece of paper to wave around so their guys know for sure they can get the property. Nobody's going to come up with six million without a piece of paper, right? So that's what we need from you – the piece of paper.'

'I really should call the agent, shouldn't I? Or a lawyer?'

'Look,' Britt said, 'I want you to be fully and completely protected. I really do. And if you call the lawyers, they're going to ask for the papers and it'll take time and there'll be all that lawyer crap, and we only have seventy-two hours. But call them. Go ahead and call them. On the other hand, you could trust me as your friend – and later we'll see that you're completely protected. I've been in this business a long time, and I can tell you, you can't do anything at all without *trust.* That's why I just want to get the project off the ground. Look – you're out here now, everyone knows I'm going to do the picture, nobody else is going to make offers on the property 'cause they know it's mine – so why should you stand in the way of our getting financing? You're just cutting off your *own* nose if you do that. And this piece of paper is *meaningless,* really meaningless. Later, we'll do it right.'

'If it's so meaningless, why do you need it? Why can't you just say I'm willing to do it if the terms are right?' I asked.

'Because you know how money-people are,' Britt said. 'They're compulsive idiots. They need pieces of paper.'

Sonny shrugged, as if to sympathize with the plight of the poor flaky artist confronted with the compulsive money-people. 'You gotta do business with idiots sometime,' he said.

'Yeah,' said Danny, 'this is a private investment group with fifteen, maybe twenty-five people in it. We can't mobilize them without *something* in writing. But we know it really doesn't count. They just don't understand the picture business. They're private investors, see.'

'Here,' said Britt, uncapping a felt pen and passing it to me with the agreement. Sonny and Danny closed in, surrounding me. What Britt said was true. Everyone knew she had my book, whether I signed or *not*, so what was I going to do – peddle it on the streets? Even my own agent had said there were no other serious takers. I signed with a sinking heart.

At the 'Hollywood party,' the next night, everyone who was anyone was there – the hosts, the parasites, and a few unclassifiable specimens – all circulating lazily in the patio of a 1920s Moorish-style Bel Air mansion built by a silent film star and now owned by Britt's lawyer. Robyn Barrow herself was there, with her saucer brown eyes and her tiny fixed nose and her hippie boyfriend from Big Sur. Robyn was said to be able to get any project off the ground – she was that 'bankable.' Her agent knew it too. Deena Maltzberg was as wide as Robyn was tall, wore pink heart-shaped specs, and had long platinum fingernails. She also had a devastating sense of humor – and although she was a wicked negotiator, she never actually lied. She had a tendency to infantilize her movie-star clients though, hovering over them and calling them 'baby.' I even heard her encouraging Robyn to eat.

'Honey-baby, at least eat some celery sticks so you don't pass out,' Deena said.

'Do I *have* to?' said Robyn in a baby voice.

'Yes baby, you do – or Mommy will be very, very cross with you,' and Deena lapsed into baby talk.

'Meet *Candida*,' she said turning to me. 'Candida, meet Candida.' And she winked at me and then at Robyn. I stood looking at this living legend, not knowing what on earth to say. When someone is that famous, you know them through so many false faces in magazines and on the screen that you can hardly see the *real* face through the blur of multiple images.

'I loved your book,' Robyn said shyly, fingering a piece of long black hair that may (or may not) have been hers. 'It must be *so* wonderful to be able to write.'

'It must be so wonderful to be able to sing,' I said. Or to make five million dollars a year. Or to have so much power. But actually I didn't believe it. I know that money never made people secure and that Robyn was probably at the mercy of her agent, her lawyer, her banker, her boyfriend, her fans. I had seen enough of fame to know that it created as many problems as it solved. And especially the sort of fame she had. She could never be invisible *any*where. That was what they paid her for – to be constantly visible, constantly available. In a culture in which popularity equals power, the more visible you are, the more powerful. But it's a strange sort of power because it also makes victims of its possessors. Better to be powerful the way Sonny Spinoza was – invisibly. There is a certain freedom in invisibility that no one ever believes in until they've lost it.

Robyn fidgeted and looked down diffidently. It was the familiar discomfort of the super famous – who always seem to look away, look down at their feet, or hide behind long hair or big sunglasses or deep-brimmed hats – perhaps because they feel so vulnerable, always being under surveillance by millions of eyes. Robyn was wearing a devastating gray chiffon chemise, slick with silver sequins, furred at the hem with silver fox.

'I love your dress,' I said.

'Oh,' she said, and shrugged as if she were wearing jeans. 'I *hate* clothes like this, but Deena thinks it's good for my image. *Yucch* ...' And she made the face of a tomboy whose mommy makes her wear organdy and Mary Janes.

'Do you wanna know something? I shouldn't tell you this but I'm so stoned I don't give a shit. Deena is my best friend in the world, I mean my very best friend in the world – like when you were twelve, you know – and made a pact in blood and pricked your fingers? And I really

228

don't know if she would be my friend at all if it weren't for also being my agent. Isn't that pathetic? I mean isn't that really pathetic?' But Robyn wasn't about to wait around for my reaction. 'Excuse me,' she said, 'I gotta pee.'

I turned around then, feeling rather lost, and caught sight of numerous other luminaries: the famous Swedish movie star Siv Bergstrom; her elegant woman 'companion,' Ninka Bernadotte (who was tall and dark and wore a black velvet blazer and silver lamé slacks); Sally Sloane, the British bird who had arrived from trendy London in 1968 and never gone home; and numerous young American stars, starlets, semistars, demistars, and their entourages. (Why stardom necessitates an entourage, I never really understood until fame touched me – but it became clear to me that when one totally lost invisibility, one also shed a degree of natural protective coloration which other people now had to supply. It was like being marked with a bull's-eye, like being a snail without its shell, a reindeer without its antlers. One needed normal, unfamous, invisible people around to lend one *their* invisibility.)

Britt stood in a tree-shaded corner of the patio, conspiring with her lawyer and snorting occasionally from her tiny vial of sugary powder. Her lawyer was perhaps the only bald man in Beverly Hills – which is, after all, some distinction in a town where hair transplants grow more plentifully than weeds. He was wearing a T-shirt with a decal that said GOOCHY. A real cutup. He could *afford* to be. In a profession so insecure that even the biggest stars can wind up too broke to pay their income taxes, the lawyers are the only members of the cast who are never out of a job and who collect fees whether their clients win or lose. Being a lawyer in Beverly Hills must be the closest thing to being a landed squire in eighteenth-century England.

The squire in question, whose name was Melvin Weston – né Weinstein? – slithered over to invite me on a grand tour of the grounds.

'Maybe you'll use it in a book someday,' he said, smirking legalistically. (Oh God, I thought, which do I hate most as a group? Lawyers or psychiatrists? A toss-up. Beware

229

of *any*one paid by the hour; they're likely to have clocks that run fast.)

But I smiled sweetly at Melvin anyway. 'I'd love to tour,' I said. Britt hurried off to make time with Deena Maltzberg; Spinoza and Dante were romancing Robyn Barrow; and Josh (who was somewhat intimidated by gatherings like this) had been taken under the voluminous wing of a very bosomy, very drunken lady agent named Maxine Medoff, attractively nicknamed 'Maxine the Knife.'

'Follow me,' said Melvin.

Just then a tall man with a familiar-looking face (now grayed with disuse) shambled over to us and said wryly, 'Can I come too?' I looked up into his weary, mocking visage, the big sea-green eyes with circles under them, and recognized Boyd McCloud, whom I'd presumed dead – though he was hardly forty. (Why is it that when people stop appearing in the press, we assume they are no longer alive? Death by publicity – or the lack of it.) Boyd McCloud had been on the verge of becoming the new James Bond – or the new Tarzan, I forget which – ten years earlier. He was an Olympic skier, a hero to the media, a poser for cigarette ads, magazine covers, screen tests, grim and masculine 'pain relief' commercials. He made one film – a turkey about an Olympic swimmer – and from there drove straight into oblivion – a victim of too much press, too little substance. Once so hot he needed three lawyers, two agents, and two publicists, he was now so cold that he was probably among those faded famous faces one sees on line at the IRS office begging for extensions.

I was surprised that Melvin had him around at all. In America in general, Hollywood in particular, failure is thought to be highly contagious – especially failure Hollywood *itself* has created. But Boyd was a client of Melvin's (in debt to him, in short, and Melvin wanted to make sure his creditors didn't skip town).

'He drives my Rolls,' Boyd said airily.

'*My* Rolls now,' said Melvin.

'In lieu of fees,' Boyd said informatively, knowing me for a neophyte.

'Hell – Boyd – that's just a down payment on what you owe me: your soul.'

'What soul?' said Boyd.

We three toured. We toured the Moorish projection room, with the huge pillows on the floor instead of seats. We toured the cavernous basement kitchens, featuring whole collections of Tiffany glass goblets, vermeil service plates, and closets full of crockery from now defunct ocean liners. We toured the cathedral-roofed, hand-leaded, art-nouveau greenhouse with a real Italian fountain in the center (and a miniature river running lazily between pots of impatiens and fragrant gardenia). We toured the swimming pool, sunken into a garden of banana palms, with large ugly cubist sculptures poised on platforms above the water. We toured the white-carpeted master bathroom with a chandelier from one of the suites on the *Ile de France* and a white marble Jacuzzi imbedded in the deep shag.

Each item was lovingly, covetously described by Melvin himself, with sinister, heckling accompaniment by Boyd – who intimated that every object had been acquired in lieu of fees from some creditor-client or other, including apparently the estate itself. Melvin denied this. 'Come on, Melvin,' said Boyd, 'you'd foreclose on your own mother in lieu of fees.'

'At least I wouldn't sue her – like some people I know,' Melvin said cryptically – they both roared with laughter.

I was afraid to ask who – in the assembled starry throng – had sued his very own mother. I really didn't think I wanted to know.

'C'mon, c'mon, kiddies,' Britt said, rounding us all up as the witching hour of nine o'clock drew near. We were due at LAX for the Red-Eye to New York, and there were suitcases to call for and people to coordinate and good-byes to be said.

'I'll drive you to the airport,' Josh said wistfully.

We stood looking at each other, not knowing when, if ever, we'd meet again.

'Good,' said Britt. 'Sonny and Danny and me go in the limo and we also gotta pick up my bags and this other writer who's going to New York with us – Shelley Granowitz – and also I'm seriously thinking of taking Cliff …'

Cliff was a new acquisition – acquired, in fact, not in lieu of fees but in just the time it had taken Melvin and Boyd to show me the premises. Clifford Bing was beautiful, glassy-eyed, and twenty-four. He had turquoise eyes and turquoise beads and the blondest hair you ever saw. And he never said a word. If I could have a twenty-six-year-old, Britt would go me two years younger. She was that competitive.

'I object,' I said weakly. 'If you take Cliff, I take Josh –'

'Babe,' Britt said, staring at me with her cold eyes, 'the budget can't afford Josh. And besides, you've got a husband in New York, remember?' And then, like a merciful executioner, she offered me a deep drag on her joint.

'I need it,' I muttered.

'Keep the whole joint,' Britt said munificently – and flounced off to say her good-byes.

Josh and I said our stoned good-byes in the car on the way to the airport, in the airport, and even at the boarding ramp.

'Write me,' I said.

'But where?'

And we both suddenly remembered that I was a married lady who couldn't exactly receive love letters at her own address.

'Two friends,' I said, 'both extremely trustworthy and dear.' I gave Josh Hope's address and Rosanna Howard's.

'I love you,' I said, 'and I don't want to go home.'

'I love you too,' he said, 'but is that *enough*?' And he stood forever smiling his crooked smile and waving at the entrance to the boarding ramp, while I walked through it backward, unable to take my eyes off him until the boarding ramp turned its inevitable corner and Josh, now tiny at the end of the tunnel, disappeared from sight.

*   *   *

The plane took off. The lights of Los Angeles flickered through the smog. I seemed to be fighting the motion of the plane. Every time we gained altitude, my fingertips ached, missing Josh. The walls of the plane appeared to be closing in as we turned and banked over the Pacific and then headed eastward, straining against all my willpower to stay there, to stand still, not to leave.

I was furious with myself for allowing Britt to rail-road me into going, for signing the option form, for boarding the plane. Britt was so definite and bossy that she could muster all kinds of support for the most absurd projects. One simply never thought of questioning her authority. How else would I have wound up – stoned – on the Red-Eye with this weird cast of characters? We were a comical caravan, a bevy of buffoons, a coven of con men, a troupe of trollops – and Britt was our leader. Our strange group appeared to have taken over the whole first-class section. Sonny and Danny, Britt and Cliff, Shelley Granowitz and her Yorkie named Bogart (whom she had hidden under her raccoon coat and who peed on me almost immediately after boarding), and two extremely faggy-looking producers named Sam Fink and Dan Fox (of Fox–Fink productions), who worked together, lived together, and just happened to join the party – though they assured me they had no interest whatsoever in horning in on *Candida*! One of them (Sam) conducted his entire analysis by telephone from Beverly Hills to New York, he told me. Every afternoon at 1:00 (4:00 for his analyst), he'd simply dial her number long-distance, lie down on the couch of his Beverly Hills office, and free-associate by phone. At 1:50 for him, 4:50 for her, the session was over. This cost him about five hundred dollars a week – but, of course, the production company paid. His analyst was known to the tax man as a 'story consultant' in New York.

'That's why I appreciate your book so much,' he told me lispingly, 'because I've been through the whole analytic *shtik* myself.'

'It's always comforting to meet a kindred soul,' I said.

The street where I lived ...

California is a wet dream in the mind of New York . . .
New York is a nightmare from which Los Angeles is trying to awaken ...

The flight from Los Angeles to New York takes only five hours, but the real distance should be measured in light-years. Los Angeles is more different from New York than New York is from London or Stockholm or Paris. Someday scientists will discover the invisible gas that fills the air in Southern California, making the most uptight, cynical Easterners relax, take off their clothes, lie in the sun, divorce their spouses, build swimming pools, take up Zen meditation, visit spiritualists, and in general behave as if they've found God through sex, nudity, and sun-worship.

To return to New York from Los Angeles is always to experience a profound psychic shock. Suddenly the streets are narrow, bodies are hidden, the sky has shrunk to a gray strip wedged between the tops of buildings – and that peculiar frenzy of chiefly useless activity (which New Yorkers call Life) returns with a rush. There is noise, dirt, hustle. People frown and guard their bodies with crossed arms, with sharp words, with heavy clothes. Women clutch their handbags. Porters and taxi drivers and washroom attendants are churlish and bristling. The sky is pressing down on them. The buildings are pressing in on them. They are indignant because of the lack of space. They have no room to move or breathe. They are all wishing they were out West.

It was only when our strange party had disembarked and we were all waiting for our baggage that I suddenly realized how cold it was in New York. I'd left Los Angeles in the same thin cotton caftan and sandals I had worn at the party. My sandals had been pissed on by Shelley's obstreperous Yorkie and my feet felt at once sticky and cold. Britt and her party were laughing and joking among themselves and I felt like a kid in camp, left out of the main clique.

They were all bound for the Sherry-Netherland. I was bound for Seventy-seventh Street, where I would have to face the remains of the life I'd left behind. I still missed Josh

237

palpably, with aching fingers and a tightness in my chest. Every ten years, I go to California and my life changes utterly, I thought, commenting to myself at the same time that that wasn't a bad first line for a book. And then I *cursed* myself inwardly for that thought. It wasn't another *book* I wanted – it was Josh. I *refused* to write another book in which the heroine reaches out for love and settles for cynicism. I had already told that story over and over again. I had told it in poems, in a novel, in a screenplay, even – and there was no point in telling it again.

Everything in me mistrusted my feelings for Josh. The Beverly Hills Hotel seemed like a dream. The long hours in bed, the funny room-service orders in the middle of the night ('Strawberry jam with no toast,' Josh had demanded so we could lick it off each other), the hours spent talking about everything under the sun, giggling, learning that for all our differences in years, we were really doubles under the skin – all this I mistrusted. It was too good, too happy. It *had* to be ephemeral. It *had* to wear off in a month – or two. But so what? What was the alternative? To go back to Bennett and write still another cynical book proving that love is an illusion? The world had more than its share of such books. All of the greatest fiction of the modern age showed women falling for vile seducers and dying as a result. They died under breaking waves, under the wheels of trains, in childbirth. *Someone* had to break the curse, *someone* had to wake Sleeping Beauty without ultimately sending her to her destruction, *someone* had to shout once and for all: fly and live to tell the tale!

'C'mon kiddies,' said Britt. 'This way to the Big Apple!' And we all piled into the limo after her.

The gray streets of Queens and a sinking heart. Usually, the sight of the Queensboro Bridge fills me with elation. It means New York, Home, a certain kind of excitement available nowhere else in the world. But this time New York just seemed dismal. It was a prison three thousand miles away from Josh. New York was the past and California was the future. I had no business being here at all. I had no business returning to the past.

Seventy-seventh Street on a chilly October morning. The museum of Natural History looming like a brownstone nightmare, the leaves blowing in the wind, the dog-walkers watching their dogs shit. This was home – but it no longer seemed like home. Home was where Josh was.

I thought of my return to Seventy-seventh Street with Bennett during the summer of '69. It was the summer of the moon shot, the summer after my grandmother died, the summer my grandfather had a major coronary and didn't seem to want to live anymore.

What drew me back to Seventy-seventh Street? On some level, it was certainly Bennett's intimidation (he threatened to leave me if we didn't accept my grandfather's co-op), but perhaps there was something deeper operating too: a need to reclaim my roots after the alienating time in Germany, a need to recapture my childhood so that I could write about it and that way transcend it, a need to make sense of my past. Maybe, too, the writer in me needed to go back to the scene of my childhood.

I had lived on Seventy-seventh Street from age two to age twelve. (Later, we moved into another rambling triplex on Central Park West – an apartment not so unlike the first – but I was older.) Seventy-seventh Street was where I got my first tricycle, where I learned to ride a 'two-wheeler,' where I first learned to cross streets on the way to school.

I came to West Seventy-seventh Street as a toddler and remember no earlier home. I remember Columbus Avenue when the bars were Irish instead of Puerto Rican; when the buses ran in two directions and cost five cents, then seven cents, then fifteen cents; when there were transfers both eastbound and westbound, costing nothing at first, then two cents, then they vanished. Nothing costs two cents on Seventy-seventh Street anymore – not even a postcard. In fact the mailbox around the corner quite frequently disappears, leaving no trace except four bolts in the cement sidewalk. It turns up, weeks later, in some tenement basement, divested of welfare checks. The idea of someone stealing a whole mailbox seems to me the ultimate symbol of urban anarchy. Muggings can be understood as a fact of city life; dogshit and blaring transistor radios can be borne or ignored, but the mail is sacred – particularly to a writer. Awaiting the mail is one of the main tasks in a writer's day. When mailboxes can be stolen from the streets in broad daylight, nothing is safe.

I remember Seventy-seventh Street during the great snow of 1947. The cars buried in snowdrifts, the museum steps obliterated, and all the local children shouting through the deep snow, making boot-holes in the white silence.

I remember trick-or-treating on Seventy-seventh Street at Halloween, watching spring return through the blossoming fruit trees in front of the museum – and of course the Thanksgiving Eve ritual, the blowing up of the giant balloons.

As a child, living on Seventy-seventh Street was like belonging to a privileged club. *Other* kids watched from a distance as balloons floated through the air; *we* saw them being blown up! Other kids came by subway to see the dinosaurs; we *lived* with them. We felt like insiders, inhabitants of a country of titans. We might be small, but we lived in intimacy with legendary giants. We might be children, but we consorted with gods.

In adolescence, of course, I disowned the old block. I wanted to live in the Village, in Gramercy Park, in Paris, in Rome. Anyplace was better. My family did, in fact, move out of their crumbling artist's apartment on Seventy-seventh Street and into a somewhat less crumbling artist's apartment on the up-town side of the museum. Not very far away – but another world. Now we were on the side of the Planetarium rather than the dinosaurs: a quantum leap.

Whatever it was that drew Bennett and me back to Seventy-seventh Street in '69 is not easy to account for. Call it fear – or call it synchronicity. Call it a longing for roots. Southern writers had their magnolia blossoms and decaying plantations, I had my dog shit and disappearing mailboxes. It might have smelled like garbage – but it was home. The tourist might see the eyesore of a welfare hotel, the bags of uncollected trash, the giant water bugs blithely crossing the street in broad daylight, the Puerto Rican stoop-loungers whining 'Hey chickie, wanna fuck?' – but I saw my childhood. What the rue des Vignes and the rue des Hospices were to Colette, Seventy-seventh Street and Central Park West were to me. My friends mocked me for still living on the street where I grew up, but I knew that at a certain point in my life, at least, it was nourishing for me to stay there.

That point had passed. Seventy-seventh Street now seemed strangling compared to California and the big western sky. My whole life there was an artifact. Josh's warm, funny smile was where I lived now.

I dragged my suitcases into the lobby and rang up on the intercom to my apartment. Bennett was there. Miraculously enough, Bennett (who never changed his schedule for anyone) had stayed home to wait for me. The farther I drifted from him, the more committed he became to me. In the early years of our marriage, when I was trying everything to make it work, he disdained me, fell silent, attacked me, turned to Penny and sent me to a shrink instead of taking me in his arms. Now he wanted to make it work – but the timing was wrong. It was already too late.

He heard my keys in the door and opened it before I could.

'Darling,' he said, and took me in his arms. After so many years of coldness, his warmth seemed counterfeit to me. His body felt strange, cold, reptilian. It wasn't the body I belonged with. I had shifted into a new sphere. I touched Bennett without somehow touching him at all – as if there were an invisible skin between us.

He had cut his hair, trimmed his drooping mustache, and had grown, in addition, a Freudian beard. A scraggy one, to be sure, but the influence of the Master was clear. His ears stuck out – or had they always stuck out? It was impossible to tell.

'Let me look at you,' he said. 'You look great.'

Couldn't he see Josh all over me? Was he blind?

'Why did you cut your hair?' I asked, drawing away from him. 'And why did you grow that silly beard?'

'Oh, I discussed it with Doctor Steingesser. I looked too much like a kid.'

'I loved your long hair.'

He dismissed this with a shrug. His analyst's opinion was what mattered, not mine.

'Anyway, what's *wrong* with looking young?'

'Not good for the patients,' he said.

'Oh, that's silly. Patients don't come to you because of your *hair*. Or because of your Freudian beard.'

'That's what *you* think,' he said disdainfully. 'I don't want to look like a kid anymore. Dr Steingesser pointed out my unconscious desire to look young. I'm forty, after all.'

'I've never understood why looking like a complete conformist helps in dealings with the unconscious. I frankly think it's a lot of shit. There's no reason why dullness and sobriety should help in interpreting people's *dreams*.'

Bennett looked irritated, but he was determined to hold it in. He had stayed home to wait for me, had cancelled patients for me – all the things that would have melted my heart had they been done years ago, even months ago. But I was indifferent. Hard, even. All I experienced in my reunion with Bennett was a painful feeling of hypocrisy. How could I convey this to him? How could I express it. I could hardly express it to myself.

He put his arms around me, ground his pelvis against mine. I could feel his erection and it only filled me with repugnance, followed by a wave of incredible sadness. Every time I had been separated from Bennett in the past, I had worried about him screwing around or finding somebody else or just deciding he didn't want me. This was the first time I was utterly sure of his loyalty to me, his missing me – and now it was just too late.

'Let's go to bed,' he said, taking me by the hand to the bedroom.

'What time is it? Don't you have to go to the office?'

'I have another half-hour or so,' he said, utterly oblivious to my reluctance. Ordinarily, I was never reluctant to go to bed. Bennett was the reluctant one; Bennett was the one who complained of my hot pants, my eagerness to screw anywhere, everywhere.

'There's so much mail piled up,' I said as we passed my study. 'Just looking at it makes me nervous ...'

'The mail can wait,' said Bennett – who *never* thought the mail could wait before. We had switched personalities, it seemed; he had become like me.

He tore off my clothes with great eagerness, began nibbling my nipples dutifully, massaging my clitoris, and thrust his cock into me, moaning about how beautiful I was, how tight my cunt was, how *good* I felt to him. My body responded in its accustomed way, almost against the will of the mind that lived in it. My cunt moistened for him, my heart raced, my nipples hardened, I came – thinking of Josh (with whom it was so hard to come). Oh Doris Lessing, my dear – your Anna is *wrong* about orgasms. They are no proof of love – any more than that other Anna's fall under the wheels of that Russian train was a proof of love. It's all female shenanigans, cultural *mishegoss*, conditioning, brainwashing, male mythologizing.

What does a woman want? She wants what she has been told she ought to want. Anna Wulf wants orgasm, Anna Karenina, death. Orgasm is no proof of anything. Orgasm is proof of orgasm. Someday every woman will have orgasms – like every family has color TV – and we can all get on with the real business of life.

'What are you thinking?' asked Bennett.

'About Tolstoy and Doris Lessing,' I said.

Bennett chuckled. This was the Isadora he knew, the Isadora he could live with, the Isadora he could control. This was the woman who cared about literature, not life. He was comfortable with that woman. I had never been more *un*comfortable with her in my life.

For the first time [I wrote in a letter to Josh that day], it seems possible to try to integrate my writing and my life. What I mean is – I think I always assumed that I had to be unhappy in order to be productive in my writing. I don't know whether I expressed this to myself – but I certainly lived that way. Now I'm beginning to wonder *why* I lived that way. Was it just to ward off the evil eye? I think that somewhere along the line, I must have

243

made a pact with myself that I would give up love, if I could have literature. Men are allowed to have both. Women almost always have to choose. And if I had to choose, I would choose writing. At least that was less likely to disappoint than love. So I lived with someone I had practically no communication with. And my rationalization for this was: *he lets me write.*

Lets me. Only recently have I begun to realize how pathetic that formulation is. Do I *let* him practice psychiatry? I would never think of letting him or not letting him. None of that is my business. Yet I felt grateful (and guilty) toward Bennett for years simply because he *let me write.* And that was supposed to make up for everything: the lack of warmth, the lack of communication, the lack of laughter.

I think it was only when I began to realize that my writing *mattered* to other people, that they were *helped* by it, that I stopped seeing it as some silly self-indulgence that my cold but indulgent husband *let me do* – and began seeing it as a birthright.

Recognition helped enormously – the recognition of readers particularly. I had a place in the world now, was connected to society in some way. I felt useful and productive as I had when I taught freshman English. I was not merely jerking-off in a dark room.

We live in a society where everyone habitually lies about their feelings – so there is an immense gratitude toward anyone who even tries to tell the truth. I suppose this is why certain authors are worshipped as cult figures. We may disdain truth in our daily lives but we are much more relieved and exhilarated when we find someone at least *trying* to express it in a book.

I've spent six months or more being miserable about my ridiculous fame, being overwhelmed by it, guilty for it, self-punishing, divided – but now (with the perspective of California and you and Kurt's longevity and Jeannie's death) I'm beginning to see that it was given to me for a purpose as a way of enlightenment perhaps, and as a path toward freedom.

Throughout my childhood and adolescence and twenties, I was consumed with ambition, sick with envy of all those who were published, visible, praised. Then when I *got* visibility myself, I was plunged into despair, terror, fear of falling – tears shed for answered prayers, all that. But now I'm dimly beginning to perceive that for a person as ambitious as I, the only way to transcend ambition was actually to go *through* the fame crazies. Only after that could I dedicate myself to what really mattered – loving someone wholeheartedly, to working at my writing instead of going up in smoke as a media personality, to *using* success instead of letting it use me ...

For the first time in my life, my head actually seems to be screwed on right. There doesn't seem to be any reason why we can't love each other and also write – and yet, even saying that I get scared. We better not be too visibly happy. The evil eye will surely get us for it ...

But in the days that followed, there were plenty of misgivings. No letters from Josh arrived. Rosanna Howard tried to talk me out of Josh, saying I was mad to get involved with another man just when I was on the verge of 'breaking my dependency on men,' just when I could leave Bennett and live with her. But how could I explain to her that Josh had nothing to do with 'Dependency on Men' or feminist politics or any doctrinal disputes whatsoever? Josh was merely the best friend I'd ever found. Then why wasn't he writing? Had I been wrong again? Had I picked another winner? The letters must have gotten lost. I believed that for one, two, three days, and then I seriously began to wonder.

Britt meanwhile was giving me grief. Installed at the Sherry-Netherland with her entourage, she was wheeling and dealing, calling me periodically to report on her various negotiations, and telling me all sorts of confusing things.

It now appeared that Spinoza and Dante were out of the picture, that she was 'in negotiation with a major studio,' that she was 'talking to directors,' that she would 'let me know what developed.' She was now speaking cavalierly of playing the lead in the picture herself. Even though she had absolutely no experience as an actress, even though

245

her voice resolutely seemed to issue from her nose, she had decided that she and she alone was the real Candida – and she had somehow convinced a major director to agree with her.

Incredibly enough, the book was selling better and better. It was everywhere. My phone never stopped ringing. Mail never stopped flooding in – and Britt was holding press conferences and interviews at the Sherry-Netherland, talking up the picture she was going to star in, riding to glory on *Candida*'s coattails, even claiming in one interview to have 'made Isadora Wing what she is today ...' Her *chutzpa* enraged me. Britt had never written a book or made a movie. She had never done anything but toot her own horn and order people around. Her whole reputation was based on one Western which she'd conned her husband (who was the heir to a brokerage firm) into investing in. Through no fault of theirs, this movie became a huge financial success, and, in the Hollywood manner, people who put up money got producer credits. Thus Britt became a 'producer' without ever having made a movie at all.

When I calmed down enough to realize what I had signed away, and how binding it was, I was desperate. On Britt's side, nothing was binding. All her talk of making a quality movie, of private financing and artistic control were conveniently forgotten as soon as she had a piece of paper from me. It turned out there had never been any private financers at all, that Paradigm Pictures had been her partner all along, and that Sonny and Danny were just a couple of guys she'd happened to pick up. They were as much Mafiosi as she was actress. Had they been real Mafiosi, they probably would have been more honorable.

My agent was no help at all. She was young and inexperienced and employed by a giant agency to whom Britt was the important client, not me. Ten percent of what I made was nothing compared with ten percent of a movie – any movie – and Britt's last movie had grossed millions.

'You need a good lawyer,' Rosanna Howard said. 'The difference in making money and being rich is having a lawyer.'

'What about Gretchen?' I asked.

Rosanna was amused. 'You don't go to a feminist lawyer for a film deal,' she said. 'What you need is the kind of lawyer they'll be afraid of. The essence of using the law to your own advantage is intimidation. Most cases never get to court anyway (and if they do, what happens has nothing to do with justice), so the question is: how much can you scare the other side? I think you were clearly intimidated and defrauded into signing something you, one, didn't want to sign and, two, didn't understand. You need a tough lawyer. And you need him *now*.'

I thought of the mansion in Bel Air where Britt's lawyer lived, of the Rolls-Royces, and the vermeil service plates, and the Tiffany glass goblets – all acquired in lieu of fees. If movie stars couldn't pay their legal bills, how could I?

'I'm not sure I can *afford* a lawyer,' I said to Rosanna.

'You can't afford *not* to,' she said.

Intuition, extuition ...

Samuel Johnson defines the
novel as 'a small tale,
generally of love.' The
French say, 'without adultery,
there is no novel.' Who am
I to disagree?

For the next week or so, my life was a constant round of lawyers' appointments, phone calls, interviews, and growing panic over not hearing from Josh alternating with a growing conviction that I loved him. Just thinking of Josh made me happy. I would skip to my appointments, skip to the Sherry-Netherland (where Britt kept assuring me to trust her, not to panic about the film, not to listen to my lawyers), run to my analyst's office (where my analyst was absolutely stumped because she couldn't seem to find anything oedipal or self-destructive about my feelings for Josh), waltz down Madison Avenue to Rosanna's house (where Rosanna tried to convince me to forget about Josh and live with her), race to Hope's office (where I would look in vain for letters from Josh and would spend hours sitting and telling Hope how absolutely wonderful he was).

I was in love. My skin glowed. I lost ten pounds in a week because I didn't seem to need food anymore. I skipped and ran and sang in the streets. Strangers smiled at me, dogs followed me, both my Jeffreys asked me what had happened in California, who *was* it? They knew. The only person who was resolutely deaf and dumb was Bennett. The only person who suspected nothing was my awful wedded husband. I had gone from lying in bed all morning staring at the ceiling and wanting to die – to waking up at six and skipping into the bathroom singing Cole Porter songs – and Bennett didn't notice at all! And how could I tell him? He would only tell me to go to my analyst and talk about it till I talked myself out of it.

After a day of frantic activity, I would come home at night and write love poems. Bennett would go to sleep and I would stay up until two and write. The poems tumbled out as if by ghostly dictation. There was no stopping them. In the morning I would bound out of bed – not tired in the least – and mail the poems off to Josh. I sent him books, photographs, letters, and poem after poem. I was so certain I'd somehow wind up with Josh that I didn't even

251

bother to make copies of some of the poems. I – who am usually so punctilious about carbon copies, xeroxes, the paraphernalia of literary immortality – just sent my scrawled copies off into the blue, with an absolute conviction they would catch somewhere, like the filaments of Whitman's noiseless, patient spider.

All my life, I had written in the hope of finding my lover, my double, my friend through the printed word. Books go out into the world, travel mysteriously from hand to hand, and somehow find their way to the people who need them at the *times* when they need them. Josh had read my poems two years before because his parents and I had a friend in common and the books had been passed along. Cosmic forces guide such passings-along. The fingertips of the book-lenders are as charged with cosmic energy as the fingertips of people at a séance. The book propels itself from hand to hand by the transmitted energy of the author's long-distance wishing. When you find a book in a rented beach house or the library of an old ocean liner, it is hardly by chance. The book is waiting there, waiting summer after salty summer, perhaps, to change your life. And the author (who may be dead by now) is still hovering somewhere in the ether to watch.

When Josh read my poems originally he'd thought, This sounds like someone I could talk to. It had flashed through his mind that perhaps I was the woman for him, but he cast this out as wishful thinking. There is intuition and extuition. Intuition is the voice of one's spiritual counselors, and extuition is the work of the evil eye. The evil eye told Josh: 'She'd never be interested in you.' So he tucked the poems in some attic of his brain and went on fucking his current girlfriend, whose tits he loved but whose mind he couldn't seem to locate. 'I discovered that you can't base a relationship on tits,' he told me.

But can you base one on poems? Or on a few days in bed at the Beverly Hills Hotel? Or on having the same childhood experiences? Or on both being born under the same sign of the zodiac? Who knows?

I only know that in our choice of friends and lovers and teachers who will change our lives, we are guided by
252

forces which have nothing to do with the rationalizations we give. Poems are the greatest proof of this. Again and again I've noticed that my poems predict my future, that I write a detailed poem about some event in my life months before it occurs. This was the case with some of the love poems I sent Josh. They referred to events that would not happen until later. It was almost as if I wrote first and then waited for my life to catch up. I, who was so indecisive about almost everything else, was utterly convinced from the moment I met Josh that this was the man who would make my life whole. Even though our fucking was not quite perfected, even though my friends considered it the sheerest madness for a 'successful' New York lady like me to join my life with a 'hippie kid' who was an unemployed screenwriter to boot, I knew it was right. My poems knew it, at any rate.

And yet, having poured out all my gut-level convictions in the small hours of the morning, my daily waking self (the self that listens to extuition, not intuition) began to falter. A week had gone by and Josh had not sent me a single letter.

'Maybe he's just not a letter-writer,' Hope said, encouragingly.

'But he's a *writer*. All writers love writing letters. It's such a great excuse for not writing whatever they're *supposed* to be writing.'

'Well, maybe they got lost somehow.'

'But how, Hope? They wouldn't get lost *here*.' (Even the mail-room lady in Hope's office was on the lookout for them.)

'Darling, I've been looking for them every day. Did you ask Rosanna?'

Hope hated Rosanna, thought she was cold and opportunistic – but it was not Hope's method to interfere with anything I felt I had to experience. I needed a lesbian experience? Well then, I should have it. Hope saw life as process, not end; therefore she was infinitely patient.

'Rosanna hasn't seen any letters either. She keeps telling me to forget Josh. She thinks he's a loser – not that she'd say so in so many words. She thinks that if I need a part-time male lover – because I still haven't completely committed myself to women – it ought at least to be someone in New York, someone rich, someone famous. She rather accepts the idea of my having a part-time lover and still having her. She says I can even get married if I want. But it ought to be *her* sort of marriage – lots of separations and houses all over the place. And that takes money.'

'You'll have money,' Hope said. 'The less you worry about it and do your work, the better off you'll be.'

'But I can't work at all now. And the movie thing is all screwed up and the lawyers' bills are already adding up – and I still haven't seen the royalties from this best seller everyone assumes is making me so rich. If I leave Bennett, I'll be broke, and Josh has no money at all. I'm not sure I can start living like a student again at this point in my life.'

'Trust me,' Hope said. 'Have I ever been wrong about anything?'

'No,' I conceded.

But I went away and once again dismissed Hope as gushy and sentimetal, because by then I was in a funk to end all funks. The week had passed. The poems were written, and the other side of my nature asserted itself. Panic returned. Panic and despair. All my feelings for Josh, all my poems, all my cheeriness I now dismissed as just another infatuation, another zipless fuck. Bennett was grim, but he was stable. Josh was a mere chimera.

'Why don't you call him?' Holly asked when I went to her greenhouse loft to cry on her shoulder.

'Because I feel like a fucking asshole. I've been sending him poems and letters all week and he hasn't written a word. It's the same old shit I've done so many times before – falling in love with a bastard and *inventing* him for myself. Who *is* Josh? A hippie version of Adrian Goodlove, maybe. Who knows. I thought I was past that – but I'm sure as hell not going to make an idiot of myself by calling him. I did that once before.'

'When? Who?' Holly asked.

'Oh, that time Gretchen and I went to London. We called Adrian in Hampstead, even drove out to his house to witness his domestic bliss with Esther. They had gotten married after all, and had a baby, a daughter with the same squint as Daddy. Adrian laughed and called me the baby's godmother. It seems she was conceived right after he dumped me in Paris. Then Adrian flirted with Gretchen intolerably – making both me and Esther miserably jealous. And finally when I asked him if we could have lunch alone – just to talk over what had happened in our lives as a result of each other – he became incredibly distant, evasive, clearly rejecting. I absolutely refuse to subject myself to *that* again. I've already made an imbecile of myself sending all those poems to him. I'll probably never even see the manuscripts again. At least with Adrian, I got a book out of my idiocy. This time, the notes are lost forever.'

'There's nothing wrong with living alone, love,' Holly said. 'You don't have to bounce from one man to another. And you don't have to fall into bed with Ms Vampira Howard, either. *Some* of us live alone ...'

'With plants,' I said.

'What the hell have you got against *plants*?' Holly yelled.

Bennett remained the only person in my life who was oblivious to the changes I had gone through during the week. He had not noticed either my manic or my depressed phase. It was true that we practically never saw each other, but even when we accidentally happened to run into each other in the apartment, he was utterly blind to what was going on with me. Superficially, our life went on. I divided my time among friends, lawyers, interviews, poetry readings, hassling with Britt about the film. Nothing was resolved on that score. The lawyers were in consultation at a hundred dollars an hour, plus long-distance phone bills; Britt was telling me to disregard them, that she was my friend, that she would never cheat me; Rosanna Howard was telling me that Britt was lying to me; Hope was telling me not worry, it would all work out; Holly was telling me to live alone and like it; and both my Jeffreys were offering what

255

they had always offered: a little lunchtime diversion, with promises of more to come. Both of them seemed so silly to me now. I was disgusted with all those people who took up the fine art of marital compromise and defended it with religious zeal. Both Jeffreys had wives they couldn't talk to; I had a husband I couldn't talk to. We were all supposed to go on forever, having our midday infidelities, our five-to-seven blow jobs in empty offices, and talking vaguely about leaving our spouses someday. But neither Jeffrey would ever leave. That was clear enough. Each of them rather liked the fragmented life he had chosen. They never had to make a commitment this way. They were not committed to their wives, not committed to their lovers, and above all not committed to themselves. They were doing precisely what Bennett had done with Penny and me, vacillated between two women, causing both of them pain – and through secrecy (or *sneak*cracy – to be exact) avoiding the responsibility of ever making a decision.

At least I had been open about Adrian Goodlove. Bennett was free to take me back or leave me. That he chose to stay – that he realized that one summer's fling was not much compared with his long, passionate, sneaky love affair with Penny – was his decision. It also strengthened his power in the marriage because I didn't know about Penny and was consequently dazzled by his generosity and magnanimity. Also, there was his famous indulgence in 'letting me write' – letting me write a book that would ultimately change my life, by leading me out of fear. I had felt so guilty throughout the writing of *Candida Confesses*. And so panicky. I had felt that I'd no right to tell the truth about my life, but some other demon drove my pen onward as I told myself, promised myself even, that I would never try to publish it. I had to get it all down, I had to get it on paper – even if it was ultimately only for my own eyes.

And then it was published – and, astoundingly enough, millions of women all over the world felt exactly as Candida felt! What a revolution it would be if all the people who led fragmented, lying, sneaking lives – justifying themselves with talk of realism, compromise, homage to the superego, civilization and its discontents – finally decided

256

to throw off their self-imposed shackles and live according to their honest feelings! They would not immediately start fornicating in the streets and killing each other promiscuously. Not at all. But they would have to face the responsibility for their own happiness or unhappiness. They could no longer blame their wives, their husbands, their children, their parents, their shrinks, their bosses. And what a loss that would be! No one to blame! That was the real reason my two Jeffreys stayed with wives they didn't like – to assure themselves of always having someone to blame. That was why most people led lives they hated, with people they hated. That was why Bennett didn't level with me and leave me for Penny. That was why I stayed with Bennett long after I knew the marriage was dead. How wonderful to have someone to blame! How wonderful to live with one's nemesis! You may be miserable, but you feel forever in the right. You may be fragmented, but you feel absolved of all the blame for it. Take your life in your own hands, and what happens? A terrible thing: no one to blame.

My feelings for Josh had shown me the possibility of a life that wasn't fragmented. I had glimpsed it briefly, foretold it in poems, written to him about it, and then – silence. He didn't write back. Now I was nowhere. I couldn't go back to my old life with Bennett, with my double Jeffrey, leading the luncheon life, wasting time, flip-flopping from one silly affair to another, hating my husband, flirting with an accidental pregnancy to somehow make my decision for me, to change my life without my having to take the responsibility for changing it. Where *could* I go?

For the moment, I seemed to be spending an awful lot of time with Rosanna.

Rosanna had a way of appearing whenever I felt lowest and whisking me off to lunch or dinner or drinks in her Corniche. Everything (with the possible exception of making her come) was easy with Rosanna. She was as cool as I was passionate, as measured as I was excessive, as stable as I was ambivalent. Her studio apartment was full of poetry books and cases of red wine. There was always music

257

on the stereo and lots of new books on the coffee table and fresh coffee in the astonishingly beautiful copper espresso-maker that took up one whole wall of the kitchen. And always there was the scent of Rosanna's musk perfume in the air.

There was even a genuine friendship between me and Rosanna. It certainly wasn't her fault that, like most people, she couldn't see beyond her own experience and wanted to justify it by pushing it on everyone else. Rosanna had been married before – to an uptight lawyer she identified with Bennett and now had found a measure of contentment in a very loose, very open marriage to a guy who liked to be away a lot and fuck around a lot. It suited both their temperaments. Rosanna was left alone with her writing, her women friends, her cool studio with hot espresso. Robert had the freedom he wanted, openly – without having to lie – and he also had the use of her fortune. I'm sure they loved each other in a sort of Harold-and-Vita way, and I know they felt terribly superior to all those poor benighted souls who couldn't get it together to have an open marriage. Rosanna naturally assumed that since this arrangement worked for her, a similar arrangement might work for me. She was hardly wishing me ill in wishing that for me. She loved me and wanted what was best for me. I think she also thought it would be great for us to live together, and she knew how to get to me – my writing.

'I *know* you'd get more writing done if we lived together,' she said. It was a Sunday afternoon, and we were lounging in her apartment, drinking wine, reading poems together, talking. The chauffeur had gone off to the airport to get Robert, who was supposed to be coming in that night. Bennett was playing tennis. I had told him that I planned to spend the evening at Rosanna's and had invited him to join us, knowing he would never do it because he didn't much like Rosanna, and anyway he had lots of reading to do for a course he was teaching at the hospital.

'Well, I certainly need to do *some*thing,' I said. 'This is no way to get a new book written.'

'We could go off to my place in Aspen,' Rosanna said. 'It's very peaceful. I even have an electric typewriter there.'

I thought about it. Though Rosanna had proposed this before, we had never gone because, somehow, I was sure that so much time alone with Rosanna was more than I could take. I liked her friendship, but I felt it had been marred by the sex. Not that I was sorry about the affair or had anything against women making love to women. It was just that there was a slight sense of compulsion in our sexual scenes just as there was a slight sense of pity with Jeffrey Roberts and a slight sense of contempt with Jeffrey Rudner. Sex had come to puzzle me. There was all sorts of sex in my life and not very much intimacy. It seemed I was forever standing outside the experience thinking about it critically – with everyone but Josh. When I was with Josh, I was utterly and absolutely with Josh – whether I came or not. We lived inside each other's brains. We knew each other by heart from the first moment we met. I could be alone anywhere with Josh and not be bored. But what was the point of thinking about Josh? He hadn't written a word.

'Well,' I said finally, 'maybe we *should* go to Aspen and try to work right after this movie nonsense gets straightened out.'

'That's the most intelligent thing I've heard you say all week,' Rosanna said. And she poured me another glass of Mouton-Cadet.

The doorbell rang. There was much noise and commotion outside, and Rosanna trotted to open the door. Who should appear but a rather drunken Robert Czerny and two friends, acquired on the plane from Washington. Robert was large, paunchy, gray-haired, and addicted to slapping people on the back. He didn't much approve of poetry, but he liked me in spite of this. And I liked him. He was unpretentious and absolutely up-front about his opportunism. No sneakracy for him. You could take him or leave him. His politics were neo-redneck and his voice was loud and booming. He actually pronounced *American* 'Amurrican.'

On the plane he had picked up two sex doctors who wrote books and collected erotic art and were old orgy-hands. They were an attractive couple in their forties –

the woman a Swedish blonde named Kirsten who had grown up in the United States and had enormous tits (between which dangled a gold pendant shaped like an erect penis, only it was pointing down – poor thing), and the man a slender Viennese named Hans who had grown up in Paris. They were terribly amiable and jolly – sexual missionaries, really (or emissionaries, as I came to call them) – and had apparently followed Robert home in the hopes of having an orgy or getting a millionaire patron for their erotic art collection – or both.

The frosty Rosanna had, at least, the intuition to surround herself with bouncy, warm people.

'Well,' said Rob, rubbing his hands together and taking off his sheepskin coat, 'what'll you have to drink?'

Hans and Kirsten were happy with the wine and cheese Rosanna and I had been working on all afternoon, but Rob wanted Scotch – a twenty-year-old variety which slid down the gullet like honey.

Then we all got around to the serious business of discussing erotica and art. Hans and Kirsten had a collection of erotic art so extensive it included everything from Hokusai to Georg Grosz. They had exhibited this collection all over the world at their own expense – but now they were low on funds and they needed a backer to provide them with the money for renting a gallery, insuring the art, mounting the exhibition (which somehow seems like more of a pun in this instance than it usually does). They were willing to share the glory and the profits with their mounters. The glory of being associated with such a business was actually rather dubious. For no apparent reason – other than Hans's and Kirsten's not particularly prurient connection with sexual matters – they had been the subjects of FBI harassments, wire-tapping, yearly audits by the IRS. As they described this, Rosanna looked extremely nervous. Much as she would have wanted to be associated with such a venture for the prestige of it, she could hardly let herself get involved with the sort of thing that might be dangerous to her tax position. Hans, who was a psychoanalyst – albeit an unorthodox one – and who picked up on people's feelings much more quickly than most of the orthodox

260

psychoanalysts I know said, said : 'Don't worry, Rosanna, that's cool. You can see the art and *then* decide. In the meantime, why don't we just have a party?'

'Terrific!' said Rob, who'd been hoping for an orgy all along.

Now, there are times when the very air is sexual, when it's dusk and the moon is hanging low over the rooftops, and the temperature of your blood is the same temperature as the air and you look at a man – any halfway decent-looking man – and you know you could go right to bed with no questions asked at all. This was *not* that sort of night.

It was cold, the participants were all rather constrained and strange to each other, and sex was not in the air. But here we all were together – and Rob was a practical fellow. An opportunity like this might not arise again. At such time, pot is invaluable. Pot and the Beatles. How many orgies might have faltered without pot and the Beatles! That clitoral trill, that thumping bass. And sweet smoke filling the lungs, the head, the cunt ... and the Beatles singing *'because the world is round ... it turns me onnn.'*

Goddamn, I *missed* the sixties. When everyone was dropping acid and their pants every two minutes, I was in Germany with boring Bennett being a 'good wife,' cooking gourmet meals, breaking my leg in penance for wanting the most natural thing in the world – my freedom. I wanted to go to parties in town with the students at the University of Heidelberg. I wanted to get stoned and fuck and act my age. But Bennett, who was routinely fucking Penny in my study twice a week, pronounced all that *'infantile'* and sent me to a shrink to 'work it out.' Then, at the dangerous age of twenty-nine I took one fling with Adrian Goodlove and came back – not dutiful this time – but, worse, cynical. Formerly submissive, I was now in-dependent – independent but resigned to never communi-cating with my husband, to never finding any love that lasted, to patching up my aching emptiness with silly meaningless midday affairs ...

Damn, damn, damn – if only I hadn't missed the sixties! If only I had sown some wild oats like Josh did.

Josh. I shut my eyes and saw Josh. I was lying on the couch, wineglass in one hand, joint in the other, when Josh's funny, warm, furry face swam into my field of vision. 'I love you too – but is it *enough*?' he was saying. He was standing at the airport, at the end of the boarding ramp. And I would never get back through that tunnel and into his arms again. Like Alice, having drunk the wrong potion, I was too big, too old, too sad, too disillusioned ...

'Want to dance?' Hans said, taking me by the hand. He had a nice bony European face – but it wasn't Josh's.

What the hell, I thought. Hans pulled me up out of the deep couch. The music had now changed to 1967 psychedelic – *Sgt Pepper's Lonely Hearts Club Band* – and it was taking me back, back, back to those years in Germany when I felt so guilty for being young, for being horny, for wanting what *every*one wants at twenty-five – while my middle-aged husband (who was *born* middle-aged) had his cake and ate it too, telling me all the while I was 'infantile.' Unforgivable!

Damn. It wasn't too late to be twenty-five! I would rather be twenty-five at thirty-two than never be twenty-five at all!

Dancing. I had almost forgotten how much I loved dancing. With a little pot and some good music and a pinch of despair as the kicker, I can get into dancing as if dancing were the only thing I ever did. My body moves right into the music as if the music were its home. And I dance – not like someone who thinks and frets and worries all the time, not like someone who analyzes and re-analyzes everything – but like someone who listens to no beat but the beat between her legs. And in a way I *become* that person.

Hans and I danced and danced until we danced into the bedroom. 'Someone has to start an orgy,' I said to him, 'and it might as well be us.'

'Agreed!' he said, laughing. Hans said *everything* laughing. Hans was jolly and clever and if I closed my eyes and forgot his bony body, his strange face, his strange laugh, his death's-head skull, his funny accent – I could almost pretend it was Josh taking off my clothes, Josh running a slick finger between the wet lips of my cunt, Josh unzipping his fly, Josh's big cock coming into me, Josh's face covering mine with kisses ... I looked up at Hans and through his face I could see – in that special way only possible to the very stoned – all the faces of the men I had loved or lusted for blending into each other. Josh melted into Bennett, Bennett into Adrian, Adrian into Charlie, Charlie into Brian, Brian into my father. They were all one man. There was no difference between them at all. I dug my nails into Hans's back and came screaming and crying and shrieking at the top of my lungs, 'It isn't fair, it isn't fair, it isn't fair!'

Hans had gentle instincts. He didn't get angry or frightened. He stroked my hair.

'*What* isn't fair, Isadora?' he asked.

But I was too stoned to explain, and by now my screams had attracted the rest of the party, who appeared, dancing like bacchantes – some wishing to comfort me, others to join in the fun. I was bleary-eyed and stoned. The music was loud ('*I'd love to turn you on ...*') and I scarcely remember who inaugurated the first combination or the second or the third – or indeed how one could *tell* one from the other.

Somewhere at the hazy beginning of it all, I was being fucked in the ass by Hans while Rosanna ate me and Rosanna's husband sucked my nipples. (Then Kirsten of the gigantic knockers appeared and preempted me in the breast department.) At a later, wetter, and sweatier point in the evening, Robert was fucking me and Rosanna was behind him encouraging him and holding his balls helpfully. I couldn't help but notice that Robert never did get very hard – and it momentarily flickered through my mind that maybe this was really the secret of *most* of the sex people – the sexual emissionaries; they really weren't very potent without (what you might call) all this peer-group pressure. At some point Robert fucked Rosanna – and I had the distinct sense that it took all the *rest* of us being there as observers for them to accomplish the simplest missionary mating.

'But was it *fun?*' my friends always ask. And the truth is, I can hardly even *remember*. Of course it was engrossing. And of course there were lots of orgasms – mine, his, hers, theirs, everybody's. And there was the added pleasure of feeling superior, liberated, special – above the common bourgeois run of uptight people, fucking two by two.

I kept thinking, Oh gee, I'm eating a *woman* while another woman eats *me*, while a man fucks her, while a man sucks him! Oh *golly*, this is certainly a first! And yet the dominant feeling of it all was that we should have had someone there directing traffic, possibly with a megaphone – because it was all so much like *rush hour*. There was a good deal of rearranging bodies so that our various human chains would be unbroken, and the positions we found were not the kind that were easy for your average amateur nonpracticing yogin or yogina to master. But we persevered – valiantly. A kind of group greediness took over – and those of us who were normally sated after one, two, three orgasms felt it incumbent upon us to have dozens of orgasms – in all positions, with everyone present.

I was astounded at my own stamina. This (by now) virtually anonymous pile of bodies became like one organism, stretching, contracting, eating, excreting, moving onto drier ground when we had soiled the last. It had ten arms, ten legs, two penises, three vaginas and six breasts – of assorted sizes – not to mention ten eyes, ten ears, and five mouths (that were practically always full). Something was always in eruption – as in a region of volcanos. Something was always being gobbled by some orifice or other. When at last Kirsten got up and went into the living room to bring wine for us, it felt like an amputation.

And yet there was also a wonderful feeling of closeness, of sheer physicalness, of being nothing but a body and that being *enough*. It was almost like the way I'd felt in California, looking at the waves roll in, feeling the balmy air, and thinking that nothing could possibly be wrong with the world if the sky was so clear you could see all the way to Japan – or Catalina.

Thinking of California made me fix on Josh again, and I was overcome with sadness. I felt I'd betrayed him. I remembered the orgy we hadn't had with Ralph Battaglia, and I felt incredibly guilty to have participated in this one. These weren't people I loved – they were *bodies*. The closeness I'd felt a minute before shifted to revulsion. The others were drifting off to sleep in various position on the bed and floor. I got up and wandered into the bathroom, where I stared at myself for a long time in the mirror over the sink, wondering what on *earth* to do now.

I must have been there for some time, hypnotizing myself with my own gaze. The bathroom door was half open, so at first I didn't even see Hans when he slid past me and seated himself on the closed toilet seat.

'Fascinating, isn't it?' he said.

I started. 'What?'

'Staring into the pupils.' He pronounced it 'poopeels.'

'Yes – you begin to think you can climb right down into those holes. Actually, I like flicking the light on and off and watching the irises contract.'

'So let's do it,' Hans said, getting up to play with the light. He switched it on and off twice while I watched my eyes respond. 'No more,' I said, 'I'd really rather talk.'

'Shoot.' He seated himself on the toilet seat, in the pose of Rodin's *The Thinker*. We were both naked, but oddly comfortable with each other in the bright light.

'Well – it's my whole life. It's a mess, a disaster. I have a husband I'm always trying to avoid, a lover in California who may not love me, an incipient lawsuit that should cost twice what I possess, a . . .'

'I thought Rosanna was your lover,' Hans interrupted.

'Rosanna is my *friend*.'

'Oh I see,' he said, chuckling. 'You mean you oblige her.'

'Not really.'

'Come on now – I'm not as dumb as most of the psychiatrists you know.' (Charmingly enough, he pronounced *dumb* 'dump.') 'It's okay. I couldn't do more than oblige her myself. She's very *cold* really . . . who's the guy?'

'A lovely, funny, gentle soul named Josh who is clever and witty and makes puns all the time and writes and draws and plays the banjo and makes me ridiculously happy. Only he hasn't written me at all. And now I feel bloody guilty about this damned orgy ...'

Hans put an admonishing finger over my lips.

'I don't want to hear you use the word *guilt* again. It's a useless word. Meaningless. As for orgies – they are what they are – neither more nor less – and certainly nothing to feel guilty about. They don't substitute for love. They're not *supposed* to. The best thing you can get out of an orgy is a little lightening of that terrible burden of the superego. If you get the *opposite* – the whole thing is wasted. *Worse* than wasted. What we did tonight is not a thing to take seriously. It's an experience. You never have to do it again if you don't like it – but at least you know what it *is*. Where's the guilt in *that?*'

'Josh would say something like that.'

'He sounds ok*ay*,' Hans said in that Middle-European way of accenting the wrong syllables in American slang words; 'Why don't you write him or call him and see what's up?'

I sighed heavily and seated myself on the edge of the tub. 'I've been *writing* letters, poems, *everything*, and he doesn't answer ...'

'How do you know he got the letters?'

'I just know.'

'How do you know he hasn't written?'

'I just know that too.'

'You know a lot,' Hans laughed.

'It's hopeless. He's six years younger – and it's utterly impractical to even think of our living together.'

'Why? He's not dead. You're certainly not. Things change, people's circumstances change. What does he do?'

'What do you think? He writes. It couldn't be *worse*. You *know* what happens when two writers try to live together – disaster.'

Hans laughed at me again. 'That's a very good scenario – and if you go on believing it, you'll make it happen and then you'll *really* feel justified. So he's six years younger, so what? And who ever told you writers couldn't live together? Kirsten and I are writers. We've been together
266

for almost twenty years, we've traveled everywhere together, we write in studios right next to each other ...
Contrary to what this night on the town may make you think, we lead a very quiet life, write all day, cut off the phones, bring each other coffee, help each other edit manuscripts. It's a *great* life. I can think of nothing *nicer* than two writers living together. In the first place, you have so much time to *be* together. Other people don't have that ... Don't make up some cheesy Hollywood script and live your life by it. So, he's younger ... big deal. Your husband – how old is he?'

'Forty.'

'And does *that* make you happy?'

'Obviously not.'

'And what does he do?'

'A shrink.'

'That's worst of all. A doctor. Security. Bloomingdale's, a co-op, so what? Does it make you feel secure? *Obviously* not. What's wrong with taking risks? Being miserable in your marriage for another year and *another* year and *another* year is a *big* risk too – only you don't *see* the risk. The risk is your life. Wasting it, I mean. It's a pretty big risk.'

I nodded.

'You know what, Isadora? Security doesn't matter, but love does. Do you want me to tell you something really subversive? Love *is* everything it's cracked up to be. That's why people are so cynical about it. Living with someone you really share things with is not only wonderful, it's actually *better* than all the love songs, all the silly movies say it is. It really *is* worth fighting for, being brave for, risking everything for. And the trouble is, if you don't risk anything, you risk even *more*. Life doesn't leave that many choices. It's really very harsh. You can stew like this forever or try it with Josh – and maybe fail – but at least you won't be at the same point you're at now – the stewing point, you know?'

'I guess it would be better to try and fail and wind up alone than to go on like this ...'

'You? Wind up alone? I hardly see it. Maybe things with
267

Josh *won't* work out, but I don't think you'll ever forgive yourself if you don't *try* ...'

'You're right,' I said, looking at the floor.

'So call him,' Hans said. 'What are you waiting for?'

'What time is it?'

'I don't know. Maybe eleven or twelve. Anyway it's not that late on the Coast. Try it. *Call.*' He took my two hands and pulled me up from the edge of the tub.

'Go,' he said, giving me a gentle pat on the ass.

Still naked and now somewhat shivering, I sat down at Rosanna's desk in the living room. 'This is it.' I said to myself, defending against the evil eye. 'Here goes nothing.' I started to dial the Los Angeles area code and then I stopped. Damn – I didn't remember Josh's number. It was in my memo book, which was in my handbag, which was in the bedroom. I couldn't go in there and wake everybody. Was this an omen? Did it mean I shouldn't call?

Call Information, you idiot, I said to myself.

I dialed Los Angeles Information, which rang and rang. Finally I got the operator, asked for the number, and began fumbling for a piece of paper to write it on. There was no pad on Rosanna's desk, no scrap paper. But what's this, under the blotter? Several sheets of brown kraft stationery. 'Can you wait a second?' I asked the operator.

'*Sure,*' she said in that California way that implies no rush, as much time as there is sky and ocean, no hassles. I pulled out one of the brown sheets and scribbled Josh's number on the back.

'Thanks,' I said to California.

'Sure,' said the anonymous western voice.

Suddenly I turned the brown sheet over and saw lettered in black block capitals at the top, JOSHUA ACE. Breathless, heart pounding, I glanced down the page ...

Isadoraitis. Prime susceptibility: 11 P.M. to 2 A.M. Contributing factors: photographs, Isadoraeuvres, daydreaming. Primary symptoms: uncontrollable desire to spill soul followed by anxiety, living-room pacing, and need to cuddle. Secondary symptoms: intense longing, chronic heartache. Temporary remedies: letters, poems, fantasies. Permanent remedies: extended, intensive doses of I.

I am living on tenterhooks, whatever those are. Your poems knock me out. I can't believe they're really for me. Will you ever come back? Or will I have to come to N.Y. and bodily remove you from 77th Street? I am destined for disappointment, but what the fuck? Come, come come. I am projecting long-distance thoughtwaves reflected to you from an aluminum pie-plate high on the moronosphere.

I laughed to myself. I was still holding the phone against my ear and the dial tone had changed to a shaky alto recording, 'Please hang up ... there appears to be a receiver off the hook ... please hang up ... there appears ...' I hung up. The moronosphere was from *Flesh Gordon*, a movie we had seen together, and the moronosphere had become a private joke between us. We had spent less than a week together and we already had hundreds of private jokes, hundreds of memories.

Isadora, my little pumpernickel, just thinking of you makes me happy. I say that and then I realize that I hardly even *know* you. Except that I *do* know you, don't I? You *have* to come back.

This last week has been an emotional 'quickie' and I am left spacey and confused, weltzschmerzy and angst. I keep on wanting to talk to you. I feel like I've been in isolation all these years and I have all these things jammed up in my head and I've spilled a little of it and then been shut off again. Like stopping in the middle of a piss. And then I want to fuck you and learn how you like it because we never really did that.

You see, the only thing I can fuck straight off are plastic pusseys of the *Playboy* variety, because they are manufactured for that purpose. It's like I said, the dichotomy of moms and lovers. Understand that you are the first, the only woman I've met who is smarter than I am and doesn't act like a cretin postcoitus. You may not know this, but despite the movement, ladies tend

269

to be lobotomized by penises. Even very hip, together ladies. Perhaps insertion of the glans into the mouth severs some chain of neurons ... I think the only substantive relationship, worth the emotional strife, is between equals. Still, it is scary. A lifetime's indoctrination is stamped in my gray matter ...

Did I say you made me happy? Yesterday I spent all evening thinking about you. I really like your hair, the way it dips in front. And you have the most intense, happy, sad worried look. All at once. I look at the picture you sent me (the one with all the hair and the Ophelia-mad eyes) and it feels like a stone in my stomach and makes me gooey to the touch. I pine (I never knew what it meant before), but I actually pine ...

There were twelve letters, or fifteen. They were about us, about the love poems, about Gurdjieff, Castaneda, Charles Dickens, movies, the hamburger as a symbol of American life, the moronosphere, my screenplay of *Candida*! (which I'd left for Josh to read), and his growing anxiety about me, his missing me, his wanting to live with me forever ...

I picked up the phone and dialed. My mind was a jumble of conflicting emotions: elation over finding the letters, disgust with myself for having doubted Josh, anger at Rosanna for having confiscated the letters, astonishment at her desperation, wonderment over whether or not she really *wanted* me to find them ...

The phone rang in West Hollywood.

'Hello?' came Josh's comical telephone-voice. Just hearing it made me sure I loved him.

'Josh? It's me, your old buddy, Isadora.'

'Baby!' A loud smooching-sound was transmitted across the three-thousand-mile cable. 'I *love* you ...'

'Oh god, I love you too. I miss you so. Oh god ...' I felt so stupid saying all those banalities. Here was the most special love affair in *history* and I sounded like an ass. Anyway, the telephone is a rotten instrument for communicating anything human. It separates lovers instead of joining them. You want to extend your tongue for a kiss and there's nothing to kiss but a black plastic maw.

'Why did you stop writing? I *love* those poems. I'm so flattered they're for me — I can't believe it.'

'I never got the letters till now — Rosanna hid them.'

'She *hid* them? God — what a bummer. But didn't *Bennett* tell you I called? I just called your house an hour ago. I thought you were returning my call.'

'No. I'm at Rosanna's. I found the letters by accident ... weird, huh?' I didn't want to tell him about the orgy on a long-distance call. I'd tell him when we were together, when I could describe it with the proper élan, and we could laugh about it.

'I *have* to see you again,' I said.

'When? Are you coming here or should I come there? I can't stand this being apart. It's *dumb* and pointless.'

'You could come here, but where would we *stay*?'

'Look — why don't you get Britt to bring you back?'

'I *hate* Britt. She's ripping me off royally and I really ought to be suing her, not taking trips with her. She's literally *stolen* my work — and now she treats me like shit. But I'll find a way to get back. Maybe Rosanna will let us use her place in Aspen and we can write there ...'

'Are you sure you want to take any favors from Rosanna after this?'

'I don't know where *else* we could go ...'

'Sweetie, just come back here. Stay with me, we'll find another place to live if it isn't big enough ...'

'I love you immensely.'

'But will you *come*?'

'I'll find a way, I swear it. I'll call you back tomorrow.'

And we exchanged lengthy smooches, and very reluctantly hung up.

Clutching my pile of letters, I tiptoed into the bedroom, where it still looked like the Decline and Fall of the Roman Empire. Rosanna was sleeping curled up spoonlike with Kirsten, clasping her lovely big tits. Robert was sprawled on his back on the floor. Hans was in the shower, singing. The three in the bedroom were dead to the world. I snatched up my clothes, my handbag, my boots, my coat, and tiptoed into the bathroom. I folded the letters carefully and put them in my handbag.

'You're wonderful,' I said to Hans through the steamy air.

'What happened?'

'I called him – and just as I was calling him, mysterious cosmic forces transported all his letters into my hands ...'

'What?' he said, sticking out his dripping head.

'I found the letters, and he loves me, and I spoke to him, and I'm going there, and you're right about everything!' I dropped my clothes, leapt into the shower, and hugged him under the spray. 'You're *wonderful*!'

Hans looked absolutely baffled for a minute, and then he smiled at me rather mischievously. 'So the letters materialized right here in Rosanna's apartment, eh? This can only point to one conclusion, Holmes ...'

'What, Doctor Watson? ...'

'You need a thorough scrubbing with Vitabath, courtesy of your favorite psychiatrist in the whole world.'

'That's a dubious distinction,' I said, 'but I'd love to come clean.' And we washed each other all over, giggling deliriously.

'I really should be furious at Rosanna,' I said to Hans as we were drying off, 'but I'm so relieved to have found the letters.'

'Clearly an act of desperation,' Hans said. 'Rosanna knows she can't keep you and she's grasping at straws. She's probably ashamed of hiding the letters – but it's the sort of compulsive act jealousy drives people to. I wouldn't rub it in if I were you. "Vengeance is mine saith the Lord ..."'

'I love you, Hans,' I said, meaning it.

My hair was still wet (and crammed into my floppy purple hat) when I sneaked into my own apartment at 1:00 A.M. and, to my astonishment, found Bennett waiting up for me – Bennett who never waited up for me, particularly on a 'school night.'

He was sitting on the white couch in the living room reading *Neurotic Distortion of the Creative Process*.

272

'You had a call,' he said ominously.

'Oh? Who?' I was trying to act nonchalant and at the same time hide the fact that my hair was wet. I came into the living room and sat down with all my clothes on – hat, coat, boots, bag crammed with love letters. I hoped he wouldn't notice the straggly ends of hair dripping into my fur collar.

'I didn't know it was raining,' he said coldly.

'Oh, is it?' I must have sounded like some sort of dumb blonde out of Anita Loos, but I was just so astonished that ordinarily deaf-and-dumb Bennett noticed *anything*. 'Who called?'

'Who do you think?'

'I haven't the faintest idea. Really, I haven't.'

'A friend of yours from Los Angeles.'

My heart pounded at the very mention of the words *Los Angeles*.

'Britt?'

'I thought Britt was in New York.'

'Oh, that's right. She is.'

'You seem pretty flustered tonight. Where the hell have you *been*?'

'At Rosanna's.'

'In the shower? Or was it just a wild party where everyone sprayed champagne around?'

'If you wanted to know so much, why didn't you come? I invited you ...' I said with massive insincerity.

'I don't happen to like your millionaire friends. Or your hippie ones.'

'Who do you mean?'

'Isadora, who the hell is *Josh*?'

The name went through me like lightning. 'Didn't I tell you? He's the son of Robert and Ruth Ace. I met him on the Coast at his parents' house. He wants me to help him with his short stories. He's just a kid, very sweet, very starstruck about writers. I promised to read his work and tell him what I thought.'

'Oh,' said Bennett, 'I was sure he was your lover.'

'Why? What on earth did he say?'

'Only that he wanted to speak to you. He seemed sur-

273

prised you were out, distressed somehow and awkward.'

'Well, he's very young.'

'How young?'

'Twenty-six.'

'And what are you going to do for him – teach him about love?'

This infuriated me for some reason. My secret was pressing against my rib cage like a trapped bird that had to fly out. I had almost gotten away with my lie, but I suddenly realized that I didn't *want* to get away with it.

'Actually, he could teach *me* a thing or two. Not to mention *you*.'

'Oh?' Bennett said, raising his eyebrows. And he smiled secretively, got up in total silence, and turned out the lights.

'Good night, Isadora. Pleasant dreams.' And he disappeared down the hall to the bedroom.

I stood there *furious*, wearing my hat, my coat, my boots, my wet hair. I wanted Bennett to *know*, I wanted to read him the letters, tell him that there were people in this world who *could* love, who *could* be warm, who didn't sit home every night reading about neurotic distortion and feeling superior to the entire world.

I ran down the hall to the bedroom after him and shouted into the darkness: 'Okay! He is my lover! He makes me happy and I'm going to *leave* you for him! We get up in the morning giggling and we talk to each other about everything! He doesn't lay guilt numbers on me and he doesn't sit around nursing his unhappy childhood and he isn't hypocritical and cynical and superior to everything in the whole goddamn world!'

Bennett sat up in bed, turned on the light, and said: 'So leave. You'll never write another book as long as you live.' Then he turned off the light and went to sleep.

I locked myself in the bathroom and wept for what seemed like an hour. Then I took two Valiums and fell asleep with all my disheveled clothes on, clutching the bag with Josh's letters to my chest, on the black leather chair in my study.

Bullwinkle's wrinkles ...

Thanksgiving Day and I am leaving Seventy-seventh Street forever. The day is cold and gray, with billowy white clouds materializing here and there on the china-blue plate of the sky. Bullwinkle and the other balloons are netted down to the street, their big bellies swelling pregnantly toward those sumptuous, sailing clouds. In two hours the parade will begin without me. I will be flying.

A street of fallen giants held down by nets and sandbags, and me dragging my beige linen luggage with the violets on it, dragging it down to the corner where I hail a cab and tell the cabbie I'm headed for Kennedy Airport.

I wave good-bye to my balloons, which are straining upward on their helium wings, trying to break free, trying, it seems, to soar. But however it may appear to credulous little children, the balloons don't really fly at all. In an hour or two, they will be tethered to tiny people in clown suits, and will be dragged along the avenues of New York like captured beasts of the wild, like Gullivers through a Lilliput of skyscrapers.

Once, only once, when I was not above three feet tall myself, the Panda balloon broke free and took off over the Museum of Natural History, over the park, over the obelisk – which we kids called Cleopatra's needle – where it hovered for a while on the verge of an explosion, perhaps, and then drifted on up up up through the clouds.

Very few New Yorkers remember that occurrence, but it is fixed forever in my memory – even if I only dreamed it, when I was very young.

EPILOGUE

They had fought ...

They had fought. A terrible fight in which he said she was a ravenous, insatiable cunt, and she said he had never satisfied her, never, and he said she might as well go out and find other men to fuck her because he couldn't satisfy her, couldn't, wouldn't, didn't care, and turned with his back to her in bed.

He would not fuck her. She could beg and plead for it and he would not. It was his power over her, over her fame, her blondeness, her money, her being older than him, and wiser (hah) and hornier – she being thirty-three and always throbbing at the cunt, he being a cool twenty-seven with a huge cock which he could give and take away at will. He was not her dildo, her plaything, her vibrator; he was her man.

He had the cock. She could cry and whimper and press herself to his hard back, but he still had the cock. He was reading, preserving his dignity, his manhood, exercising his mind, pretending he didn't know that her cunt was wet for him, that her arms and legs ached and her pelvis felt like someone had knotted the bones.

She could go into the bathroom and masturbate with the end of a douche nozzle or a bottle or a handheld shower head – but he would lie there coolly in bed reading, a young river god with reddish hair on his long body, with his small red mouth meditative above his copper beard and his greenish hazel eyes dreamy behind his glasses.

She wanted to weep and tear her hair and masturbate over and over and bite him and pummel him and sink her perfect white teeth into his neck and bite until she opened the jugular vein. But she held back. Instead she composed herself and said: 'You have never satisfied me, never, you make me so nervous that I come and feel nothing, or I don't come, or I don't come at all.'

Then he was hurt. The red mouth quivered like a wound. The hazel-green eyes looked as if they would fill with tears. Even the copper beard looked defeated. And she was triumphant having hurt him, her baby, her love, and she opened her arms to him and took him in. 'I love you,' she said. They both hugged, shaking with sobs.

But still he would not fuck her, not that night. That was his power, not to be lightly yielded. He held her and hugged her and rocked her, but the cock belonged to him.

She was wet for him. She took his hand and brought it between her legs to the place where the lips were slippery as rocks covered with moss at the edge of a lake, and said, 'This is for you,' and he drew his hand away.

She wanted to bite him, kill him, draw blood, but instead she hugged him tighter and tighter, thinking of the man up the beach whom she thought of when she masturbated, whom he was jealous of, the actor with the sea-blue eyes and the cadlike ways with women, and the broad shoulders, and the (probably) enormous cock. She didn't even want him. That was the thing; that was what made her so mad. She wanted *this* one, this copper-colored lover, *this* pink cock. The cunt is a very selective organ. It had settled on this man, it had molded itself to this cock, it had come home to this particular embrace, these arms, this big bearish hairy hug. Her eyes squeezed shut and tears broke out as if they should shriek as they did.

She fell asleep with her head on his chest, with his fleecy chest hairs tickling her nostrils, and the tears slipping, trickling down from her cheeks into the fleece on his chest.

Nightmares, apparitions, the waves stacking up to crash, crashing, stacking up again, the black cat from next door stalking rabbits, field mice, lizards, other pulsating small creatures he could torture for a long time before he killed.

In the morning, she still wanted him. He had a headache, hugged her briefly, saying so, got up out of bed almost brusquely and stomped into the bathroom to the shower. For a long time the water cascaded, faucets squeaked, bottles rattled, she lay in the water bed, masturbating with a sticky finger, circling round and round on her clitoris, sticking another two fingers deep, deep inside, and thinking of the blue-eyed actor up the beach whom she didn't like.

284

He drove into town with the top down. He was wearing the cap she gave him the first week and pressing his foot down to the floor on the accelerator and thinking of a girl in town he used to go with and maybe ought to go back and fuck. She was no threat, adored him, was nice and homey and ordinary, a librarian with lascivious tastes in bed and a small son, not yet quite housebroken, who used to surprise them in bed. Women liked him. Too much sometimes. They fell in love with his boyishness, his baby face, his wounded eyes, his vulnerability. He could leave her, he could always leave her. He was not yet a complete captive. He was still his own man.

Later, missing her, he called her from town. 'I love you,' he said. 'I love you immensely,' she said.

He came home. She was writing letters with her secretary, another lady who obviously liked him. All afternoon, the three of them worked together in the beach house, writing, making coffee, marinating things for dinner, telephoning. She wrote in the sun for a while, letting the sound of the waves screen out her secretary's typing. The hot sun on her back made her horny and she went into his study, where he too was writing and she straddled his knees and tickled his balls, gave him a hard-on, and then skipped away.

The secretary left and the dinner guests had not yet arrived. They were to come any minute. She stood in the kitchen peeling a ripe avocado for the salad, feeling the outside of the slimy green fruit, slippery like her cunt that had throbbed for him all day. She had masturbated once, twice, three times, but still she needed him. Only his cock inside her could give her peace. The rest were just spasms.

Her fingers were slippery on the green fruit, and she called to him to help her slice it. He came, took over the slippery slicing, while she rinsed her hands, dried them on a paper towel, and then slid them under the waistband of his jeans, into his crotch, around his balls, which were so perfectly rounded, so smooth, so tenderly pink. Then she darted her tongue in and out of his ear and she licked the avocado from his fingers. 'I'm so hard for you,' he whispered, 'do we have time to fuck?' 'They're coming any

285

minute,' she teased him. She was perfumed, powdered, her hair brushed out, and wearing high-heeled sandals and a half-buttoned caftan with nothing underneath. He felt for the soft mound over her cunt. 'Fleecy pudenda,' he said, repeating an old phrase from the first delicious month they'd lived together. 'God I'm hard for you – don't we have *time*?' 'Not now,' she said, enjoying teasing him. His cock was bulging under the copper buttons of his jeans, making her think of high school, finger-fucking in the living room, all the delectable lore of guilty adolescent sex. 'I can't answer the door like this,' he said, pointing to his impressive erection, which she squeezed again, to feel its hardness. 'Stop,' he said, but not sternly.

The guests left. The coffee table was littered with full ash-trays, stained wineglasses, empty bottles of Mouton-Cadet, dried cheese, soggy soda crackers, half-eaten petit fours, an empty brandy bottle, two snifters with little splashes of brandy still glowing golden in their bowls. 'We don't have to clean up, do we?' she asked. 'I guess not,' he said. 'We can do it in the morning.'

She was tired now. Almost too tired to fuck. That was ironic, wasn't it? She went in the bathroom to splash her face with water and brush her hair and perfume herself.

'I'm not sure I trust Joanna,' she said, speaking of the people they'd spent the evening with. 'She's really very tough, isn't she?' She was thinking that everyone was tougher than she was, more savvy, less likely to get duped, less open, more self-protective. Perhaps even *he* was – for all his sweetness. Perhaps he was really tough too.

'I'm not sure I trust you either,' she said, from the dressing room.

'What?' he said, hurt, put off.

She came to bed and looked him in the eye.

'That's a hell of a thing to say to a man who's about to make love to you,' he said.

'I didn't mean it the way you thought. And besides you don't have to make love to me.'

'I know I don't have to. I *want* to. But I won't unless you tell me why you don't trust me.'

286

All sorts of things whirled through her head. Her shattered marriage, her constant yearning for this man who doled himself out to her, making sure she knew who was boss, her tenderness for him, her fear of feeling so open and vulnerable, her fear of needing him so much. It was impossible to explain all this to him – even though he was kin to her, even though he was the man who understood her almost better than she understood herself, the man who was her best friend in the world. Even here, even in this closeness and tenderness they had shared for almost a year, there was division, a failure of empathy, the snake in the garden.

'I didn't mean it the way you thought. And if I explain you'll only misunderstand more. Sometimes I wonder if, under your sweetness, you aren't also somehow tough. That's all. It isn't important. I can't even explain it ...'

He looked hurt. 'I wanted to fuck you,' he said. 'I felt so warm towards you and so horny. Why are you building this wall?'

She didn't know. He got up and turned off the lights. He brought a pine-scented candle from the living room and fumbled with his cigarette lighter, trying to light it.

'To create a romantic mood,' he said sardonically. The candle wouldn't light. She lunged across the waterbed, leaving him bobbing in the wake. She fumbled with the lighter, inverting the candle, burning her fingers, and covering them with green wax – but not managing to light the wick.

'Here – I'll get another candle from the living room. Why don't you put on that great black nightgown?'

On one of their trips she had bought a bunch of silly underclothes to indulge his girlie-magazine tastes. There was a black satin corset with red ribbons and wide black lace trim, long garters, black seamed stockings. There were several filmy black nightgowns, one with pink satin ribbons under the wired bosom, which pushed up her breasts, until the nipples teetered over the edge of the black lace top. The nightgown was split up the front. She put it on now without the bikini pants that matched it. Her cunt was dripping. She met him again in bed. The candle was lit.

287

'Can you doubt how much I love you?' he asked, as if he knew not to pursue the other topic, trust, hurt, toughness.

'No,' she said. He was her love, the only man who'd made her feel totally womaned, totally entered, opened, vulnerable. Womb, woman, ovum, open, vulva, vulnerable. When he touched her cunt she felt as naked as the peeled avocado she had held in her hand earlier that evening.

'It's a flower,' he said, circling his fingers on her clitoris, touching the tender place just behind the opening, bending down to continue circling with his tongue.

'It's wet for you,' she muttered.

She didn't want to think about fucking or coming or fights or anything, but just of his tongue revolving on the crest of her cunt, of the slipperiness, the avocado slipperiness, and the rocking of the waterbed, and the ocean thundering outside. She bent to his penis and began teasing it with her tongue, darting her tongue around his balls, around the shaft, touching the skin, then not touching it, then touching again, until she heard him moan, as if she could draw speech and groans and song from his cock as well as sperm, as if she could make it speak.

Then he was sucking her nipples, molding her breasts where they swelled up over the black lace cups. She opened her eyes for a split second and looked at him sucking her breasts, this red-bearded baby with the huge hard cock, this man, this prodigious miracle, this wonder.

It was no good. All her feminism, all her independence, all her fame had come to this, this helplessness, this need. She needed him. She needed this man.

When he entered her, when his cock slid into her, she was moaning something about that, about surrender, and how ashamed she was of needing him so, of loving him so desperately. 'But I need you just as badly,' he said. 'I can't do this without you, I need you too.'

At first she was on top of him, sliding up and down rhythmically on his cock, while he held her clitoris between two slippery fingers, and pushed another finger up her ass. The whole world went out except for the throbbing in her cunt, which seemed to her like a universe, a galaxy, a deep black hole in space. She came the first time with a shuddering that made her scream and bite his shoulder. It was almost as if the orgasm was not only in her cunt, but in her throat, her voice, her whole body, and the scream was part of it, part of the release. He turned her over roughly but tenderly and began fucking her from above. And she thought, feeling that cock slide in and out of her as if it owned her soul, that if she died then, if she died that very minute, it would be all right, she would have known most of it, have lived, have felt it. There was more: she wanted his baby, their baby, she wanted to feel that pain, that pleasure, but still, if she died at this very moment, life would not have cheated her.

She was coming again. She told him. Could he wait? she asked. Could she stop moving for a minute? he asked. She slowed, she squeezed his cock with the muscles of her cunt, he moaned. His mouth was very tender and soft on hers, his eyes were wide enough to let all the darkness in. He rolled her over again, putting her on top, holding his cock very still, his hips very still. She was squeezing his cock with her muscles but trying not to slide up and down on it until he quieted down somewhat.

And then they both began to move again, interlocking, cock and cunt, and nothing else in the world mattering. She came with a shudder that shook her whole body and released another scream from her that scarcely seemed human. Everything released as she screamed and came; she also peed, and was embarrassed and apologized. 'I love your pee, your farts, your shit, your tight snatch,' he said, digging his nails into her ass, and then he pulled her cunt down on his upraised cock like a glove over a finger. 'Do you want my sperm,' he asked, rhetorically – because of course she wanted it, wanted to feel it spurt straight up to her womb, her heart, her fingertips, and he moaned and began to come, sobbing, shaking, crying, and she felt the base of his penis throbbing as all the filaments flew flew flew into her womb and hopefully caught.

They lay not moving in the absolute peace after the earthquake. She felt a small sun glowing in her solar plexus, and her legs and arms too heavy to move, mercury-filled moon suits, leaden limbs. He held her to him even as his cock grew soft and curled away from her. 'I'll never leave you,' he said, 'never.'

'Do you suppose,' she said, her voice hoarse from screaming, weak with love, 'that many lovers felt this and then died anyway?'

'It doesn't matter,' he said, 'it doesn't matter at all.'

'That means *yes*, doesn't it?'

He hugged her very tight.

THE LOVE POEMS

The Puzzle

They locked into each other
like brother & sister,
long-lost relations,
orphans divided by time.

He bit her shoulder
& entered her blood forever.
She bit his tongue
& changed the tone of his song.

They walked together astonished
not to be lonely.
They sought their lonelinesses
like lost dogs.

But they were joined together
by tongue & shoulder.
His nightmares woke her;
her daydreams startled him.

He fucked so hard
he thought he'd climb back in her.
She came so hard
her skin seemed to dissolve.

She feared she had no yearning
left to write with.
He feared she'd suck him dry
& glide away.

They spoke of all these things
& locked together.
She figured out
the jigsaw of his heart.

& he unscrambled her
& placed the pieces
with such precision
nothing came apart.

The Sad Bed

This is the sad bed
of chosen chastity
because you are miles
& mountains away,
over canyons, under jet-streams,
where the cirrus clouds streak
from east to west,
& the cumulus clouds
copulate to spite us,
& the hard cock of the wind thrashes
the bellies of planes.

We are not in flight,
& we sigh on our sad beds.
Three thousand miles apart
but memorized in each other's eyes & hips,
so full of each other,
we are empty to the world.

I could find a cock to fill me,
but it would never make me fly.
You could find a cunt to clutch you
but you would not cry
& bite her shoulder
wanting entrance to her blood.

So instead the whole country is a bed
in which we lie on opposite coasts,
divided by the obdurate mountains
of our obstinate love,
& wishing for an earthquake
to shake the continent,
& collapse us into each other.

The Long Tunnel of Wanting You

This is the long tunnel of wanting you.
Its walls are lined with remembered kisses
wet & red as the inside of your mouth,
full & juicy as your probing tongue,
warm as your belly against mine,
deep as your navel leading home,
soft as your sleeping cock beginning to stir,
tight as your legs wrapped around mine,
straight as your toes pointing toward the bed
as you roll over & thrust your hardness
into the long tunnel of my wanting,
seeding it with dreams & unbearable hope,
making memories of the future,
straightening out my crooked past,
teaching me to live in the present present tense
with the past perfect and the uncertain future
suddenly certain for certain
in the long tunnel of my old wanting
which before always had an ending
but now begins & begins again
with you, with you, with you.

The Muse Who Came to Stay

You are the first muse who came to stay.
The others began & ended with a wish,
or a glance or a kiss between stanzas;
the others strode away in the pointed boots of their fear
or were kicked out by the stiletto heels of mine,
or merely padded away in bare feet
when the ground was too hard or cold
or as hot as white sand baked under the noonday sun.

But you flew in on the wings of your smile,
powered by the engine of your cock,
driven by your lonely pumping heart,
rooted by your arteries to mine.

We became a tree with a double apical point,
reaching equally toward what some call heaven,
singing in the wind with our branches,
sharing the sap & syrup
which makes the trunk grow thick.

We are seeding the ground with poems & children.
We are the stuff of books & new-grown forests.
We are renewing the earth with our roots,
the air with our pure oxygen songs,
the nearby sea with the leaves we lose
only to grow the greener ones again.

I used to leap from tree to tree,
speaking glibly of Druids,
thinking myself a latter-day dryad,
or a wood nymph from the stony city,
or some other chimerical creature,
conjured in my cheating poet's heart.

But now I stay, knowing the muse is mine,
knowing no books will banish him
& no off-key songs will drive him away.

I being & begin; I whistle in & out of tune.
If the ending is near, I do not think of it.
If the drought comes, we will make our own rain.
If the muse is grounded, I will make him fly,
& if he falls, I will catch him in my arms
until he flies with me again.

Time Zones

I start my day when dreams are strangling you,
your eyelids flutter with the melon breasts
of women too enormous to be true.
You are fucking, muttering, loving in your dreams;
I am in a taxicab downtown.

And then you wake – and I sit down to lunch,
bored by another boring interview.
I interview the self I know by heart.
My luncheon partner interviews his dreams.

Meanwhile you pour your soul into your fingers
& type the night's accumulated dreams.
& then once more I find myself a cab.
The driver drives himself – thinking it's me.

At three o'clock, I find myself alone.
You are running on a beach under the sun.
You are lying in the glare & seeing me.
I tap the keys to reach you through the clouds.

& then I go to dinner; you are home
writing to me & writing to yourself.
The two are one; we don't require carbons.
I feel your thoughts before you write them down.

& so to bed – I lie there until three –
to phone your midnight bed before I sleep.
I dreamily embrace you through the maze
of multicolored continental cables.

I'd put the telephone between my thighs
or wrap the cords & wires around my waist
if it would bring you closer
but the time
is wrong, is wrong –
we have to chase the sun
from east to west
before we both come home.

I Sleep With

I sleep with double pillows since you're gone.
Is one of them for you – or *is* it you?
My bed is heaped with books of poetry.
I fall asleep on yellow legal pads.

Oh the orgies in stationery stores!
The love of printer's ink & thick new pads!
A poet has to fall in love to write.
Her bed is heaped with papers, or with men.

I keep your pillow pressed down with my books.
They leave an indentation like your head.
If I can't have you here, I'll take cold type –
& words: the warmest things there are –
but you.

The Wingless & the Winged

the wingless thing
man . . .
— E. E. CUMMINGS

Most men use their cocks
for two things only:
they stand up pissing
& lie down fucking.
The world is full of horizontal men —
or vertical ones —
& really it is all the same disease.

But your cock flies
over the earth,
making shadows
on the bodies of women,
making wild bird noises
from its tiny mouth,
making music
& food for thought.
It is not a wingless thing
at all.

We could call it Pegasus —
if it didn't make us think
of gas stations.
Or we could call it Icarus —
if it didn't make us think
of falling.

But still it dips & dives
through the sky like a glider,
in search of a meadow,
a field,
a sun-dappled swamp
from which (you rightly said)
all life begins.

Her Mouth, His Seed, Her Soul

My mouth seeded
with your sperm,
I talked back
to the interviewer.

It may also be this way
with God.

Approach with a mouthful
of stones; you will be mute.
But speak semen & seed
& the words will flow.

Is heaven
a television show?
Everything points to it:

flickering circles of light,
the cloudy dots
that piece the rounded puzzle
of the sky.

'What is your soul about?
Describe it for the viewers
who can't read.'

My mouth is hot
with your seed.
& so I speak
as freely as
the Delphic oracle
still stoned on laurel leaves.

'My soul is about a girl
who finds herself.
My soul is growing up.
My soul is no longer
afraid to fly.'

(My soul is mine;
my mouth belongs to you.)

The Cornucopia

Always before
there was the holding back:

don't show your love too much
or he will run away.

Give the words like little gifts
& never say:

I love you
too soon, too soon.

Anytime was always
much too soon.

But I heaped you with love
& you kept on coming back.

& I talked & talked & talked
& you kept on talking back.

& I heaped my love on you
& you kept on heaping yours.

What did you think we were *holding*
by holding back?

Why did we think it *safe*
to hoard our love?

The cornucopia returns
upon itself.

The fruits fall out.
We eat them & they grow.

We Learned

the decorum of fire ...
  — PABLO NERUDA

We learned the decorum of fire,
the flame's curious symmetry,
the blue heat at the center of the thighs,
the flickering red of the hips,
& the tallow gold of the breasts
lit from within
by the lantern in the ribs.

You tear yourself out of me
like a branch that longs to be grafted
onto a fruit tree,
peach & pear
crossed with each other,
fig & banana served on one plate,
the leaf & the luminous snail
that clings to it.

We learned that the tearing
could be a joining,
that the fire's flickering
could be a kindling,
that the old decorum of love —
to die into the poem,
leaving the lover lonely with her pen —
was all an ancient lie.

So we banished the evil eye:
you have to be unhappy to create;
you have to let love die before it writes;
you have to lose the joy to have the poem —
& we re-wrote our lives with fire.

See this manuscript covered
with flesh-colored words?
It was written in invisible ink
& held up to our flame.

The words darkened on the page
as we sank into each other.

We are ink & blood
& all things that make stains.
We turn each other golden as we turn,
browning each other's skins like suns.

Hold me up to the light;
you will see poems.
Hold me in the dark;
you will see light.

Doubts before Dreaming

Contending with the demon Doubt
when all of life heaves up into your mouth,
the lies you spat back with your mother's milk,
the men you loved & hated & betrayed,
the husbands who slept on through windy nights,
the rattling at the panes ...

Pain, doubt, the ache to love again.
The man you cuddled to your chest
who went away ...
The demon Doubt comes back to haunt your life.
You chose to live, & choosing life meant pain.

*

Throw out the generalizations!
What you meant – you liar poet –
lyre in your mouth ...
You mean: I loved him once
& can no more.
You meant: I kept confusing guilt with love.

*

This is the problem: that we live;
& as we live each body cell must change.
We dream, & as we dream our dreams must change.
We eat, & in devouring life, we change.

*

We dream we read our lives in some huge book.
Our dreaming eyelids flick the pages past.
The muse writes through our dreams
& dreams our lives.
The book has pages torn & broken type.

*

& as we dream, some paragraphs are blurred.
& as we read we re-invent the plot.
The eyes are dreaming cells, the eyelids move.
The cells divide as lovers fall apart.

*

They slide away to sleep, he slips from her.
He sinks into her dream, her dream is filled.
& as she fills with him, her eyes are changed.
He dreams a woman he has never met.

*

Nothing can stay: the cock grows soft by dawn.
& she seals over like a virgin raped only by dreams.
However much they cling, they drift apart.
Their hands are joined, their dreaming hearts are severed.

*

They dance the dance of dreamers as they sleep.
This dreamers' dance: the pattern of their lives.
The partners change, yet always stay the same,
the partners bow, their hearts collide & break.

*

Slippers beneath the bed, bare toes toward heaven.
Soles cradled in the sheet, the dancers sleep.
They dream they dance & dance & dance again.
They dream the dance of dreamers without feet.

*

What is the question here? I cannot say.
I am asleep, my tongue is blurred by death.
I spit the pits of death across the bed.
I love my love, yet eat him while he sleeps.

*

Death is confusing, life more confusing still.
Alive, we dream & dead, who can be sure?
Since all we have are dreams, let's join our beds.

Total Eclipse

Not wanting to write
for fear that anything –
the passion for the page,
the love of carbon ribbons & erasers –
will distract me from your face,
from your eyes green
as the flickering base of flames,
& your tarnished copper hair.

My love is thick as rust
& just as hard to scrape off.
It glows like the green roofs of Paris:
it shines in the sun like dropped pennies.

I fix on your face
until I am blurred & bleared,
until my eyes cannot focus
& all words become one.

Oh let me write you into my life!
I am afraid of rust & tarnish,
but even more afraid of this gleam.

When my eyes have taken you in,
when my body has eaten
& spat you out,
when my heart remembers to beat
& my fingers remember the pen –

will I still remember you then,
boyish & sly –
yet a total eclipse of my sun?

The Dirty Laundry Poem

This is the dirty laundry poem –
because we have traveled from town to town
accumulating soiled linen & sweaty shirts
& blue-jeans caked & clotted with our juice
& teeshirts crumpled by our gloriously messy passion
& underwear made stiff by all our joy.

I have come home to wash my clothes.
They patter on the bathroom floor like rain.
The water drips away the days till you.
The dirty water speaks to me of love.

Steamy in the bubbles of our love,
I have plunged my hands into hot water
as I might plunge them
in your heart.

After years of spots & splatters,
I am finally coming clean.
I will fly to you with a suitcase of fresh laundry,
strip my clothes off, heap them on the floor,
& let you scrub my body with your love.

Property Settlement

As we bought the furniture
we thought it would root us together:
every chair would be a child,
every mirror a glass for our passion,
every painting a patch of cracked wall
covered & covered forever.

But now we are moving on –
& all our treasured junk
which seemed so solid, so unmoveable,
is like ashes in the fist of a mourner
outside the crematorium.

Scatter it over the sea!
I am moving to a bare house on a bluff
overlooking the Pacific.
I will furnish it with the multicolored love
of my red-bearded, green-eyed lover,
with the crushed kaleidoscope of our passion,
& the bottle glass we find along the beach,
& the pure unclouded sunlight that we pour
over & over each other.

If we don't have a bed,
we will make nourishing love
on the sunstruck kitchen floor.
If we don't have a chair,
we will rock
on each other's thighs.
If we don't have a table,
we will eat out of each other's
delicious bodies.
He will lick honey from my cunt,
I will cover his cock with jam
& suck it off like a hungry baby.

Take the desk, the analytic couch,
the posters we bought in dead Vienna.
Take the scholarly journals, the brokerage receipts,
the money, the money, the money,
& churn your worthless stock.

Put coins in your pocket;
they will not buy you love.
Make a blanket of bonds & passbooks;
they will not keep you warm.
Quilt yourself over with checks;
they will not bounce for you as I did.

You will be solvent & sane
huddled in the coinage of your coldness –
but I am gone.

Sailing Home

In the redwood house sailing off
into the ocean,
I sleep with you –
our dreams mingling,
our breath coming & going
like gusts of wind
trifling with the breakers,
our arms touching
& our legs & our hair
reaching out like tendrils
to intertwine.

The first time
I slept in your arms,
I knew I had come home.
Your body was a ship
& I rocked in it,
utterly safe in the breakers,
utterly sure of this love.

I fit into your arms
as a ship fits into water,
as a cactus roots in sand,
as the sun nestles into the blazing horizon.

The house sails all night.
Our dreams are the flags
of little ships,
your penis the mast
of one of the breeziest sailboats,
& my breasts floating,
half in & half out
of the water,
are like messages in bottles.

There is no point to this poem.
What the sea loses
always turns up again;
it is only a question of shores.

Living by the Sea

The truth is: I never understood anyone's
messages ... Only the ocean existed.
— PABLO NERUDA

Now that you're here
I'll have to finish the book
on my back,
hard to write love poems
when no pens flow up,
hard to write love poems
in the midst of it,
hard to write at all
with you in bed.

I used to fill
my empty bed
with words for you.
Simile sheets
& warming metaphors.
In the caesura of our love,
I wrote to you
I linked our thighs with words;
our hips pumped ink.

Now we are living by the sea —
which has no rhyme.
Now our bed is salty & the sheets
are printed with white messages.

Only the ocean exists —
& you & me.
We write in foam
upon each other's lips.

Living Happily Ever After

We used to strike sparks
off each other.
Our eyes would meet
or our hands,
& the blue lightning of love
would sear the air.

Now we are soft.
We loll
in the same sleepy bed,
skin of my skin,
hair of my head,
sweat of my sweat –
you are kin,
brother & mother
all in one,
husband, lover,
muse & comforter;
I love you even better
without sparks.

We are pebbles in the tide
rolling against each other.
The surf crashes above us;
the irregular pulse
of the ocean
drives our blood,
but we are growing smooth
against each other.

Are we living happily ever after?
What will happen
to my love of cataclysms?
My love of sparks & fire,
my love of ice?

Fellow pebble,
let us roll
against each other.
Perhaps the sparks are clearer
under water.

The Surgery of the Sea

At the furthermost reach of the sea
where Atlantis sinks under the wake of the waves,
I have come to heal my life.

I knit together like a broken arm.
The salt fills in the crevices of bone.
The sea takes all the fragments of my lives
& grinds them home.

I wake up in a waterbed with you.
The sea is singing & my skin
sings against your skin.
The waves are all around us & within.
We sleep stuck to each other's salt.

I am healing in your arms.
I am learning to write without the loss of love.
I am growing deeper lungs here by the sea.
The waves are knives; they glitter & cut clean.

This is the sea's surgery.
This is the cutting & the healing both.
This is where bright sunlight warms the bone,
& fog erases us, then makes us whole.

After the Earthquake

After the first astounding rush,
after the weeks at the lake,
the crystal, the clouds, the water lapping the rocks,
the snow breaking under our boots like skin,
& the long mornings in bed ...

After the tangos in the kitchen,
& our eyes fixed on each other at dinner,
as if we would eat with our lids,
as if we would swallow each other ...

I find you still
here beside me in bed,
(while my pen scratches the pad
& your skin glows as you read)
& my whole life so mellowed & changed

that at times I cannot remember
the crimp in my heart that brought me to you,
the pain of a marriage like an old ache,
a husband like an arthritic knuckle.

Here, living with you,
love is still the only subject that matters.
I open to you like a flowering wound,
or a trough in the sea filled with dreaming fish,
or a steaming chasm of earth
split by a major quake.

You changed the topography.
Where valleys were,
there now are mountains.
Where deserts were,
there now are seas.

We rub each other,
but we do not wear away.

The sand gets finer
& our skins turn silk.

OUTSTANDING WOMEN'S FICTION IN GRANADA PAPERBACKS

Muriel Spark
Territorial Rights	£1.25	☐
Not To Disturb	£1.25	☐

Toni Morrison
Song of Solomon	£1.50	☐
The Bluest Eye	£1.25	☐
Sula	£1.25	☐

Erica Jong
Fear of Flying	£1.50	☐
How To Save Your Own Life	£1.50	☐
Selected Poems	95p	☐
Selected Poems II	£1.25	☐
Fanny	£1.95	☐

All these books are available at your local bookshop or newsagent, or can be ordered direct from the publisher. Just tick the titles you want and fill in the form below.

Name _____

Address _____

Write to Granada Cash Sales
PO Box 11, Falmouth, Cornwall TR10 9EN.

Please enclose remittance to the value of the cover price plus:

UK 45p for the first book, 20p for the second book plus 14p per copy for each additional book ordered to a maximum charge of £1.63.

BFPO and Eire 45p for the first book, 20p for the second book plus 14p per copy for the next 7 books, thereafter 8p per book.

Overseas 75p for the first book and 21p for each additional book.

Granada Publishing reserve the right to show new retail prices on covers, which may differ from those previously advertised in the text or elsewhere.

GF1381